This Book is ~~Donated~~
for Profane
Content.

THE ART OF A LIE

ALSO BY LAURA SHEPHERD-ROBINSON

The Square of Sevens
Daughters of Night
Blood & Sugar

THE ART OF A LIE

A NOVEL

LAURA SHEPHERD-ROBINSON

ATRIA BOOKS
New York   Amsterdam/Antwerp   London
Toronto   Sydney/Melbourne   New Delhi

An Imprint of Simon & Schuster, LLC
1230 Avenue of the Americas
New York, NY 10020

For more than 100 years, Simon & Schuster has championed authors and the stories they create. By respecting the copyright of an author's intellectual property, you enable Simon & Schuster and the author to continue publishing exceptional books for years to come. We thank you for supporting the author's copyright by purchasing an authorized edition of this book.

No amount of this book may be reproduced or stored in any format, nor may it be uploaded to any website, database, language-learning model, or other repository, retrieval, or artificial intelligence system without express permission. All rights reserved. Inquiries may be directed to Simon & Schuster, 1230 Avenue of the Americas, New York, NY 10020 or permissions@simonandschuster.com.

This book is a work of fiction. Any references to historical events, real people, or real places are used fictitiously. Other names, characters, places, and events are products of the author's imagination, and any resemblance to actual events or places or persons, living or dead, is entirely coincidental.

Copyright © 2025 by Laura Shepherd-Robinson

All rights reserved, including the right to reproduce this book or portions thereof in any form whatsoever. For information, address Atria Books Subsidiary Rights Department, 1230 Avenue of the Americas, New York, NY 10020.

First Atria Books hardcover edition August 2025

ATRIA BOOKS and colophon are trademarks of Simon & Schuster, LLC

Simon & Schuster strongly believes in freedom of expression and stands against censorship in all its forms. For more information, visit BooksBelong.com.

For information about special discounts for bulk purchases, please contact Simon & Schuster Special Sales at 1-866-506-1949 or business@simonandschuster.com.

The Simon & Schuster Speakers Bureau can bring authors to your live event. For more information or to book an event, contact the Simon & Schuster Speakers Bureau at 1-866-248-3049 or visit our website at www.simonspeakers.com.

Map of Parish St. James's reproduced by Motco Enterprises Limited.

Manufactured in the United States of America

1 3 5 7 9 10 8 6 4 2

Library of Congress Cataloging-in-Publication Data
Names: Shepherd-Robinson, Laura, author.
Title: The art of a lie / Laura Shepherd-Robinson.
Description: First Atria Books hardcover edition. | New York : Atria Books, 2025.
Identifiers: LCCN 2025005903 (print) | LCCN 2025005904 (ebook) | ISBN 9781668083093 (hardcover) | ISBN 9781668083109 (paperback) | ISBN 9781668083116 (ebook)
Subjects: LCGFT: Detective and mystery fiction. | Novels.
Classification: LCC PR6119.H4655 A88 2025 (print) | LCC PR6119.H4655 (ebook) | DDC 823/.92—dc23/eng/20250211
LC record available at https://lccn.loc.gov/2025005903
LC ebook record available at https://lccn.loc.gov/2025005904

ISBN 978-1-6680-8309-3
ISBN 978-1-6680-8311-6 (ebook)

For Billy,
who stole the buttons

Parish of St James's, Westminster

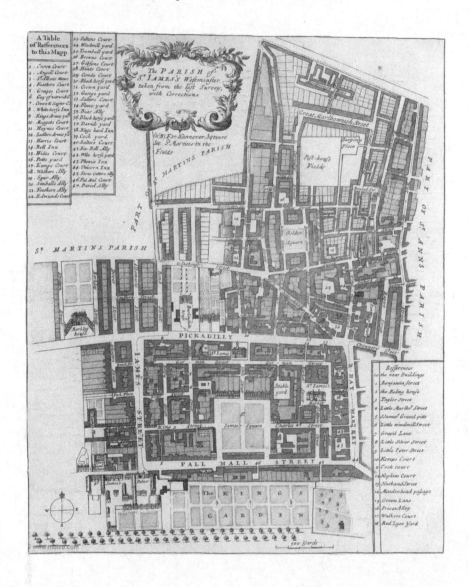

PART ONE

The Mirror

A lover, when he is admitted to cards, ought to be solemnly silent, and observe the motions of his mistress. He must laugh when she laughs, sigh when she sighs. In short, he should be the shadow of her mind.
A lady, in the presence of her lover, should never want a looking-glass; as a beau, in the presence of his looking-glass, never wants a mistress.

Henry Fielding, *Love in Several Masques*, 1728

CHAPTER ONE

Nine times out of ten, when a customer walks into the Punchbowl and Pineapple, I can guess what will tempt them. It is the confectioner's principal art, anticipating wants and needs—and people betray their desires in countless small ways. For a young lady taut with nerves, dressed to make a house call, I suggest a pretty basket of French macaroons to impress her friends. For a young buck in the first flush of love, seeking a gift for his mistress, I propose a *petits puits d'amour* (the name and oval shape might make him smile, though I act oblivious to any indelicate connotations). For an older gentleman—picture one crimson from hunting and port—a rich plum cake spiced with cinnamon and mace. For a widow in mittens, a box of scented violet wafers—or if she is bent with the rheumatism, bergamot chips. For a little boy with a cough, I prescribe a *guimauve*: a soft cake of honey whipped with the sap of the marsh mallow plant. And for his governess, a sweet syllabub, to be eaten at one of my tables, while she ponders how life's misfortunes brought her here.

That day, the fifteenth of June 1749, I was watching a gentleman in the mirror behind my counter. He'd just strolled in, escaping the bustle of Piccadilly, remarkably unsullied by the dust and heat of the day outside. His finger hovered over my golden nests of spun sugar, each filled with marchpane eggs and topped with a sugar-work bird—a new creation I'd put my hand to whilst the shop had been closed for mourning. Like my birds, he was a colorful creature—his coat a smoke-blue silk with silver embroidery at the collar and cuffs, a topaz pin in his cream cravat, and a plump meringue of a periwig beneath a smoke-blue hat adorned with a peacock feather. The patina of the mirror speckled his tawny skin, the warp of the glass distorting one golden-brown eye.

Not a sugar nest, I thought, not unless he was looking for a present for his wife—and he had taken a stool at my counter, which suggested he intended to eat. An apricot tart, I decided. Refined, yet unadventurous, like most of my customers.

To my surprise, he pointed to a silver tureen, where half a dozen glass goblets of ice shavings nestled amidst larger shards of ice. "Is that a Persian sherbet?" he said. "I haven't had one in years."

"Perfect for the weather, sir," Theo said.

I could imagine how she'd be looking at him. Fifteen years old, and men still a mystery she presumed delightful. "The goods are behind the counter," I'd sometimes remind her. "Not in front of it."

"I'll do it," I said, turning. "Go see to the balancing pan."

"Yes, Mrs. C." Theo gave me a pert look, and threaded her way, hips swaying, to the door at the back of the shop.

Undistorted by the mirror, the gentleman appeared slightly familiar, though I couldn't quite place him. Perhaps from church? A carriage moved on the street outside, and a shaft of sunlight gilded his face, revealing a few delicate lines of age around the eyes and mouth. He put up a hand to shield his gaze, signet ring flashing.

I poured a syrup of rosewater over one of the goblets of ice, adding a scatter of dried rose petals and ground Turkey pistachios. The gentleman handed over the coins and while I weighed them, he plunged in with his spoon.

"Your girl wasn't wrong," he said, after a moment. "That's perfection right there."

I inclined my head at the compliment. "Most find the flavors too exotic."

He grinned. "Round here they still say that about a peppercorn."

He'd get no warm words from me, a widow of nearly thirty. Yet I was still pondering the mystery of where I had seen him before. Once I'd secreted the coins in my money-drawer, my curiosity got the better of me. "Do I know you, sir?"

His smile faded. "We've not been introduced, but I attended your husband's memorial service. William Devereux is my name. My condolences, Mrs. Cole. Jonas was a general, a true force. I can hardly believe that he's gone."

People think it's what you want to hear. To know that the man you loved mattered. That his qualities were recognized, that he is remembered. How could they know that every morning when I awoke, I put my shoulder to the grindstone of forgetting? Here in the shop, I could pretend that none of it had happened. That Jonas was out on parish business, or had popped upstairs to fetch a spool of ribbon or a clean apron. It brought me a measure of peace, just for an hour or two, until some well-meaning customer like Mr. Devereux brought it all back. The punch in the gut, the sick wave of fear for my own future.

Mr. Devereux was watching me with evident concern. "I have something for you," he said, holding out a folded piece of paper. I found myself gazing at an official-looking document with a stamp and a seal.

"I advise gentlemen on the prudent investment of their money," he explained. "Jonas was a client of mine. Acting upon my counsel, your husband placed ten pounds with the Culross Iron and Coal Company. I am pleased to say that this is the dividend from the first quarter." He smiled and handed me a silver crown.

"Ten pounds?" I said, knowing nothing of this investment, trying to keep the eagerness from my tone. "Is it possible to redeem that money now?"

"Not for the moment, I'm afraid. But all being well, you can expect to see around five or six shillings every quarter, with the stock becoming redeemable in nine months' time."

Five shillings was still five shillings. Every penny mattered now. Since reopening the shop after Jonas's murder, everything had proved a struggle. Summer was always the worst time of our year—the nobility and gentry having fled the swelter of the city for Bath and Tunbridge Wells—and widowhood had brought new challenges to my trade.

"I'd only known Jonas a few months," Devereux went on. "We met by chance in the bank and got to talking. It led to a fledgling friendship. We drank together sometimes—at the Running Horse or the

Star and Garter." He sighed. "Are they any closer to finding the villains responsible?"

I shook my head rather bleakly, and Devereux had the good grace to look away, rattling his spoon against his glass to scrape up the last of the syrup. "Delicious," he pronounced. "Though it's iced cream that I truly dream of in this weather."

Grateful for this rather clumsy effort to change the subject, I studied him quizzically. "Iced cream, sir?"

"My mother used to make it when I was a boy. She was raised in Italy, and it is a great delicacy over there. Mother used to flavor the cream with peach or elderflower and then it was frozen almost solid. I used to think it was like biting into a snowball—though snow never tasted so good."

His words intrigued me. Even before Jonas's death, I'd been convinced that our shop required innovation if we were to stand out from our competitors. Now my need to entice new customers through the door was rather more pressing.

"Do you know how it is done?" I asked. "Freezing cream, I mean?" I had never seen, nor heard of frozen liquids other than water.

"I am afraid I only ever enjoyed the end result," Devereux said. "Many years later I tried it again, on the Piazza della Signoria in Florence. But it was sold from a pail, so I saw none of the preparation."

A woman in a wide yellow hat approached the counter and I noticed her steal a second glance at Mr. Devereux. "What is that?" she asked, pointing.

"A simple pound cake, madam," I said, "but filled with a Seville orange cream. It's like a burst of sunshine in your mouth."

Her lip quivered. "I'll take six of those almond wafers."

I turned to box up her purchase, and Devereux met my eye in the mirror. "Too exotic," he mouthed.

I was still frowning at his presumption when Theo returned. "Mr. Brunsden is come to settle his bill." She set down a tray of lemon jellies and smiled at Mr. Devereux.

Restraining a sigh, I excused myself. As I passed through the shop, my little jewel box of gilt-edged mirrors and pistachio paneling, I exchanged a few words with my regular customers. Entering the hot, sweet hell of my kitchen, I found Oscar sweating over the pastry table, stamping out almond hearts. Not quite trusting Theo with the shop's money yet, I told Oscar to watch the counter and to send in Felix to take the goods down to the cellar. Then I smoothed my apron, and walked out into the yard.

Roger Brunsden was resting upon his cane in the shade of the old vine that had colonized my back wall and those of the neighboring yards. His boys trooped in and out of the alley, grunting under the weight of sacks of flour and salt, sugar loaves wrapped in blue paper, boxes of dried figs and currants.

He greeted me with an elaborate bow, then handed me his bill. "That time again, I am afraid, Mrs. Cole."

Brunsden had the manners of a marquis and the accent of a Thameside stevedore. Sweat crawled from beneath his periwig, staining his cravat yellow with some kind of scalp oil. His pink, piggish eyes, fringed by bristling white lashes, traveled over my purple gown.

"Black was rather too somber for my customers," I said, regretting it immediately. I didn't owe Roger Brunsden or anyone else an explanation.

"Not for me to judge," he replied, unsmiling.

I studied his bill. "But this is more than a usual month," I cried. "We only reopened two weeks ago."

"The price of sugar isn't what it was," he said. "Nor the price of wheat."

I didn't believe his excuses, not for a moment. He just didn't like women in trade—and was seeking to take advantage of my lack of experience with the books. Nor was he the only one. Between him, the fruiterer, and the egg man, I'd be lucky to break even that month. "Give me five minutes with a paring knife," I'd exclaimed to Oscar in frustration, "and I'll pit their stony hearts like Morello cherries!"

Reluctantly, I parted with my coins and returned to the shop. Mr. Devereux had gone, and Oscar glanced pointedly at a gentleman of middling years who was sitting in his place at my counter. Fearing he'd also come to collect on a bill, I slowed my pace.

His broad shoulders were hunched, his giant body contorted awkwardly upon the stool, one tree trunk of a leg stuck out to the side as if it was injured. His clothes were very fine—burgundy silk, a good French lace—but rather disheveled in the wearing, his cravat and wig askew, his coat misbuttoned. The intensity of his gaze suggested a fierce curiosity about the world, whilst the imperious jut of his long chin (which nearly met his long, curved nose) and the curl of one great fist upon the counter implied a determination to leave his stamp upon it.

He turned as I approached. "Mrs. Hannah Cole?" he said. "My name is Henry Fielding, the chief magistrate of Westminster. I'd like to talk to you about your husband's murder."

CHAPTER TWO

We sat in my parlor, Mr. Fielding taking Jonas's elbow chair. Theo brought up a tray of refreshments from the shop and I poured myself a bowl of tea, trying to still the rattle of the pot. Why was Fielding here and not the constable who'd come before? What had he learned?

His eyes traveled over my furnishings—the imitation Persian carpet, the mahogany card table with its silver-plated tea caddy, the japanned cabinet of our best China—coming to a rest on the shelf of books next to his chair. "I commend your taste, madam."

"I have always admired your novels, sir," I said, feeling my cheeks color. "*Tom Jones* is my favorite one yet."

"Alas," he said, "my new calling as Bow Street magistrate leaves me little time to write at present. But on the rare occasions that I do pick up my pen, I find I have plentiful inspiration for human wickedness. And all good stories start from there, do they not?"

I nodded uncertainly. "Please, tell me why you are here. Have you caught the villains who killed Jonas?"

He smiled sympathetically at the catch in my voice. "I'm afraid not, madam. But I am here to tell you that I intend to redouble Bow Street's efforts. To that end, I am taking personal charge of the case."

A pulse throbbed in my temple and I took a moment to compose myself. "I am glad of it, sir."

He paused to take a bite of his Piccadilly Puff, washing it down with a generous gulp of green walnut wine. It is a favorite choice of the sybarite: the silken sweetness of the custard, the crunching layers of puff paste, the dusky depths of the spices mingling with the sourness of lemon. I might have guessed that Mr. Fielding was a man who struggled to keep his appetites in check, even if I hadn't read the more unkind stories about him in the newspapers. His appearance bespoke his pleasures: his prominent belly, his beveined cheeks, and his gouty foot. A magistrate was not so very different from a novelist, I reflected. They both held the fate of the principal characters in their hands.

Fielding dabbed at his mouth with a napkin. "If you feel able to, Mrs. Cole, I would like to revisit the events surrounding your husband's murder. I want to make certain that I have all the details correct." From his coat pocket, he produced a bundle of documents.

I sighed. The story was simple enough and I had told it many times. "On the night of the twenty-sixth of March, Jonas went to meet some friends at the Running Horse in Mayfair. I am told he left the tavern at around ten o'clock, but he never returned home. I reported him missing the following morning. My apprentices and I spent two days scouring the streets and visiting the hospitals. Then your constable called at the shop." I drew a breath. "He said that Jonas's body had washed up on a Wapping beach. That he'd been attacked and robbed in the street, beaten severely about the head, and probably died of his injuries before he was thrown into the river."

"It says here that Jonas told you he was intending to visit a friend later that night, after the tavern?"

"That's right," I said. "The constable thought it might have been someone who lived near Whitehall or the abbey—because of their proximity to the river. Jonas had a lot of friends in that part of town, but I don't know all of their names. He was often out late."

Mr. Fielding adopted a grimace of compassion. "It passes, madam," he said. "The first time my memories of my late wife brought me more consolation than despair, that was the moment I knew I would endure."

He gazed at the portrait hanging over the fireplace: Mr. and Mrs. Jonas Cole, dressed in their best. My husband had found the artist at a little studio in Leicester Fields. It was the new thing, someone had told him, for a rising man to have his portrait painted. The artist had captured his prominent jaw and nose, his heavy dark brows. But not the energetic light in his eyes, nor the force of his will. I had protested the entire endeavor, for I'd feared we'd look ridiculous and I'd had a fondness for the Dutch oil that had hung there since my grandfather's day. It had depicted a platter of oysters, a bowl of olives, and a peeled lemon. Two flies crawled along the edge of the platter, and Jonas had said they made him feel sick.

"It's supposed to look real," I'd told him. "Life has flies, Jonas."

Now they swarmed.

"Your children must have also brought you consolation," I said. *And your money*, but I didn't say that.

Fielding inclined his head. "But you are still young, madam. In time—"

"No," I said, rather too fiercely. "I will never marry again."

He smiled. "Perhaps one day you will feel differently. I know I did." He leafed through his documents. "I understand several items were missing from your husband's body? Hence the presumption of a robbery?"

Presumption. What did he mean by that? "That's right. Jonas's purse strings were cut, and his watch and ring were missing."

"The watch was engraved with a double-headed eagle. Is that right?"

"The Russian imperial crest," I said. "Tsar Peter gave it to my grandfather during his Great Embassy to London."

Fielding raised an eyebrow. "It is a sad truth that due to Bow Street's limited resources, not all crimes receive the diligence they deserve—especially where there are no witnesses to the act in question. But due to your husband's prominent position on the parish committee, and the consequent interest of the newspapers in his murder, my constables gave this matter their utmost attention. Given the distinctive appearance of your husband's pocket watch, they circulated a description to various jewelers, pawnshops, and other places where stolen goods are sold—as well as to our informants in the thieving gangs. Despite Bow Street's offer of a substantial reward, nobody credible has come forward to claim it."

"Does the noise bother you, sir?" I asked, springing up from the sofa, pointing to the three large windows that overlooked Piccadilly. "I don't like to leave them open, but it gets so hot."

"Not in the least, Mrs. Cole. Please sit down. Now, my visit to you today has been prompted by a curious matter that has lately come to light."

I frowned. "A curious matter, sir?"

"As is required by probate, your husband's executor recently submitted a preliminary valuation of his estate to the Prerogative Court."

"His cousin, Daniel," I said.

"Quite so. I was surprised to learn that as well as this property and its contents, your husband had over fifteen hundred pounds deposited with Messrs. Campbell & Bruce, a banking house on the Strand."

I stared at him. "That cannot be true. Our life savings amount to less than two hundred pounds."

"So you did not know?"

Wondering why Daniel had said nothing of this to me, I shook my head mutely.

"Could the money have come from your shop?"

"No," I replied, faintly. "Our takings are ten pounds a week at most. Less in the summer. After the shop and household expenses, only a pound or two is left."

I confess my heart had soared at the thought of all that money. As his nearest male relative, Daniel was Jonas's principal heir, but under the terms of his will and my marriage contract, I was entitled to a third of his estate, as well as this house and shop, which had belonged to my father. All my financial problems solved. My debts cleared. The business safe. But where *had* it come from? What else had Jonas been hiding from me?

Mr. Fielding was silent, perhaps waiting for me to come up with an explanation. When none was forthcoming, he pressed on: "Our fruitless endeavors to find the watch, combined with this large and unexplained fortune, have led me to consider the possibility that your husband's murder might not have been the result of a street robbery after all. That the watch and his other possessions might have been taken to give that appearance, when the motive was something else entirely."

Again, I stared. "I don't understand."

"I have to consider the possibility that Jonas was killed by someone he knew." Fielding paused to take another bite of his pastry.

"Surely not," I said, struggling for words in that horrible moment. "Jonas was well liked. Respected."

"Even the best of men can inspire resentment. Upon which subject I must ask . . ." Fielding paused again to lick his fingers—"did Jonas have any enemies that you know of?"

I was trying to think. "He could be hard in his business dealings," I offered at last. "Sometimes he was late paying our suppliers. And sometimes he would be accosted by a ratepayer unhappy about a decision of the parish committee. The amount of their poor rate or an order to improve their pavement. But I never knew of any serious falling out." I studied Fielding's face. "Do you have a theory, sir? About this money?"

"Just supposition at the present time. Can I ask if one of your husband's friends owns a midnight-blue carriage with brass trim?"

I was convinced he did have a theory and I wanted to know it. Why was he asking me this? I forced myself to breathe.

"His friends are—were—shopkeepers and tradesmen for the most part. None that I know owns a carriage, except for the Smithsons and theirs is brown. But Jonas knew a lot of prominent gentlemen from the parish committee. Perhaps one of them?"

He nodded. "I ask because on the night your husband disappeared, just before he left the Running Horse, he requested that the landlord look outside for such a vehicle. He said it belonged to friends who might be waiting to give him a ride home. The man remembered it because Jonas had made a similar request just two nights earlier. Also, because he thought it an odd arrangement. The carriage just dropping by like that, when Jonas was so close to home, and on the latter night in very inclement weather. Both times, there was no vehicle waiting there and Jonas left the tavern alone."

Fielding was right. It did seem odd. Jonas had always extolled the virtue of a walk, whatever the weather. There was still so much about his final days that I didn't understand. I'd tried to push it all to the back of my mind, but how could I now?

"One possibility is that Jonas was afraid he was being watched," Fielding went on. "And that's why he asked the landlord to look out for that carriage. Some of the men he was drinking with that night say he seemed tense and rather snappish in the weeks preceding his death. Was that your impression too?"

I paused, uncertain what to say. "Perhaps a little—but Jonas could get like that sometimes. Curt with the apprentices. Even with me. I put it down to overwork. Between the shop and the parish committee, his responsibilities put quite a strain on him."

"You have three apprentices, is that right?"

I nodded. "Oscar is our trade apprentice. He has been with us for five years, learning the art of confectionary. Felix and Theodora are pauper apprentices from the workhouse. We took them on in September last year."

"You are to be commended, madam."

"We had room. This big house. All those abandoned children. I only wish we could have done more." I put my hands in my lap to stop them tugging at the lace of my cuffs. "We had a maidservant too, but she left about three months ago, not long before Jonas died, and we never got around to finding a replacement. Times are a little difficult right now, or I should have seen to it." Aware that I was talking too much, I smiled apologetically.

"I may need to speak to your apprentices at some point," he said, "but I have an appointment to get to now. Perhaps in the meantime you could ask them if they ever remember seeing such a carriage in the vicinity of this house? You can write to me at my residence on Bow Street."

"Of course."

"Then that is everything for the time being."

As we rose, my head swam, as if my life was spiraling away from me. Fielding bowed, and then gazed at me solicitously. "Be assured, Mrs. Cole, that I shall not rest until your husband's murderer is hanging from a rope."

CHAPTER THREE

I HAD TO see Daniel. Had to find out what he knew about this money. My emotions were a wave. Up and down. Fielding's appearance in the shop. The news that he was no nearer to catching the killer. Him taking personal charge of the inquiry. His revelation about the money. His theory that Jonas was killed by someone he knew . . . I hurried downstairs and grabbed my hat from a peg in the cloakroom.

Leaving Oscar in charge of the shop, I strode along Piccadilly, the street choked with shoppers and servants and delivery carts. When Parliament was sitting, grand carriages were a familiar sight, but now there were only one or two open-top chaises heading in the direction of Hyde Park. I turned onto St. James's Street, a sloped avenue of shops with curved windows: the finest cobblers, tailors, vintners, and tobacconists in all of London—and the little post office receiving house above which Daniel lived and worked.

I waited impatiently while the postmaster served a customer from his booth lined with pigeonholes stuffed with mail. Once I had his attention, I asked him to fetch Mr. Cole. When Daniel came down and caught sight of me, his face lit up with a broad smile. "Hannah, dearest," he said, in his plummy Ulster brogue. "What fortuitous timing! I was going to call by the shop later on."

"I need to talk to you," I said.

Hearing the urgency in my tone, he suggested we take a turn about the park. On the street outside, he raised his hat to a party of gentlemen leaving White's chocolate house. Jonas had used to say that half the cabinet met there to plot against the other half, but he would have sold his eyeteeth to become a member. In much the same spirit, he'd taken great pride in having a cousin who had been raised as a gentleman on an Irish plantation and educated at Cambridge—though if you'd seen him and Daniel together, you'd never have thought they were related. Where Jonas was tall, lean, and dark, Daniel was stocky and fair. Where Jonas spoke with a quiet authority, Daniel had an expansive charm surely destined for the bar or the pulpit. Yet despite a spell at one of the inns of court, he'd found the law to be "duller than Dorset," and thought the church an unambitious calling for a man of his talents. The idea of high government office was much more to his liking, and so Jonas had used his connections in the parish to obtain him a sinecure overseeing the Westminster post offices, which we'd all hoped would lead to better things.

"Do I take it Henry Fielding has been to see you?" he said. "I spoke to him this morning and he said he was coming to you next."

"He told me Jonas had over fifteen hundred pounds in the bank. Is that true?"

"Yes, it is."

"Why didn't you tell me?"

"Because I didn't want you doing anything rash like telling Henry Fielding. Regrettably, he has found out of his own accord."

"I don't understand." A familiar phrase of late. Curse all these men for keeping things from me.

"The wretched man has ordered a stay on the passage of probate. I'd been hoping it would all be wrapped up by the end of next week."

That wave again, crashing down upon my little world. "All of the money is delayed? Even the savings from our shop?"

"I'm afraid so."

"Why would he do that?"

Daniel hesitated. "He suspects that Jonas came by that money through nefarious means. He says if it rightfully belongs to somebody else, then they'd have a claim to it. It's possible he will try to confiscate the lot."

"Oh, Daniel." I couldn't afford this. The court had advanced me a small amount to live on in the weeks after Jonas's murder, but it wasn't nearly enough. With the shop closed and a mounting pile of bills, wages to pay, mourning clothes to buy, I'd been forced to borrow more. Only nobody wanted to lend to a woman unproven in business, except at extortionate rates, secured against the house and shop. Then the alembic I used to make the shop's distillations had cracked. The cost of a new one had added greatly to my debt, the lender only too happy to let the interest mount. I'd been counting the days until probate was granted, when I could use my third share of our savings to clear that debt.

I shook my head. "Why didn't Fielding tell me any of this?"

"I presume he didn't want to upset you—not until he has evidence of his suspicions. I have spoken to my lawyer, and he says all we can do is wait. If Fielding wants our money, then he has to prove wrongdoing."

"How can he hope to prove it? Jonas is dead."

"He intimated to me that villains usually have accomplices. Men they trust, who are privy to their secrets. One theory he has is that Jonas might have fallen out with someone he knew within the criminal fraternity. But Jonas wasn't a thief, he was a respectable tradesman. I told Mr. Fielding that in no uncertain terms."

Villains. Accomplices. Secrets. I felt sick. "So where did that money come from?" I asked.

"I haven't the first idea. All they could tell me at the bank was that it had been deposited over the course of the last two years in small amounts. Fielding seemed to think that was significant. I hear he has an appointment at the vestry hall this afternoon."

"Then he must think the money came from the parish?"

"I would think so. The newspapers are always full of stories about corrupt committeemen fiddling the poor fund." Daniel gave me a comforting smile. "Try not to worry, Hannah. What else can we do?"

I knew Daniel had debts too, presumably on better terms than mine. But a gentleman always had ways and means of obtaining more credit. Beg a loan from one of his rich friends, or his wealthy relatives on his mother's side. I tried not to resent the cheerful insouciance with which he greeted life's adversities. Hadn't I depended upon that same steadiness after Jonas's murder? While I'd been numb with shock, Daniel had dealt with everything: the funeral, the constables, the court, the memorial service. And unlike everybody else, he'd supported my decision to reopen the Punchbowl and Pineapple, declaring that the worst thing a person could do after a bereavement was wallow.

We were walking in the direction of the park, past a little crowd gathered outside the red-brick gatehouse of St. James's Palace. The royal standard proclaimed that King George the Second was in residence, having chosen for once to summer in London rather than Hanover. Theo liked to come down here on Sunday afternoons to try to catch sight of the king and his mistress, the Countess of Yarmouth. We turned into the narrow alley between the palace and the Lutheran church, raising our voices over the stamp of guardsmen's feet.

"I heard Fielding is trying to get a bill through Parliament to establish a *police* like they have in France," Daniel said. "The little despot wants a private army at his disposal, made up of paid constables, able to arrest anyone in London across parish boundaries. He put it to the Duke of Newcastle, who asked why he should support a measure so manifestly unpopular, when Fielding couldn't even find the murderer of one confectioner. The cabinet read all about Jonas's death in the newspapers, you see. A hardworking shopkeeper, backbone of the nation, a dedicated servant of his parish, cut down in his prime. Some of them knew him too, from the parish committee. I imagine Fielding thinks that if he can find the murderer, and at the same time prove that Jonas had been tempted away from the path of righteousness by villainy and corruption, it will be the perfect advertisement for his *police*." He smiled thinly. "And it will give the newspapers something to write about other than Fielding's antics with his maid."

"She is his wife now," I said distantly, still trying to make sense of it all.

"Fielding had little choice in the matter, not once she was carrying his child," Daniel went on. "All those plays he wrote casting philanderers like himself as the villain of the piece. Abandon her, and the world would have called him a hypocrite. Doesn't mean he has to like it though. I heard he tried to pack her off to the country, but she refused to go any further than Twickenham."

"The poor woman," I murmured. Some of my neighbors had advised me to sell up and retire to the country. Marry again in time, to a kindly widower with a few acres. Except the shop was my home, the only one I'd ever known, and it was much more to me than my livelihood, it was Father's legacy.

We crossed into the park, weaving our way between the avenues of lime trees and a rather boisterous game of pell-mell, onto the parched yellow lawns. Jonas had always encouraged me to walk in the Green Park, where the people of quality strolled, but I preferred St. James's, where nobody judged what you wore. The world seemed to be enjoying the weather: little boys flying kites, tradesmen's wives gossiping in pairs, soldiers on leave flirting with maidservants dawdling on errands. We walked along the ornamental canal in the direction of the parade ground.

"Jonas had an investment that I didn't know about," I said. "A gentleman came into the shop this morning and gave me five shillings. Two thirds of it is yours. I assume the relevant papers went astray."

I tried to keep the resentment from my tone. At least Daniel hadn't tried to challenge my right to a third of the money and the shop. The newspapers were full of stories about male heirs who'd done just that.

"Do you think Jonas could have had other investments?" I asked. "Maybe that's how he came by the money?"

Daniel looked skeptical. "Surely we would have found a record? Contracts? Stock certificates? They can't all have gone astray."

"I don't know. But I could ask Mr. Devereux—if he comes into the shop again? Or we could seek him out?"

"Devereux? Who's he?"

"The gentleman who gave me the money. He said he was a friend of Jonas's."

"Never heard of him. But I suppose it's worth a try."

"Can you think of anyone else we could talk to? Someone Jonas might have confided in?"

Daniel frowned. "Let's not get carried away. Do Fielding's job for him."

"Why not? He talked about how few resources he has. If we could prove that Jonas acquired that money honestly, then Fielding would have to lift the stay on probate. And it might affect his thinking on the murder?"

"Well, for one thing it might be dangerous," Daniel said. "These accomplices Fielding talked about. Villains." He shuddered.

"I thought you said there was no truth in any of that."

When Daniel didn't at first reply, I wondered if he was quite so convinced by Jonas's innocence as he'd claimed. I certainly wasn't under any illusions about my husband. Respectable he might have seemed, but Jonas had never scrupled overly about trifles like taxes and the letter of the law. I found it hard to imagine him risking everything by turning thief, but it wasn't completely beyond the realm of possibility.

"What matters is finding the devils who killed him," Daniel said firmly. "However Jonas came by that money, a street robbery still seems to me the most likely explanation for his murder. And even if Fielding is right and Jonas was killed by someone he knew, there are plenty of other places he might look. That's what I told him."

"What other places?" I asked, turning sharply.

He waved a hand. "Jonas was fearless. Always locking horns. Who knows what enemies he might have made over the years."

I studied his face, thinking it bland and rather evasive. It made me wonder if he was keeping something else from me.

"All I'm saying is that we need to think of our future," Daniel went on. "It's what Jonas would have wanted. Best to leave everything else to Mr. Fielding."

By "our future" he meant the money, I supposed. His lion's share of the fifteen hundred pounds. Perhaps he was afraid of what we might find if we looked too hard.

"I hate this," I exclaimed. "Not knowing what's going on when it concerns our lives."

"It's all very vexing," Daniel agreed. "When I found out about the money, I had my name put down for White's. Am I a suspect, do you think? I suppose we all are now."

"Oh, Daniel, don't say that. Of course you're not a suspect."

Frustrated by his levity—and his refusal to act—I thought of Jonas:

striding across the park like he owned the place, swinging his cane, raising his hat, on familiar terms with men far above him in rank and station. Was Henry Fielding right? Did he have a more sinister acquaintance too? Villains with whom he'd quarreled? I gazed back across the park in the direction of St. James's church and the vestry hall, wondering what Mr. Fielding was discovering there.

CHAPTER FOUR

I was at work in the kitchen, not long after the shop had closed, when Felix burst through the door, dragging a mop and bucket after him, slopping dirty water onto the floor. "A gentleman gave me this to give to you."

Biting back a reminder about good manners, I took the note he held out. The paper was thick and expensive, smelling faintly of civet scent. A neat, round-handed script. A recipe for peach iced cream.

"You must mean Mr. Devereux," I said. "I need to talk to him."

"He's already left in his carriage. Said to tell you he went down to St. Paul's to find a dealer in Italian books. That's his translation from a volume of recipes, right there." Felix tossed a coin into the air and caught it. "Gave me a shilling."

"How strange that he would go to so much trouble," I murmured. Also frustrating that I'd missed him, given the questions I wanted to ask him about Jonas's investments. "Did he say if he would be back?"

"Said he hoped he'd be able to try iced cream tomorrow."

"Then I'd better make some." Despite all my other anxieties, as I set about the recipe—grinding sugar, boiling it to a syrup, then clarifying it with egg white to draw off the impurities—I tasted a sweet edge of hope. My customers often proved resistant to change, and yet this frozen delicacy promised innovation married to the familiar. After all, what could be more English than peaches and cream? I knew instinctively that it would prove more popular than Persian sherbet, and more suited to this weather than apricot tarts. Yet reading the recipe, which advised freezing the peach cream by surrounding the pots with ice, I grew rather doubtful. When I chilled water or wine with ice, it didn't freeze, it simply grew cold. And surely this mixture would be much thicker than water, which my instinct told me would make it harder to freeze?

Theo was writing labels for wormwood wine in the cramped script she'd learned at the workhouse, chattering away about the earl of this and the countess of that. Oscar was cutting out lemon pastilles, taking too long in his efforts to make their size precisely even. Felix was down on his knees with the blacking pot, getting more upon himself than on the oven doors. I judged it a good time to tell them the news.

"You probably already know that Mr. Fielding came by the shop today," I began. "He tells me that new evidence has come to light in Bow Street's inquiry, and he now believes Mr. Cole might have been killed by someone he knew. He may want to talk to you in the coming days."

They stared at me. "Why would he want to talk to us?" Felix asked.

"In case you know anything that might help him."

"Well, I don't."

His black brows were drawn together, his fist clenched tight around the blacking brush. It had been Theo we'd wanted, when we'd gone to the workhouse last year, seeking a pauper apprentice. She was a little scrawny from the workhouse gruel, but she had the right look for a shopgirl: all big, honest eyes and dimpled cheeks. Only she'd refused to come without her brother, and the beadle thought she'd run away if we tried to separate them. When I'd said we should take them both, I'd expected Jonas to refuse, but to my surprise, he'd thought that Felix might suit us too.

"I've been saying for a while that we need a fellow on the door to move on vagabonds and discourage thieves," he'd said. "This one's got a savage look. And he'll be useful in helping with the heavier jobs around the place. Oscar struggles to lift a preserving pan."

Now I couldn't help seeing that decision in a new light. Had Jonas wanted a savage-looking fellow around the place because he'd been afraid? Of whoever was in that blue carriage? His accomplices? His enemies? It might help explain one or two of the things I didn't understand.

"He wanted me to ask you about a midnight-blue carriage," I said. "One with brass trim. Did any visitors ever come to the house in a vehicle like that?"

"Oscar saw it, didn't you?" Felix said.

Oscar's hand jerked, sending sugar all over the table. Felix sniggered. My trade apprentice had never liked being the center of attention. A strand of lank brown hair was plastered to his sweaty cheek, and he brushed it aside before stammering out his answer.

"That was Theo," he said. "She told Mr. Cole."

I turned. "Theo?"

She answered me with apparent reluctance. "Mr. Cole said that there had been a spate of burglaries in the street and he asked us to watch out for a dark blue carriage that had been involved. I told him I'd seen it a few days earlier, just across from the shop. I think he thought that they might have been watching the place."

I hadn't heard anything about a spate of burglaries. "When was this?"

She considered. "The beginning of March, I think."

A few weeks before the murder. "Did you get a good look at the driver? Or the men inside?"

She shook her head.

"Did Mr. Cole seem concerned by what you told him?"

"I think so. He said I wasn't to mention it to you."

I frowned. "Did he say why not?"

"I suppose he didn't wish to frighten you."

My voice grew taut. "Is there anything else he ever ordered you not to tell me?"

She flushed. "No, Mrs. C."

My fear for the future often made me short with them. It ate away at everything good: sleep, civility, trust.

"I'll write and tell Mr. Fielding," I said.

"Watch out," Felix said to his sister. "Fielding will be looking to stick that murder onto someone." He mimed putting a noose around his neck, pulling it tight, lolling his tongue in a death grimace.

"Don't be a child," I said, sharply.

I pulped the peaches and then stirred them, together with the sugar, into three pints of cream, tasting my mixture until I was satisfied with the sweetness. Then I went into the shop, where I'd left the key to my spice box. In the half-light of dusk, I surveyed the marble tables and the gilded chairs; the silver punch bowls, the crystal lamps, and the gilt-edged mirrors. A large pineapple, the symbol of our shop since my father's day, was in pride of place on an ivory stand on my shelves. It was surrounded by glass jars with serpentine handles containing lozenges and sugar drops, glittering like jewels. The fixtures and fittings of my shop cost almost as much as the building itself. But my customers demanded the best, and if I sold anything to meet my debts, word would get out that I was in trouble. Then my suppliers would want paying in advance, which would only mean more debt. I knew my moneylender believed that I'd be forced to sell up eventually, and I suspected he already had a buyer for the shop in mind. Parasites, my father had called them. He'd thought only fools borrowed money. But he'd never worn a widow's weeds, never known how the world conspired to punish a woman for the crime of wanting to earn an honest living.

As I returned to the kitchen in a despondent mood, the voices of my apprentices carried to me in the cloakroom. They were talking about me and Mr. Devereux.

"He went to St. Paul's especially to find it," Oscar said. "Probably searched for hours. Why would he do that?"

Felix barked a laugh. "Why do you think?"

"Because he wants to marry her?" Theo said. "She's still quite pretty and she has no children. And she has this shop."

"It's not the shop he's after," Felix said. "You should have seen his chaise. Bang-up, it was. Lacquered all over, fine black horses, the coachman in good livery. Devereux's a wealthy gent."

"Then what does he want with Mrs. C?" Theo asked.

I shall not repeat Felix's reply. Except to say it contained the usual unkind slanders about widows and the supposed laxity of our morals. Theo squealed with laughter and Oscar snapped at them to be quiet lest I hear.

As I walked into the kitchen, fixing them with a hard glare, they fell silent. I unlocked the spice box and grated a little nutmeg into my mixture. Then I arranged twelve tin pots on a tray and filled each one to the brim with my peach cream.

"When you're done with that, Theo, chop the nuts for the pistachio prawlongs. Felix, if you use any more of that blacking, it's coming out of your wages."

Carrying my tray, I descended the stairs to the cellar, where I was hit by a welcome blast of cool, spice-scented air. The first room, on the Piccadilly-side, contained the coal and wood stores; the ash bins; bottles of wine and spirits for the shop's distillations; and sacks of flour, salt, apples, carrots, and beets. The room to the rear contained the stairs, our ice-store, and rows of shelves holding conserves and marmalades; jars of marinating fruits; cakes and puddings wrapped in muslin; goods from the dairy, sugar loaves, and other groceries. I set my pots down on a vacant shelf, and went over to the ice-store. A sulfurous waft rose up to greet me from the culverted river that gurgled away ten feet below. Originally built as a well at the time the house was constructed, the river water had soon grown too polluted to drink. When I'd been a girl, we'd simply emptied our chamber pots into it. It had been Jonas who'd remarked how cold it was down there in the shaft, and had the idea of repurposing the old well into an ice-store.

Using both hands to turn the handle, I raised the large wooden tub up from below. Almost as wide as the shaft itself, the tub could hold seventy pounds of ice when full, but I had only one small block left. I'd have to buy more tomorrow, and the price had gone through the rafters with all the hot weather. Lifting out the ice, wincing at the chill even through the flannel wrapping, I carried it to the butcher's block nearby. A rack on the wall behind it held saws, picks, and other ice tools. Mr. Devereux's recipe was rather vague, but it clearly required larger pieces than the shavings in a Persian sherbet. I selected a pick of medium size and set to work with my mallet, filling a pail with the fragments I mined.

"How long will it take to freeze?"

Oscar. A heavy lad of nearly eighteen years of age, he had a surprising ability to creep up on a person like that.

"The recipe says four hours," I replied, rather shortly.

Oscar put his stack of boxes down on one of the shelves, and with a heavy sigh, set about rearranging the jars of pickled peaches. Felix's work, I presumed.

"He never does what I tell him," Oscar said. "And if I threaten him with a thrashing, he just laughs."

Poor Oscar. He'd been hoping for a compliant young shopgirl to order around and look up to him, and instead he'd got Theo, who answered back, and Felix, who terrified him. Not that he was above a subtle insult, many of which flew right over Felix's head, gibes at his lack of breeding and education. Sometimes my shop felt like a front in the Indian Wars.

"There's a lesson for you there against making empty threats," I said. "But there are better ways of getting a person to do what you want than a thrashing."

He sighed again. "If there are, I haven't found one."

"If you run headfirst into a wall, don't just do it again. You have to work out how to get around it. Show Felix that it's in his best interests to help you. You'll learn all this fast, once you have a shop of your own."

Oscar's father, a master cabinetmaker in the City, already had a premises in Cheapside picked out for him. "He's an odd lad," he'd told Jonas, when we'd first met to discuss his son's apprenticeship. "Give him a hammer and a plane and you'll end up with splinters, but he can do things with sugar that would put a king's table to shame. Our cook says there's money to be made in that now."

Jonas had thought that Oscar had a weak character, but even he couldn't deny the boy's talents. I was going to miss him when he was gone. Thinking about the burdens of widowhood and Felix's gibes, I screwed the pots of cream into the ice rather forcefully. Then I set about sealing them with muslin.

Oscar lingered by the ice-store. "Theo has a loose tongue, you know. You should hear some of the things she says about our customers when you're not here. Stories she reads in those scandal sheets she buys. You never know what she might say to Mr. Fielding about our business."

I studied his anxious face. "What business do you mean? I'm sure we have nothing to hide."

Oscar held my gaze for a moment, then looked away.

CHAPTER FIVE

LATER THAT NIGHT, in my sweltering parlor, my apprentices upstairs in bed, I could think properly for the first time that day. Assess things rationally—however hard that might be. Had Daniel been keeping something else from me? Something he'd shared with Mr. Fielding? And what had Oscar meant by his cryptic comment? I shivered, the sweat on my skin suddenly cold.

I thought of Fielding sitting here earlier. His condescending manners. Yet he was sharper than the constable who'd come before. A man familiar with stories, who had an ear for the lies people told to cover their tracks. I thought of his raised eyebrow when I'd said that Peter the Great of Russia had given my grandfather his watch. The irony being, that part was true.

Jonas had loved that watch. He was forever bringing it out in public—"Oh, is that the time?"—and then telling the story of the tsar's Great Embassy to London. Peter's retinue had included two clocksmiths, seventy soldiers picked for their height, four dwarves (presumably also picked for their height), and a monkey. He had paid several visits to my grandfather's shop, where his dwarves ate so many coffee cream wafers they ran amok overturning tables and breaking glasses.

When the time came for the tsar's departure, he asked my grandfather to return with him to Moscow as his imperial pastry cook. My grandfather politely declined and was afraid he'd given offense, but the tsar kissed him on both cheeks and presented him with his watch in recognition of his talents.

Back then, in the last years of King William's reign, there were open fields to the north of Piccadilly. People had said that my grandfather was mad to open his shop there. The grand nobles who'd built mansions near to St. James's Palace were too busy at court to shop and the king had his own army of confectioners. Better to have bought a premises on the Strand, where gentlemen had shopped for generations, or in Covent Garden. But my grandfather had believed that the rest of the nobility would follow in the wake of the courtiers. Then the gentry would follow the nobles, the lawyers and the physicians would follow the gentry, and soon every luxury tradesman would want a shop on Piccadilly. So it had proved. Now the mansions of Mayfair sprawled all the way to the Tyburn Road, and there were six confectioners within a mile's radius.

One of my earliest memories is of my father holding up that watch by its chain, the case spinning, catching the light, sending golden circles gliding across the walls like wandering suns. The scents of my childhood—toasted almonds and cinnamon, blackcurrant and clove—bring back my father's deep voice, and the comforting touch of his calloused hands. I never knew my mother, who had died not long after I was born. My father and the Punchbowl and Pineapple: that was my world. I would run home from the Academy for Tradesmen's Daughters, our poor housemaid calling after me to slow down, in time to help Father serve our last customers and close up the shop. He was a big, gentle man—bigger even than Mr. Fielding. After supper I would climb onto his lap, and he'd tell me stories about the Sleeping Beauty of the Wold and the ogress who planned to eat her in a raspberry sauce. He taught me how to tally accounts and how to spin sugar into spirals. Not to confuse wealth with honor. Nor good fortune with hard work.

I was twelve years old when Jonas came to live with us. He was the first apprentice my father ever took on. Father said it was because the shop was doing so well and he needed another pair of hands, but I could see how he'd started to tire carrying sacks of flour, and held his arm awkwardly when beating a meringue. When I think of Jonas now, it is as he was then. Fifteen years old, long, awkward limbs, his hair spiked up like a sweep's brush. Intrigued by this interloper, I would watch him in the kitchen with a critical eye, unimpressed by his work with sugar and pastry. Sometimes he would tell me stories too. About men he knew from the newspapers who'd made themselves a fortune out of nothing. Cotton kings and engineers, silk merchants and shopkeepers like Father. Fascinated by his dreams, my world grew a little larger to encompass him.

Jonas improved the fortunes of the Punchbowl and Pineapple in countless small ways. His real talent lay with figures and he soon took over the books, pointing out to my father where he could make savings, who was overcharging, and who was skimping on their measures. He dealt with such men more forcefully than my father ever could, and it brought me a frisson of excitement watching him do it. To my regret, he spent most of his evenings in the taverns (of which my father didn't approve), getting to know the footmen from the grand houses. If he learned that the Countess of Chesterfield liked almond prawlongs, then that lady would receive a pretty box of them the next day with the compliments of our shop. When her footman appeared at the counter with an order, Jonas would offer him a healthy discount.

"He'll be back," he'd say with satisfaction.

"Why wouldn't he be back?" I said. "You're all but giving our goods away—to our richest customers."

"Sometimes you have to spend money to make money. People want to shop where the grandest people do. They like to feel a proximity to their lives."

I liked to feel a proximity to Jonas's life. He took me to see the lord mayor's procession when my father had taken to his bed with a fever. Jonas had climbed a wall and hauled me up so I could see. We'd eaten chestnuts from a bag and he'd pointed out all the important men of the City. I tried to impress him by talking about Shakespeare, but he said he wasn't interested in stories people made up.

I tried not to mind when he laughed at my singing. And I pretended his blancmange was better than mine. Was this love? To care so much about one man's opinion?

For his eighteenth birthday, I made him a castle out of gingerbread and sugar paste.

"It's Windsor," I told him, proudly. Father had an engraving of that fortress on the wall in his book room.

Jonas circled it admiringly. "When I'm rich, I'll take you to Windsor in my carriage."

I smiled. "How will you be rich?"

"I'll buy the shop next door and knock them into one. More customers means more profit. I'll buy another shop then, in Berkeley Square. Maybe one in Bloomsbury too."

I clapped my hands. "An empire!"

He grinned. "You'll have to call me Jonas the Great."

A flaw in his scheme occurred to me. "But it's Father's shop. Will you buy it?"

"I won't need to," he said. "I mean to marry you."

He said it as though it was obvious. My stomach turned over.

"Because you want the shop?"

"Because you're beautiful."

In the heady months that followed, I became aware that others were complicit in this design. Jonas's parents and my father too. On the day Jonas asked for my hand, Father had presented him with the tsar's watch. "Give this to your firstborn son," he'd said.

By then, we all knew that my father was dying. Nobody spoke of it, but his speech was slurred, his head often slumped, and he could no longer work in the shop. Jonas and I had been married just six weeks when I walked into the parlor to find Father lying on the floor. Jonas had held me as I'd wept, and I remember how tightly I'd clung to him, seeking his durability in my shattering world.

He was my world now. I grieved, but I also soared.

Sometimes I still think of those early days of our marriage. The dawn sunlight upon his skin, still a foreign land to me, the things he used to say to make me blush.

"You're my Windsor." His palm grazed my bare breast, making my breath quicken. "I'm going to conquer you, Hannah Cole."

I remember wondering how I could be so happy at such a time. I remember thinking: *this is what love is*. I remember pitying all those girls who'd never been adored by Jonas Cole.

But that's the trouble with stories, especially the ones you write for yourself. Sometimes you think they've ended, when they've barely begun.

*

Jonas died twice, I always think. The first time he died slowly like my father had. His decline began only a year into our marriage. For weeks, ever since my courses had stopped, Jonas had been talking about all the things he would one day do with our son. Send him to a school for gentlemen, put him into one of the professions, marry him well.

"He's not even born yet," I'd cry. "Give the poor lad a chance."

On that dreadful day, not long after supper, all those dreams drained away into a bloody chamber pot. When I told Jonas, he turned around and left the room. I wept for an hour, alone, waiting for him to return. When he did, he sank to his knees, placing his head in my lap. Relief coursed through me.

"We'll make another," he said. "Let's start right now."

I'd count the days with a feverish obsession, checking them off in a little book. Then a bloody moment of despair, and I'd have to begin all over again. Teas of calamint and sage, visits by the rector, who talked about the barren fig tree and the fruitful vine. We knew the fault was mine, because we took the Barley Test: each steeping a handful of grain in our urine, then planting the seeds in soil. When his took root and mine did not, I told myself not to give up hope—and isn't hope the best storyteller of all? The books advise against salted meat, against being too fat, or being too thin. The midwife told me sad women couldn't conceive—that you could kill a child with longing. The rector talked of Sarah and Rachel and my namesake, Hannah—about the scourge of bitterness and the balm of patience. As the years went by, his smile grew more fixed, and he talked more of bitterness and less of patience.

At least he still smiled. I don't know when Jonas stopped. Oh, he had smiles for his friends and our customers, but when we were alone his face was a stone. If Jonas set his mind to something, he expected the world to bend to his will. When he wanted a seat on the parish committee, he went about befriending the right men. Then he engineered the displacement of one of those men, so that he could take his place. But you can't fix a woman's womb like you can fix an election. More than anything, I think Jonas resented me for his powerlessness—to obtain the one thing that he wanted most.

By then, he was always out late on parish business. His dreams involved politics now, rather than our shop. One day, I confronted him as he was putting on his coat.

"Please, Jonas, stay home. Just for one night."

He pulled out my father's watch. "I have to see the committee officers about a problem with the Court of Burgesses."

"Tomorrow, then?"

"Tomorrow I have a meeting about the workhouse."

Needless to say, all these meetings took place in taverns. What else went on there? Dice? Dancing? Critical conversations about wives? Other women? My mind worked away at these possibilities.

"A good husband spends time with his wife," I cried out in despair.

He studied me then, as though I was suddenly an object of interest. "You think to lecture me about being a good husband, when you can't even fulfill the most basic function of a wife?"

Then he walked out, leaving me with an aching void in my chest and the realization that the man I'd loved was gone.

As for the man who'd taken his place, my enemy with his cruel words and cold eyes, he died on the twenty-sixth day of March 1749 when I beat his brains out with the mallet I use to break up ice.

CHAPTER SIX

KILLING JONAS WAS not an act of pleasure, but rather of necessity. I'd been over it all in my mind many times, and I did not see that he had left me very much choice. It was a clear-cut case of self-defense, even if the law wouldn't see it as such. I concede that this last detail is an important one.

If my own motivation was clear, Jonas's was more of a mystery. I knew he was planning an act of great wickedness—one that needed to be stopped—but I didn't know why. Did the fifteen hundred pounds in his bank have something to do with it? Or whoever owned this blue carriage?

One thing was for certain: I had been complacent in thinking that everyone had believed my fiction of a violent robbery. Now that Henry Fielding had shattered that illusion, I could no longer take refuge in ignorance. If that money had been acquired honestly, which I certainly didn't rule out, then I needed to prove it quickly. Steer Fielding back to pawnshops and footpads, before he stumbled upon evidence that might have him poking around in the dark corners of my marriage. And if Jonas *had* stolen that money, if he *did* have a villainous acquaintance, then anything I could learn that might help point Henry Fielding in their direction rather than mine, was all to my benefit. Everything else paled into insignificance, even probate and the looming shadow of my debts.

Early the following afternoon, I told Oscar to mind the counter again while I went out. Felix was slouched against the wall outside, eating one of Mr. Fortnum's "scotched" eggs. When I ordered him to stand up straight and not to eat while he was on duty, he simply said "Right you are, Mrs. C" and crammed the rest of the egg into his mouth.

Yet I couldn't deny his efficacy as a doorman. The urchins gave our shop a wide berth now, and the one time a thief masquerading as a gentleman had tried to walk off with a pineapple—Felix told me the villains call such men "spruce prigs"—he had dragged the fellow out by the ear, kicked him hard in the buttocks, and sent a volley of curses after him as he'd hopped off down the street. Impressed, I'd attempted to smarten him up a little, giving him one of Jonas's old wigs to wear, and a hat and coat with brass buttons that I'd found at the Oxford market. The wig was too small and the coat too big, but Felix swaggered around in them nonetheless.

Mrs. Brunsden, Mrs. Fortnum, and Mrs. Howard were talking outside the Howards' lace emporium on the other side of the street. I gave them a nod, wondering if they were talking about me. Most of the wives didn't like my decision to reopen the Punchbowl and Pineapple any more than their husbands did. In the City it would not be seen as strange—many widows ran businesses there—but St. James's had unwritten rules designed to preserve its rarefied status. Judgmental fools, I thought, as I stomped along Piccadilly in the direction of the Haymarket. Wait until you find yourself alone without a husband.

In this bleak and ungodly humor, I approached St. James's. Churches are often a fitting match for their congregations, and St. James's was suitably elegant and imposing. Set a little way back from the street behind a railing, built of red brick like the palace, the sun gleamed on its dressings of white Portland stone. The vestry hall, where the parish committee met, was one of several buildings in the courtyard.

I had only been inside it once before, when I'd attended a dinner for the committeemen and their wives. I'd found it an intimidating place. Many lords and members of Parliament sat on the parish committee in order to keep their streets well maintained and their poor rates low. Jonas had given me so many instructions about who to talk to and what to say, that I remember wishing eternal fire would consume them all. I had embarrassed him that day, quite without meaning to, and he had refused to speak to me for over a week.

Today the vestry hall was a quieter place. An ecclesial chill crept across my perspiring skin. Half a dozen stern portraits of rectors past gazed down to tally my sins. Seated at a large oak table, busy writing in a ledger, was the parish clerk, Mr. Twisleton.

"Mrs. Cole," he said, rising, when he caught sight of me hovering by the door. "Do come in. Won't you sit down?"

Jonas had begrudgingly admitted Twisleton's competence in administrative matters. He was a young man, from a long line of parish clerks, his deep-set eyes, wide nostrils, and sunken cheeks giving him an unfortunate resemblance to a memento mori skull. Yet he was amiable enough, and at church on Sundays; despite the fashionable congregation around us, he had always made a point of wishing me good day. I declined his offer of refreshment and he gazed at me, concerned. "How have you been? You have been in my prayers."

"In truth, Mr. Twisleton, I have been better. Yesterday Henry Fielding came to see me."

He nodded gravely. "Yes, I too had that pleasure. If that's the word."

"This money," I said, twisting my handkerchief in a simulacrum of distress. "I don't understand where it came from. Daniel said Mr. Fielding made certain insinuations about Jonas. But I cannot believe—" I broke off, dabbing at my eyes.

"It grieves me to know that he has occasioned you further suffering," Twisleton said. "Rest assured I told Mr. Fielding that there is no possibility that the money in question came from this parish."

"Are you sure?" I said, my heart rising a little. How much easier things would be if Jonas had come by the money honestly. Then Fielding might be persuaded to think again.

"Quite certain. I would know if such a large sum were missing from the parish funds. I showed Mr. Fielding the books and the figures prove it. He then suggested that the money might have been misappropriated in some other way—that certain sums I was showing him might not have reached their intended destination."

"Like the poor fund?" I asked, remembering what Daniel had said.

"Quite so. But our entire poor fund amounts to only four hundred pounds annually, and so I cannot see how Mr. Cole could possibly have enriched himself to the tune of fifteen hundred pounds. We captain a rigorous vessel here, the rector and I. Oh, I don't deny that occasionally some act of minor wrongdoing by one of our overseers comes to light. A poor-fund claimant who doesn't exist, or a pension for a man dead long ago. But the bad apples get rooted out and the barrel is sound. I told Mr. Fielding not to believe everything he reads about parish corruption in the newspapers. That the name of a good servant of St. James's like Jonas Cole should be besmirched . . . why, it is akin to the defamation of Nehemiah."

Rather bewildered by this onslaught of metaphor, I wished I had more confidence in Twisleton's judgment. His pleasure of choice, whenever he came into the Punchbowl and Pineapple, was a large nugget of Holland candy, the crystallized sugar containing glittering fragments of angelica, pistachio, ginger, and chocolate—treasures to be mined from their sweet bedrock by a determined tongue. It is a confection for a man who takes a child's delight in the world, and I envied Twisleton his optimism about human nature, even as I scorned it.

"I find this greatly reassuring, sir," I said. "And yet I would feel better if I knew for certain where this money *had* come from. You knew my husband well. Have you any idea?"

He hesitated, not quite meeting my eye.

"What is it? Please tell me. I need to know."

He nodded understandingly, his lips drawn back onto his teeth in a rictus smile, one that suggested his idea might not be to my liking.

"One possibility that I suggested to Mr. Fielding was that Jonas had won that money at play. Please don't be distressed, Mrs. Cole. I know gaming houses are illegal, but there is barely a gentleman in the kingdom who hasn't stepped foot in one at some point in his life. I know I have—though please don't tell the rector. Not all such establishments are disreputable, quite the contrary."

I wished he would stop talking and get to the point. "What makes you think Jonas frequented such places?"

"A rumor I heard. That he had been entertaining some of the more prominent members of the parish committee in the local gaming houses. He aspired to sit in Parliament one day, as I'm sure you know. An astonishing ambition for a shopkeeper, one might think, but with Jonas you felt that anything was possible. However he came by that money, I'm sure that was its intended purpose. To fund his campaign."

Bribes, he meant. Jonas used to say that a man didn't get into Parliament without buying off the right people.

"Do you know the names of these gaming houses, sir?"

"I'm afraid not. As I say, it was only a rumor. I had a word with Jonas about it—just a quiet warning that the rector wouldn't like it—but he laughed it off."

"Did Mr. Fielding seem convinced when you told him about this rumor?"

"Not entirely." Twisleton scratched his temple, one finger sliding beneath his wig. "He asked me a lot of questions about Jonas's work for the parish. And also enquired about your household and Jonas's friends. I suppose he has to consider every possibility."

My pulse quickened. Was Daniel right? Was I already a suspect? Had Fielding's inquiries included questions about my marriage?

I forced the sort of smile that clever men like: supplicating, deferring to their knowledge. "I confess I hardly comprehend Jonas's work for the parish at all. He used to say that it would bore me—and perhaps it would have done. But now that he is gone, I feel a need to better understand that part of his life."

Twisleton looked rather relieved, evidently preferring this topic to unsavory rumors concerning dead husbands. "The workings of the parish are really rather simple, though I appreciate it might sound a little complicated at first. The St. James's committee is unique in its form. We guarantee representation to all ratepayers, the membership elected in thirds: peers of the realm, gentlemen, and tradesmen. It is the committee itself that does the electing, not the ratepayers—we owe rather more to Rome than Athens here in St. James's! As the lords and most of the gentry are only resident for part of the year, the bulk of the work of the parish falls upon the tradesmen. The rector and I divide the various areas of responsibility up between them. In Jonas's case, he served as a sort of envoy between the parish and other bodies of relevance to our work: our neighboring parishes, Parliament, the various government ministries, the Common Council of London, the magistrates of Westminster and Middlesex, and so on. Jonas met with them periodically, apprising them of our work where it overlapped with their own, and reporting back. We liked to think of him as our intelligencer—I don't believe that's too grandiose a word."

"I see." Given Jonas's parliamentary ambitions, all these connections would undoubtedly have proved very useful to him. But Fielding clearly thought there was more to it than that.

"And of course," Twisleton went on, "Jonas was a great supporter of our philanthropic works. The charity school and the workhouse, in particular. That was the manner of man he was, Mrs. Cole. Pray don't listen to any speculation to the contrary."

I thanked him again for setting my mind at rest.

Twisleton rose. "While you are here, I have something for you." He disappeared through a door, returning with a red silk coat in his hand. "I found this in the cloakroom the other day, when I was having a tidy. I was going to drop it by the shop, but I wanted to choose the right time."

As I took it from him, I caught a waft of Jonas's lemon scent. It made me feel sick. Taking my leave from Twisleton, I walked back along Jermyn Street, holding the coat at a distance, as if it was an unclean thing. I entered the shop via the alley and the kitchen, and was about to hang the coat in the cloakroom with my hat, when instinct gave me pause.

Jonas's pockets were always full of life's detritus. In the old days, I'd emptied them fondly. Later, as suspicion had crept in, I'd rooted through them seeking evidence of betrayal. It felt strange to be doing the same thing now, when our account had already been settled in all its finality. The little pile I accumulated on the kitchen table was familiar enough: gentlemen's calling cards, trade cards, and other scraps of paper scribbled with reminders and appointments in Jonas's hand, a handkerchief, two clay pipes, coins, a tinderbox, sticks of sealing wax, a battered packet of cinnamon comfits from the shop—and what looked like a trinket:

a little fish made of porcelain with painted scales of gold. I picked it out, holding its cool weight in my palm.

Gamblers played with gaming tokens shaped like fishes. I'd seen them at the Vauxhall Gardens when Jonas had taken me there: the gamblers hunched feverishly over the tables, little piles of fishes in front of them. Those fishes had been flat and made of ivory, but who was to say they didn't come in different forms? This one certainly looked distinctive. I slipped it into my pocket.

When I walked into the shop and Theo caught sight of me, her expression betrayed her agitation. "The carter is waiting, Mrs C."

My trip to buy ice! What with everything else, I had forgotten it entirely. Hurrying outside onto Piccadilly, I found Felix slouched against the wall again. "Carter wouldn't wait," he announced. "Said he had to be in Kensington for four."

Uttering a soft cry of frustration, I gazed up and down the street. If I couldn't buy ice, the cream would sour and the butter would melt. Spotting a hackney carriage, I waved it down, trying not to think about the expense of the journey out to Willesden. But the driver only sped past me, raising a cloud of dust from the cobbles that dirtied my dress. A molten heat rose behind my eyes, the shop fronts and the carriages blurring together. Then I heard a shout and a clatter of hooves. Glimpsed the sleek black flanks of a pair of horses and the lacquered yellow wood of a fine four-wheeled chaise that halted beside me.

"Can I convey you anywhere at all, Mrs. Cole?"

I looked up into the enquiring face of William Devereux.

CHAPTER SEVEN

Heads turned as we rattled along Piccadilly in Mr. Devereux's open-top chaise. *Not three months since her husband died,* I could imagine them saying. *And you should have seen her companion!* In theory, as a widow, I was committing no great transgression by taking a ride with a gentleman upon a matter of business. But try talking about theory to the good people of St. James's.

Unwise, given everything—and yet I needed to buy ice and I wanted to talk to Mr. Devereux about Jonas's investments. Perhaps mindful of my reputation, he had moved to the rear-facing seat. I had also summoned Felix to act as chaperone, now sitting up front with the liveried driver, wearing a broad grin at the prospect of a journey in this fine carriage. We turned into Tyburn Lane. On our left Hyde Park, as bleached and white as the Desert of Sinai. On our right, the mansions of Mayfair, shuttered for the season. Mr. Devereux discoursed pleasantly about the weather, about a hazelnut cake he'd eaten in Paris, and about the merits of Mr. Handel's new oratorio. As we rounded the gallows at Tyburn, marking the northwest corner of the city, I averted my eyes.

"I am very grateful to you, sir," I said. "This is quite an imposition."

"Oh, I have only ulterior motives, I assure you."

Mindful of my apprentices' conversation the previous evening, I must have looked momentarily shocked, because he burst out laughing. "The iced cream," he declared. "I hope I might claim my reward when we return?"

"Oh," I said. "I'm afraid it didn't work."

I explained that I had checked on the pots first thing that morning, and discovered that the peach cream, whilst very cold, had remained resolutely unfrozen. I'd repurposed the cream into a cheesecake, but the ice had gone to waste.

Devereux frowned. "That is a great shame. I was very much hoping to try it again. And yet the recipe must be possible, for I have tasted frozen cream myself. We must be doing something wrong."

Bridling a little at his implication of a shared destiny, I spoke rather curtly. "Well, it can't be helped."

Oblivious to my displeasure, he passed a hand across his chin. "There's a man we might consult: Professor Becker. Have you heard of him? He is currently appearing at Hickford's Long Room. Might I convince you to accompany me there tomorrow night?"

I had heard of Professor Becker. The newspapers were full of acclaim for his chemistry show. But I didn't countenance Devereux's proposal for a moment. His invitation had convinced me that Felix was right, this was all a transparent ruse to conceal his true desire: that "one thing" which the guides to widowhood referenced so obliquely, and that Felix had cited last night with rather less decorum. My tone bore a resemblance to the product we were heading to buy. "Mr. Devereux, I am in mourning."

Immediately, he looked contrite. "Yes, of course," he murmured. "Forgive my enthusiasm."

I might have spoken more sharply still, had I not been sitting in his carriage with questions to ask him. We rode in silence for some time, until I judged that the awkwardness of my refusal had passed. By then we were out in the countryside, rattling along beside a long parade of taverns and tea gardens advertising the waters in the Kilburn wells. Their owners aspired to draw genteel customers from the nearby resort of Hampstead, but the patrons came instead from the pleasure garden at Belsize: a rough crowd who preferred bear-baiting and bare-knuckle boxing to string quartets.

Ignoring the brazen stares of the drinkers in the street, I focused on Mr. Devereux. "Can I ask you a question, sir? Did my husband ever make any other investments on your advice—apart from the one you told me about yesterday?"

"No, he did not. Although we did discuss the prospect of him doing so."

"Could he have made investments on the advice of others? Or upon his own initiative?"

"He might have done," Devereux said. "Though if he did, he never mentioned it to me."

I seized on this possibility. "Could a person invest around two hundred pounds and turn it into fifteen hundred pounds over the course of just two years?"

Devereux raised his eyebrows. "Not unless he is a magician. A good rate of return is ten percent a year on an investment, which is what I anticipate from the Culross Iron and Coal Company. I've known of a few extraordinary speculative ventures in which a man might double his money within a year, but that is rare indeed, and is usually due to an anomaly in the market. Most of the time such schemes are dreamed up by sharpers and other fraudsters. I counsel you to be wary of anyone suggesting such a thing."

"Oh no, you misunderstand me. Jonas had a large sum of money in the bank when he died that I knew nothing about. I am simply trying to ascertain where it might have come from."

Devereux frowned. "I presumed it was an inheritance."

"It couldn't have been. His cousin, Daniel, was his only living relative." I studied his face a moment. "Then Jonas told you about that money?"

Devereux nodded. "There is a syndicate I am involved with, a very profitable scheme, and Jonas wanted to be a part of it. Our minimum investment is a thousand pounds and I was surprised to learn that he had such a sum at his disposal. Even so, I had to refuse him, though the decision was not mine. It was a difficult conversation, and afterwards he avoided my company. I regret bitterly that he died when we were on bad terms."

Then it didn't sound as if the money could have been accrued through investment or speculation. Rather despondently, I watched the world go by. Before too long, we passed the boundary marker for the parish of Willesden, an unfashionable stretch of countryside between Hampstead and the town of Harrow. "The manor's just here on the left," I told Mr. Devereux.

He twisted round to instruct the driver, who slowed the horses as we approached the gate-lodge. The porter had been let go a year earlier and the gates were left unlocked during the day. Felix jumped down to open them and then scrambled back onto the box. We jolted along the rutted drive, between wide lawns of dying grass, until the red-brick moated manor house came into view. At my direction, we turned onto a spur of the drive that rounded the house, leading to a few acres of neglected woodland on the north side of the estate. Mr. Devereux turned to inspect the brambles and the dead deer in the moat.

"I know the wilderness garden is à la mode right now, but this seems a little much even for Willesden."

"Jonas said Mr. Marsh would be forced to sell up within a year," I explained. "His family have owned this place for generations. He's trying his hardest to cling on, and maybe he will, given this weather. The butter costs a third of the price of the ice I buy to cool it."

The woods brought welcome respite from the sun, and our chaise moved more easily over this softer ground. When we came to a horse and cart tethered to one of the trees, I called out to the driver to stop. He tied up the horses, fitted the steps, and Mr. Devereux handed me down. He insisted upon accompanying me along the path, birdsong mingling with the distant rasp of a saw. The ice house, a low, domed brick structure covered in moss, always conjured my father's stories about trolls who lived in burial mounds, who kidnapped little girls and ate their fathers. Various tools were propped against the boulders that stood either side of the rusting gate, and a large wheelbarrow was drawn up on the grass. The gate stood ajar, and when I called out a greeting, the sawing stopped. Mr. Onslow soon appeared at the top of the stairs that led down into the interior of the ice house.

I introduced him to Mr. Devereux. "Mr. Onslow is Mr. Marsh's man of business." I forbore from mentioning that he also seemed to be butler, land steward, and, for all I knew, kitchenhand as well. "I'd like a little more than usual, Mr. Onslow. This weather . . ."

He mopped his brow with a handkerchief. "So does everyone, Mrs. Cole. It's sixpence a pound, I am afraid."

"So much?" I cried. I'd hoped that once the great households had left town for their country estates, the price would drop.

"Every merchant in the City wants ice at the moment. I've had buyers come from as far as Stratford le Bow. Then the Duke of Newcastle's man came this morning and took five loads for Newcastle House. A new Swedish ambassador is in town apparently." The sound of sawing resumed. "I have a load ready to go, but I expect you'd like to choose your own?"

Led by Mr. Onslow, we passed through the gate, and descended the stone steps by the light of several lanterns. We emerged into the vast ice pit, the portion aboveground only a fraction of that below. A narrow circular walkway surrounded the pit, where many tons of ice were stored. The two laborers Onslow employed looked up from their sawing and touched their caps.

"There's a drain at the bottom of the pit," Onslow informed Mr. Devereux. "Carries the meltwater back to the lake."

One of the laborers got to his feet, puffing out a sigh, and drew back the flannel covering to expose more of the ice. They knew me, and how particular I was. I made a full circuit of the walkway, inspecting the surface. "That bit there," I said, pointing. "But that part there looks brackish. I want none of that." The laborers exchanged a not-so-surreptitious roll of the eyes.

"They harvest the ice from their lake in winter," I told Mr. Devereux. "Give them a free hand and you'll be taking home a frozen squirrel."

We climbed the steps back up to the shade of the yew trees, where I paid Mr. Onslow and we made polite conversation while my fifty pounds of ice was cut into blocks and wrapped in flannel to minimize melting on the journey home. When the laborers had loaded it onto their barrow, one of them wheeled it along the path to the chaise.

Mr. Devereux's liveried coachman was leaning against the carriage, smoking a pipe and talking to Felix. A tall, lean man, his cheeks a little scarred from the pox, he evidently had the lad in his thrall—something about a sword fight at Hatton Garden. Between the pair of them, they loaded the pallet of ice onto the chaise, we all climbed aboard, and the coachman flicked his whip. Soon we were on the Edgware Road once more, heading back towards London.

The road was clear, the sun fierce, tempered a little by the breeze as we rode. The carriage swayed gently and Mr. Devereux closed his eyes. Soon I began to wonder if he'd fallen asleep. Studying the angles of his face beneath the shadow of his hat, the cords of his hand upon the side of the carriage, I found myself wondering about his circumstances—where he was from, whether he was married, and so on. I had refrained from asking him any of these questions, lest they be mistaken for undue interest on my part.

Devereux was about forty years old, I judged. He dressed and spoke like a gentleman, seemingly cultured and well educated—and yet banking, stockjobbery, and the other financial occupations inhabited that uncertain terrain between the accepted gentlemanly professions and the horrors of trade. Perhaps he was a rising man, as Jonas had liked to think himself, his money enabling him to move in circles far above his origins. On the other hand, I'd read about gentlemen from old families of good name who had turned to banking and stockjobbery in an effort to repair their diminished fortunes. As I pondered into which category Devereux fell, his eyes opened and he caught me looking. He smiled, and rather flustered, I turned away.

The carriage had slowed, caught up in a queue of traffic just outside Kilburn. Soon we had halted entirely, and after a little while one of the other drivers in the queue went to the front to find out the cause of the delay. When he returned, he informed us that a fight had broken out in the street.

"They should close this place down," Devereux said. "I have high hopes that Mr. Fielding will bring the rougher elements of the town to heel. Though I can't imagine he will venture out as far as this."

"What do you know of him?" I asked. "Beyond his novels, I mean."

Devereux thought for a moment. "He has a great reputation for infallibility and integrity when it comes to matters of justice. I know it must be true, as I have read it in the newspaper, and none could know Mr. Fielding better than the author, for he wrote it himself."

He grinned. "I've heard it said that he desires to create one body to combat crime across the whole metropolis. The current muddle serves nobody, he believes, and he's probably right. Watchmen and constables are appointed by lot from the parish. They are mostly unpaid and unwilling, which leads to corruption. Responsibility for their work is divided between the magistrates and the parishes, who are usually too busy squabbling amongst themselves. You can see why Fielding believes that change is necessary. But there is great opposition in Parliament, so who knows if it will ever come about."

"Parliament don't want to combat crime?"

"Oh, in theory, they do. But they fear Mr. Fielding's proposals will lead to tyranny. The Crown and the ministry able to drag their critics from their beds at night and clap them in irons. Englishmen are nothing if not staunch in defense of their liberties, even when that liberty means the freedom to be robbed in the street. But if anyone can talk Parliament round, then it is surely Mr. Fielding. He is said to be a very persuasive fellow."

"And a tenacious man," I murmured, as the carriage moved off again.

"Well, something needs to be done," Devereux said. "Street robbery is a blight upon the nation—I hardly need tell *you* that. Gin and gambling too—though I won't pretend I am a complete stranger to the taverns and the gaming houses. But a little wine and play for recreation now and then is different to this." He gestured to a man lying unconscious by the side of the road, his friends trying to rouse him by pouring beer onto his face. "So many people impoverished, leading sad and brutal lives. Little wonder, really, that some of them turn to villainy."

"You think crime can sometimes be justified? If one's circumstances demand it?" I'd asked myself this question countless times since the murder.

"Not justified precisely, but I think many crimes are preventable—with the right measures to improve the plight of the poor."

"And where there is no excuse? If a person isn't poor, but simply wicked?" I was thinking about Jonas now. How easily my thoughts slid between the two of us, weighing our respective crimes like sugarplums and marchpane bites.

"Then I suppose one must hope that justice prevails."

I could tell he was thinking about justice in its narrowest sense: courts and lawyers and magistrates like Henry Fielding. How like a rich man to suppose that the law would be on his side. But there was biblical justice too. A tooth for a tooth. I thought of Jonas's teeth scattered across my cellar floor.

"You said just now that you are a patron of the gaming houses?" I said.

"I was in my youth. Back in the Dark Ages." Devereux grinned again.

"It was suggested to me that Jonas might have won his money at play." I reached into my pocket for the little porcelain fish. "I found this amongst his things. Does it look like a gaming token to you?"

He took it from me and examined it. "Some of the golden hells use fishes made of silver and mother-of-pearl. Perhaps porcelain too? I'm not sure."

"Golden hells?"

"That's what they call the very best gaming houses. Copper hells are for tradesmen and laborers. Silver hells are for the lower to middling sort of gentlemen. Whilst your golden hell is the preserve of the nobility and the richest gentry."

"Mr. Twisleton, the parish clerk, said he'd heard Jonas entertained the great men of the parish at gaming clubs," I said. "I can't imagine they would have wanted to go anywhere except the best."

Devereux gave me an appraising glance. "This money gives you cause for concern?"

I debated how much more to say. "Mr. Fielding thinks it possible that it has a connection to Jonas's murder. That he might have been killed by someone he knew."

Devereux looked taken aback. "I thought it was a street robbery?"

"They haven't found his watch. Then there's the money and a suspicious carriage." I told him what the landlord of the Running Horse had said. "But Cousin Daniel still thinks that a robbery is the most likely explanation. Which is partly why I'm so anxious to assist Mr. Fielding. I hate to think of him wasting his time looking in the wrong place. If I could find out where Jonas used to play, then I could pass that information on to him."

Devereux considered. "There is a young gentleman of my acquaintance, a client of mine. Or rather, his father is a client: the Marquis of Morrow. Lord Richard is his youngest. He is a good lad, but for a time he fell in with a bad lot. His father has asked me to keep an eye on him over the summer, whilst he is away at his estate in County Durham. One of Lord Richard's many vices was the gaming houses. I imagine he's seen the inside of every golden hell in town. He might be able to tell us where this fish came from—if indeed it is a gaming token at all."

"You would ask him?"

"I was thinking rather that we might ask him together. I could invite him to the chemistry show tomorrow night. We could talk to him and to Professor Becker about the iced cream. Kill two birds with one stone. Come, what do you say? I will bring a chaperone along: an old family friend, Mrs. Parmenter. It will all be perfectly respectable."

So that was the way it was to be. If I was to get what I wanted from Mr. Devereux, information that might lead me to the source of Jonas's money, then I had to play his little game: open myself—or pretend to be open—to the possibility of a seduction. Well, I was good at pretending. Hadn't I kept a smile on my face for years when Jonas was tearing my heart in two, because I'd read that no man falls back in love with a sad wife? Didn't I pretend every day to be a grieving and virtuous widow, and nobody—with the possible and worrying exception of Oscar—had come close to imagining the truth?

I would go to the assembly rooms and act suitably grateful and enthralled, just until I had the information I wanted. But hell would be an ice house before Devereux attained his "one thing." On that point, at least to myself, I was quite certain.

CHAPTER EIGHT

I KNEW RIGHT away that I did not like Mrs. Parmenter. She was all smiles, patting me with a lace-gloved hand, when Mr. Devereux handed me into his chaise and made the introductions. But I caught a glitter of judgment in her little blue eyes. Mr. Devereux had explained to me the day before, on the return journey from the ice house, that she was the widow of his mentor and former business partner. They had shipped jade, porcelain, and tea from the Indies and China, he'd said, and Mr. Parmenter had taught him everything he knew about trade and speculation. It had been the death of that gentleman which had prompted Devereux's return from the Far East last year, where he had acted as agent for their company.

"William has told me about your loss," Mrs. Parmenter said. "How brave of you to venture out so soon. And in purple already. How times change."

Rather less subtle were the pinched faces of Mrs. Brunsden, Mrs. Fortnum, and Mrs. Howard, who watched us ride past from their usual station across the street. Mrs. Brunsden had been into the shop earlier to tell me that Mr. Fielding had called on her husband yesterday. And this morning, she'd said, Fielding was visiting two tradesmen who'd sat on the parish committee with Jonas and used to drink with him. All day I'd been wondering what they might have told him.

"I have heard all about your little shop." Mrs. Parmenter smiled. "You must be terribly sure of yourself to even think of running it alone."

I put her age at about seventy, her neat gray curls secured with a blue silk ribbon and a diamond brooch. Tiny in stature, she was wizened as a currant, to my mind hollowed out by an excess of malice. Yet what did I care for her good opinion? Neither she, nor her precious Mr. Devereux, meant anything to me. Their company was merely to be endured in the interest of my inquiry.

Mr. Devereux sat back upon the carriage seat, his face golden in the evening sun. His emerald-green silk coat was unbuttoned to display a waistcoat embroidered with hummingbirds, a black silk solitaire tied around his neck. Had he made an effort for me? I rather hoped he had. It gave me a frisson of pleasure to imagine his face later tonight once he discovered his elaborate plan of seduction had all been in vain.

"I am glad to see you smiling," he said. "You look very well tonight, Mrs. Cole."

I inclined my head, though inwardly I deplored his lies. The gown I was wearing, the finest I had in purple, was a velvet affair more suited for winter than a hot summer's evening. As we turned into the regrettably misnamed Air Street, I was already perspiring. Thankfully, it was only a short ride to Hickford's Long Room, the most fashionable place of assembly in all of London. We alighted from the carriage amidst an elegant crowd of ladies and gentlemen and their servants, and a queue of handsome equipages much like our own.

"Thank you, Tom," Devereux called up to his coachman. "Bring the carriage around at nine, will you? I promised Mrs. Cole that I would not have her home too late."

I'm sure he thought I'd change my mind, once the subject of the full force of his charm and persuasion. Pretending not to notice the arm he offered, I made my own way into the hall, where I attempted to pay for my own ticket. Upon discovering, to my astonishment, that entrance cost a half-guinea, I fell silent and allowed Mr. Devereux to pay. Mrs. Parmenter smiled thinly.

The Long Room had a soaring ceiling, a painted gallery above the main floor, and elegant moldings picked out in gold. Arrangements of tables and chairs faced the stage, around which the fashionable patrons milled. I recognized a few of my customers, who gave me half-nods of recognition, perhaps unable to place me, or confused as to why I was there. We had taken only a few paces into the room, when Mr. Devereux was confronted by a shabby-looking gentleman in black, who clasped his hand in both of his and shook it hard.

"Sir, Mr. Devereux, it is an honor to see you again. If you only knew—"

"Please," he said, looking a little awkward, "think nothing of it."

"Nothing?" the man said. "No, sir. It is everything."

Mrs. Parmenter ushered me to a vacant table, where she summoned a waiter to bring wine. When Devereux joined us, she gave him a reproving look. "Giving your money away again, William?"

"There's more to life than money," he said. "Brereton's work is shockingly underfunded and I am proud to support it."

"It is underfunded because it is an affront to right-thinking people."

Beneath Devereux's smile, I detected a trace of irritation. "Right-thinking people should be more affronted by the poverty and desperation that drive women to such extremes."

Mrs. Parmenter turned to me. "That tatterdemalion in black has established a home for fallen women," she explained. "All well and good, one might think, but he seeks to reintroduce them to polite society, where they might be employed by or even marry unsuspecting men. You are surely with me on this, Mrs. Cole?"

Though I considered both parties my adversaries, in this particular instance I knew whose side I was on. "On the contrary," I said, "it sounds a very worthy cause. I commend your generosity, Mr. Devereux."

Any further discussion upon the subject was curtailed by the ringing of a bell. Everyone hastily found their seats, and the master of ceremonies walked onto the stage. He announced that Professor Becker of the university at Leiden was to demonstrate a series of chemical marvels, after which there would be an interval, followed by a concert of vocal and instrumental music. Mr. Devereux had explained to me earlier that he had written a note to Professor Becker that morning begging leave to consult him after his show. He'd received a reply saying that Becker was already due to meet some gentlemen from Oxford and Cambridge during the interval, but that he would grant us an audience once he was done. Though my principal interest that night was golden hells and the porcelain fish, I was genuinely intrigued by the puzzle of iced cream, and I hoped that Professor Becker might be able to provide a solution.

Becker made his entrance onto the stage to much applause. A portly, well-dressed man in a brown periwig, he appeared quite different to the gaunt alchemist in singed robes that I'd imagined. "All that you will see tonight," he informed us in a heavy German accent, "will appear beyond nature. My experiments will excite, they will surprise, and they will astonish. Yet all are the product of natural causes: no tricks, no magic, only the wonders of chemistry."

He gave a signal and two assistants appeared, carrying a large model between them, which they placed on the table in front of him. A clay mountain, with many tiny white buildings at its base, sat upon the shores of a bay of sculpted blue water.

Becker gestured to the model. "Here you gaze, as did the gods, upon the town of Pompeii and the volcano named Vesuvius. Pliny the Younger tells us that in the seventy-ninth year of Our Lord, Vesuvius erupted most violently, engulfing Pompeii in a terrible fire." He picked up a blue-glass bottle and poured a substance into the volcano. Then he added a few drops from a little phial, before adding a measure of clear liquid from a third bottle. "Oil of vitriol," he announced, standing back from the table.

At first nothing happened, and I began to think that his experiment hadn't worked. Then smoke started pouring from the volcano, flames and sparks burst from the top, and a blood-red substance like lava spurted out, spilling over the sides to submerge the town below. We applauded, waving the smoke away from our faces.

For the next hour, Professor Becker amazed us with stinks and bangs, liquids that changed color or burst into flames, and powders that exploded without a tinder. After he had taken his bows and the applause had died down, a waiter came over to enquire if we desired refreshment. I was tempted to try the ratafia cakes to assess the quality, but that would have meant removing my gloves, when my hands were calloused and scarred from my work in the kitchen.

"Aha," Devereux said, as the waiter poured the wine he'd bought, "there is Lord Richard. If you'll wait here, ladies, I'll bring him over."

He returned accompanied by a slim, dark gentleman of around the age of majority. Dressed rather rakishly, his cravat askew, his white dress coat unbuttoned, Lord Richard had downturned black eyes and a sulky mouth. When Devereux made the introductions, his friend eyed me with some impertinence.

"Well, Willie, you've kept this one quiet and little wonder." He kissed my hand, holding it rather too long. "Mrs. Parmenter."

From that lady's expression, she did not think much of him either, which made me like Lord Richard a little more.

"We have a question for you," Devereux said, addressing the young man. "In your time at the tables, did you ever come across a house that played with porcelain fish? Do you have it, Mrs. Cole?"

I passed the token to Lord Richard, who brushed my fingers as he took it.

"The Goldfish," he exclaimed. "Best golden hell in town. I lost three thousand acres there once. Don't tell my father."

"Where is this place?" I asked.

"St. James's Square," he said. "Lucky number seven."

A stone's throw from the Punchbowl and Pineapple. I wondered how often Jonas had frequented the place. Could he really have won fifteen hundred pounds at play? I wanted to believe that he had. Then Mr. Fielding might abandon his theory about the murder. As gaming houses were illegal, he might still try to confiscate our money, but I'd have to hope that Daniel could persuade him to let us keep the savings from the shop.

"There you are," Devereux said. "Didn't I tell you that Lord Richard was our man?"

"Your servant, madam. The Goldfish does not permit ladies, or I would offer to escort you there tonight. Yet if it is an evening's play that you desire, I know another establishment that would serve."

"You misunderstand," Devereux said, a little sharply. "Can't you see Mrs. Cole is in mourning? And remember all those promises you made to your father."

"Can't blame a fellow for trying." Lord Richard grinned. "Willie, do you have a moment? Sir James would very much like to talk to you about matters Arcadian."

Devereux frowned. "This isn't the time or the place to discuss business."

"No time like it," Lord Richard said. "Please, I said you would."

Devereux restrained a sigh. "Ladies, do you mind?"

Of course, we said that we did not, and they crossed the room to join a tall, fair man, with a large mole on his nose, who began talking to Devereux in a very animated fashion.

"Poor William." Mrs. Parmenter sighed. "Everyone always wants something from him. There are times I wish he was rather less obliging."

"Gentlemen often seek his advice on financial matters?"

"Or an introduction to men of consequence. And some want his money, of course: an investment, or a donation to a charitable cause. Then there're the women, swarming like wasps and him the honey."

"Mr. Devereux is unmarried?"

She gave me a look, as if to say surely I knew that already. "There was an engagement once, a long time ago, but it came to nothing. I believe William intends never to marry, which is a great tragedy in itself, but it doesn't stop these ambitious girls from trying. His friends have an eye for the fortune-hunters, I assure you of that."

Bridling inwardly at her implication, I smiled sweetly. "Then I am fortunate to be the exception. For it is Mr. Devereux who wants something from me."

She looked momentarily confused. "Oh, and what is that?"

"Iced cream," I said, delighted to confound her. "A frozen delicacy that Mr. Devereux desires to try again. Apparently his mother used to make it. I have attempted the recipe myself, so far without success. Mr. Devereux hopes that Professor Becker might have the answer."

"Oh," she said. "Yes, of course. Dear Antonia." She fanned herself, looking pleased to have the upper hand again. "We knew the family well, my husband and I. Poor William was only eight years old when he lost her—and his father was a brute, no comfort at all. Her birthday fell around this time, which surely explains his sudden enthusiasm for your shop."

Having lost my own mother at a young age, my heart went out to Mr. Devereux. I watched him across the room as he shook the tall man's hand, afraid that I might have misjudged him. Was his preoccupation with iced cream genuine after all? Did he merely desire to pay tribute to his late mother? Had I been presumptuous in suspecting an unseemly interest on his part? From what Mrs. Parmenter had said, there was no shortage of young ladies who'd greet his attentions with rather more kindness than I had shown.

These thoughts were uppermost in my mind when Mr. Devereux rejoined us a few minutes later. This time I returned his smile with more warmth.

"Professor Becker will see us now," he said, gesturing to the footman hovering behind him. "Will you join us, Mrs. Parmenter?"

"If you don't mind, I see Mrs. Knight over there. My housekeeper wants her still-room maid's recipe for lavender-water."

Relieved to be deprived of her company, I followed Mr. Devereux and the footman through a door, down a short corridor, and into an anteroom with a parquet floor. Professor Becker was seated at a table before a stack of leatherbound books and pages covered in a close Germanic script.

"Herr Devereux, I presume," he said, rising to bow. "And you must be Frau Cole." He kissed my hand.

Once we were all seated around the table, Mr. Devereux explained why we wished to consult him.

"This is the recipe we used," I said, taking out Devereux's paper. "I followed it to the letter, but the cream wouldn't freeze. It simply grew cold."

The professor studied the recipe a moment. "Little wonder," he said. "You have neglected to unlock the hidden heat within your liquid."

I frowned, confused. "But the cream is cold. There is no heat."

Becker smiled. "All liquids contain a latent heat concealed within themselves. Even when they feel cold, they are secretly hot. You must withdraw that fire by means of the frigorific method."

I didn't even attempt to repeat the word. "It all sounds rather complicated."

"On the contrary," Becker said. "It is simplicity itself. What you require, my dear lady, is salt."

CHAPTER NINE

THE FOLLOWING MORNING, before the shop opened, I made iced cream again, this time guided by Professor Becker's notes.

To freeze liquids solid by means of the frigorific method, take a pail and lay some straw at the bottom. Use several pounds of ice, some broken very small, some in larger pieces. Put the larger fragments in the bottom of the pail, and sprinkle liberally with bay-salt. Set your liquids in the ice in pots and lay more ice and salt between them. They must not touch, and the ice must lie around them on every side. Lay a good deal of ice and salt on top, cover the pail with straw, and set it in a cellar where no sunlight comes.

Last night, Mr. Devereux had proved the perfect gentleman. His driver, Tom, had brought the carriage around at nine as instructed, and his master had attempted no liberties upon my person on the way home. That would teach me to listen to the gossip of apprentices. I could hardly explain my contrition to Mr. Devereux, but I hoped I could at least give him a pot of iced cream the next time I saw him.

As I tidied away the ice tools, my gaze fell upon the mallet. Looking down, I had a sudden vision of Jonas slumped at my feet, blood spilling from his broken skull onto the flagstones. It could overwhelm me like this sometimes, the enormity of what I had done. Going through his pockets, cutting the strings of his purse, easing his ring off his finger, taking out his watch. My father had once told me that the culverted river at the bottom of our ice-store was a tributary of the Tyburn, which flowed into the Thames. Fathers tell their daughters many stories, some of them true.

Now, as I wrapped the block of ice back up in flannel, I placed my hands on my neck and forehead, trying to cool my burning skin. The ice tub had a funneled section built into the base, to enable the meltwater to run off through a hole in the bottom. Before lowering the tub again, I slid my hand through the hole, feeling about in the cavity inside. My fingers found the oilskin packet and my breathing calmed a little. I took comfort from the cold, hard contours of my grandfather's watch.

*

All day long the shop was quiet, troublingly so. As six o'clock approached, with only the odd customer to serve, I asked Oscar to mind the counter again. Theo gave me a sharp look, and I could tell she was getting curious about my comings and goings.

Piccadilly was still a furnace: topless urchins running about, begging for water from the shopkeepers; a dog dying by the side of the road outside Burlington House. I cut through the churchyard onto York Street, a thoroughfare of fine houses that would ordinarily be described as large, were they not dwarfed by their magnificent neighbors in St. James's Square. The pretty garden at the center of the square was locked up and deserted. Most of the mansions had their shutters closed, their residents decamped to their country estates or to the spa—though a few showed signs of life: a servant beating a rug, or a carriage dropping off a visitor. At number seven, home to the Goldfish, the curtains were drawn. Boldly, I approached the door and lifted the brass knocker.

I waited for a long time. Eventually, I heard a light tread in the hall, and the door opened about four inches. A little brown face peered out. Whether butler or doorman, I wasn't quite sure.

"My name is Hannah Cole. I would like to speak to the proprietor of this house."

The door opened a little wider. "You looking for work?" he said, in an accent that might have been Spanish. The man's dark eyes traveled over my face and gown.

"No," I said, wishing I'd worn a shawl despite the heat. "I think my husband visited this establishment. His name was Jonas Cole. Perhaps you remember him?"

He glared at me. "There's no one of that name here."

"I know," I said, patiently. "My husband is dead. I'm just trying to find out if he ever played dice or cards here—"

Before I could finish, he slammed the door in my face. I knocked again, several times, but nobody answered. Determined, I withdrew to the opposite side of the street, standing in the shade of the trees at the edge of the garden, keeping watch. About ten minutes later, the door of number seven opened again, and a lady came out. I walked back across the road to intercept her.

"Excuse me," I said. "Might I speak with you a moment?"

She turned in a waft of attar of roses, and I saw that she was young—perhaps not yet eighteen years old. Elegantly attired in yellow silk trimmed with white lace, she peered at me from beneath a painted parasol. I repeated everything that I'd said to the doorman.

The girl glanced back at the house. "I can't talk to you. I'm sorry." She was trying to sound like a lady, but she'd convince no one.

She kept walking and I hurried along by her side. "Please," I said, "I'm not meaning to cause trouble. I'm just a widow trying to learn the truth about her husband."

She turned, without breaking her stride. "If your husband's dead and he came here, then the truth is you're well rid of him. Now please, in all kindness, leave me alone."

I stared after her, darkness edging out the brightness of the day. She was like the girls I'd imagined, when I'd thought of Jonas in the taverns. Young and pretty, probably pliant when she wasn't being pestered by a desperate woman in the street.

"Is anything the matter, madam? Can I help at all?"

Turning, I saw a large, ungainly gentleman of late middle age. The door to the Goldfish was closing again, and I gathered he'd just come out. He was rather crumpled in dress, and looked as if he hadn't slept in days. Yet his expression appeared genial and his bloodshot eyes kind. "Alexander Arbuthnot," he said, lifting his hat to make a bow. "At your service."

Cautiously, I introduced myself, once more explaining the business that had brought me there. As he seemed more inclined to listen, I gave him a description of Jonas and a few facts about his life that he might have shared with an acquaintance at the gaming tables.

"A shopkeeper?" he said. "We don't get many of those at the Goldfish." He frowned. "Jonas Cole . . . Yes, I remember him."

I gazed at him hopefully. "You do?"

Like the girl, he glanced back towards the house. "Not here, if you don't mind. The Goldfish doesn't appreciate gossip outside of the pond. Walk with me for a moment, if you will."

He offered me his arm, and though I was reluctant to take it, I was also eager to learn what he had to say. We walked briskly back up York Street towards Piccadilly, until we came to the entrance of the alley named Apple Tree Yard. Steering me firmly inside, he halted a little way down.

"There," he said. "Now we won't be disturbed."

To my horror, he pressed me against the wall, pushing his mouth against mine. I tried to shove him away, but he gripped me by the shoulders, forcing me back. I froze in panic, until his hand pressed between my legs, and instinct took over. My hand slipped into my pocket, finding my little pastry knife. I jabbed it into his stomach, just below the V of his waistcoat. He howled, stepping away, and I held the knife in front of my face. "Get away from me," I shouted, my voice cracked by fear.

"You bloody harpy," he said, pawing at his bulge to examine the wound.

I backed away, still holding the knife, until there was a good few feet between us. Then I turned and ran. His shouts carried after me: "You're too old for my taste anyway. I'd sooner have Noah's wife. Ugly bitch."

I hurried up York Street, past the church, onto Piccadilly. The crowds were a blur, my head and heart pounding. What a fool I'd been to think that I could visit a place like that without consequence. I didn't believe that man had ever met Jonas in his life. Someone cannoned into me, and a volley of curses followed me down the street. I could still feel the imprint of the man's thumbs upon my shoulders. Determined not to stop until I reached the safety of my shop, I almost collided with a gentleman just outside.

"Mrs. Cole? Whatever is the matter?"

It was Mr. Devereux. I tried to tell him it was nothing, but I was trembling too hard. It was as if all the feelings that I'd been keeping in check these past few months had suddenly spilled out of me.

"Come inside," Devereux said gently. "You need to sit down."

For once, I was relieved by the dearth of customers inside the shop. Devereux exchanged a few words with Oscar and Theo, and then led me into the kitchen. When I was seated upon a stool, he disappeared through the door, shortly returning with a glass of *Perfetto Amore*. He placed it in my hands, and then crouched down, gazing at me solicitously. "Now, please," he said, "tell me what happened."

Somehow I found the words between my gulps for air. "That blackguard," Devereux exclaimed. "But what on earth were you doing, going to that club by yourself? You heard what Lord Richard said—it's no place for a lady. I thought you were going to give the name to Henry Fielding."

I was silent a moment, seeking an explanation he would both believe and understand. "I am ashamed to say that I wasn't entirely honest with you before. Mr. Fielding clings to a different theory about that money and I didn't believe he would give the club his due attention."

"Whatever can you mean?" Devereux exclaimed.

"Mr. Fielding believes that Jonas might have come by that money dishonestly. He is so convinced by his theory that he has put a stay on the passage of probate. I am told that he may confiscate all of my money. And I cannot afford it—I have too many debts—I might lose my shop."

Devereux's smile had faded. I wondered if he'd walk out, disgusted to be associated with the wife of a man suspected of criminality. But when he spoke, he did so no less kindly. "I am appalled on your behalf— that he should speak ill of Jonas like that. And it is doubly distressing that you are being made to suffer financially."

"I thought if I could prove that Jonas won that money at play," I said, "then Fielding would have to revisit his theory. You think me very foolish, I suppose?"

"I think you brave," he said. "But you must promise me that you won't put yourself in danger again. Let me go to the Goldfish. I have no engagements tonight. I'll see what I can find out and report back to you tomorrow. That way we can decide what to do next."

Had I still believed that Mr. Devereux was after that "one thing," I shouldn't have had a moment's qualm in playing him along by accepting his offer. Yet it seemed plain to me now that he simply wanted to assist the widow of his dead friend, perhaps out of a misplaced sense of guilt after his argument with Jonas. Or perhaps he was just a decent, honorable gentleman—there had to be a few of them left in this world. Was it wrong of me to take advantage of such a man? To make him an accomplice to my attempts to conceal my crime? Surely it was—and yet desperation is a ruthless friend.

"I couldn't possibly ask you to do that," I said.

To which an honorable gentleman could have only one response: "But I insist."

My conscience prickling at Devereux's kindness, I suddenly remembered why he had come. The iced cream, his mother's birthday. Eager to make amends for my deceptions, ignoring his protests that it could wait, I insisted on going down to the cellar to inspect my creation. Lifting out one of the pots, brushing off straw, ice, and salt, I untied the muslin covering to examine the surface of the cream. To my great excitement, it appeared to be frozen solid. Returning to the kitchen with two of the pots, I found a pair of spoons. Mr. Devereux and I exchanged a smile of anticipation.

"You first," I said.

Devereux took a mouthful, savoring the flavors. "Oh, Mrs. Cole," he said, his eyes alive with a golden light. "It is just as I remembered."

I took a spoonful myself and almost gasped at the sensation. The cream coated my mouth, sweet and cold and rich. Truly, it was like nothing I'd tasted before.

"What do you think?" he said, eager to learn if my reaction mirrored his own.

"I think success has never tasted so sweet, Mr. Devereux."

He laughed—and for the first time since Jonas's murder, I laughed too. I couldn't have diagnosed a single cause. The fading tension of that moment in the alley. Mr. Devereux's kindness. Our victory in this endeavor. That heavenly texture and flavor. The boyish enchantment on his face. A fleeting vision of what iced cream might mean for my shop. It was as if a bottle had been unstoppered, and all those dark emotions that had bubbled inside me for so long were suddenly expelled in this rare moment of fermented delight.

Which was how I appeared—every inch the merry widow—when Henry Fielding walked through my kitchen door. He looked from me to Mr. Devereux. "I do hope you don't mind my calling unannounced."

My words tripped over one another: "You are most welcome, Mr. Fielding. Allow me to name Mr. Devereux, a friend of my late husband. He advised Jonas upon his investments. Mr. Fielding is the Bow Street magistrate, the man who's going to catch Jonas's killer."

"Your reputation precedes you, sir," Devereux said, bowing gracefully. "Mrs. Cole, I can see that you have important business to discuss. I shall not intrude upon your time and patience a moment longer. Yet I will call again tomorrow—once I have the information you seek, regarding that financial matter we discussed." He turned to Mr. Fielding. "Be sure to try Mrs. Cole's iced cream, sir. You'll divide your days between the before and after."

Fielding raised his hat, his gaze following Mr. Devereux to the door. When he turned back to me, his expression was thoughtful. "Perhaps we might adjourn to your parlor, Mrs. Cole? There are one or two questions I'd like to ask you about your marriage."

PART TWO

The Dance

Dancing begets warmth, which is the parent of wantonness.

Henry Fielding, *Love in Several Masques*, 1728

CHAPTER TEN

DID YOU EVER meet a bigger cunt than Henry Fielding? As soon as I saw his face, his beady inquisitor's gaze looking from me to Hannah Cole, I knew I had a problem. Or at least, I already knew I had a problem the moment she told me that scribbling cunt had put a hold on her money. But seeing him there in her kitchen, Hannah all a-flutter with nerves, I knew that problem wouldn't resolve itself anytime soon.

I hadn't needed the carriage that day, and I walked back through Leicester Fields, trying to work out how much trouble I was in. Amidst the crowds and the music, the cries of brandy-and-tobacco-men, beggars, sharpers, and whores, my heart slowed and my head began to clear. I remembered Hannah's rich burst of laughter, a refrain of heavenly music to my ears. Not just her laugh, but her grateful eyes when I'd offered to go to the Goldfish later tonight. I told myself that Fielding's intervention presented an opportunity as well as a threat. I certainly couldn't afford to walk away now. Not how things stood.

The streets beyond Leicester Fields were crowded with people heading for the theaters. As I passed Fielding's crib on Bow Street, I gave it a resentful glare, wondering what questions he was asking Hannah right at this moment. Solve this problem for her, I reasoned, get Fielding to hand over her cash, and she'd open up to me like jasmine in moonlight. Easier said than done, you might think, and you'd be right. The minds of smug fucksters like Fielding, who think themselves Shakespeare, Aristotle, and Galileo all rolled into one, are the hardest to change. Every thought they possess has the sanctity of a holy writ, merely because they were the ones who dreamed it up. But when all is said and done, they are just like everybody else. You simply have to learn the right steps to make them dance.

The playhouse crowd gave a wide berth to the nest of alleys around the back of the Theatre Royal, home to brothels and bathhouses, gin shops and squalid taverns. The residents started drinking over breakfast and then kept going. Groups of ragged men stood about on corners. One lot were fighting, skidding in vomit. Half-naked women leaned from the upper windows shouting encouragement. One of the Jezebels scowled like Hannah Cole, which made me remember our trip to Willesden—but when she had laughed just now in her kitchen, her eyes alive with hope and possibility, she'd reminded me of a painted Madonna that I'd once seen on the wall of a Florentine palace. The guide had told me that she had the face of a lady the artist had loved, that he'd fought a duel for her hand and had lost his life. I would tell Hannah about the resemblance, once she believed in herself a little more. Only I must remember to give the story a happier ending.

Glancing behind me, I saw that I had company. Two young ruffians I didn't recognize, probably new to the neighborhood, dogging my heels at a distance. My hand dropped to my coat pocket where I kept a fistful of pepper. My face is my trade, and a broken nose could see me ruined. Blind your opponent and run—that's my method.

The ruffians drew a little closer, and I braced myself for their attack. Then I heard a noise, half-click, half-kiss, and they melted away. Turning, I saw Whispering Pete propped up in an alleyway, enjoying a concerto from some young lad, down on his knees, playing the skin flute. "Right, Billy," he said, giving me a grin. I guessed the ruffians must have been part of his gang, because I reached the door of the Black Lion in Vinegar Yard unscathed.

Twenty and Pig patted me down for weapons at the door. Twenty was named for the number of men he was said to have killed, whilst Pig was short for Pygmalion, a name he'd earned due to his love of carving men's faces. Always tip a man who would happily piss on your bleeding corpse. I asked after their children and headed inside.

I still felt a shot of joy at being home after Bath and Tunbridge Wells. In the spa towns, I sometimes caught the eye of an adventurer or a woman on the make, a discreet recognition of a kindred spirit. But here in the Black Lion's taproom, I could find a legion of my people. Thieves and actors, most a bit of both, all looking the part of ladies and gentlemen and liveried servants.

"Billy," somebody cried. "I hope I passed muster?"

Wesley Ball, last seen at the chemistry show. "You did very well," I told him.

Ball rubbed the mole on his nose, eyes lighting up with relief. He'd always been an anxious sort. First-night nerves.

Not Sylvia. She was drinking from the little silver cup they kept for her behind the bar. Her usual tipple: redcurrant gin.

I spread my hands wide. Sylvia liked to be adored. "A better performance than your Lady Macbeth back in 'twenty-nine."

"One aims to please." Sylvia preened, her wrinkled lips stained red from the gin. "She's sharp, your Mrs. Cole. I like a girl who fights her corner. I gave you a tragic past, by the way. A broken engagement."

"She asked?"

"Oh, yes. Wanted to know if there was a wife."

I smiled. Sylvia had always been my favorite chaperone. She never pushed too far or too fast. Let them do the running.

I looked around for John James, wanting to thank him too. Never neglect the minor players in your ensemble. I spotted him in a corner, his tongue down the throat of some doxy. Doing his bit for the fallen women of London again.

Then all I could see was Amy, her black hair curled, her breasts plump, a red silk flower to match her dress, Bristol stones sparkling everywhere. She threw her arms around my neck and kissed me hard.

"I've missed you, Billy," she murmured. "Take a girl out on the town?"

"Later," I told her. "I have to talk to Tom."

She pouted, always got like this when I was on a job. "There's a baronet who offered me ten pounds to join him for supper after the theater."

"But he won't give you half the performance I will." I grinned. She'd wait.

Tom was at a table near the bar, talking to a young Lascar I didn't recognize. I wormed my way through the crowd towards them, pausing to buy a beer. As the tapman filled my pot, I half-listened to their conversation.

"That old fellow there," Tom was saying, "the man with the white hair. He's one of the finest knuckles you ever saw."

"A knuckle, sir?" the Lascar said, in accented English.

"It means he can talk his way in anywhere. His specialty's a colonel. The opera, Parliament, even the palace once. Stole a ruby bracelet under the nose of the king's guard."

The Lascar looked impressed.

"And that young sharper over there plays a good clergyman. Any denomination you want. A sham wedding or a funeral, whatever you need."

"And the beautiful lady by the door?"

"That's Emily, our altar girl. She's been married sixteen times. Has every fish in town swimming into her net."

I turned, beer in hand, to join them, and Tom raised his arm in greeting. "Meet Spruce Billy," he said to the Lascar. "He's the man in charge. Bill, this here's Nazim. Just spent a year aboard an Indiaman, which put him off sailoring for life. Now he's looking for more gainful employment."

Nazim certainly looked the part. About twenty years old, with soft black hair and proud, patrician features.

"Perfect," I said to Tom, as I shook the boy's hand.

Nazim studied me with interest. "And what is your specialty, sir?"

I met his gaze with a grin, still thinking of Hannah Cole's laugh. "I have a certain way with the wealthier widow."

CHAPTER ELEVEN

Contrary to what you might think, I don't hate women. I couldn't do this job if I did. I love women and I always have. The smell of them, the taste. The way they shed their caution like a second skin. Their generous hearts.

Just to clear up any doubts, I'd never met Jonas Cole. During the period we were supposedly friendly, I was in the arms of a widow named Penelope Felton at a little house I'd rented just outside Bath. That association had left me seven hundred pounds the richer, which had paid off most of my debts and funded a couple of months of generous living back in London. I first heard the name of Hannah Cole two weeks prior to my first visit to the Punchbowl and Pineapple. I have a clerk at the Prerogative Court to whom I pay a retainer to keep an eye out for suitable widows. He told me that Jonas Cole's estate was a sizable one, surprisingly so for a shopkeeper. We both presumed his fifteen hundred pounds had come from an inheritance. His widow, Hannah Cole, was set to receive over five hundred pounds of that money, and she'd also inherited their house and shop on Piccadilly.

Lest you mistake me for the worst kind of villain, I never take everything—even when they are willing to hand it over. I planned to take only four hundred of Hannah Cole's pounds, leaving her enough money to clear her debts, and a little more besides. A woman's trust is a sacred thing—and only a bounder would leave her penniless and humiliated. The beauty of my method, you see, is that most of my widows never even realize they've been robbed. It all comes down to the art of a lie, the right story for the right woman. Sometimes I weave two or three of them together, until I learn which one will find a willing audience. But one thing never varies: when I tell them their money is lost, I spin them a tale to believe in. A disastrous investment or a sunken ship or a villainous partner. That way they get to tell themselves they've simply been the victim of a chance misfortune. Stories again. Nobody likes to feel a fool. We believe what we want to believe, which is whatever serves us best. Always the gentleman, I tell them that the only thing that matters more to me than my heart is my honor—which lamentably demands that we must part. Often they insist that the money is nothing compared to our love. There's something beautiful in that, if you stop to think about it.

Occasionally, one of my widows grows angry and questions my motives. Penelope Felton of Bath was one such woman—very unkind in her assessment of our time together. But even when they do suspect me, what woman wants to show herself up as a gull by making a complaint? Risk their friends and family finding out? Becoming an object of pity and scorn in polite society? Not to put too fine a point on it, they cannot divulge the loss of their money without revealing the rest. Shame is a weakness I've always lacked, but one that others seem to feel and fear most keenly. Being a liberal sort of fellow, I deplore society's double standards when it comes to the act of physical passion. And yet the fact that a lonely widow who has the audacity to take a lover faces censure, even ostracization, should it become known, does rather work to my advantage. Most prefer to curse my name in private, rather than invite a public scandal. One or two have gone further and involved a magistrate, but I've always been able to talk my way out. I change my name, travel around, and if I ever encounter any of my former widows who have quietly nursed a grudge, their dislike is easily dismissed as the pique of a woman scorned. Those double standards again! In my experience, ladies can often be the most eager to apply them.

But the unhappy women are the exception, not the rule. For the most part, not only do I leave my widows with their pride intact and their fortunes only somewhat diminished, they are happier and more contented than they were before I met them. You probably don't believe me, but I have studied women and their workings for years—just as Professor Becker studies his powders and potions. The truth is all widows are broken in their own way. Those who loved their husbands feel the loss of him most keenly. He was counsel and confidant, lover and friend. For them, each day of widowhood is an eternity. They believe themselves incapable of ever feeling that way about another man—until I take their hand and gently guide them into a new world. When the next fellow comes along, one infinitely more worthy than me, they will know how to open their hearts and love again.

Conversely, those who were indifferent to their husbands mourn their squandered years, the loss that hurts is the waste of their youth and beauty. They worry that no man will ever look at them again with desire, and they pass through life with a weariness that often moves me. To build a woman like that back up takes some doing. But to watch her confidence unfold, to see her preen and flirt and come alive, is like watching a butterfly emerge from a cocoon.

Finally, there are the women who hated their husbands, often hard, brutish men who made their days a living hell. Those widows mourn the loss of their purpose in life, which was to imagine all the ways that he might die. You would think they'd be easy pickings, but they can often be the hardest of all. Cynicism does not sit easily alongside trust. Experience has taught them that men are cruel, unfeeling creatures, and there are indeed too many like that in this world. Yet there are also good men out there, and they only need to believe that I am one of them. So many do, long after their money is gone.

I hope you see by now that my services are akin to those of a physician. Diagnose the malady, provide a suitable cure. When you look at it like that, why shouldn't I get paid?

*

I first saw Hannah Cole at her husband's memorial service in St. James's church. It obviously makes my work easier when I'm not having to summon enthusiasm for a woman knocking on the lid of her own coffin, or one who would make a looking-glass crack—and there was certainly much to admire about Hannah Cole. She was not a tall woman, but she had a rather regal bearing as she sat dabbing at her eyes in her pew. Her hair was dark brown, sleek as an otter, neatly pinned, a black ribbon providing the only ornamentation. I couldn't see her face clearly from that distance, but I could tell she had not overly indulged of her wares, possessing a shapely waist and a small round bosom modestly covered by an embroidered fichu. I found myself rather envying that little scrap of lace, and looking forward to the days and weeks to come.

By the time I saw her again, that first day in her shop, she was already in purple. The color lent a luster to her eyes, which were a vibrant blue—and if the shadows beneath them bespoke sleepless nights, that was hardly surprising given her situation. Full cheeks and lips, her chin and nose small and shapely, good teeth. I imagined she received her share of male attention, which was the part that did not delight me. Such women are never grateful, you see, like the plain ones often are.

I am sometimes asked at the Black Lion how I can simply stroll in off the street and into a woman's life. They don't realize that the Hook is the easy part. People are naturally resistant to strangers—not only pretty women—and you have to give them a reason to let you in. With Hannah Cole, I used two of the most reliable weapons in my arsenal. Nobody is ever rude to a friend who admired their late husband, and nobody mistrusts a man who has come to give them money.

The next stage is the hard bit: how to turn that spark of an introduction into a kindling flame with the potential to ignite a conflagration. I call it the Mirror. Sometimes the dead husband is sufficient. Where he was loved and missed, you become a looking-glass that reflects his glorified light. I talk about his qualities, the void he has left in my life—and soon I start to fill the void in hers. But when I talked about Jonas Cole on that first day in the Punchbowl and Pineapple, she closed me down. By then, I knew a little more about her husband. It was possible their marriage hadn't always been easy.

I'd read all the accounts in the newspapers about Cole's life and death, and I'd discreetly asked around in the local taverns, finding out where he had drunk and shopped, about his friends and his involvement with the parish committee. When I discovered that he had banked at Messrs. Campbell & Bruce, I decided that this would be the perfect explanation for how we'd met—away from his usual haunts in St. James's. Cole's acquaintances had painted a picture of a canny, striving fellow, the sort of man who is respected, sometimes feared, but not well liked. His death had shocked the neighborhood, but nobody seemed overly grief-stricken. Their talk was of the parish committee—who would fill Cole's place—and their disapproval of poor Hannah for reopening her shop. His vices were predictably mundane: drink, though not to excess; gambling, the same; and other women—sometimes whores from the local brothels, sometimes the wives of his friends.

Far worse to my mind than his infidelity, he talked disrespectfully to his friends about his wife. I never do that with my widows, even when it's a struggle to like them—and with Hannah it wasn't a struggle at all. She was worth ten of her husband, but she didn't seem to know it—I suspect because he'd leached all the confidence out of her. Bad husbands often do that—with their fists or their words or their quiet contempt. Despite her looks, Hannah struggled to believe that William Devereux could be interested in her. Or rather, she'd thought I was after her body, when it was her mind I truly coveted—and her money, of course.

You can spot the little clues to a person's nature if you train yourself to look. A swift glance around her shop at the barberry jellies, the preserved cedrat, the exotic fruits in syrup, the candied jujube, and the Turkish jellies told me that she was a woman of adventurous taste—which suggested an open mind and a liberal heart. Naturally, I ordered a Persian sherbet, though I would have preferred an apricot tart, and we bonded in opposition to her conventional customers. Nothing unites two people more than a common enemy. I decided that this incarnation of William Devereux would be well traveled, his trade having taken him as far as India and the Japans.

It was in this spirit of exoticism that I'd first mentioned iced cream. And there it was: my Mirror. I saw it right away. Her face suddenly alert and interested, eager to know more—the irony of ironies that it should have been my fucking mother who inspired it. The taste of that iced cream stuck in my craw, I can tell you. But Hannah was determined to show her detractors that she could run that shop and run it well, and she saw a potential in iced cream that I was only too happy to nurture. Hence my visit to St. Paul's to track down a recipe. Show me a shared goal and I grab hold of it with both hands.

The following day, when I'd returned to the shop to try it, Tom and I had pulled up in our hired chaise at the carriage stand opposite her shop. A carter was waiting there, in conversation with the ferocious-looking lad who guarded Hannah's door.

"I don't know where my mistress is," the lad was saying. "Can't you wait?"

That prompted a lot of grumbling on the driver's part, but eventually he agreed. Until the boy returned to his post and I fixed the driver with a broad smile.

"I should like it very much if you'd tell that lad you've changed your mind," I said. "Make an excuse. Anything will do."

The carter squinted at me suspiciously. "And why should I do that?"

As if conjured from out of nowhere, a half-crown appeared in my hand. "I'd like to take a drive with Mrs. Cole."

A lascivious grin spread over his face. "Widows," he said. "Make it a crown and you've got yourself a deal."

It was on that trip to Willesden that I'd learned that the iced-cream recipe hadn't worked. My mother really had grown up in Italy, and she really had used to make me iced cream, but I was damned if I could remember how she'd done it. I didn't know if Professor Becker would have the answer, but I thought it was worth a try—and it was the perfect excuse to get Hannah out of her shop and into my orbit. I'd been surprised to learn that Henry Fielding thought her husband had been killed by someone he knew—like everyone else, I thought he'd been murdered in a violent street robbery. But given what I knew of Cole's philandering, and the manner of man he was, I guessed there would be no shortage of likely candidates for his murder. Beyond using it to my advantage to convince Hannah to come to Hickford's, I hadn't given it very much thought.

All told, that night was a great success. Sylvia, Mrs. Parmenter, is an old hand at this game. You might think it mad, to have an old lady tell my gull that she wasn't worthy of me. But very few women will accept that premise—even the browbeaten ones. Much more often it has the opposite effect. They start thinking about all the ways they *are* worthy, and before they know it, they have accepted the terms of the question. Luckily, Sylvia loves to play the villainess. Knowing her history as I do, her convincing contempt for the Jezebels of London still makes me smile. In the course of my research, I'd discovered that Hannah had once embarrassed her husband at a dinner at the vestry hall by speaking ardently about the plight of fallen women. Even Amy had liked Hannah better when I'd told her that. Naturally, I made Mr. Devereux a generous supporter of that cause, in the face of Mrs. Parmenter's fierce opposition.

Finally, Hannah had discovered that I was not the libidinous wretch of her suspicions, but a grieving son who only wanted to honor his mother's memory with iced cream. It was touching, how badly she felt for having misjudged me. Perhaps she pictured the lost, motherless boy she imagined I'd been? Since then, my Mirror had shone with a warm and balmy light—and our success with iced cream had paved the way to a new joint enterprise. I speak, of course, of our common enemy: that cunt Fielding. If he confiscated her money, then everything I'd worked for would be lost. Nearly three weeks' labor, not to mention all the blunt I'd outlaid on my minor players, on the hire of the chaise and horses, on Hannah's five-shilling return on her husband's "investment," on the entrance to Hickford's and all the rest. I certainly wasn't looking forward to telling Tom.

But Hannah Cole was desperate, that was the silver lining. Not pewter polished up, but the genuine article. She feared losing her shop, everything her grandfather and her father had built. I'm sure she wanted the rest of the money too, whatever she said. Thanks to that fat old fuck from the Goldfish who'd tried to ravage her in the alley (not my design, that one was down to luck), she'd come to the conclusion that she couldn't do this alone. Which meant I could take the lead in the Dance to follow.

I don't deny that it helps to have a pretty face. Hannah Cole had noticed mine, be in no doubt about that. On that first day in her shop, I'd seen her looking me over in the mirror—and the speed with which she'd sent her shopgirl away so that she could serve me! Then again on the carriage ride back from Willesden, when I'd pretended to be asleep. How flustered she'd been, when I "awoke" and caught her looking. I doubt she'd admitted her attraction even to herself. Widows often deny their feelings, right up to the moment they fall—and nothing beats that moment of capitulation. To hold that fire in your hands, Prometheus unbound. No wonder the gods were jealous, is all I'll say.

Perhaps you think Hannah Cole is a fool, that you wouldn't be taken in by my tricks, that you'd see right through me? I am entirely content for you to think that, because one day soon I might stroll into your life and have you heading for your bank inside six weeks. What you have to understand is that I'm very, very good at what I do.

CHAPTER TWELVE

Two hours later, I was back in St. James's, knocking on the door of that temple of chance named the Goldfish. The two fellows on the door took one look at me and called the director over. Miguel, a little brown Portuguese with eyes that shone like an oiled blade, studied me without much interest. "Desperate times, Billy?"

That day in the carriage to Willesden, I'd pretended not to recognize Hannah's porcelain fish. Partly because William Devereux was supposed to be an upstanding fellow, and partly because it had been a good incentive to get Hannah out to Hickford's. But I knew the Goldfish well, along with many other similar haunts. Sometimes, when I was down on my luck, Miguel gave me work here, or at one of the other golden hells owned by his master, a stone-cold villain named Patrick Musgrave. By "work" I mean he employed me as a puff, a gentleman who hovers around the gaming tables, playing the part of a dissolute rake, occasionally winning big to entice foolhardy men into play. It gave them confidence the games weren't rigged—which naturally they were, making me highly skeptical that Jonas Cole had won his fifteen hundred pounds here. Yet I was curious as to how Cole had got through this door in the first place. The Goldfish was as exclusive as golden hells came. I'd seen baronets and Irish peers turned away. But I knew better than to ask Miguel, who'd report my interest back to Musgrave, a man I preferred to keep at a certain distance.

"I'm looking for Lord Richard," I said. "Is he in yet?"

"In and nearly out. The way we like them."

"I'll keep him playing as long as I can. It's in my best interests if he's short of blunt."

Miguel grimaced. "Members only. You know that."

"Lord Richard is a member."

He shook his head. "The man upstairs won't like it."

Whilst I have been known to palm a card or cog a die from time to time, I'm not so big a fool as to try that here. It's rumored that if you cross Patrick Musgrave, he crosses you right back: a crucifixion with nails and a crown of thorns. Which might be an exaggeration, but not one I'm eager to test.

"Tell him I'll do a night's puffery for nothing once this job is done. So what do you say?"

I can talk my way in or out of almost anywhere. That isn't braggadocio, I really can. It's why things that might daunt a different man, don't daunt me. Even Tom, my "coachman," who knows me better than anyone, gives in to his doubts from time to time. Like just now in the Black Lion, when I'd told him about Henry Fielding and the money. He'd listened, his face increasingly stony, as I'd laid it all out.

"Jesus, Billy," he said.

"It's all in hand," I told him. "Our sweet widow and I are going to find out where that money came from and head Fielding off at the pass."

"And what if it *is* stolen? They say Fielding can't be bribed. He'll confiscate that money for sure."

It was the reason Fielding's name was spoken with such contempt in the Black Lion. If he caught you out in a felony, he'd aim to hang you. He couldn't try the more serious cases himself—that had to be done by a Crown Court judge—but he could commit you for trial and then appear as the principal prosecution witness against you. Unsurprisingly, perhaps, his inflexibility had made him enemies—as had his proposals for judicial reform. Most people have learned to rub along with the world they know, and they don't appreciate those who seek to turn it upside down.

"Don't trouble yourself about Fielding. I'll talk him round."

"How?" Tom demanded.

"I'll think of something."

Tom shook his head. "I don't like this, Bill. You don't want Fielding looking too closely at you."

"He won't be looking at me. He'll be looking at Jonas Cole and his murderer. Hannah laughed today, Tom. You should have heard it. She was transformed."

"Look at my face," he said. "I'm not laughing. We should cry quits."

"After everything we've already invested? It's not as if we're overburdened with other options."

That was the trouble with London in the summer. All the rich widows fled to Bath and Tunbridge Wells. But I'd spent too much time in the spa towns lately, and Hannah Cole was by far the best prospect my clerk had suggested in London.

"Have I ever failed you yet?" I said, seeing that Tom was wavering. "Faint heart never won four hundred pounds."

Not that anyone was winning here at the Goldfish—only the puffs and the house. Once Miguel had capitulated and let me in, I strolled through the entrance hall, with its mosaic floor and grand chandelier, into one of the gaming rooms. The three tables were surrounded by players, hunched over their porcelain fish at the altars of fortune. It was quiet tonight: the rattle of dice, the whisper of cards, the creak of leather, the glug of brandy. I nodded to our host, the Earl of Whitelaw, who was sitting in a chair by the fireplace, beneath a painting of his father triumphant at Blenheim.

If you're confused as to why it is that the earl owns this house, but everyone in it either works for Patrick Musgrave, or pays him to be here, then you're supposed to be. Gaming houses might be illegal, but an Englishman's home is his castle. Try stopping private play amongst friends, and the politicians would soon regret it. Not that they ever would, because most of them enjoy a hand of faro as much as the next man. That being so, should Henry Fielding or one of his overzealous constables ever beat upon this door, the earl would claim that all these good people were his invited guests, come to supper and cards—and every gentleman present would swear the same. The Goldfish had operated here for two years now, and it was rumored that the earl wouldn't clear his debt to Musgrave for another five. Every time I saw him, he looked older, his expression more dazed. Not all crucifixions are done with nails.

Lord Richard was sitting at the E & O table, with only two other players for company—and I was pretty sure that one of them was a puff. It might surprise you to learn that Lord Richard really is the youngest son of the Marquis of Morrow. Up to his eyes in debt, terrified his father will cut him off if he finds out, he's always open to schemes that keep his head above water. But it isn't just about the money with him. Lord Richard is the sort of blueblood who enjoys the company of rogues and sharpers—and he loves the thrill of playing at one himself.

The woman presiding over the table gave me a curt nod of recognition. Virginia, I recalled. Red hair, six foot in her stockings, round as a Rubens. Lord Richard was gazing at her like she was Juno, strolled down from Mount Olympus.

"That faro table's hot as Hades," I announced, as I sat down. "Just my luck I'm out."

The other player at the table glanced across the room, then scooped up his pile of fish, and headed over to join the fray. Gamblers are so easy. Always chasing the win that might get away. The puff considered Lord Richard's dwindling shoal, then collected up his own fish and followed his quarry.

Virginia spun the wheel vigorously and dropped the ball. E & O was still relatively new to London, though I'd seen it twenty years ago in the *casini* of Florence. Some find it dull, but it's the best odds you'll ever see. If the house was playing it straight, of course.

"I want ten guineas," Lord Richard said to me, not taking his eye off the ball as it leapt from slot to slot. "And another half-guinea to get my father's house steward out of the way. He reports on my every move to the old bastard."

The ball came to a rest in one of the slots. "Odd," Virginia said.

Lord Richard muttered a curse.

"Six guineas," I said. "But you can have two of them tonight."

He thought for a moment, and then rubbed his fingers together in what I took to be a gesture of encouragement. "Anything gets broken or stolen, you're footing the bill. And our arrangement still stands, even if you can't get her there."

"I'll get her there," I said, "don't you worry about that. I'm just not sure when."

"I'll need at least a week's notice." Lord Richard pushed his guineas towards Virginia, who replaced them with another little pile of fish.

"I like your Mrs. Cole," he went on, as she spun the wheel again. "Reminds me of the wife of our old stablemaster. She taught a boy a thing or two, I can tell you."

I often used Lord Richard to play the rake around my widows. His job is to make me look worthy by comparison. Not that there's much acting needed on his part. There's an irony in paying a man to play himself.

"You talking or betting?" Virginia said to me.

"Talking." I placed a half-crown on the table. "You ever meet a man in here named Jonas Cole?"

She regarded my coin thoughtfully. "Maybe."

"I know he used to play here." I placed another coin next to the first. "Who did he play with?"

"Why do you want to know?"

"The usual," I said. "A rainbow, with a pot of gold at the end of it. Doesn't matter to him, does it? He's dead."

We watched as Lord Richard pushed his entire pile of fish onto the square marked "Odd." "Does this have something to do with Henry Fielding?" she said.

"Why do you ask?"

She shrugged. "I heard his informants have been asking around the clubs about Cole."

"You did know him, then?" I put down a third coin.

Appearing to come to a decision, she scooped up my money. "I knew who he was. Everybody did."

I looked around me. "Miguel's standards are slipping. Letting a shopkeeper through the door."

She spun the wheel. "Like you, he had grand friends. Lords, members of Parliament."

"Except I heard that it was him who did the inviting. Did he ever win big?"

The rattle of the bouncing ball filled the silence. "Won a little, lost a little. He didn't come here to play. Wanted to impress his friends. Politics." She might have said *excrement*.

"What else did they get up to?" I asked. "Girls?"

"Sometimes. If that was what his friends wanted."

"The girls can't have liked that. No one works here to bed a shopkeeper."

"They do what they're told. Miguel said to keep Cole happy—whatever he wanted."

"Not like Miguel to care about a shopkeeper's happiness."

Lord Richard stared at the wheel and banged the table rather hard. "That damned bitch fortune."

"Careful," I said. "She might take offense."

Virginia swept the table clean. "Miguel also does what he's told."

I stared at her. "Cole had dealings with *Musgrave*?"

Lord Richard was gazing rather morosely at the space where his fish had used to swim.

"Sometimes the wheel spins hot," Virginia told him consolingly. "Sometimes it spins cold. This table here," she held my gaze, "it's cold as a grave."

It was the kind of cheerful thing people said when Musgrave's name came up in conversation. Musgrave and Cole. All sorts of possibilities came to mind. As well as his many gambling clubs, catering to men of every rank, Musgrave owned a string of brothels, taverns, pawnbrokers, and gin shops. He's the richest man in London you never heard of.

Lord Richard was going through his pockets, searching for coins. A flash of gold, and Virginia was counting out fish again. I placed a hand on his shoulder. "I'll need you before the supper. One night this week. Usual terms."

He bowed, a mocking gaze. "Yes, My Lord."

As I walked back into the entrance hall, the footmen and Miguel sprang to attention. Doubting that I had inspired this display of diligence, I turned to see Patrick Musgrave and two of his henchmen coming down the stairs. I picked up my pace, but it was too late. Musgrave's voice rang out: "You been playing at my tables, Billy-boy?"

It didn't help that Musgrave reminded me of my father. That same heavy, square face, hard eyes that saw everything. The unpredictability of that yellow-toothed smile. Musgrave must have spent upwards of three hundred pounds on his suit of pewter silk, but he still had the look of a Smithfield prizefighter, one who refused to fight by Broughton's Rules.

"I wouldn't dream of it," I said. "Your tables are plain unlucky."

If you've learned it the hard way, as a child, there are certain instincts you never lose. Musgrave's fist shot out without warning, and I jerked my head to take the blow on the top of my skull. But Musgrave opened his hand at the last moment to straighten my cravat. "Try your tricks on my customers, and I'll break your fucking legs."

His henchmen laughed sycophantically. Giving them a moment to sweep past me, I emerged onto the street in time to see Musgrave climbing into a carriage. It looked black in the half-light, but as the vehicle moved off and its brass trim caught the light of the burning torches outside the Goldfish, I realized the shade was midnight-blue.

CHAPTER THIRTEEN

If you can judge a man by the company he keeps, you can also judge a man by the book he writes. *Tom Jones* by Henry Fielding is the tale of an orphan of dubious origins. Except I had just flicked to the end of the final volume of the novel and discovered that Tom was in truth the nephew of the wealthy squire who had raised him. Interesting. It told me that class mattered to Fielding—he couldn't bear for his amiable orphan to come from unworthy stock—which was something I might make use of when the time came. Tom might be the principal character, but the word "hero" might better be applied to his uncle, Squire Allworthy. No saint has fewer flaws, no king was ever so admired—and what does this paragon do to merit such respect? You guessed it, he's a magistrate, a model of integrity and compassion, Solomon himself. Fielding only went and put himself in his fucking book.

I was sitting at the tea-table in my rooms, feet up on another chair, an argument between two carters drifting up to me through the open window. I took a bite of my breakfast, sheep's tongues and mustard on toast, thinking about Fielding's novel and what else it revealed about the man. Take young Tom—not my Tom, the one in the book. He had spent his early years whoring with promiscuous women. Given what the world knew about Fielding's own appetites in that regard, it wasn't hard to make the connection. People contain contradictions, I've always thought. The grieving husband who beds his wife's maid, the public servant who indulges in private vice. Those who cry "hypocrisy" are too simplistic, in my opinion. Every man has a private struggle and in this novel, it seemed to me, Fielding had laid his own struggle bare. Duty versus desire. Good Squire Allworthy versus the roguish Tom. In Fielding's eyes, I judged, true heroism was man's triumph over the desires that endangered his soul. Another insight I might make use of when the time came.

Danger made me think of Patrick Musgrave. That midnight-blue carriage might have been a coincidence, but I didn't think so. If Jonas Cole had been in business with Musgrave, and the pair of them had fallen out, I was only surprised that his end hadn't been worse. I knew what Tom would say. That I was mad to even think about going through with this business now. Fielding on one side, Musgrave on the other. Like that monster and the whirlpool, each looming to swallow you up. But that was precisely why I had no intention of telling Tom.

Hannah was due at my rooms at midday. Tom had taken her a note that morning, asking her to call upon me then, and she'd given him a note in reply saying she'd be there. Of course, I could have simply dropped by the Punchbowl and Pineapple, but I wanted to change the terms of our acquaintance. I've already told you how much I learned about Hannah from a few short moments looking around her shop. People inhabit their homes like they inhabit their skin. By the same token, with a bit of thought, your home can tell a story about you. One you write yourself, without too much regard for the truth. My rooms were on the first floor of a fine, yet unostentatious house on Bruton Street in Mayfair, the setting for many a seduction over the years. The place is just about affordable, a convincing home for a wealthy bachelor who doesn't think too hard about domestic comfort. The landlord lives upstairs and is drunk most of the time, meaning he doesn't pay much attention to my comings and goings. An archway to the side of the property leads to a carriage house and stable and has a discreet side entrance with stairs leading directly to my rooms, enabling a lady to enter and leave without being observed.

I have five rooms in all: a sitting room, a bedroom, a dressing room, a pantry, and a second bedroom downstairs, ostensibly for Tom, though most of the time he stays over with his girl, Beth. Amy had helped me improve the cornicing and furnishings with a bit of gold paint and some silver-gilt cord, and I hire bronzes and paintings from a dealer whenever I need them. Another fellow who owns a printing press in Cripplegate helps me out with anything I need. In this case, prospectuses of companies and stock certificates like the one I gave Hannah. I'd strewn them around my sitting room, together with a few other props: an abacus, account books, and a few volumes on finance and the law. The other day, I'd taken myself off to Messrs. Campbell & Bruce and deposited the sum of ten pounds in their vault. I placed the official-looking documents they had given me on prominent display, though I'd discreetly doctored them to turn my ten pounds into a thousand. Wealth begets confidence, which begets trust. There's no rhyme nor reason to it. A rich man has no more morality than a beggar—and sometimes a great deal less in my experience. But for whatever reason, the more familiar a man appears to be with money, the more likely a person is to entrust him with their own.

But don't make the mistake of thinking it's just about money. I've already talked about the Mirror. Hannah Cole struck me as a practical woman, not the sort to sit around imagining the beau of her dreams. She probably didn't even know she had one. Not until she met me.

Thinking of her adventurous side, I'd swapped out some of my usual paintings for maps of the Near and Far East. I'd also taken a trip down to the docks at Limehouse Hole where I'd picked up a few carvings in ebony and sandalwood, some jade and ivory pieces—Buddhas and pagodas—and a stuffed parrot. The other day when we'd been to the ice house, Tom had set about cultivating Hannah's young ruffian of a doorman, a lad named Felix. He'd told Tom how Hannah had taken him and his sister on from the workhouse and even paid them a small wage on top of their bed and board. Coupled with Hannah's concern for the plight of fallen women, and her interest in my remarks about poverty and crime in the carriage, I felt this was a seam we could mine further. I'd had Tom pick up a few pamphlets soliciting donations for charitable causes: the Foundling Hospital, the Marine Society, and all the rest. Perhaps I'd ask Hannah which one I should donate to? There's a thrill to power like that. Experience a little, and most people crave it more.

My gaze fell on Fielding's book again, and the letter keeping my place in it. After Felix had told Tom how Mrs. Cole liked to read stories, I'd borrowed a little library of novels from my book dealer. They'd been intended just to set the scene, but since yesterday's discovery, I thought Fielding merited a little research himself.

I'd told Amy all about it, when I'd gone to her rooms after the Goldfish. "To write a novel I think you'd have to imagine yourself in another man's shoes. Not so different to what we do. Except the honest man usually wins."

She'd laughed, rather contemptuously. "I don't understand why people pay good money to be told lies."

"There's comfort in a lie," I said. "You know that."

Which was when she'd reached into her pocket and given me the letter. It had come for me at the Black Lion, she'd said, not long after I'd left. Nothing unusual about that—I often use the place for correspondence, when I don't want a person knowing my real address. Except that this one was addressed to William Cullen, my real name. The only person who knew it, and who would write to me at the Black Lion, was my father's solicitor, Mr. Thornhill. And as my father had died four years ago, leaving me the grand sum of fuck nothing, I couldn't think what else he'd have to say.

"Well?" Amy had said, when I'd read the letter through twice.

"My stepmother is dying. She wants to see me."

"Think she's leaving you some blunt?" It was like Amy to get to the point.

I shook my head, eyes traveling over Alice's spidery hand. "She's got nothing in her own right. It all went to my half-brother. I should go, I suppose. She was kind in her own way. Used to tell me that my father loved me really."

"There's comfort in a lie." Amy grinned.

Now, at my tea-table, I studied the letter again, not relishing the prospect of Hackney. Especially now that my cunt of a half-brother had got his hands on the spoils. I'd go in the carriage, of course. Take Tom dressed up in his livery. I wished I'd done it when my father had still been alive.

A knock at the door roused me from these thoughts. When Tom showed Hannah in, I saw she had come alone, which I thought interesting. To call at a gentleman's rooms without a servant, even upon a matter of business, was taking quite a risk with her reputation. Perhaps she wasn't as convinced of her husband's innocence as she'd claimed, and didn't want her apprentice overhearing any hint of scandal? Or perhaps her heart was already running in front of her head . . .

I dismissed Tom, who had work to do, and showed Hannah to the seats by my fireplace, a more intimate setting than the table. She had brought me a box of ginger cakes, but declined any refreshment for herself. I could sense her nerves, though she hid them well—talking just a little too fast when we exchanged niceties. She told me that the iced cream had sold out inside an hour and she had already prepared some more.

"I charged three shillings a bowl, and was worried it would be too much. But now I am thinking it might not have been enough." She'd been looking around the room, taking in all my props, but now she gazed at me directly. "You said that you had news for me, Mr. Devereux?"

She listened intently as I told her everything I'd discovered the night before, omitting only her late husband's whoring and my suspicions about Patrick Musgrave. I didn't want her doing anything rash like giving his name to Henry Fielding. I'd given the matter a great deal of thought since last night—debating what use a man like Cole might have been to Musgrave—and I told Hannah the theory I'd settled upon.

"From the sounds of it, Jonas was treated as an honored guest at the Goldfish. Which is unusual given his circumstances. But I don't believe that he won that money there, and I'm afraid I think that Henry Fielding might be right in thinking it wasn't acquired honestly. My best guess is that Jonas was acting as a middling man between the gambling houses and the magistrates. Corruption is rife on the Westminster bench and the gaming clubs have deep pockets."

Hannah clutched her wrist, frowning thoughtfully. "You think Jonas made his money facilitating bribes?"

"That is my suspicion, though I have no evidence to prove it. In his role as parish intelligencer, Jonas would have been a familiar figure at the courts. And his work with the other parishes seems to have taken him all over London. I think Henry Fielding has the same suspicion. He's been asking around the clubs about your husband."

Many of which belonged to Musgrave, and unlike the Goldfish, were housed in winehouses and taverns which could be raided at a moment's notice.

Hannah seemed to take the news rather better than I'd thought she would. "The men who own these clubs are very villainous, I should think? Men who wouldn't shrink from murder?"

"They are undoubtedly more familiar with violence than you or I."

She nodded soberly. "And there are a lot of them? These clubs?"

"Dozens across the Westminster parishes."

"Then I don't imagine it will be easy for Mr. Fielding to investigate all the suspects. He might hunt for months and never find the guilty party."

"I'm afraid it also means that he may lay claim to your money," I pointed out. "That seems very unfair to me—after everything you've been through."

"Surely he would let Daniel and me keep the savings from the shop?" she said. "I would like to keep the rest of it, Lord knows, but the most important thing is that those villains who murdered Jonas are caught."

"I don't think you can guarantee anything," I said. "Not whilst all the power lies in Fielding's hands. I know he deplores corruption on the bench more than anything."

"Without that money to repay my debts, I will lose the shop," Hannah said, rather despondently.

I waited just long enough for this prospect to sink in. "What if there was a way to help Fielding catch the murderer *and* for you to keep your money? I don't just mean your savings, I mean all of it."

She studied my face. "How could I do that? You just said that Mr. Fielding deplores corruption."

"First, I think we need to ascertain for certain what Jonas was up to. At present all we have to go on is my suspicions."

The truth was, I didn't yet know how I'd convince Fielding to hand over the blunt. But there is always a route to getting what you want. Fielding's desire above all else was to catch Jonas's killer and get the nod from his political masters for his precious *police*. Knowledge was power, I reasoned, and it was something one could trade. Of course, the shadow of Patrick Musgrave loomed large over my thinking now. If he'd had a hand in Jonas's murder, then I was dicing with danger to even think about getting involved. But until I knew the facts, I couldn't make a judgment upon that score. Only once you know your terrain, can you see all the angles.

"How could we find out more?" Hannah asked, not unreasonably. "The men who own these clubs are hardly likely to admit it. Nor these corrupt magistrates."

"Did anyone ever come to the house to give Jonas money?" I asked. "Or to receive it?"

"Only our suppliers. Jonas didn't conduct parish business at home. He was busy in the shop during the day and in the evenings he went out."

"He would have wanted to make these transactions discreetly," I said. "Can you recall anything he ever said or did that seemed unusual to you? Anything that struck you as strange or out of place?"

She thought for a moment. "There was one thing that I always thought rather odd. A regular delivery we made from the shop. Once a week, a dozen champagne biscuits and a box of candied fruits to a Mr. Fox. Jonas always insisted upon packing the delivery himself, when he never helped me with any of our other orders. I asked him why he took such care with it, and he said Mr. Fox was a friend from the Westminster bench who was going to help him get into Parliament. The order never went out with our regular deliveries. A boy came to collect it."

"You think there might have been money in those boxes?"

"It's a possibility, don't you think? After Jonas died, that boy never returned. Nor was there any record of a Mr. Fox in Jonas's papers. I looked because I couldn't afford to lose him as a customer. I even went down to the magistrate's court to see if I could find him, but nobody knew his name."

"Given all the precautions Jonas was taking, I wonder if it was a pseudonym."

Her face fell. "Then we'll never find him?"

"I didn't say that." I smiled. "Let me see what I can do."

Color flooded her face rather becomingly. "I don't know how to thank you—except with iced cream. I wanted to bring you some today, but it would have melted on my way round. Perhaps if you came by the shop? I have been trying out new flavors."

How I love the breathless flutter of a grateful woman. "I am eager to try your iced cream again, but there is no need to thank me. Whatever Jonas was up to, he was still my friend. I owe it to him to assist you, and if it helps to catch his murderer, then so much the better."

Again, she looked away when I spoke of her dead husband in these terms—and with her next breath, she changed the subject: "How did you come to be in your line of business, Mr. Devereux? Speculation, investments?"

It's always a good sign when a woman starts to ask you questions about yourself. "It's fair to say that it wasn't the path my father intended for me," I said, solemnly. "He was a gentleman, a landowner in Middlesex, and he envisaged that I would live like him, squeezing every last sou out of my estates. We argued—about many things, but principally because I wanted to improve the lot of our tenants. By then my father had remarried, and he discovered that he liked his new son rather better than me. We had one argument too many and he cut me off."

"That was cruel," she said, with feeling. "Especially after losing your mother. Mrs. Parmenter told me how young you were when she died."

I was silent a moment. "Please don't blame Mrs. Parmenter—I'm sure she was simply trying to protect my family's reputation—but that isn't true and I don't like to deal in falsehoods. My mother didn't die, at least not when I was a child. She might even be alive today for all I know."

Have I mentioned that the truth can often be a useful tool in crafting a lie? I like to make use of it wherever I can. My mother's story is a case in point. Bitch has to be good for something. Real emotions always work better than the ones you feign.

"I think I told you before that my mother grew up in Italy," I said. "Her father was an English merchant in Verona, and when she was sixteen, she fell in love with a man her parents didn't approve of. The family returned to England in order to separate them, and a few years later, thinking that her first love had forgotten her, she married my father. But when I was eight years old, her Italian came to England to find her. I awoke one morning to find her gone." Hearing the catch in my voice, I willed a tear to my eye, losing myself for a moment in those old feelings. "My father divorced her for adultery. I blamed myself for years. Had I been better behaved, she might not have left."

When a man bares his soul like that to a woman, she is usually touched by his gift of trust. And if she feels unworthy of that honor, which she surely should on such short acquaintance, she often tries to earn it by laying bare a few truths of her own.

"Oh, Mr. Devereux, it was not your fault."

They always say that. As if they could ever know.

"How could a mother do such a thing?" Hannah went on, in a quiet, sad voice. "When you went to Italy, was that to look for her?"

I nodded, rather bleakly. "I searched Venice, Verona, and Rome, but I never found any trace of her. Then one morning, I was walking through Florence, just as dawn was breaking. You have never seen light like it. The sun catching the marble statues in the Piazza della Signoria. I realized then that there was a world out there for me." I laughed, as if embarrassed that I'd said so much. "But you don't want to hear about that. Lord Richard always tells me that I forget to be charming."

"Lord Richard is wrong," she cried, gazing at me with a trace of outrage that warmed my heart. "I would rather talk like this, with honesty, about the things that truly matter, than all the foolish frivolities people come out with when they cannot think of anything more interesting to say." She drew a breath. Here it comes, I thought. "My own mother died when I was just six months old. I think about her often, though one cannot truly mourn those one cannot remember. But my father, the loss of him . . ." She stared out of the window. "You remind me a little of him. He could not abide a lie either. Though I'm afraid he also said the same about speculation."

"Many do." I smiled wryly. "And indeed, there are vultures on the Exchange, eager to feast upon the entrails of the unwary. Though in my case, I had an honest teacher, one who valued ethics above all else. I speak of Mr. Parmenter, who trained me up in his business trading in the Far East, as I told you."

Hannah's gaze roamed the room again, taking in all the maps and paintings and trinkets. "I always wanted to travel," she said. "Just to Paris to see their confectionary. But Jonas said we couldn't leave the shop for so long. I had to content myself with books." She was gazing at my own bookshelves now. "It is rare to meet a man who reads novels. Or, at least, one who will admit to it. Jonas thought they were trivial things. He only read the newspapers."

"You can only learn so much from a newspaper," I said. "Or even a novel, for that matter. To truly experience a place, you have to see it for yourself. I hope you get to visit Paris one day, Mrs. Cole."

She smiled at me then, a proper meeting of the eyes, before she lowered hers demurely. Was she feeling it yet? I sensed she was. Watching a woman wage war on her own desires always makes my heart race. I could already tell that this fire would be fierce when it surged. In the meantime, I basked in the glow of that kindling flame.

CHAPTER FOURTEEN

The white Norman keep of the Tower of London stood stark against the azure sky, like a castle on a flag. Tom was leaning against the ramparts up ahead, smoking a pipe. From this heightened vantage point, I could take in the vast sweep of London, the river flashing in the sun, great oceangoing ships like children's toys. One of those days that makes you treasure the air in your lungs.

"We've got a problem," Tom said, with a face that suggested he was rather less enamored of his surroundings than I was.

"Good day, Bill," I said. "How did it go with Mrs. Cole? Easy journey here? Nice weather we're having."

"I'm serious," he said. "I had a letter this morning. One of my friends in Bath. Penelope Felton has laid a complaint against you with the magistrate there."

I whistled. "I didn't think she had it in her."

It had taken all my talents to conjure a smile from Penny's thin lips. An embittered woman of forty-two, Penny had weathered two dead sons and years of caring for her much older husband. I'd admired her resilience, though not her temper. Masquerading as a wealthy baronet, I'd woven her a tale that soon had her enticed: an investment I'd made in an iron foundry owned by an old friend—and his secret government contract that had already made me a small fortune. Soon she was begging me to get her in, and parting her from her seven hundred proved as painless as podding peas. When I'd told her that it was all gone, I had endured the full force of her anger—which I always take as a professional failing on my part. Yet the thing Penny had cared about most—other than her money and Sir William Truscott (as I was then)—was her position in Bath society. Penny and her friends presided over the pump room like cardinals in a conclave, and they liked nothing better than a scandal involving one of their number. For that reason alone, I'd thought it unlikely that she'd report me.

"So we'll stay away from Bath for a couple of years," I said. "No great loss there. Too expensive."

"My friend says she's now in London. That she's come looking for you here."

"You know where we haven't been in a while," I said. "The Lakes. Lovely skin the ladies have up there. Though you have to get their shoes off early to check for webbed feet."

"This is no joke, Billy. Not with this Fielding business too. What if he gets to hear of it?"

"I don't see why he'd make a connection. I was Sir William Truscott, baronet, in Bath. William Devereux grubs around on the Exchange to make a living. Trust me, Tom." I grinned. "Doctor knows best."

Dr. William Lamont had been my name when I'd first met Tom in Norwich, over ten years ago now. He'd been working as a footman for real then, in the household of a wealthy and reclusive widow who suffered from a dropsy of the legs. It just so happened that Dr. Lamont was a renowned authority in the treatment of that very same condition. When I'd first examined Tom's mistress at her large townhouse by the river, I'd thought her legs didn't look so very bad to me. A few treatments from my medicine chest—containing a wide variety of pills and phials of colored water purchased from the quacks of Covent Garden—and she was claiming how much better she felt. I concluded that there was nothing wrong with her except unhappiness and boredom, and Dr. Lamont proved an exceptional cure.

Most women desire money as the means to an end. A bigger dowry for a beloved daughter, a carriage to keep up with the neighbors, a Mayfair townhouse to gain entry into London society. But my Norwich widow loved the filthy lucre just for itself. I adore a greedy woman. The slightest whiff of temptation and they're yours.

With such ladies, I often make use of the Spanish Prisoner lay. It's been around for a hundred years and more, but it still works like a charm. I tell my widow that a Hapsburg count of my acquaintance has been imprisoned in Spain under a false identity (in this case, I claimed the count was a former patient whom I'd treated during a spell at Baden-Baden). The prisoner cannot reveal his identity, or he will be killed. But if I am able to raise the sum of five hundred pounds (more if my widow is good for it), I can secure his release. Should I do so, he will double my money, just as soon as he has recourse to his bankers in Vienna. Naturally, I never have sufficient funds to help my poor friend, and as I recounted this tragic tale to my miserly matron of Norwich, her eyes lit up.

The next day, I'd called at her house, expecting her to have the money ready, but she fobbed me off, saying there had been a delay. I kept a smile on my face, but I won't deny I was concerned. In the hall, as I was putting on my coat, one of her footmen sidled up to me. "I've smoked your lay," he said.

Tom was little more than twenty then. Lean as a lizard, and with his sharp jaw and cheekbones, pox-scarred skin and cunning eyes, not entirely dissimilar in appearance.

"I'll bet you're not even a doctor," he said.

"There're professors in Edinburgh and the Sorbonne who would beg to differ," I replied, haughtily.

He only laughed. "You don't fool me. She wants to consult her sons about that money. Asked me what I thought."

I heard this in some alarm. Relatives are the absolute worst.

"I told her I'd think it over. That she shouldn't give you the money today."

I knew a pitch when I heard one. "How much?"

"Thirty," he said.

We settled on twenty, and two days later, after I'd taken possession of her seven hundred pounds, Tom turned up at my lodgings to collect his cut. "I expect you spend a lot of time thinking about what people want," he said, as he pocketed the money. "But not enough time thinking about what you need."

"And what is that?" I said.

"A partner. Someone to watch your back."

"I'm touched by your concern. But I work alone." Don't get me wrong, often I'd hire a bit player or two. Sometimes a whole host of them. But a junior partner was different.

"That's a mistake," he said. "A gentleman should have a servant. She thought it odd that you didn't."

There was truth in his words, but an accomplice meant dividing the spoils—and a witness to bear evidence against me.

"Servants talk to other servants," he said, as if reading my mind—a trait that I admire in a man. "There's value in information. Give it six months, and I bet I save you more than I earn."

"I can see you're good at telling a man what he wants to hear." I smiled. "But it isn't easy playing a part for days at a time."

"You think I don't know that? I've been pretending to like that old bitch for nearly three years now. I could do with a new challenge."

In the end, it was strange how little thought I gave it—and it turned out to be one of the best decisions I ever made. Tom had more front than Buckingham House, and a ruthless mind for a situation. It certainly wasn't like him to be so chary as he was today.

"The way Hannah looked at me," I said, up there on the Tower's ramparts. "She held my gaze two seconds too long. It'll be a quick one, Tom. I can already feel it."

He grunted. "What about Fielding and the money?"

"All in hand." A slight overstatement. I'd just come from the Palace of Westminster, but the magistrate's court had already finished for the day. They were reconvening tomorrow, and I intended to be there.

"When we're done, let's go to Bavaria," I said. "You like the spa in autumn. Or we could have some fun with the mesdames dowagers down in Nice?"

Tom didn't smile, only knocked out his pipe on the wall. "Come on," he said. "Let's go down."

We descended the steps that led down to one of the Tower's courtyards, and walked past a pair of guards in Tudor costume on the gate. Ignoring their hard stares—I'd earned their resentment by refusing to tip them on my way in—we knocked on a blue door beneath a sign of a painted lion. A little African lad opened the door and we gave him our names.

"Entrance is a shilling," he told us.

"We're friends of Kit Fowler," I said.

"Oh, right. He told me about you. It's still a shilling."

Grumbling a little, I paid him, and he jerked a thumb over his shoulder. "You'll find him by the monkey house. Past the cages on the left."

A curved half-moon of a passage was lined with stone cells in which exotic animals gloomily resided: a leopard pacing, a sorry-looking bear with molting fur, a wolf who followed our progress with his yellow gaze.

A livelier scene greeted us at the end of the passage. To one side of a cobbled yard stood a much larger cage, domed like a canary's. Kit Fowler stood in the center, spooning orange slop from a bucket into a wooden trough. Monkeys swarmed around him, chattering, squeaking, some swinging from the bars, one sitting on his shoulder, pulling at his graying beard.

I lifted a hand in greeting. "And there was me thinking you never had any luck with the ladies."

He grinned. "Not what your sister said, the last time I saw her."

Tom and I had met Fowler in a tavern, where he'd been selling parrots' feathers from a bag. I'd added his details to my little book, which is filled with the names of men and women with interesting jobs, who might come in handy one day. And today my plans for Hannah, which were already taking shape, meant that he had.

Fowler came out of the cage, wiping his hands on a rag. "The little lad's over here," he said. "But don't get too close. The mother had a lady's arm off last year."

We halted next to a large circular pen surrounded by a railing that to my mind didn't look high enough, given the tiger reclining at its center. I had never seen one in the flesh before, and I regarded her with a measure of awe, the power of body and limb manifest even in that sedate pose. The cub was nestled close to his mother, just as sleek and beautiful, but rather less likely to bite your head off. Still, I regarded him rather doubtfully.

"Are you sure he's safe?"

Fowler considered. "He might swat you with his paw, and if he bites you, you'll know it, but no worse than a dog. Keep him collared and on a chain and you should be all right. Just the one night, you said?"

Tom nodded. "We're not sure when yet. A half-guinea, is that right?"

"We said a guinea," Fowler said, his eyebrows raised.

A little boy ran up to the railing, cradling a tabby cat in his arms. He lifted the creature up so the tigers could see it. Both mother and son regarded it with some interest.

"That's sweet," I said. "I wonder if they think they're related."

Fowler gave me a look. "We let people in for free if they bring a cat or dog to feed to the tigers."

Deciding that I didn't want to stick around to watch, we agreed that I'd give Fowler a day's notice when I needed the cub, and we shook hands.

"I'll tell you something else Felix told me," Tom said, as we made our way back down the half-moon passage. "Something Mrs. Cole doesn't like."

He glanced pointedly at the lad on the door, as he opened it to let us out.

"She doesn't like Africans?" I said. "Don't sound like her."

"No," Tom exclaimed. "I mean slavery. Felix said some Quaker came into her shop, handing out pamphlets. He was set to throw the fellow out, but Mrs. Cole stopped him. Said she wanted to hear what he had to say and afterwards she told Felix's sister that she wished she could buy her sugar from someplace else."

I digested this information. "Good for Mrs. Cole."

Sometimes we had runaway slaves come into the Black Lion. Usually beaten or otherwise abused, the idea of giving a little payback to the likes of their former masters rather appealed to them.

"Think we can use it?" Tom said.

"Maybe." It was all grist for the mill. "You know, you should speak to that girl direct. There might be things she hasn't told her brother. The way she looks at a man you'd have her on her back inside five minutes."

Tom answered me rather forcefully. "Not this time, Bill."

I gave him a quizzical look. "Oh?"

He halted a little way from the guards by the gate, as if he had something important to say.

"Look," he said, "it's Beth. I've been meaning to tell you, but I haven't found the right time. She's going to have a baby. We're getting married."

"Congratulations." I couldn't think what else to say.

"I wasn't sure what to think about it either, when she first told me. But I came round to the idea. Every man has to hang up his hat sometime, don't you think?"

I studied his face. "What are you saying?"

"I'm not coming with you. To France or Germany or wherever. I need to be here."

"Fair enough," I said. "What about afterwards?"

He sighed. "It don't sit well with her, Bill. What we do. It never has."

"I see." I knew better than to argue with him. Tom's will was cast from steel, and if his back was against the wall, it had an edge like a blade. But he'd change his mind, I told myself. A few weeks with a squalling baby, and he'd be begging me to take him back. If he lasted that long.

"What about you?" Tom said. "Don't say you haven't thought about it. Making an honest woman of Amy."

I laughed. "I'm a man, not a magician."

"I'm serious. Anyone can see the girl adores you."

"She's a good actress. Don't be fooled."

He examined me a moment, though I wasn't quite sure what he was looking for. "You can't really mean to go on doing this forever?"

Beth had really got under his skin. Women could be manipulative like that when they were expecting. I threw an arm around his shoulder, feeling the hard muscle beneath. "As long as I have teeth in my head, Tom. What else would I do?"

CHAPTER FIFTEEN

For those unfamiliar with London, the Palace of Westminster isn't one big mansion like St. James's or Buckingham House, but rather a sprawling jumble of buildings on the banks of the River Thames. Norman stone, Tudor brick, Stuart timber, and everything in between, bristling with spires, pinnacles, turrets, buttresses, and weathervanes. Half the buildings are falling down, and the stables smell of shit—a fitting metaphor for Parliament, some might say. The dark passages and dirty courtyards between the buildings contain an assortment of taverns, chophouses, shops, and stalls selling everything from books to spectacles to signet rings. Someone has to relieve the robber barons of their ill-gotten gains.

By this, I don't just mean the politicians. The courts of the King's Bench, Chancery, and Common Pleas all meet beneath the hallowed hammer-beam roof of Westminster Hall. The lesser courts—Exchequer, Requests, Wards and Liveries—convene in the buildings that surround it. Sit in any one of those courts for more than twenty minutes and you'll see that half the judges in the place are on the take.

Their poor relations, the magistrates of Westminster, occupy an anonymous house on the shabbiest side of Old Palace Yard. I had to fight my way past a gaggle of "straw-men," professional witnesses offering testimony for a fee, to get a seat in the public gallery. A paper upon each chair listed the day's cases: men and women charged with beggary, blasphemy, whoring, and brawling—and the keeping or frequenting of gaming houses. Word in the Black Lion said that my new nemesis, Henry Fielding, believed such establishments to be nurseries for much more serious crimes. He had convinced the Duke of Newcastle to lean on his fellow magistrates and they'd initiated widespread raids against the gamesters.

At the beginning of the session, in between sips of port, the justice chairing the bench that day delivered a stern sermon against gambling, that he presumably hoped would be well received around the cabinet table. "I have heard tales of footmen now worth fifty thousand pounds, raised up by the preposterous wheel of fortune. Whilst others, born to greatness, descend by the same method, until all distinction and propriety is lost."

Yet once the cases were heard, it was a different story. One after another, a string of men accused of keeping gaming houses were acquitted, even where the evidence was as cut-and-dried as a herbalist's wares. The only conviction involved a taverner from Tothill Fields, who had been running three shovelboard tables and a game of thimbles and balls in his cellar. He was fined forty shillings, but by my reckoning he must have been making ten pounds a night from play, which seemed like a bargain. Still, he looked furious, and I could only presume he hadn't been paying off the right people. Who the right people were, was what I was there to find out.

At two o'clock, the justices retired to Waghorn's, a chophouse within the palace precinct. I followed in their wake and observed them as they ate, the dining room echoing to the chink of glasses and the pop of corks. Once I judged the magistrates to be suitably lubricated, I sent over a bottle of good brandy, and as I'd hoped, they invited me to join them. Amidst a cloud of tobacco smoke, I introduced myself as William Canning, adding that I was new to town, having lately purchased two winehouses in Covent Garden.

"My friend, the late Jonas Cole, suggested that I make your acquaintance," I said. "Given your responsibilities for the licensing of my trade."

The gentleman who'd chaired the session, a fat fellow by the name of Enright, grimaced. "Fielding hasn't caught the brigands yet, I see. Hanging's too good for them. I'd draw and quarter them too."

The high bailiff proposed a toast to Jonas Cole and we all drank. For a time, we discoursed about the scourge of crime, until I judged it time to make my play. "Before he died, Cole said I should meet a friend of his named Fox. He is a useful fellow, I was told, full of good advice about how to protect one's business against misfortune."

"You mean insurance?" Enright said, as he filled his pipe.

"Insurance is certainly the word for it," I said. "Only a fool wouldn't put his hand in his pocket to buy peace of mind. Do any of you know where I might find him?"

I noticed a few of the men exchange surreptitious glances. One of the justices, a man with a long chin and a rather scabrous skin condition, studied me over his glass of claret. "I believe I know your Mr. Fox," he said. "Met him at Ranelagh Gardens once or twice. He is a regular there, I'm told. Attends the Rotunda every Saturday night after nine o'clock."

Which was as good as an invitation to my ears. Satisfied that I had run my quarry to ground, I sat back, sipping my wine, hearing the bay of hounds and the blast of a horn.

*

The ball of iced cream was nestled in a crystal dish. A pale orange in hue, it was studded with bright green pistachio kernels and glistening slivers of lemon peel. The flavors mingled in my mouth, sweet orange, sharp lemon, and the earthy bitterness of the nuts. Better than anything my mother had made. I forced it down.

We were in Hannah's kitchen. She smiled at the look of rapture on my face. "I tried beating it periodically while it was freezing. It has greatly improved the texture. I am trying out other ideas too."

How innovative she was. I smiled at her fondly. The queue had been out the door when I'd arrived, and iced cream was the demand upon everyone's lips. Hannah had three flavors on sale now: peach, raspberry, and the one I'd just tried, which she had named "Royal Ice."

"You have no idea what you've done for me, Mr. Devereux," she said. "My shop will turn a pretty profit this week, and that is down to you."

See how I had already improved her lot? Hannah glanced anxiously at the door. "I had better not be long. Oscar and Theo are run off their feet and it is all Felix can do to keep the customers in line."

Despite her concern, wanting to prolong our time together, I spun my story out. "It seems our Mr. Fox will be at Ranelagh Gardens tomorrow night," I concluded. "I hope you do not have a prior engagement?"

She stared at me aghast. "But I cannot go to Ranelagh. I am in mourning."

I had anticipated this objection. "I understand, and yet I think it essential that you are there. Mr. Fox was your husband's accomplice, perhaps his friend. He is far more likely to open up to you than he is to me. Especially once he discovers that I have lied to him."

I was, of course, quite certain that I could have got the answers I wanted from Mr. Fox without Hannah there. Bribery or blackmail—one will usually suffice. Yet Ranelagh happened to be the perfect setting for the next act I had in store for Hannah Cole. It took me a little while to talk her into it, but her desire to find out who'd killed her husband and her anxieties about her money soon won her round.

"But you must promise to take me home directly we are done with Mr. Fox."

Of course, I gave her my word that I would. Unable to detain her any longer, we made our way back out through the shop, where a stocky gentleman of fair complexion rose to greet her.

"Well," he said, in an Ulster accent rich as chocolate, "what a sensation you are causing, my dear. I'm told three customers came into the receiving house this morning talking about your iced cream." He produced a bundle of letters from his coat and handed them to Hannah.

"Mr. Devereux, allow me to name Mr. Daniel Cole, my late husband's cousin," Hannah said. "He has charge of all the post offices in Westminster. Daniel, you remember I told you about Mr. Devereux, Jonas's friend?"

"The stockjobber," Daniel said, gazing at me without much warmth. "I was at Cambridge with a Jonathan Devereux. Is he any relation?"

"Only very distantly," I said. "I belong to the Middlesex branch."

"I have Mr. Devereux to thank for my iced cream," Hannah said. "He told me all about it and found me a recipe at St. Paul's."

Again, I felt Daniel's cold-fish gaze upon me. "A veritable Galahad," he said.

"I merely convinced Mrs. Cole of its merits," I said. "The effort was all hers."

"Then I applaud your powers of persuasion," Daniel said. "Not least in persuading Jonas to part with his money. Never an easy task. I'm surprised he never mentioned you to me."

Like I said, relatives are the absolute worst. Sometimes you can make a conquest of them, especially the females of the flock, but the men tend to be resentful of good-looking members of their own sex—far worse than women in that regard, in my experience.

"I am often a well-kept secret," I said. "The Marquis of Morrow frequently says that he is terrified his friends will find out all about me and I'll put up my fees."

I sensed it took all Daniel's self-control not to look impressed by the name. "Maybe I'll give you an interview myself, once probate is granted."

Pompous ass. The thought of taking his money was delightful, but widows are my métier and I never work on more than one job at a time. "Regrettably, I am not taking on new clients at the moment," I said. "But if that should change, I'll let you know." I raised my hat.

"Mrs. Cole, it has been a pleasure."

As I walked out onto the street, I turned to see Hannah watching me through the window. I touched my hat again, holding her gaze, with very little concern for Daniel Cole's deepening frown.

CHAPTER SIXTEEN

And so we embarked upon the Dance. Imagine leading a lady in a minuet, turning her this way and that; a bound here, a reverse there, only the steps are all in your mind. It is a remarkable thing to witness a woman move to your own design. And what better place to take to the floor than Ranelagh Gardens?

You could hear the music a quarter of a mile away. Ordinarily I would have arrived in Chelsea by boat—there is a delightful intimacy to a glide along the Thames—but the carriage was an essential part of the evening's plan. Hannah had told me that she had never been to Ranelagh before, and as we strolled along the tree-lined avenue from the ticket booth, her eyes widened at the lights and the mirrored fountains and the pleasure-seekers flaunting the latest Parisian fashions. Unlike the Vauxhall Gardens, which could be a riotous, bawdy place, at Ranelagh refinement was the order of the night. A gentleman went to Vauxhall to tumble a shopgirl in the bushes. He came to Ranelagh for romance under the stars.

I sent Tom and Felix off to the gated part of the garden where servants were permitted to drink while they awaited their masters. Hannah appeared a little fretful and I guessed she was worried about being seen in my company. But not so worried that she'd neglected to dress and pin her hair, securing it with a pretty comb inlaid with colored glass. I had taken great care with my own appearance too, having purchased a coat of ivory silk embroidered with the iridescent green wings of beetles, that I was assured by my tailor was a popular fashion for men in the India trade. We strolled arm in arm towards the domed Rotunda, which was modeled upon the Pantheon in Rome.

I had to pay an additional fee to get us through one of the Doric porticoes, and I told the footman on the desk that we were joining Mr. Fox. He consulted his list, and then summoned another footman to escort us to our table.

Hannah was gazing around. "Why, it's magnificent," she exclaimed.

The footman grinned. "First time? The walls and ceiling are Canaletto. It takes six men to raise and lower each chandelier, and a party of twelve over an hour to light all the lamps."

In the center of that vast round space stood a giant square pillar, decorated with Moorish arches and other moldings. As well as supporting the roof, it incorporated a large balcony upon which the orchestra were playing. The acoustics were dismal, but nobody let that spoil the fun. Groups of patrons perambulated around the interior in a rather monotonous circular walk, exclaiming over one another's gilt lace and jeweled buttons. A more sedentary crowd looked on from the double tier of supper boxes around the walls, waving fans, drinking wine, gossiping away.

The footman led us to one of the supper boxes on the lower tier, and I recognized its occupant right away: the clerk of the peace who had presented the indictments in the sessions at Westminster Palace. It took me a moment to remember his name: Mr. Mitford Banks.

He rose and we bowed. "Mr. Canning, I presume?"

"And you must be Mr. Fox. Though I believe you went by a different name in court the other day."

"Let's stick to Fox, shall we?" Banks said, with a little smile.

About twenty-five, he had soft, downy skin and a face every woman he met would want to mother. He wore the anonymous dark suit of the Whitehall placeman, which he had enlivened with a large nosegay in his buttonhole. At ease with himself and the world, a sharper's glint to his eye, I liked him immediately.

Banks's gaze fell upon Hannah and he turned to me enquiringly.

"My wife," I said. "She plays an essential role in our business."

"Very modern," Banks said. "I am all for modernity. The steam engine, the pianoforte, and Mrs. Canning." He bowed again.

I had told Hannah in the carriage that initially we would disguise both our motives and our identities.

"But I thought you hated deception of any kind?" she'd said.

"Not where it concerns the well-being of my friends."

She'd frowned. "I don't like the idea of lying."

"Neither do I," I assured her. "But I fear it may be the only means to obtain what we want."

She had seemed to accept this argument, and had raised no objection to my proposal that we pretend to be husband and wife. Of course, there was no real reason for any of this deception, but I hoped our act of sham intimacy would foreshadow the real thing. We had rehearsed our lines together on the journey, though I was ready to step in should Hannah falter under pressure.

The booth was decorated with a droll painting of Satyricon goings-on in a glade, and as we took our seats, a waiter appeared to pour wine. Once he had departed, our host got down to business.

"My sources tell me that you are in the wine trade, sir. Do I take it that you are looking to expand your business into other quarters?"

"I am indeed," I said. "Mr. Cole had offered to help us in that regard, but his untimely demise curtailed our association before our dealings ever came to fruition."

"A great tragedy for all concerned," Banks pronounced solemnly. "Yet I am pleased to tell you that Mr. Cole's death caused only a temporary setback for my business. I have a new partner now, and our enterprise flourishes once again. I take it Mr. Cole explained how it all works?"

I glanced at Hannah. This was her moment and she took it. "He merely said that you could help us insure ourselves against the unwanted attentions of the Westminster bench," she said.

I gave her a smile of encouragement. She was a natural!

"Oh, indeed we can," Banks declared happily. "When it comes to the laws against gaming—forgive me, madam—Parliament is an ass! Happily many of our magistrates believe that too. One or two of them even own gaming establishments themselves. Given the right inducement, which I should be pleased to facilitate for a small fee, those gentlemen will ensure that I learn about any imminent raid upon your establishment. I will then pass that information on to you, via my partner, at which point you can decide whether to pay a further sum to avert the raid entirely, or simply take steps to ensure that when the constables come calling they will find nothing untoward."

Whilst Banks had been talking, I had taken hold of Hannah's hand. Immediately, I'd felt her stiffen, but I gave her hand a little squeeze to indicate that it was part of the act.

"You can guarantee it?" I said. "That we'll never be raided without advance warning?"

Banks pulled a sorrowful face. "Alas, there are never any guarantees. A few of the Westminster magistrates are men of a reforming nature. And Henry Fielding has whipped them into a lather. Then there are the ambitious fellows eager to curry favor with the ministry. Sometimes they turn secretive, holding the meetings to plan their raids *in camera*. But should you ever have the misfortune to find yourself before a hostile bench, there are other measures we can take to protect your livelihood."

"Oh?"

Banks grinned. "I can ensure that the jury which hears your case will consist of understanding men, customers of the gaming houses themselves. I already know that you are a betting man, sir, and I can promise you'll never find better odds than this."

"How much does it all cost?" Hannah asked.

"A woman who gets right to the point." Banks beamed. "A guinea a week for information. More if I need to arrange a jury, or pay men off to avert a raid. That includes my cut and that of my partner."

I had already given some thought to the question of why Cole had been living in fear of Musgrave's blue carriage. Listening to Mitford Banks describe their operation, I wondered if Cole had been skimming money off the top. Charging the gaming houses to avert raids that didn't exist. Or failing to warn them and then charging them extra to arrange a compliant jury. Had Musgrave smoked his lay? Was Mitford Banks in on Cole's treachery? If so, I was surprised to find him in such rude health.

"It all sounds very reasonable to me," I said. "But if we are to do business together, I shall require something more from you. I'd like to know the name of every gaming house owner on your books, and every man on the Westminster bench who has taken your bribes."

Banks laughed. "I cannot oblige you there, sir. My associates insist upon my utmost discretion."

"And yet I insist that we exist upon terms of perfect honesty," I said. "Allow me to go first. I regret to say that we have lied to you. I am not in the wine trade, and my name is not Canning. This good lady is not my wife. Her name is Mrs. Cole, the widow of your late partner."

Hannah removed her hand from beneath mine and glared at Banks. "I believe you are rather partial to my champagne biscuits, sir."

He stared at her and then at me. "I don't understand."

"Henry Fielding is suspicious about the source of Jonas's fortune and has delayed the granting of probate in the matter of his estate," she said. "It is possible that he might seek to confiscate my money, and we are seeking to dissuade him."

"I am sorry for your predicament, madam, and for your loss," he said. "I had nothing but respect for your late husband. But you must see that I cannot help you. What use would that list be anyway? It would only confirm Fielding's suspicions."

I wasn't sure yet. But if the men on that list were enemies of Fielding, then it was possible that they might be allies of mine. It was time to show this Fox that we had him cornered. "Did you know that Mr. Fielding believes this enterprise of yours might have had some bearing upon Jonas's murder?" I said. "Should he learn your name, I imagine he would want to talk to you. I've heard his interrogations can be rather fierce."

Banks paled visibly. "I had nothing to do with his murder."

"I believe you," I said. "But what matters is what Fielding believes. Even if he accepts your pleas of innocence, there's still the small matter of your misconduct in public office. If Fielding can't hang you for it, he'll certainly have you dismissed. Or you can give me what I want, and I promise that he'll never learn your name from our lips."

The prospect of unemployment and the shadow of the gallows tree seemed to make up Banks's mind. Taking a little book and a pencil from his coat pocket, he wrote studiously for a few minutes. Tearing out the page, he handed it to me. I studied it for a moment, being familiar with most of the names of the gamesters and magistrates on the list. Interesting.

Had I been alone, I might have questioned Banks further. Find out if my suspicions were correct, and Cole had been skimming money off the top. Find out whether Banks knew more about the murder than he'd volunteered. But I didn't want to talk about any of that in front of Hannah. She would feel compelled to tell Fielding, and the last thing I wanted was Musgrave thinking I'd had a hand in turning him in. I could always find Banks another time, should I feel the need. All told, Cole's murder was low on my list of concerns. Armed with Banks's information, I knew precisely what I planned to do with it.

Hannah fixed Banks with a hard stare. "If I were you, sir, I'd keep to honest work from now on. You don't want to end up like my poor husband."

Doubting that Banks would follow her advice, I escorted Hannah back across the Rotunda. I'd thought she might tell me off for taking her hand, or quibble with me about my promise to Banks, but she only gave a shaky laugh. "For a man unaccustomed to lying, Mr. Devereux, you are remarkably good at it."

"You were rather adept yourself," I said. "What perfect sinners we are."

She gazed at me rather anxiously. "We must give that list of names to Henry Fielding."

"I concur," I said. "But I think it would be a mistake for you to give it to him. He may suspect that you had knowledge of Jonas's corruption. It might make him more inclined to confiscate the money, rather than less. Whereas I could talk to him, gentleman to gentleman, on your behalf."

She hesitated, but seemed to accept the logic of my position. "You will be sure to tell him everything we have learned about these villains? All that you said about their violent nature? I get the impression that Mr. Fielding's inquiry into the money is just one of several theories that he is pursuing. He's been talking to my friends and neighbors too, and I hate to think of him squandering his time like that."

Oh Hannah! Such loyalty to so undeserving a wretch. But I imagine she didn't know the half of it. Perhaps she was too busy with the shop to suspect Jonas's infidelity, or simply too trusting. The latter is a trait I value highly in a woman.

"Of course I will," I said, as we emerged from the Rotunda into the moonlight.

"How will you tell him that you came by those names? If you intend to keep that young rogue out of it?"

I waved a hand. "I'll think of something. Now I promised that I'd take you home directly, and I always keep my word."

She smiled. "You are good to remember it, sir."

We walked back towards the gate, Hannah absorbed in her thoughts, apparently oblivious to the noise and revelry surrounding us. I gave a message to the man on the door of the servants' enclosure, and soon Felix and Tom appeared. I ordered Tom to have the carriage brought round to the front gate, and Felix went with him to assist.

While we awaited their return, I asked Hannah if her iced creams were still selling well. She was in the middle of telling me an amusing story about the astonished reaction of one of her customers, when she broke off. "Oh, that little boy. I think he is lost."

A child, about five years old, was standing in the middle of the crowd, looking about himself and weeping.

"Probably belongs to one of the traders," I said, gazing around. "No one else would bring a child to a pleasure garden."

Hannah was by the boy's side in a moment, drawing him close, soothing his sobs. I watched, taking note of this scene of maternal concern, until a man in a blue uniform hurried up to them and embraced the lad. As he carried his son away, Hannah gazed after them with a wistful smile. Jonas's friends had talked about her infertility and the strain it had placed on her marriage. I didn't imagine her husband had been a paragon of understanding.

Tom and Felix were heading back through the crowd towards us. "There's a terrible to-do in the carriage park, sir," Tom said, as he reached us. "An overturned dray, vehicles backed up. If we try to leave now, we'll be sitting there for an hour at least."

Felix nodded eagerly. "It's a right mess, Mrs. C."

Tom's plan had been to square the boy while we were busy in the Rotunda. Make up a story about an overturned carriage, and spend another hour drinking beer on William Devereux's coin. It seemed Felix hadn't needed very much persuasion.

"I'm so sorry," I said to Hannah. "It sounds as if there's nothing we can do except wait."

"It is hardly your fault," she said, though that note of anxiety had crept back into her voice.

"Be sure to come and find us the moment the blockage is cleared," I instructed Tom. "Mrs. Cole and I will be by the canal. If we are forced to wait, it might as well be with wine in our hands."

I offered Hannah my arm again and we walked back into the garden. The wind stirred the lanterns in the trees, starlight and music to arouse the passions. Easy as getting a dog to lick a dish.

CHAPTER SEVENTEEN

WE STROLLED ALONG the edge of the ornamental canal, where boats with carved prows scudded up and down, gentlemen heaving upon the oars to impress their ladies. Drinking booths lined the far bank, and as we reached one end of our promenade, Hannah clutched my arm a little tighter.

"Oh look, there is Lord Richard. He is waving. See there!"

I'd thought she was never going to notice him. "So it is," I said.

"And isn't that the same gentleman you talked to at the chemistry show?"

Wesley Ball. I felt a twinge of anxiety about his ability to carry off his part tonight—though when he was on form, he was very good indeed.

"His name is Sir James Mountford, baronet," I said. "A new friend of Lord Richard's. And that's Lady Mountford and her sister, Sophia Soderley. The Marquis of Morrow will be pleased. You wouldn't have wanted to meet Lord Richard's old set. Do you mind if we go over? They will think it rude if I do not."

"Very well," she said, looking rather pensive. "Only I hope they do not think ill of me, being here, like this with you."

"Oh, Sir James is a very liberal fellow, I assure you."

Lord Richard rose to welcome us into the booth. "Mrs. Cole, I thought that was you. Will you join us?"

Hannah glanced at me, perhaps hoping I'd refuse. Alas, I found myself conveniently distracted by some horseplay upon the canal. The silence drew out, Lord Richard gazing at her expectantly, until politeness demanded she reply. "If Mr. Devereux has no objection . . ."

Again, she gazed at me, rather hopefully. "Object to a lady's desire?" I declared. "I never would."

Lord Richard made the introductions. "Mrs. Cole has a shop on Piccadilly. Selling confectionary, I think you said, Willie?"

"The best in town," I replied. "She has a new delicacy on sale this week. Iced cream."

"Oh, we should go," Lady Mountford cried, clutching Miss Soderley's arm. They really were sisters: Anna and Mary Saunders. Both had done a stint on the London stage, though there was only so much call for twins, and they'd found more success as a double act in the Mayfair brothels. Amy had taken charge of their hair and gowns. Anna was a picture in blue silk and peacock feathers, Mary in white satin embroidered with Bristol stones.

"Do you know, I have never tried iced cream," Lord Richard declared. "Though I believe my grandmother once tasted it at the table of the second King Charles."

"That's not all she tasted that night, from what I've heard," Sir James said.

That's it, Wesley, I thought. Ease your way in gently.

"You must excuse my husband, Mrs. Cole," Lady Mountford said. "A glass or two of Rhenish and he fancies himself amusing."

Hannah smiled politely.

"I have a capital idea," Lord Richard said. "Mrs. Cole could make us iced cream for the supper next month." He turned to Hannah. "It's just a small affair at Morrow House, to celebrate the success of our syndicate. My father is regrettably away, but the Countess of Yarmouth will be there."

Drop the name of the king's mistress into conversation and you were guaranteed a reaction. Some at court sang her praises, for she was skilled at acquiring peerages for her friends. Others resented her influence, or considered her presence at court a scandal, especially those who had been close to the late queen. But for luxury shopkeepers like

Mrs. Cole, the countess's patronage, so rarely bestowed, was guaranteed to send sales soaring—and might even lead to a royal warrant. Hannah's eyes widened at the prospect of the countess trying her wares.

"I should be honored," she said.

Lord Richard grinned. "I'll send my father's butler along to your shop. He'll make all the arrangements. I'm afraid he's a frightfully ugly fellow. His mother should have thrown him away and kept the stork."

When the laughter had subsided, we conversed for a time about inconsequential things: a riding dress of blue camblet trimmed with squirrel fur that Miss Soderley was having made; Sir James's plans for the landscaping of his park; and a new stuccatore Lord Richard's father had brought over from Venice, who was said to be a da Vinci of plasterwork. Hannah's cheeks grew a little flushed from the wine—and perhaps from the thrill of conversing as equals with these fine ladies and gentlemen.

"Do you know any scholars, Mountford?" Lord Richard said. "My father's library-keeper is barely literate. You'd sooner put a eunuch in charge of a bacchanal."

"Lord Richard," I said reprovingly, but my lip twitched as I met Hannah's eye. It was a test to see how she'd respond to that sort of talk. Seeing that she'd face no censure from me, she allowed herself a half-smile.

"What?" Lord Richard protested. "The ladies don't mind a joke."

"Indeed," Miss Soderley said sweetly. "We have tolerated you all evening long."

To my delight, Hannah laughed. How joyous it was to see her coming out of herself.

Lady Mountford rose from the table. "I think I shall take a turn about the stalls. Sophia, Mrs. Cole, will you join me?"

Hannah glanced at me. "Well, I don't know—"

"Tom said it would be an hour," I reminded her, "and I can always come and find you should he return."

For a long moment, we awaited her reply. The entire expense of that night would be wasted if she refused.

"Oh, do come, Mrs. Cole," Miss Soderley cried. "I want to hear all about your confections, so I can tell my friends."

The prospect of new customers seemed to make up Hannah's mind. "Very well."

"I shall accompany you," Sir James announced. "I said I'd buy a fan for my sister."

When we were alone in the booth, Lord Richard grinned. "How are we doing, do you think?"

I frowned. "Keep your damn voice down."

I always got agitated in moments like this. When I couldn't be the one leading the Dance. Tom was always telling me to have more confidence in our people.

We had rehearsed Anna's lines last night, with Amy playing the part of Hannah.

"It is a delight to finally put a face to the name," Lady Mountford would say, drawing Hannah aside, whilst her husband and her sister toyed with the fans. "The woman who has captured William Devereux's heart at last. If my sister is a little *froide*, don't take it personally. She is positively green—and I'm sure she won't be the only one. Your back will be a perfect pincushion from all the knives."

At which point, we anticipated, Hannah would protest that she had done nothing of the sort. That I was merely a friend of her late husband, and all the rest.

"Oh, you are quite wrong there," Lady Mountford would say. "You must have remarked the way he looks at you? He is quite smitten, my dear. Why, only the other night at whist, Lord Richard speculated about William's intentions towards you, and William bit his head clean off. And then Lord Richard said . . . No, perhaps I should not say any more. My sister always says that when God gave out discretion, I was last in line."

Of course, Hannah wouldn't be able to leave it there. When pressed for the end of the story, Lady Mountford would smile. "Well, first Lord Richard said that Mrs. Parmenter would have William's heart, liver, and lights, if he was enticed by a shopkeeper into marriage. And Mr. Devereux grew quite cross. He said—and let me see if I've remembered this correctly—that Mrs. Cole was in mourning for her husband and he was quite certain that no thought of marriage had ever entered her mind. But *then* he added that whilst he had known you only a short time, it was already apparent to him that as well as undeniable beauty, Mrs. Cole possessed charm, intelligence, resilience, and kindness. That any gentleman of his acquaintance should be proud to have a wife like her, and that if anything, it was he who was unworthy."

Words like that will burrow into a woman's brain like a beetle. To be admired, championed, by a man as dashing as William Devereux. To have him speak of marriage in the same breath as her name. She'll remember a conversation like that over and over again.

Hannah's face was a picture when they returned. I swear she glowed. Would she mention her conversation with Lady Mountford to me? On balance, I didn't think so. She kept herself close, did Hannah. Sometimes I struggled to work out what she was thinking. But now, looking at her face, I could almost hear the echo of Lady Mountford's words in her mind.

"What perfect timing," I declared, as they reached us. "There is Tom."

Did I detect a trace of disappointment on Hannah's face, as we bid our farewells? Did she wish to linger a while longer in this new world? Or did she welcome our walk back to the carriage alone? Tom strode on ahead of us, while I took a more sedate pace. Hannah, I noticed, did nothing to hurry us along. Lights twinkled in the trees, courting couples all around us. I gazed down at her and smiled.

"I hope you did not feel browbeaten by Lord Richard over our supper," I said. "Say the word and I shall get you out of it at once."

"No, please, I will enjoy the challenge. But can I ask you a question? What is Arcadia?"

"It is a commercial syndicate," I said. "That is why we are holding the supper—to celebrate ten years of successful trading in the Far East. Why do you ask?"

"Just now, when we were returning to the booth, Sir James spoke to me about it. He seemed to think that I might be able to exert influence over you, though I cannot think why."

"Sir James would like to join our syndicate, but he was rebuffed in his overtures. The decision was not in my gift and I told him so." I frowned. "He should not have sought to involve you in our business."

"Was Arcadia the same venture that Jonas wished to invest in? The one that you argued about?"

It's always easier when a woman possesses curiosity and intelligence. When they don't, it can be like getting a slow horse to jump.

"Yes, it was," I said. "Arcadia is a very profitable venture and when men hear rumors of our success, they often wish for a part of it. Sometimes, like Sir James, they won't take no for an answer. Neither did your husband, I regret to say."

"Jonas didn't like anybody to tell him no," she said.

"Even you?"

"Especially me," she said, looking away.

I liked that she was opening up to me, but this wasn't the time for her to be dwelling upon her dead husband. "What else did Sir James have to say?" I asked.

"That you didn't say no to Mrs. Parmenter. Even though she had less than a thousand pounds to invest. He felt it very unfair."

"That was different," I said. "And it wasn't easy to convince the others to let her in. I had to use all my powers of persuasion."

"Different in what way?"

"Mr. Parmenter had neglected his affairs in the years before his death. There were debts, other difficulties. She was going to lose her home. I couldn't stand by and watch that happen."

Little points of light danced in her eyes like fireflies. "You are a good man, Mr. Devereux." Again she held my gaze a moment too long. "Mrs. Parmenter told me that your return from abroad has created quite a stir. Gentlemen hoping you'll transform their fortunes. Young ladies wishing the same . . ."

"Oh dear," I said, looking abashed. "Mrs. Parmenter can be rather overprotective, I'm afraid."

"Do you need protecting, sir?"

Ah, the Dance. I smiled at her playful tone. It's a lovely moment when they start to flirt. "That's why I have Tom. Ladies flee from the sight of his sword."

"I am quite sure he wouldn't want you advertising that fact."

I don't know which surprised me more: her bawdy riposte or my laughter. Tom, who knows me too well and can spot the genuine article, turned, eyebrows raised. Whether it was the wine, or the example of the conversation in the booth, this was a different Hannah—one I liked very much. She wore her desire openly now and I could all but taste her heady mixture of fear and elation. But I'm not some halfpenny seducer, drumming on the door of a woman's virtue. She has to truly want me first, so badly that she fears she might die from the longing. Hannah would acknowledge her feelings soon, if she hadn't done so already. A few more nights like this and she would throw open that door herself and invite me in.

CHAPTER EIGHTEEN

THE FOLLOWING DAY, I wrote a short letter to Henry Fielding begging an audience. He wrote by return to grant me one that evening, and, at the allotted hour, I presented myself at his townhouse on Bow Street. With the slum rookeries of St. Giles and Seven Dials to the north, and the fleshpots of Drury Lane and Covent Garden to the east and west, Fielding's home—where he also presided over his courtroom—was described by the newspapers as a last bastion against the barbarian hordes.

A manservant showed me into his master's study. Fielding was sitting in an armchair by his fire, his leg up on a stool. "Forgive me if I don't get up. Damn gout." He studied my face. "I thought I recognized the name. I met you the other day, in Mrs. Cole's kitchen."

"That's right." I took the seat opposite him, and he called to the servant to pour more wine. "Have you tried Portland's Powder?"

"The Duke of Newcastle swears by it," Fielding said, rather gloomily. "Not me. I've tried everything. Nothing seems to help."

Had I been masquerading as Henry Fielding, or a man like him, I would have fitted out my rooms in precisely this way. A lot of dark wood and leather. Paintings of dogs and horses. Busts of Roman emperors and Greek philosophers. And a great many books, Fielding's own volumes on prominent display. The claret glasses were engraved with the crest of Eton College, school of the most self-satisfied fucksters in the kingdom. And the pamphlets in the box on the table between us, which Fielding had evidently been reading, appeared positively lewd in nature. A gentleman disordered in his own life and habits, seeking to impose order upon others.

"Forgive me if I am unfamiliar with your name beyond our fleeting acquaintance," Fielding said. "You are some sort of stockjobber, is that right? I'm afraid my time in the City has been rather limited. Though of course I know the lord mayor and the principal aldermen."

Of course. Men like Fielding dropped names with the subtlety of anvils. Just to let you know where you stood. The irony being that his father was as big a crook as mine. Or at least, that was the talk of the Black Lion. According to the rumors, Edmund Fielding had tried to steal his children's inheritance from their grandfather, and neglected them in pursuit of women and fast schemes. Eventually, his dead wife's mother had fought him in court for custody of the children. It was easy to see how Fielding had been pulled in two directions. Was he his father's son, a man of loose morals and dissolute habits? Or the grandson of the crown court judge? The answer seemed to be: a bit of both. In lust, he'd bedded his maid, but duty had compelled him to marry her, a greater sin still in the eyes of polite society. The scandal had caused him enormous ridicule, and many of his former friends would no longer receive him. With advancement to high office blocked, he had chosen to throw himself into public service. The toll of which he appeared to be mitigating by drinking himself to death.

"I was a stranger to the City too, when I started out there," I said. "My father was a landowner, my grandfather a judge."

Fielding grunted. "Mine too."

Fancy that. "I had a gift for figures, and as my father's estate was rather encumbered, I thought I should put that talent to good use."

Fielding smiled a little more warmly, now that he believed we were from similar stock. "I admire any gentleman who has managed to turn his fortunes around through ingenuity and hard work."

I'd heard that his own finances were not precisely comfortable. Integrity comes at a price, and Fielding had forgone all the income from bribes that normally came with his office. You can imagine, then, what he thought of his fellow magistrates who did not show quite the same degree of restraint. He'd tried to have some of them removed from the bench, with only limited success. I imagined Jonas's dealings had angered him deeply and he considered that fifteen hundred pounds to be a personal affront. Which meant that I would have my work cut out.

"As I explained in my letter," I said, "I was acquainted with Jonas Cole and for a short time I advised him on his financial affairs. Since his death, I have made the acquaintance of his widow and have been advising her. Mrs. Cole informs me that you are trying to ascertain the source of her husband's money. I believe I am in a position to help you there."

Fielding studied me curiously. "Go on, sir."

"It's important that you understand that I considered Cole a friend, as well as a client. He told me that he had received a substantial inheritance that he was looking to invest, though he made only one small investment with me at first. I imagine he wanted to see how it would do, before he committed the rest of his money. I would certainly have acted for him in that capacity, had I not received a letter shortly before Cole died."

I took a gulp of wine, as if steeling myself to go on.

"The letter was anonymous and I never learned who sent it. The author stated that Cole's money was not acquired from an inheritance at all, but in a corrupt and villainous fashion." Briefly, I explained Cole's role as a middling man between the gaming houses and the corrupt magistrates, keeping my promise to Mitford Banks to leave his name out of it. "Naturally, I confronted Cole, as any gentleman of honor would. I'd expected him to deny it, but he only laughed. He said he'd never thought me naive, that near every placeman in London was on the take. That might be true, I said, but corruption was not a source of amusement to me. In short, sir, I told him to take his dirty money, and find another man to invest it. We argued forcefully, and almost came to blows. Nothing gets my blood hotter than a man who behaves dishonorably to his friends. Corruption is a canker on the body politic, and the thought that I might have unwittingly profited from such an enterprise was just too much!"

Fielding nodded soberly. "I only wish there were more like you in this world, sir. As it happens, this information tallies neatly with my own inquiries. I have also learned that Cole was robbing the gamesters blind. That's why he was so afraid for his life. I arrested my principal suspect this morning, the owner of a carriage said to have been watching Cole before he was killed. Regrettably, the man has a good alibi and expensive lawyers. Did you know they allow them into the courtroom now? Let them cross-examine witnesses? I have to tread carefully when prosecuting men with money."

In the interests of self-preservation, I had removed Musgrave's name from Mitford Banks's list. But it seemed Fielding was already on to him. It was a good reminder not to underestimate the man. Interesting that Musgrave had an alibi that Fielding hadn't been able to shake. I wondered if that meant he was innocent of the murder after all?

"There is one other matter that I hoped to discuss with you, sir. Mrs. Cole's share of her husband's estate. She is dismayed by the delay on the passage of probate. If it is not granted soon, she might lose her business and her home. Given that nobody is likely to make a claim on that money, I was hoping you might be willing to release it?"

"I regret to hear it," Fielding said. "But I am afraid I cannot oblige you there. Now that I know the source of Cole's wealth, I intend to confiscate the lot."

"I see," I said, unsurprised by this news. "Yet you must know that Mrs. Cole never sought to profit from anything underhand. She is dedicated to her trade, honest work at which she excels. Our nation would benefit from a thousand like her. And it could be in no way improved by putting her out of business."

"It would send a message," Fielding said. "To all those tempted by the fruits of corruption. You said yourself that it is a canker. I could put that money to good use, combating crime."

"And yet the law is rather moot when it comes to corruption in public office, is it not?" I had read up on it that afternoon. Those legal volumes had come in handy. "It is not at all clear that you have any right to that money."

"I assure you that Common Law—"

"Is a tricky filly to master. I feel duty bound to inform you, sir, that if you seek to go down this route, Mrs. Cole's friends, myself included, will not abandon her. I imagine Mr. Daniel Cole too will seek to challenge your actions. I believe he has trained at one of the inns of court."

"Then so be it," Fielding said, looking somewhat disgruntled. "It is high time that light was brought to bear on the darkest corners of our public realm. The spectacle of a court case might be precisely what we need."

"But are you sure you want to shine that light upon this particular corner?" Reaching into my pocket, I produced my list of the gaming house owners and corrupt magistrates. "This came with the anonymous letter." I handed it to Fielding, who studied it, frowning.

"I have already looked into some of these gaming-house owners," he said. "But there are several names here that are new to me, and will warrant further investigation. As for the magistrates, some are of little surprise. Others are . . . more disappointing."

"Many of those gentlemen sit in Parliament, as well as on the Westminster bench," I said. "For the most part they vote with the ministry and they have friends in high places. Many more have brothers and cousins who sit in the House, men whose votes you'll need if you are ever to obtain what you truly want. I speak of your judicial reforms, sir, of which I am an ardent supporter. I should hate to see you jeopardize that enterprise in a possibly fruitless pursuit of Mrs. Cole's money. You will see that two names on that list have a close connection to your own patron, the Duke of Bedford. And two more are under the patronage of His Grace, the Duke of Newcastle." The very man whose support Fielding needed above all else, if he was ever to get his reforms through Parliament. "Is now really the right time to be making new enemies? There will be opportunity aplenty to fight corruption, once you are in a stronger position to act."

Fielding was silent a long time, still studying my list. When he looked up, I could see that he was wavering. "You are certain about Mrs. Cole's character, are you, sir?"

"Entirely," I said, a little surprised by the question. "She knew nothing of her husband's crimes."

"I don't mean that." Fielding paused to refill our glasses. "When I questioned Daniel Cole, he told me that his cousin had kept a mistress, a pretty little thing of Huguenot stock. Her name is Annette, just seventeen years old—she'd caught Cole's eye in the Poland Street workhouse apparently. He put her up in rooms in Shepherd Market. I found her a couple of days ago. That's how I know that Cole was robbing his associates blind. Annette told me that he believed his treachery had been discovered, and he was so afraid for his life, he decided to change his name and run off to Scotland. Planned to take his mistress and his money with him. Annette is carrying his child, you see, and others have testified how badly Cole wanted a son. The plans for their departure were all in place. They were due to leave on the first of April. Then Cole was killed."

Poor Hannah. Jonas Cole really was a first-rate fuckster. "The knowledge grieves me," I said. "But beyond being a personal tragedy, I don't quite see what this has to do with Mrs. Cole?"

"Annette is convinced that she killed her husband," Fielding said.

I stared at him a moment, then burst out laughing. "Why on earth would she think that, given all that Cole had said about his enemies? It's simply ludicrous."

"Cole told her that his enemies would kill him slowly and savagely if they ever caught up with him. Torture and all the rest. Whereas in the event, his murder was bloody and brutal, but fast. Did you know that Cole had no defensive injuries to his hands? Despite all the precautions he was taking, he never even fought back. My physician says he was probably struck the first time from behind, perhaps taken by surprise in a place where he thought he was safe. A woman could have struck those blows, he says. Especially one accustomed to physical labor."

"You cannot be giving credence to the girl's suspicions?"

To my dismay, Fielding pulled at his upper lip. "If Mrs. Cole had learned of her husband's plans, then you cannot deny that she had a good motive. And she is clearly a determined woman. Her decision to keep open her shop is testament to that. Some of the neighbors have told me that they overheard arguments between the couple, and her apprentices say that he treated her most unkindly. Mrs. Cole says that their squabbles were no more, no less, than those of any married couple, but then she would say that. I'm sure you've noticed that she's already in purple."

It was all so unexpected, I struggled to get my arguments in order. "How would she have transported the body to the river, if she'd killed him at home? Dragged him through the streets? She owns no carriage."

Fielding seemed to concede the point. "And yet I do find it strange that Cole's watch hasn't come to light. It was highly distinctive, as I'm sure you recall, and worth a lot of money, perhaps twenty guineas. If Cole had been murdered by villains from the gaming houses, I'd expect them to have sold it."

"You just said it yourself," I said, leaping upon the inconsistency. "It was highly distinctive. The killers probably guessed you'd look for it and they're biding their time. Or they sold it abroad. Or the killer might have kept it as some sort of macabre trophy."

"Or whoever killed Cole couldn't bring herself to dispose of it. Mrs. Cole told me that it was given to her grandfather by the tsar of Russia. A family legend, no doubt, but it clearly meant a lot to her."

This had the potential to turn into a bigger disaster than the delay on probate. "Though I have known Mrs. Cole less than two weeks, I count myself an excellent judge of character—and I tell you that you are chasing a chimera here. I doubt Mrs. Cole is capable of a hard word, much less a murder. Her primary concern is that her husband's killer is caught and punished. These are just the wild allegations of a grieving doxy."

Fielding drained his glass. "You are probably right," he said, much to my relief. "Your conviction is certainly reassuring. I place great weight upon the word of a gentleman—certainly more than on that of a common Jezebel." He studied me curiously, with a slight smile. "I too count myself a very good judge of character, and I fancy that you rather like Mrs. Cole."

"I hope you are not implying that anything improper has occurred," I said, rather curtly.

Fielding held up a hand. "I suggest no such thing. But the heart cannot always help what it wants. *Love is to itself a higher law*, and all that."

People often make the mistake of assuming that other people are a mirror of themselves. Fielding had diddled his maid when his wife's corpse was barely cold—perhaps much earlier if the crueler tongues were to be believed. I decided to play up to his suspicion. Let William Devereux bare his heart, if it would make him a more worthy witness in Fielding's eyes.

"It is true that in Mrs. Cole I find much to admire," I said. "She is a woman of intelligence and virtue, both dutiful and kind."

"And handsome." Fielding wagged a finger. "Don't tell me that has passed you by, or I shan't believe you."

I gave him a rueful smile. "Guilty as charged. But even if Mrs. Cole were ever minded to accept me, I fear that my family and friends would never understand."

"Hang your family and friends," Fielding said, rather fiercely. "Follow your heart, sir. You'll not regret it."

I fancied he was trying to convince himself about his own absence of regret. But if he was prepared to set aside his suspicions of Hannah, in his determination to win a convert to the cause of true love across the classes, it was a small price to pay.

"My circle might be convinced to accept Mrs. Cole were she not so easily dismissed as a fortune hunter," I said. "If she possessed her own money, she could be seen to have made her choice freely."

"And so we return to the subject of probate." Fielding raised his glass. "Nicely done, sir."

I spoke passionately for some minutes more, reiterating my arguments that it was in the best interests of his judicial reforms to let Mrs. Cole keep her money, stressing the weakness of the laws against corruption, and the abilities of my barristers.

In the end, Fielding raised his hands. "Mrs. Cole should count herself fortunate to have such a champion. Very well, I submit. The lady shall have her money. Never let it be said that Henry Fielding stands in the path of true love. But in return, I ask that you do one thing for me."

I barely heard him over the choirs of angels singing hallelujahs to my talents. "Name it, sir."

"I'm going to have to talk to Mrs. Cole's household again. To see if any of the apprentices were aware of his plans to flee to Scotland. There's always the possibility that Cole's enemies were tipped off. Which means it is inevitable that Mrs. Cole will learn the truth about her husband. The mistress and so on. The baby. I had planned to tell her myself, but I think, given your friendship, that it might come better from you."

Coward, I thought. But as it happened, it suited my needs perfectly. "It is not a task I relish, but one I shall undertake."

"Good," Fielding said. "In the meantime," he waved my list, "there is much here to keep me busy."

I rose from my chair and we shook hands. "There is just one thing more," I said, producing the first volume of *Tom Jones* from my coat pocket. "Would you mind terribly? I think it your finest work."

Fielding beamed, reaching for his inkpot and pen. What a likable and discerning fellow, I could see him thinking. The feeling was almost mutual. It had been a most productive evening. All told, I had rather warmed to the cunt.

CHAPTER NINETEEN

Not wanting Hannah distracted again by the shop, I wrote to her the next morning, suggesting that we meet at her house that evening. Given that all my other arrangements were progressing nicely, I decided to grasp the nettle and have Tom drive me out to Hackney. I sat next to him on the box, as we headed east along the great thoroughfares of the city: Oxford Street, High Holborn, cutting up onto Old Street. Once past Hoxton, we joined the Hackney Road, which took us north into open countryside. The clean air and the scent of hay gnawed at my nerves. One last time, I told myself. Then the devil take Hackney.

Still, when I caught sight of the old mill house on the banks of Hackney Brook, I almost told Tom to turn the carriage around. My cravat felt tight, remembering my father's grip on my collar. His heavy-set face, dark with passions that I never understood.

"Are you still afraid, lad? Are you?"

His spittle flecked my face. I was very small for my age then. Terrified to speak. He had me at an angle, feet upon the bank, my body forced backwards over the millrace. Two weeks earlier, I'd seen old Mrs. Mallaghan's white corpse dragged out of Hamlet's Pond, and I'd been fool enough to tell my father that I was afraid of the water.

"Well?" He shook me.

The spray was in my eyes. "No, sir."

"Open your damn eyes and look at my face. I'm not afraid of anything in this world. Do you believe me?"

"Yes, sir."

He grinned, those pointed, yellow teeth. "That answer right there. That's the only one that matters. Do you understand me?"

I nodded frantically.

"The trouble is, lad, I don't believe you. Which leaves only one path left to understanding."

Then I was falling. The knife-cold shock of the water. Blackness all around me, kicking, swallowing water. The current snatching me up, whirling me around. Trying to swim, my chest hurting. Up towards the light. Then my father's shadow moving, blocking it out.

"Bill?"

Tom's voice cut through my thoughts. The sun was nearing its zenith. Meadows, cow sheds, brick kilns, market gardens.

"I said you like her. Mrs. Cole. She made you laugh."

I turned. "It's always better when I like them. You know that."

"How long until the Catch?"

That's our word for the physical act of seduction, the pivot upon which our enterprise turned. "A week maybe." I shrugged. "She's getting her confidence back. Starting to believe that a man like me would really want her."

"Not too much confidence, I hope. We don't want another Penelope Felton."

I laughed. "We're a long way from that. She has a real tenderness about her, Tom. Told me I was a good man."

"More fool her."

I gave him a look. "Now that's unkind. Without me, Fielding would have confiscated her money for sure. This way she gets to keep a hundred—and we get the rest."

We were passing my old school, a red-brick prison with a bell tower to remind you how much time you had left to serve. Hackney was twice the size it was when I was a boy, but still a town of outcasts: Huguenots and Jews and the odd villain like my father, self-made men with money, but not the respectability they desired. The school had taught me things that my father despised for their effeminacy, but that he recognized as a passport to the drawing rooms of Mayfair. Music and French, dancing and deportment, how to fence and write a verse. As boys, we'd swapped tales of London, the city a thrilling, fetid smudge on the horizon. Not all who wander are lost, we used to say, but those who wander to Hackney almost certainly are.

The house looked just the same. Oakhaven, it was called. A fucking irony right there. Weathered gray stone, pigeon shit on the gables, box windows so drafty the flags wore a sheen of ice in winter. As I climbed down from the box, Tom lit a pipe.

"I won't be long," I said. "Just say my farewells."

A dog I didn't recognize bounded out to bark at me. A servant I didn't recognize took my hat and gloves at the door. The place was musty with the smell of ancient hatreds.

I was shown into the parlor, where Simon rose to greet me. "I don't know why she asked for you," he said. "Nor why you have come. She has no money, so don't go getting any ideas."

He had my father's square jaw, but none of his bulk. Hooded eyes, a warty growth on his cheek. I observed the tension in his shoulders, and I hoped I was the cause of it.

"It's good to see you too," I said. "How's your wife and your little lad?" The house was very quiet, and I guessed they were out.

"I have three now. All boys," he said, proudly, as if it was hard to stick your cock in a woman—though in his case maybe it was. His hand rested on the mantelshelf next to the Wainwright medal for excellence in mathematics. The one miserable triumph of Simon's dismal life. My father had displayed it there just to spite me.

Alice and Simon had come to live with us not long after my mother had left. I had been eight years old at the time, Simon was seven. It had taken me a year to realize that when he called my father "Pa" he wasn't being simple.

"We put her in the morning room," Simon said now, leading the way to the back of the house. "Can't manage the stairs."

The room's shutters were closed, the gaps between them casting slats of light onto the bed. Alice had always been thin, but her illness had stripped the flesh from her bones. At the time of my father's funeral, her hair had still held a flaxen sheen. Now it was perfectly white, her skin greasy like tallow. Her eyes took a moment to focus upon my face.

"Billy," she said. "Just look at you. How proud your father would have been."

"What you need is beef tea," I said. "Put some meat back on your ribs. Soon we'll have you dancing a sarabande."

She laughed, breaking into a cough. Simon frowned. "Don't go tiring her."

"Always making people laugh," Alice said. "You got that from your father, I suppose."

In the old days, I'd have said that she was mad. Now I wondered whether there was another side to him, one that I never saw. I'm quite certain that she knew nothing of my father's business. Property in London, was what he told people. Slum landlord, was what he didn't. Plus a few pawnshops, the sort where stolen goods are sold. I'd found out by listening at doors, asking around. I'd thought he might have seen my potential, when he caught me pilfering guineas from the lockbox in his desk drawer. Instead, he'd taken a horsewhip to me in the barn.

Alice sighed, perhaps at some distant memory of their courtship. "Do you still have that big heart, Billy? I hope you do."

"Beating away, Alice." I took out a box of rose almonds that I'd bought in Hannah's shop.

She stroked my hand. "You cared so much it hurt. Always bringing me flowers and little gifts."

I shifted uncomfortably, remembering her face lighting up with pleasure. She'd wanted to be a second mother to me, and I'd worked out how to feed that desire. Didn't want her running off like my own mother had, and someone worse taking her place.

Alice rose slightly from the bolster, wincing at the effort. "Leave us, Simon. There's something I want to say to Billy."

Simon's frown deepened, probably afraid she'd stashed something away for me. Perhaps she had. I grinned at him. "Don't worry. She'll be perfectly safe with me."

Reluctantly, he left the room, and I closed the door behind him. When I returned to the bed, Alice gripped my hand again. "I need to tell you something about your mother."

Christ, I knew I shouldn't have come. "There're more comforting topics, I'm sure. How do you like being a grandmama? Bet you spoil them rotten? Am I right?"

She let out another sigh. "You think you know everything. That's your father again. But you don't." She gazed at me rather intently. "He lied to you, Billy."

"That much I know," I said, forcing out the cheer. "One day all this will be yours. He had me there."

"He had your mother put away," she said. "In a house for the mad."

I studied her face, wondering if the canker had worked its way inside her skull. "What are you talking about? My mother wasn't mad. Not unless you count her taking up with that wretched Italian."

"There was no Italian," she said. "Your mother never had another suitor, never took a lover. It was just a story your father told you to protect you from the truth." With a shaking hand, she reached under the bolster and drew out a packet tied with a ribbon. "After he died, I found these letters. Reports on your mother's condition, bills, everything. She was there eighteen years before she died."

A sour swill flooded my mouth. "My mother wasn't mad," I said again, remembering the touch of her hand on my hair, her big sad eyes.

Alice looked away. "Your father must have thought so. Why else would he have done it?"

Did she take me for a fool? I stared at a crack in the flagstones, trying to make sense of it all. He'd had my mother locked away, so that he could bring Alice and Simon into this house. And if he was a liar and a cunt, then he was in good company. Finding the letters after his death—pull the other one, Alice. She'd known all along, I thought. The secret had probably scoured at her conscience all these years.

"Your big heart," Alice murmured. "You got it from her. From your mother."

"Well, it wasn't from him," I said, rather savagely, but Alice had closed her eyes.

As she slept, snoring softly, I sat there, reading those letters. Phrases leapt out at me: . . . *cold water treatment . . . gentle discipline . . . screams at spectators . . . weeps at night, calling for her son.* The last letter was dated the sixteenth of May, 1735. *Regret to inform you that Mrs. Cullen died by her own hand last night. Please advise, by return, of any funeral arrangements you would like made. I enclose our final bill for lodging and treatment.*

The shadows of that room with its stench of death crowded in on me. Alice's breathing was very shallow. She didn't stir when I rose from the bed. I put the letters in my coat and went out into the hall, where Simon was hovering. "Well? What did she say?"

I glanced at him distractedly. "That your real father was the idiot who milked the cows and I was to be nice to you on account of it."

He stared at me, little black eyes like flies on a turd. "Come back again and I'll set the dogs on you."

When I emerged from the house, temporarily blinded by the light, I thought of the sun on the white marble in the Piazza della Signoria. My father's shadow looming over the millrace.

"You look pale as ash," Tom said. "Everything all right?"

"Never better," I said, leaping aboard.

Tom lifted his whip and the carriage moved off. Think of the moment, I told myself. The past has nothing to say to you now. Picturing Hannah Cole's lovely face, I asked Tom a fusillade of questions about our people and the arrangements for the Rope. By the time we passed the millrace again, I was cracking jokes, making Tom laugh. Reaching into my coat, I took out the Wainwright medal for excellence in mathematics. Tossed it into the water, and smiled at the ripples it made.

CHAPTER TWENTY

To my annoyance, the Punchbowl and Pineapple was still open when I arrived. The cause of it was immediately apparent. About a dozen open-top carriages were drawn up outside in the evening sun, the ladies seated within eating iced cream from crystal bowls. Gentlemen leaned against the doors, also eating iced cream, discoursing with the ladies as they might in a drawing room. Hannah's apprentices, Felix and Theodora, hurried back and forth from the shop carrying more bowls. Given that respectable women forswore taverns and were mostly barred from coffeehouses, this freedom of association attracted a few scandalized stares from passers-by. I paused for a moment to watch, thinking through all the opportunities that might arise in the future, were I able to simply introduce myself to a lady like this in the street.

The shop was packed, and I had to fight my way past the queue. Hannah's face lit up when she saw me, though I detected strain there too. I could see how anxious she was to know what had happened with Mr. Fielding.

"I need to talk to Mr. Devereux," she told her trade apprentice, a pudgy, pasty-faced lad who eyed me curiously. "Let them have just ten minutes more. Then we really have to close."

As Hannah led me upstairs, she chattered away about the day's trading. "It was quite extraordinary. I don't know where they've all come from."

Crossing the threshold of a woman's home is always an intimate act. Hannah's parlor was a testament to the restrained taste of the aspiring middling sort, the furnishings and ornaments passable imitations of their betters—rather like me. A portrait of Jonas and Hannah hung over the fireplace—and if it was designed to flatter, then Christ knows how much the artist had been drinking. I wondered how long it would remain there after Hannah learned what I had to say.

"Would you care for a glass of port?" she said.

"Only if you'll join me." I'd happily see more of that bold Hannah whom I'd taken to Ranelagh.

She went next door to the dining room to see to it. A scent of lavender filled the air, and I moved the vase on the table next to me further away. Concentrate, I told myself. But the day had been a strange one. Memories assailed me on all sides. My mother weeping. My father shouting. My footsteps pounding down the hall, lavender stalks gripped in one sweaty hand.

"We'll put them in the window overlooking the lane, where passersby will see them," she'd said, scooping me up, pressing her damp face to my hair. "And then everyone will be as happy as you make me."

The port glass, cold in my hand. Hannah's voice, urgent in its desire: "Please, tell me. How did you get on at Bow Street?"

Digging a nail into my palm to cut through my thoughts, I told her the yarn I'd spun Fielding to explain how I'd come by that list. "He'll have his work cut out now, but he appears confident that he'll find the murderer eventually. And I also convinced him to lift his delay on probate. That five hundred pounds will soon be yours."

"Oh, Mr. Devereux," she cried. "I've been so afraid of losing my shop. You have no idea what this means to me. I'll be able to take on a maid again. And perhaps another shopgirl. If business keeps up like this, then I will need one."

And then everyone will be as happy as you make me.

"There's something else," I said. "Something Daniel told Henry Fielding."

Daniel didn't like me, that much was obvious, and anything I could do to drive a wedge between him and Hannah suited me just fine. I'd decided to say nothing of Fielding's suspicions about her involvement in her husband's murder. Apart from anything else, I was confident that I had laid it to rest, and the last thing I wanted was her getting agitated about all that nonsense. But I told her everything else: about Jonas's mistress and her rooms in Shepherd Market. How Jonas had robbed his associates and ended up in fear of his life. It gave me a twist in the guts to do it, Hannah's shoulders tensing, her lovely smile wiped like a stain. When I came to the part about Scotland, she rose from the sofa and went to the window. I suspect so that I couldn't see her grief.

A betrayal only acquires the name when it is known. Without that knowledge, a person might live their whole life in happy ignorance. But once it is discovered, betrayal cuts deep and is slow to heal. When Hannah turned, I could see the pain writ large on her bewildered face.

"Mr. Fielding tells me that Jonas's mistress is with child."

A visceral noise escaped her throat, more groan than sob. Recognizing my moment, I was across the room in two swift strides. Drawing her away from the window, I pulled her close. "Your husband was a fool," I murmured into her hair. "He did not deserve you."

I had many more lines that I might have used, but when she gazed up at me, her body shaking, eyes liquid with vulnerability, they dried in my throat. I was still looking at her, trying to find them, when she rose up on her toes and kissed me. It took me entirely by surprise—I hadn't thought she was quite there yet—but my news about her husband must have tipped her over. Her lips weren't yielding, as I'd imagined, but hard, pressing, eager. Taken aback by her hunger, I tried to inhale the scent of her, but all I could taste was fucking lavender. I pulled away sharply and she stared at me, confused.

"Forgive me," I said, taking a step back. "I have to go."

She started to say something else, I don't know what. Only that I couldn't bear to hear it. Grabbing my hat from the table, I made for the door.

*

At home, I poured myself a glass of Geneva. Knocked it back, then poured another, washing away the taste of lavender, the taste of her. I couldn't explain it. The Catch had been there for the taking, and I'd walked away. Tom would have an apoplexy if he knew. I pulled off my cravat and used it to mop my face.

After the fourth drink, I felt a little calmer. All this stuff with my mother had unsettled me, that was all. I told myself that tomorrow I'd put everything right. I was still mulling my madness, when there came a knock at the door. I wasn't expecting anyone, and I presumed it must be Tom, forgotten his key again. Straightening my wig and waistcoat, I headed downstairs. When I opened the door, I had a vague impression of bulk—not Tom's lean frame—before it was barged wider with great force, knocking me backwards onto the stairs. I looked up into the face of an angry-looking golem, and behind him the malevolent smile of Patrick Musgrave.

As it turned out, there were three of them. The angry golem and his friend, equally gargantuan and angry, dragged me upstairs and sat me down. One of them leaned upon my shoulders, while the other produced a very large knife, which he held close to my face. Musgrave wandered around my rooms, picking things up and putting them down. His eye fell on a bottle of the very finest Armagnac eau-de-vie. I'd bought it mainly to dress my rooms, to add to the illusion of wealth. But on every London job, after the Catch, I allowed myself a measure in celebration.

"May I?" Musgrave said.

"Be my guest." I gestured weakly to the glasses on the bookshelf.

He sat in one of my elbow chairs, swilling my brandy, holding it up to the light. "This is good stuff," he said. "Mellow on the nose, and then it hits you like—"

A fist collided with my head. Blackness washed over me and for a moment I thought I was going to pass out. "Rather like that," I heard Musgrave say.

Pain brought me back to myself. That, and the fellow shaking me.

"Are you seeing double?" Musgrave asked. "I'm always alive to men who do. Those who pretend to be my friend, but who are secretly my enemy."

"I'd never presume to call myself either," I managed to say.

"Standing neuter, is it? I'm afraid I don't believe in that. A man is either with me or against me. That's what I say."

"With you," I said, my tongue large and slow in my mouth. "All the way."

Musgrave picked up one of the volumes of *Tom Jones*. "I was arrested yesterday, on suspicion of the murder of Jonas Cole. Your friend, Mr. Fielding, had rather a lot to say about his treachery. I know you were asking around my club about Cole. And I know that a man, who sounds very much like your good self, visited Fielding at his home last night."

It seemed Musgrave had his own doubles—men in Fielding's employ. As to how he had learned I was asking around about Cole, I presumed he'd got it out of Virginia at the Goldfish. Or perhaps Lord Richard had talked. He was into Musgrave for thousands.

"I didn't say anything about you to Henry Fielding," I said, trying to keep the panic out of my voice.

"Believe me, if you had, you'd be doing more than seeing double."

Recalling all those stories about Musgrave and his crucifixions, I swallowed.

"Did you know that Jonas Cole was stealing from me?" Musgrave asked.

I hesitated and the knife brushed against my cheek. I flinched from the blade and the golem holding it rolled his eyes. "Fancy a shave, pretty boy? No? Then answer the question."

"Not until Fielding told me," I said. "Though I knew Cole was being watched by a man in a carriage that sounded like yours."

"I wasn't watching him," Musgrave said. "And I didn't kill him either. I was at Belsize House that night in front of three hundred witnesses."

Was he lying? I didn't know. Nor did I care. I just wanted to get Musgrave out of my rooms and out of my life.

"Then I suppose one of your competitors must have done it."

Musgrave gave me a long hard look. "What has all this got to do with you?"

"Cole's widow," I said. "That's all. Fielding delayed her money in probate. I needed to get it released."

He studied me with interest. "How much did she get?"

"Five hundred," I said. "Her widow's portion."

"And you intend to steal it." Musgrave sipped the Armagnac, savoring the flavor. "There's just one problem, Billy-boy. If Cole was stealing from me, then that's my money."

My heart sank. "Be fair, Musgrave. Don't do this to me. I knew nothing of your involvement when I started this."

"You know now," Musgrave said. "And I will count it a personal favor when that money is returned to me. The sort of favor a friend would do a man, but a double never would."

I gazed at him in despair, the knife blade hovering at the edge of my vision. "I have people to pay. I have to eat. Don't leave me with nothing."

"Twenty percent commission," Musgrave said. "One hundred for you, four hundred for me. I think it remarkably generous under the circumstances."

All Hannah's money. Most of my profit. But what else could I say? "Very well."

One of the golems patted my cheek. His master drained his glass and held up the bottle. "That's not half-bad."

The knife man nudged me. "Please, take it," I said.

Musgrave smiled. "I need more friends like you."

As they descended the stairs in a great clatter, I sunk my head into my hands. Then I poured another glass of Geneva to steady my nerves. If I took five hundred from Hannah, then she'd lose her shop for certain. But if I didn't take my cut, then I couldn't pay Tom or the others. I'd never get anyone to work for me again. I was still sitting there an hour later, trying and failing to find an angle, when Tom walked through the door.

"That bitch Penelope Felton has been down to Petty France to see Dick Britten," he announced. "She knows you once called yourself William Everhart."

The name I'd used back in my soldiering days, after Hackney. Even amidst everything else, the news startled me out of my thoughts. "Christ, how did she find out about that?"

"How should I know? Dick came to the Black Lion to warn you. She gave him this card with her address in London." He tossed it onto the table. "Said she was going to be staying in town until she found you. I gave him a guinea."

Dick was an old friend from those days, one of the few who'd remained loyal. We knew too much about one another's pasts for him to ever give me away. But it troubled me that Penny had found him. That she wasn't giving up.

"Let me take care of Felton," Tom said. "Now that we know where to find her." Reaching inside his coat, he produced his thin, sharp blade. Mimed pulling an arm across the throat of an invisible enemy—then in and up, under the ribs.

Sometimes he unnerved me. Never quite sure when he was joking—or where his limits lay. "Not a chance," I said, firmly. "I'd never hurt any of my widows. Penny didn't mention Devereux or Cullen? Or the Black Lion?"

"He says not."

"Then we're all good," I said, trying to appear calm. Only good was the last thing we were. And I didn't see how I could keep the news from Tom.

"There's something else I have to tell you. You'd better sit down."

Tom looked increasingly appalled as I told him about Musgrave's visit. "Don't worry," I said. "You'll still get your share."

"I'm more worried about Musgrave not getting his."

"It's all in hand," I reassured him. "Hannah kissed me tonight." It all seemed so long ago. Her hot, sticky parlor, the taste of lavender. I poured out another long measure, drank it down.

"Get this done and fast," Tom said. "Before Musgrave loses patience. Before that Felton bitch catches up with us."

I thought of the bailiffs in Hannah's shop, her being forced out onto the street. Her face just now in her parlor, so vulnerable, stripped of pretense. Then I thought of her embracing that little lad at Ranelagh, and the noise she'd made when I'd told her about Cole's pregnant mistress.

"Tom," I said, "can you find me a child?"

PART THREE

The Rope

The extremes of grief and joy have been remarked to produce very similar effects; and when either of these rushes on us by surprise, it is apt to create such a total perturbation and confusion, that we are often thereby deprived of the use of all our faculties.

Henry Fielding, *The History of Tom Jones, a Foundling*, 1749

CHAPTER TWENTY-ONE

A WOMAN ALWAYS knows. She might try to look away, to avoid the evidence of her ears and eyes, but she knows. It might drive her to a frenzy—wanting so desperately to believe his lies—and yet she knows. I knew. Not about the baby. Not until William Devereux told me. That grotesque moment of humiliation, soon to be compounded by another. But I had known about that bitch, Annette, for many months.

She was not the first of Jonas's whores. I knew that too. The clues are always there. Little lies that get found out. The locking of his book room door, so that a prying wife couldn't read his letters. A lack of interest in conjugal duties once undertaken with delight. I watched Jonas flirt with the wives of our friends, or smile at women in the street. I'd wonder if they'd already lain together, tormented by the thought of their coupling bodies. What's a wife to do? Ignore it? I tried that. Yet a woman has her limits and Jonas found mine. Confront him? I tried that too. His contempt was fierce to behold. It was beneath me, he said, to question his fidelity. To my shame, I ended up apologizing to him. Begging him just to hold me, to comfort me with kind words. But he only left the house, saying he could not stand to be in the company of a wife who did not trust him.

And he was right. I didn't. Because I knew.

Though Annette was not the first, she was different. The first clue was when Jonas stopped eating sweetmeats. They had always been an indulgence of his, and for many years this habit did not trouble his lean frame. But since he'd sat on the parish committee, he'd acquired a little paunch. I watched that paunch diminish and I knew. There were other clues too. He took more care with his clothes and wigs. One time, the Spanish perfumier, Mr. Floris, delivered my quarterly bottle, only it wasn't my usual scent, but one that I had never worn. I took it into the shop to return it, and I saw the confusion on Mr. Floris's face—then understanding dawned, which he attempted to conceal by saying it was his mistake. I wondered who she was, this woman who was wearing my perfume, letting my husband put himself inside her.

The change in Jonas troubled me. One day I followed him to Shepherd Market and I glimpsed the woman—or rather, the girl—who came to the door of the house at which he called. Young, tall, fair, beautiful—different from me in every way you can imagine. Except that from the way her face lit up when she saw Jonas, I could see that she loved him too. I asked around in the local shops, and I found out her name: Annette. Two hard, cruel syllables. A net in which to be caught and drowned. Did she bathe in his admiration, as I had once done? Did she feel sorry for all those girls who were not adored by Jonas Cole? Did she ever think about me, as I thought about her? Had she ever come into the Punchbowl and Pineapple to take a look at me? Sometimes I pitied her. She must have desired my life, even as I desired her death. Did she imagine mine? I think she must have done.

I told myself that Jonas would soon tire of her. That given time, he would come back to me. And yet, by then, I'm not sure that I believed it. Sometimes I worried that Jonas would do something foolish. He'd never be able to afford a divorce, but he could put me into the country. Move Annette in under a pretext, to take my place—just as he'd displaced that man on the parish committee. I didn't doubt that he was capable of it—the way he sometimes looked at me now. But a public scandal would jeopardize everything he'd worked for: the shop, his position on the parish committee, his dream of Parliament. I told myself that he was stuck with me, for better or worse.

About a month before I killed Jonas, he started behaving even more oddly. He'd been curt with me for years, but now he was curt with everyone. Jumping at shadows, peering out the window, furtive and afraid. I watched, fear balling in my throat, sensing the impending rush of events that I didn't yet understand. I needed to understand them. To guard myself against any consequences his secrets might have for me. In this spirit, I tried to pick the lock of the book room door, but I swiftly discovered that I was not cut out for burglary. So I went to the apothecary and told him that I'd been having trouble sleeping at night. It was only the truth, after all. He gave me a tincture, and I mixed it into a bottle of Jonas's wine, which he liked to drink after he came home from the taverns. That night, he fell asleep on the sofa, and I took the ring of keys from his waistcoat pocket.

I unlocked the door to the book room with trembling hands, and went directly to Jonas's letter box on the desk. I sat in his chair for hours and I read all the letters he had been sent, learned all his secrets. Or rather, nearly all his secrets. There was nothing relating to his corruption in there, of all the money he was making—I don't imagine he'd have wanted that written down. When I'd learned about it from Mr. Fielding, that first day in my parlor, it had only compounded my anger. Because given all that money, what Jonas was planning to do was even more wicked. You'd think a heart already fractured could not break again, but as I read about Jonas's arrangements to run away with Annette, it was as if those fragments were being ground into dust. The houses he'd been enquiring about in various locations outside Edinburgh; the two carriage tickets north that he'd reserved under a different name; the furniture he'd ordered, including a harpsichord for his wife who loved to play.

Still, I would have let him go. Steeled myself to accept abandonment and scandal, a life without love, without him. I'd still have had the shop, have had a purpose to my life—which might have been enough to make up for my unhappiness. Except that in that box was another letter, one that provided the final proof of my husband's cruelty and greed. It was from a man named Sadler, a confectioner of our acquaintance in Golden Square, accepting Jonas's "most generous terms indeed" for the swift sale of our shop.

My shop. My home. The house that my grandfather had built. Legally, there was nothing I could do to prevent it. As a married woman, I had few rights, and those were easily circumnavigated, the courts slow to enforce them. All I would be able to demand was that Jonas support me financially, and if he'd changed his name and fled to Scotland, how could I even do that? He was planning on leaving me with nothing, to be cast out onto the street. I knew then that Jonas would have to die.

I thought about doing it there and then, as he slumbered upon the sofa. I could strangle him while he slept? Or beat him to death? But he might wake up, or the apprentices might hear, and beating would create an almighty mess. Thus it was caution, rather than moral qualm, that stayed my hand. I needed to think everything through, step-by-step, like one of my recipes. It took me three days to put my plans into place. The river at the bottom of the ice-store was shallow, gently flowing. I doubted that it could carry a body away. But on days when it rained heavily, that river could become a roiling torrent, one that filled the culvert entirely, sometimes backing up into the shaft.

For a week, I prayed for heavy rain, like some desert tribesman. When eventually it came, I stared out of the window at the deluge, overwhelmed by the thought of it all. That night, Jonas went out to the taverns as usual, and I went to bed early at a quarter after nine o'clock. But a little later, after I was sure the apprentices were asleep, I put on an old gown and took a candle downstairs to wait for him. Jonas came in the back way, as he usually did, and as most of our neighbors kept proper hours and the weather was so inclement, I was confident his return would go unmarked.

"What are you doing down here?" he said, with little pleasure when he saw me.

"Water is backing up in the ice-store," I said. "I'm worried it might flood the tub, and the mechanism is jammed."

He swore under his breath, but he took the candle, and I followed him downstairs. Earlier, I had removed the ice tub in anticipation of this moment, hiding it in the room next door. Jonas leaned over the shaft. "Where's the damn—"

Which was when I struck him very hard, from behind, with the mallet. The first blow knocked him sideways and he hit his head on the side of the low wall surrounding the shaft. He was starting to rise when I hit him again.

Life has flies, Jonas.

I hit him a few more times, just to make sure. There was blood, of course, and teeth and bone—but I had no more horror left to give. He had drained me of everything, of all that I ever was. The only remnant of our love were all his lessons in how to lie.

CHAPTER TWENTY-TWO

Worst of all was lying to William Devereux. I hated playing him for a fool in the face of his kindness, but what choice did I have? Ever since Henry Fielding had told me that he was taking personal charge of the murder inquiry, I had felt the chafing of the hangman's rope around my neck. On that second visit he'd paid to the Punchbowl and Pineapple, when he'd walked into the kitchen and caught us laughing—how I had chastised myself for that moment of ill-discipline!—Fielding had questioned me at length about all the things he'd been told by my so-called friends. Arguments overheard, frustrations expressed in unguarded moments, all Jonas's little barbs and cruelties that—crueler still—might now be used to hang me. He'd insisted on speaking in private to each of my apprentices that day, and I didn't like not knowing what they had told him. I still thought of Oscar's cryptic words to me in the cellar with unease. Every night, as I struggled to sleep, I pictured the smile of Jack Ketch, the executioner. In the mornings, I speculated feverishly about what Henry Fielding might learn that day.

Which was why I'd needed William. I had to protect myself, and my visit to the Goldfish had proved to me that I could not do it alone. William pitied me, I could see that, once I'd realized that he was not the cad I'd originally taken him to be. The grieving widow of his friend, vulnerable and alone, her money about to be stolen by Henry Fielding. I'd played up to it, of course. All big eyes and heartfelt sighs. A helpless woman inspires gallantry in an honorable man. It felt different to the lies that I'd told Daniel and Fielding and everyone else. Every false word left a scratch on my tongue.

Yet I could not deny that placing my life in William's hands had elicited results. I could never have tracked down that odious fellow, Mitford Banks, without him. And not only had William convinced Mr. Fielding to hand over my money, our information had helped to point him in the right—or rather the wrong—direction. There were a great many villainous gaming-house owners on that list to keep Fielding busy.

If only that were the end of it. If only I had never set eyes on William Devereux. He was handsome, of course. Throat-catchingly so. The way women turned to look at him, his crinkled eyes, his infectious smile. But it wasn't only that which had drawn me to him. Such tenderness he possessed, such thoughtful, quiet concern. Though he had wit and spark, I detected a sadness deep within him. Because of his mother perhaps, or the broken engagement that Mrs. Parmenter had told me about.

That day he had invited me to his rooms, I'd gone alone because I hadn't wanted Felix hearing what he'd have to say about Jonas's money. But later, I'd asked myself if there might have been more to it—if I'd *wanted* to be alone with him—even if I hadn't realized it at first. The way he'd bared his heart to me about his mother—in all our years of marriage, Jonas had never once let down his guard like that. I'm not sure I knew that men were even capable of such revelations about themselves. Had William ever told anyone that story before—like that, with a tear in his eye? How was it possible that this gentleman, whom I'd known less than a week, had seemed to understand me, to look into my very soul? The passions that moved me: my desire to travel, how I longed to help those who had nothing, even the stories I'd read. When our eyes had met that day, I'd felt something stir within me.

I was worried others could see it too. Felix observed us with detached amusement, but only because he thought William's intentions were dishonorable. The gossips had doubtless observed our comings and goings. And Daniel, that day William had come into the shop and I'd introduced them.

"Well, he's pretty as a picture," Daniel had said, after William had left. "I'll bet he has every foolish woman he meets imagining that he's in love with them. I thank heaven that you're too sensible for all that."

I told myself that I was. William was a wealthy gentleman. Mrs. Parmenter had told me that he could have any woman he wanted. Not that I wanted him. I told myself that too. I was merely using him, to get what I wanted from Mr. Fielding. Hadn't I sworn it to myself? Never to entrust a man with my happiness ever again?

Then Ranelagh. How astonished I'd been when he'd taken my hand in the Rotunda, the gentle pressure of his fingers against mine. If it hadn't been for that overturned carriage, I liked to think that I would have been saved from myself. But it had thrown us together, strolling under the stars like a courting couple. I hadn't enjoyed sitting with his friends by the canal. It had simply brought home to me our difference in rank. Until, that is, my conversation with Lady Mountford . . .

You must have remarked the way he looks at you? He is quite smitten, my dear.

Could it be true that he thought of me in such terms? Even though I'd been married to his friend, and was still in mourning? Could his head be wrestling with his heart, just as mine was? Was that why he had taken my hand in the Rotunda? I knew nothing with any certainty. Only that I was now utterly lost.

Lord knows I tried. To focus upon the only things that mattered: my business and my liberty. But everything reminded me of him. My trials with iced cream. Every time a man laughed in my shop, like I'd made William laugh at Ranelagh. Every smile of intimacy that passed between a married couple. At night, God help me, I thought of that "one thing," craving his touch with a wanton intensity.

Still, I think I would never have acted upon my feelings. Were it not for that moment in my rooms, when he'd told me that Fielding had found Annette. That she was with child. A searing pain deep in my breast, as if something had torn. That noise I made, like a dying animal. Worse still, to have William witness my distress. But then his arms were around me and all was light. Even now, I touch my lips remembering.

Those few short seconds of everything, before there was nothing. The expression on his face as he'd pulled away. Confusion, disgust. Then he'd walked out and all I had left was the memory of that moment, and the knowledge of what a fool I'd been to imagine he could ever love me.

*

The next morning, having barely slept, I struggled to concentrate in the shop. Miscounting change, getting the orders wrong. Every time the bell over the shop door rang, I looked up, hoping to see him. Fool that I was. He wouldn't come. Nor did he.

All day long we were run off our feet. I had six flavors of iced cream for sale now, having added pistachio, jasmine, and maraschino to the list. Many of my customers were determined to try all six. I had put my prices up, but still they kept coming. In the end, we ran out, and I had to turn customers away. "There'll be more tomorrow," I promised each disappointed face.

Which meant I needed to buy more ice, a much larger load than usual. I dispatched Felix to fetch the carter, and once he returned, I instructed him and Theo to close up the shop. I told Oscar to start work on the flavored creams, which we would freeze upon my return with the ice. The jolting of the cart along the Edgware Road recalled my journey in William's carriage. His smile, the sun on his skin. His hand on the side of the carriage. What I would give to have that time again.

I was so distracted in the ice house that I almost let Mr. Onslow give me a dead owl. I looked down at the poor creature, entrapped in his frozen tomb, and my affinity with his suffering intensified the ache in my heart. I exchanged a few sharp words with Mr. Onslow, and then went back up the stairs, telling myself not to be such a weak and foolish woman. I'd known William less than two weeks. It wasn't possible that I loved him. This was a ridiculous infatuation that would surely pass.

As I neared the top of the steps, I saw a man standing on the grass, a few feet from the entrance. The light was dazzling and I couldn't make out his face. Then my eyes adjusted, and I saw that it was William. I froze, thinking that my fevered mind had conjured him up. Then he took a step towards me and another, his eyes so full of longing it made me tremble.

CHAPTER TWENTY-THREE

WHEN A CUSTOMER walks into the Punchbowl and Pineapple, I want it to feel like they are crossing into a magical world. That first week, after the ice house, was like that with William. We would meet at his rooms, after the shop had closed. His building had a discreet side entrance, but it was still a desperate risk, especially with Mr. Fielding sniffing about. What manner of grieving widow takes up with a new beau, just three months after her husband has died? From their covert glances, when I left the shop each evening, Oscar, Theo, and Felix had a very good idea of where I was going. But after that bleak vision of my life without William, a thousand redcoat soldiers could not have stopped me.

I desired him like an opium-eater. It was as if my body had been made for this moment. Instinctively, he knew just where to touch me and where to kiss me. If it was a sin to have him inside me, then I wanted to sin and sin again. Where had he learned to love like this? In a sultan's seraglio? At first it had made me nervous—that he might find me wanting in some way. But with every word and gesture, he coaxed me to a new understanding of myself. Not a submission, but an affirmation—of joy, of life, of everything! I was a woman reborn—even as I stared death in the face every day.

I'd watch William stride about his rooms, just as nature had intended, and I'd drink in the sight. I liked him better without his wig. A private William just for me, one that all those admiring ladies had never seen.

"Why did you never marry?" I asked him once, the breeze from the window stirring the curtains of his bed, cooling the sweat on our burning skin.

"I was engaged to a lady once," he said. "A long time ago. But her parents did not approve, and I suppose she could not have loved me as much as I thought. After she broke off our engagement, she married one of my best friends. That's when I left England to live abroad." He sighed. "I was a coward, I suppose. I never wanted to give another woman the power to wound me ever again."

I touched his face with my fingertips. "I could never hurt you." Then I flushed at the presumption. "I don't mean to say that this compares . . ."

He raised himself on one elbow to look at me. "No, it doesn't compare, but not in the way that you are thinking. There is honesty here. Truth. You would never lie to me, or deceive me like she did."

How could he know that every word was a skewer through my conscience? If William could see the real me, a murderess, he would never trust his heart to another lady again. This man who dealt in truth and honor, who could not conceive of being lied to in the way that I had.

To cover my discomfort, I laughed. "I'm not a saint, William."

"Oh, I know that," he said, with that grin which made my stomach turn over. "A saint wouldn't let me do this . . . or this . . . or this . . ."

"A man came into my shop today," I said, very much later. "He owns a grocer's off St. James's Street and he offered me a much better price for sugar than Mr. Brunsden. Better even than we were paying before Jonas died. All he wants in return is that I display a sign in my window: *Our iced creams are made with sugar from John Pickering, grocers*. Isn't that strange?"

"Your fame is spreading," William said. "It's only natural that other people will want a piece of it."

"I cannot wait to see Mr. Brunsden's face when I tell him. There will be nothing sweeter. You should have seen the queues today, William. They were even longer."

"All that pleasure you bring to people." He kissed me on the lips. "Whereas I have only one customer."

I smiled. "Are you saying you want paying for your services? Thanks to you I will soon be able to afford it."

"I merely require that you display a card in your window: *Mrs. Cole's smile brought to you by William Devereux, Esquire.*"

I glanced regretfully at the clock on the mantelshelf. "I should be getting back." I hated to leave him, but I could hardly stay out all night. He would have Tom follow me at a distance, to make sure that I got home safely.

While I dressed, William rose from the bed and went to the window. There was a scent of bonfire on the air, the night thick and close and dark. I observed him surreptitiously, that distant look in his eyes again. I'd seen it two or three times in the past few days, and I believed I knew what it signified. He was thinking about our gulf in station—how there could be no future between us. I reminded myself of that fact over and over again. I was merely his mistress, little better than that harlot, Annette. And yet I was already condemned to burn for my greater crime, and so I lived for this new and delicious present.

*

Living for the moment proved easy at first. The hard part was striving not to show it. I thought about William constantly. Sometimes I trailed off mid-sentence, recalling something he'd said, or that moment when he'd kissed me by the ice house. How he'd compared me to a beautiful contessa that he'd seen in an Italian fresco, how she'd eloped with the artist and they'd lived happily until the end of their days. Other memories of our time together that would make me color up and burn like a woman on fire.

When William walked into the shop one afternoon, Lord Richard by his side, I could hardly bring myself to look at him. How to act normally in front of all these people?

Lord Richard kissed my hand. "What a dazzling day it is outside.

Though not quite so dazzling as inside. You are looking remarkably well today, Mrs. Cole."

William held my gaze, our eyes speaking a new private language. "A pleasure as always, Mrs. Cole."

I showed them to a vacant table, and took their hats and gloves to the cloakroom. As I could have predicted, Lord Richard asked for a fluted glass of *chocolat de crème*, which I now served alongside a ball of chocolate iced cream flavored with a grain of ambergris and two grains of cinnamon. A rich and decadent choice for a rich and decadent man.

"Surprise me," William said.

I sent Oscar out to help Theo, while I prepared the order. When I returned with them to the table, Lord Richard dove in with his spoon.

"My word, Mrs. Cole," he said, "your iced cream is as extraordinary as everyone says. And this *chocolat de crème* might be the most delicious sin ever committed."

I glanced rather shyly at William. "Your turn. You have to guess the flavor."

He ate a spoonful and frowned. "I confess I am rather flummoxed."

"First tell me if you like it. It is a trial, so I won't be offended if you don't."

He took another mouthful. "Do you know I rather do? The sourness took me by surprise at first, but now I find it works rather well."

"It is Parmesan," I said, enjoying the look upon his face. "I had the idea of serving it in a wedge, like cheese, with a little burnt sugar on top to resemble the rind. Too exotic for St. James's, I fear, though it's much the same principle as a cheesecake."

"If anyone can bring them to frozen cheese," William declared, "then it is you."

They had come to discuss the arrangements for the supper next week. Lord Richard's father's butler had already been into the shop to hear about my requirements in the kitchen and the practicalities of transporting the iced cream to Morrow House. Determined to impress the Countess of Yarmouth and make William proud, I'd used some of my profits to commission a new mold from my pewterer.

"We will be a dozen guests in total," Lord Richard told me now. "Including yourself, of course."

"But I will be needed in the kitchen," I said, astonished that he would want me there.

"Surely your apprentices can take care of the serving arrangements?" William said.

"Come, say that you will," Lord Richard said. "My guests would love to hear all your secrets."

William was gazing at me imploringly. The thought of dining with all those fine people filled me with trepidation, but a refusal would have been the height of rudeness. "I should be delighted."

We talked a little more about the supper, and I might have sat there all day, hardly hearing Lord Richard, just gazing at William. But Oscar and Theo were run off their feet, and needed more iced cream brought up from the cellar. "I should be getting on," I said, reluctantly.

William rose from the table. "I'll fetch our hats and gloves," he said to Lord Richard.

I knew he wanted to talk to me alone. In the cloakroom, shielded from the hubbub of the shop, he took my hand. "Will you come tonight?"

Alas, it was the first Thursday of the month, the day Jonas and I had always played whist with the Smithsons, who owned the glove shop on St. James's Street. Daniel had offered to make up our four, my first official engagement since the murder. I wished I could get out of it, but if I made an excuse, it might draw attention to my nocturnal comings and goings. I explained all this to William, fearing he would grow sullen, as Jonas always had whenever I'd disappointed him.

"I shall die from longing," was all he said. "Please say you'll come tomorrow and resurrect me."

"Of course I will."

He smiled. "And may I take you for a drive on Sunday? After church? There's someone I want you to meet."

I presumed he must mean another friend, and though I was secretly disappointed that we would not be alone, I said that nothing would give me greater pleasure. He caressed my hand, and I wanted to lean against the wall and have him raise my skirts right there. Then a shadow fell across the doorway, and we sprang apart.

It was Daniel, come to deliver my letters, as he so often did these days. "There you are." He looked from me to William. "You are becoming quite the regular, Mr. Devereux."

"I have always had a taste for sweet things," William said, and I was grateful the light was too dim for Daniel to see me blush.

CHAPTER TWENTY-FOUR

Daniel set the tray down on the table in my kitchen and moved the dirty glasses. The Smithsons had just left. Theo had been dead on her feet after the rush in the shop that day, and I'd told her to go up to bed, saying I would tidy up. Daniel had insisted on staying behind to help.

"Well, that was an enjoyable night," he said, watching me as I bustled around the kitchen.

"I fear I made a poor partner." I went over to the fire to check the cauldron of boiling meltwater. Given the price of salt, and how much we were getting through making iced cream, I'd started evaporating the water, drying out the salt each night to reuse it.

"I hope you'll forgive my distraction," I went on. "I kept thinking about what Mrs. Smithson said about Mr. Fielding. I hope it doesn't divert from his efforts to find Jonas's killer."

In truth, of course, I'd been thinking mostly about William—though Mrs. Smithson's intelligence had also been interesting to hear. She'd said that last night there had been a riot of sailors at a bawdy house on the Strand and that Mr. Fielding was very busy interviewing all those who had been arrested. I could only hope that along with the gaming-house villains, those miscreants would occupy his attention for some time to come.

"I have good news," Daniel said. "I visited the Prerogative Court this morning. The clerk tells me that Fielding has said that probate can move forward. Assuming there are no more delays, we can expect to see our money in a week or two. We should celebrate, don't you think?" He raised the bottle of wine.

"I'm not sure it would feel right under the circumstances."

I'd hoped he would take the hint and leave, but he refilled his glass, watching me over the rim as he swilled it. "Hannah, can we talk openly? I am tired of all this pretense."

I gazed at him in alarm. Daniel had been privy to some of my marital arguments in the past, and he had consoled me once or twice when Jonas had spoken to me harshly. William had also told me that Daniel had known about Jonas's mistress—that he'd been the one who'd told Fielding all about her. Presumably that's why he'd been so evasive in the park the other day. It angered me, that he'd known and hadn't told me—though I supposed that Jonas had put him in an invidious position. But what did he mean by pretense? My heart racing, I endeavored to keep my tone light.

"Whatever do you mean?"

"Our situation," he said. "Jonas's death. How we are left."

My voice was a rasp. "Daniel—"

"I have said nothing. I have done nothing," he declared. "But I cannot let it go on. A man knows what is right and what is wrong—and I must speak."

"Whom will you tell?" I asked, surprisingly calm in that dreadful moment. "Henry Fielding?"

He frowned. "Fielding is the last man I would tell. Only you, dearest Hannah. Other people won't understand, not for the moment. They will say it is too soon, but they can know nothing of the human heart."

As understanding dawned, I shook my head most vigorously. "Daniel, I fear you are mistaken—"

"You are concerned about propriety," he said. "You needn't be. It will be our secret, a most delightful one. In six months or so, we shall be able to tell the world how we feel. And before you ask, I care nothing for our difference in rank. I am sure you have worried about that. Such a modest little thing, you are."

Was it really me he wanted? Or the rest of the money and the shop?

Perhaps both. I wasn't sure. Only that this new complication was one I needed to put a stop to right away. "But there are no feelings," I told him. "Not on my part. Not like that."

"You are fighting it," he said, nodding. "I did too, at first. Because of Jonas. And yet if he looks down upon us, I am sure it is with sympathy for our situation. I think God will smile upon us too—it isn't always the woman's fault, you know. And if it is not to be, I would never hold your barrenness against you, as Jonas did."

I spoke firmly, in order that there could be no misinterpretation. "I am grateful for your friendship, Daniel, truly I am. But there can never be anything more between us. Never."

The finality of my words must have hit home, because his smile faded. "This is because of him, isn't it? That fellow, Devereux."

I held his gaze. "What do you mean? I barely know Mr. Devereux."

"Don't give me that." Daniel almost spat the words. "I saw you in the cloakroom earlier. And before—the way you looked at him."

I wondered if this was why he'd decided that he couldn't afford to wait to declare himself. I cursed myself for missing the signs, for unwittingly giving him encouragement. But I'd had so much else on my mind, it was the last thing that had occurred to me.

"He's just toying with you," Daniel went on. "You cannot think that he has honorable intentions?"

I lifted my chin. "I owe a great deal to Mr. Devereux. And so do you. It was he who convinced Mr. Fielding to lift the delay on probate. You should be thanking him."

Daniel was breathing heavily, a little red in the face. "I'll bet he did. Wanted to make sure of the money before things went any further. I know Devereux's sort. He's just an adventurer."

"Now you're being preposterous," I cried. "Mr. Devereux is a wealthy gentleman. He has a fine carriage and a set of rooms on Bruton Street. My money is nothing to him."

"Are you sure?" Daniel said. "I've asked around my acquaintances, friends with interests in the City, and nobody has ever heard of him."

"That is hardly surprising," I said. "He only lately returned from the Far East. But I have met an old friend of his parents and Lord Richard, the son of the Marquis of Morrow, and several other friends of his, all gentlemen and ladies of high rank."

"Oh? And where was this?"

"At Hickford's Long Room," I said, reluctantly. "And at Ranelagh. We went there as part of our inquiry into the source of Jonas's money."

Daniel laughed rather unpleasantly. "And I thought you barely knew him. Have you seen the inside of these rooms on Bruton Street?" He studied my face. "Oh, you have. It takes no great feat of wits to imagine what went on there. And here was me thinking you were concerned about propriety."

"I don't have to answer to you," I said. "How dare you speak to me like that. I want you to leave."

He took a step towards me, and my gaze darted to a knife lying on the table. But he only set his glass down rather hard, wine sloshing over the brim.

"Oh, I'm leaving," he said. "Don't you worry about that. But you'll regret your decision tonight, I can promise you that."

CHAPTER TWENTY-FIVE

I TOLD MYSELF that Daniel's threat had been uttered in the heat of the moment. That calmness would prevail. That he would come into the shop tomorrow, full of remorse, and I would accept his apology with good grace.

But he did not come. There had been another riot in town the previous night, and my shop was full of talk about the harsh treatment that the rioters could expect at the hands of Henry Fielding. I prayed that the crisis might make him forget about Jonas's murder entirely. Yet I kept hearing Daniel's words and I fretted and I feared. William could tell that something was wrong.

"What is it?" he asked me that night, during a pause in our lovemaking. "I hate to see you frown."

"Nothing," I told him. "Just some wranglings with a supplier."

I knew he didn't believe me. I hated hurting him with my lies. But how could I tell him the truth? I put my head on his bare shoulder and closed my eyes. Wished that I could stay like that forever. But that dark feeling of foreboding followed me around for days like a familiar.

*

On Sunday, I looked for Daniel in church, but he wasn't there. As I listened to the rector talk about treading sins underfoot and hurling iniquity into the sea, I prayed that the Lord would deliver me from Henry Fielding. I had dressed carefully that day, in anticipation of my excursion with William. A tortoiseshell comb to secure my hair, a dab of scent from Mr. Floris, and a new silk shawl that I'd bought at the St. James's Market. I hoped that this friend he wanted me to meet wouldn't look down their nose at me like Mrs. Parmenter, or watch me lewdly like Lord Richard.

As it turned out, I needn't have worried. When I greeted William at the door to my shop, he was holding the hand of a little boy.

"Hannah, I want you to meet Edward, though he prefers to be known as Teddy. Officially we are cousins, but he has always called me his Uncle William."

He was the most angelic-looking child I had ever seen. A head of golden curls, a darling little suit of striped satin, and soft brown eyes. "How old are you, Teddy?" I asked, crouching down to talk to him.

"Six," he said solemnly, his eyes alighting upon the jars of colored candies on my shelves.

"Then you may choose seven candies, one for each year, and one for luck."

Of course, his face lit up. He made his selections—an orange tablet, a golden dragée, a ginger pastille, a raspberry bonbon, a chocolate pistachio, a candied gooseberry, and a cherry almond—and I packaged them up in a bag with ribbon. I smiled at William. "Teddy is the person you wanted me to meet?"

"I could not think of a better way to spend an afternoon than with the two people I like best in the world. But I also wanted to show you something." He took his watch from his pocket. "We'd better get going, or we shall be late."

Teddy insisted on sitting up on the box with Tom. The pair of them chattered away, while the boy made short work of his candies. Once we were beyond the turnpike at Hyde Park Corner, Tom let him take the reins.

"His father was a cousin on my mother's side," William told me in a low tone. "Christopher was a promising youth, though his family were poor. I paid for his education and he was intended for one of the inns of court—but he made a poor marriage, against my advice, and ended up a clerk for an insurance broker. I like to think that he would have made something of himself regardless, but he was taken from us in the typhoid epidemic three years ago."

"The poor child," I said. "And his mother?"

William frowned. "She was always a selfish creature. Pretty in countenance, but not in temperament. Last year she remarried, and it was clear to me from the first that her new husband didn't care for Teddy. He often speaks harshly to the boy in my presence and sometimes I notice bruises. When I questioned Teddy about them, he said his stepfather often punishes him with a rod."

"Such cruelty," I exclaimed. "It shouldn't be allowed."

"I had words with the man, as you can imagine," William said, in a quiet, angry tone. "He only told me to mind my own business. Now Teddy's mother is with child again, and I have made her a proposal: that Teddy come and live with me as my ward. She is amenable to the plan, but it will necessitate a few changes upon my part. A new place to live. A proper household."

"Teddy is fortunate indeed to have such an uncle," I said.

Hyde Park was full of carriages, parading in the sunshine. I'd wondered if William intended for us to join them, but we continued along the road, crossing the Knight's Bridge over the River Westbourne, towards Kensington. Several grand mansions had been built along this stretch of road in the past few years, and as we reached one particularly impressive example, Tom slowed the horses.

"Well," William said, gesturing, "what do you think?"

The mansion was built of pale stone, seven bays wide and three stories high. Pillars between the windows gave the illusion of supporting a triangular pediment that was adorned with marble urns and statues of nymphs.

"It is the prettiest house I have ever seen," I said. "You don't mean—"

"I am considering making an offer," he said. "But I wanted you to see it first. A woman might think of things that a man would not. And I value nobody's opinion more than yours."

Warmth flooded through me, as it often did when he said such things. Jonas hadn't paid me a compliment in years, and certainly hadn't valued my opinion. Whereas the other day, William had donated a hundred pounds to the Foundling Hospital, just because I'd said it was a worthy cause.

Tom pulled the horses to a halt on the graveled forecourt and a rotund little man in a black velvet bag-wig came out of the house to greet us.

"Mr. Abelard, allow me to name Mrs. Cole. Mr. Abelard is the agent conducting the sale on behalf of the owner."

For the next hour, we toured the house, it taking that long to proceed through all the rooms. In the library, I admired the white and gold shelves with their panels of pink scagliola and I marveled at the vast marble fireplaces in the drawing room. It seemed so odd to me to be venturing an opinion on all this splendor, but William listened seriously to everything I said. Teddy followed us around, good as dew to flowers, at one point slipping his hand into mine. That old familiar ache. The dear child could not have known how it would make me feel. How I'd always watched my neighbors with their children, wanting to scream with rage at the world. How bitterly I'd envied them their complaints about motherhood and the workload it brings.

"The Palm Room," Mr. Abelard announced.

The astonishing sight distracted me from those dark memories. In a feat of ingenuity, the decorator had brought the gardens into the house, turning the pillars into painted palm trees of green and gold. More palms framed glass-paneled doors that led out onto the terrace.

"It comes with five acres," William said. "I'll take you out there once we've seen the rest of the house."

I spoke with more convincing authority in the kitchens and the domestic offices. "You will need at least a dozen servants to keep this place in order."

"More, I would think," William said thoughtfully. "I have already spoken to one of the recruitment offices in town. Well, what do you think? Should I buy it?"

"I think you could be very happy here," I said.

Upstairs, William drew Mr. Abelard aside to discuss the terms of the sale, while I pointed to birds in the garden, telling Teddy all the right names. Snatches of their conversation drifted over to me: sums in the thousands, bankers' drafts, legal terms. I'd known William was wealthy, of course, but not to this extent. The window tax alone would be a small fortune. It made Daniel's suspicions seem all the more ridiculous.

Once their business was concluded, William informed Mr. Abelard that we were content to view the gardens alone. We walked out onto the terrace and down a flight of steps onto the lawn. Passing through a parterre with lozenge-shaped beds ablaze with flowers, we came to a halt on the shore of a small lake.

"We shall race model boats here, Teddy," William said. "Would you like that?"

Teddy tugged at my hand. "Hannah come too?"

I wasn't sure what to say, but William smiled at the boy and then at me. "I very much hope that she will."

Beyond the lake, topiary hedges divided the lawn into four quarters: a Dutch garden, which William told me would be resplendent with tulips in spring; a rose garden; a herb garden; and an Italianate garden with a beautiful sundial at its center. Finally, at the far end of the grounds, a flight of stone steps led up a hill to a Grecian temple at the summit. When we reached the top, Teddy ran inside to investigate, whilst William and I gazed back at the house, admiring the prospect.

"It was important to me to choose somewhere close to Piccadilly," William said.

The way he looked at me as he said this left me in no doubt that he wanted me to remain his mistress. I thought of bucolic days here with William and Teddy. But how could I possibly maintain such a life? I was taking too much time away from the shop as it was. Rumors would soon start, if they hadn't already, and a scandal would not only be ruinous for my reputation, it might damage my business.

"William," I said, "I have enjoyed these past days in your company more than I ever should have done." I felt myself blushing. "But—"

"Don't say *but*," he cried. "Please, never do that." He seized hold of my hands. "If I have not spoken yet of the future, it is only because you were so lately widowed. I know that I must wait until it is proper to do so. But don't imagine that I don't think of it. That's why I wanted you to meet Teddy. To see this house. It's why I wanted to be near to

Piccadilly. I know what your shop means to you, and I would never expect you to give it up. Not unless you wanted to. I wish to give you everything you want."

Was he speaking of marriage? I stared at him. To be mistress of his heart and this mansion too. To spend the rest of my life with him, honorably and openly. To be a mother to Teddy. And yet how could I marry him, in all good conscience, given what I was? He was gazing at me expectantly. I knew that I had to refuse him. But how could I refuse him this glimpse of a perfect future, when I couldn't refuse him anything?

It was Teddy who saved me from the horns of this dilemma. There was a howl of pain from the temple. Hurrying inside, I found him on the floor where he'd taken a tumble. Scooping him up, I carried him back outside, where I stroked his hair, telling him he was the best boy, and that his Uncle William loved him dearly.

Looking up, I glimpsed a strange emotion upon William's face. Something dark and rather desperate in his gaze, so that I feared I had hurt him deeply by my lack of reply. I wanted to tell him that I loved him, that I had never felt this way before, not even in the early days with Jonas. I wanted to tell him how happy we'd be, the three of us living here. But then the cloud passed from his face, and he smiled at me with such devotion.

"Teddy looks more content in your arms than I've ever seen him."

CHAPTER TWENTY-SIX

MY FEAR AND my conscience made for uneasy bedfellows. How could I pledge myself to William, when I might be unmasked as a murderess at any moment? How could I marry him, knowing that my arrest would shame him forever? And even if I wasn't arrested, if my efforts to throw Henry Fielding off the scent proved successful, surely that secret would come between us? A lie as big and monstrous as any that was ever told. Surely God would never reward me for what I had done?

The thought of William learning the truth, seeing me for what I truly was—made me want to vomit. To imagine his pain upon discovering that he had been deceived once again by a woman he loved—it was worse even than my thoughts of the hangman's rope. And yet, my head was also filled with dreams of a life beyond all this. Waking up to William every morning. Able to call him mine. And little Teddy! How neatly his hand had fitted into my own. How could I in all good conscience deny that boy a mother who would love him? Perhaps it was God's purpose after all? My barrenness, Jonas's cruelty, even his murder? Perhaps He was offering me a chance of redemption: to raise this child to be a good man like his uncle?

In this desperate mood, vacillating between duty and desire, I sought refuge in my shop. I had been placing too much responsibility on Oscar's young shoulders, leaving him in charge of the counter and the takings rather too often, putting Theo and Felix under his supervision when I slipped out at night to see William. Was that the cause of his downcast expression? Or was it Mr. Fielding's inquiry, and whatever it was that he had alluded to down in the cellar?

"There," I said to him, as I finished checking the crystal bowls and silver spoons, each polished to a sparkling shine. "I think we're about ready. Will you bring the iced creams up from the cellar? Get Theo to help you."

There was already a queue outside the door. Whilst Oscar was gone, I inspected the display pineapple on its ivory stand. Each fruit cost me forty pounds apiece, but when they were nearing the end of their natural life, I could turn them into marmalade, sugar drops, and jellies. By eking out the flesh in this way, I made a small profit on each pineapple—and yet I had more ambitious plans for this one here.

A trough of ice was standing ready to receive the basins of iced cream, and when Oscar and Theo returned, we nested them inside. Bergamot, saffron, and muscat were the new flavors we had on offer that day. I straightened the chairs at the tables, and then turned to give everything a final survey.

"Where is that layabout?" Oscar said. "The size of that queue, we need him on the door."

"We also need a little more ice, I think." I examined the trough critically. "If I send Felix in, can the pair of you open up? I won't be long."

Theo had already returned to the kitchen. I could hear her talking to Felix in the low voices they used when they didn't wish to be overheard. Instinctively, I slowed my pace, wondering if they might be talking about the conversations they'd had with Mr. Fielding.

"You keep at that bottle," Theo was saying, "and she'll throw us out. I like it here."

"I don't," Felix said. "Not any more. She has us run off our feet with that damned iced cream. Little wonder I need a drink at the end of the day."

Inwardly, I sighed, knowing I'd have to do something about Felix, but not knowing what. I didn't want to lose Theo, but her brother seemed determined not to knuckle down to his life here. "What did you expect?" Jonas had said to me once. "That they'd run into your arms and call you *Mother*?"

The clank of a bucket and a rattle of coals drowned out Theo's reply. Felix laughed. "She don't know nothing. She's a flat. All wrapped up in her Mr. Devereux." He made kissing noises. "I could be robbing her blind and she'd be lost in her cunny-cock-dreams."

My cheeks burned. Even though I'd suspected they'd guessed what we were about, to have confirmation delivered in such crude terms was hard to hear.

"If you go near her takings, I'll box your ears, Felix Smith. You know what they do to apprentices who steal from their masters."

Felix laughed again. "It's not me she needs to be worrying about."

His words perturbed me. Did Felix mean Mr. Fielding? Or did he share Daniel's suspicions of William's motives? Either way, I'd heard enough. Sweeping into the room, I ordered Felix sharply to his position by the door and Theo, a little more kindly, to help Oscar with the counter. Then I descended the stairs to the cellar, where I leaned against the newel post. Everything felt thick again, like treacle.

Vigorously, I worked the handle of the ice-store's pulley, hoping labor would banish that feeling of foreboding. When the tub reached the top, I took out a block of ice and carried it over to my butcher's table. Taking up my pick and mallet, I hacked away, filling a pail with pieces of ice to take upstairs. Between these blows, I happened to glance up and was startled to see Henry Fielding watching me from the stairs. I almost dropped the mallet.

"Your girl told me where to find you," he said. "I do hope you'll forgive the intrusion. Did Mr. Devereux tell you that I needed to talk to you again? I would have come sooner, but I've been busy with this wretched riot."

"Yes, he did," I said, very conscious of the mallet in my hand. Despite the chill of the ice, sweat prickled beneath my arms. "Let me take you upstairs where it is more comfortable."

"Oh, I don't mind," he said, ducking beneath the beam at the bottom of the stairs, coming more fully into the cellar. Standing just a few feet from the ice tub, where my grandfather's watch was concealed. He worked a quid of tobacco in his cheek, a habit I have always deplored. "We can talk while you work."

I thought about arguing with him, but worried it might seem as if I had something to hide. Fielding nodded at the ice on the block. "There's quite a line outside your door. My congratulations upon your success. Did you know we've had complaints? Men and women mingling freely over your iced cream? I've been told it is immoral." He smiled. "I told them that once I'm done with the thieving gangs and the pimps and the gambling houses and the counterfeit rings—then I'll extend my jurisdiction to iced cream."

"Some men fear anything changing," I said, striking the ice again with rather less force.

"Some women too."

I didn't like the way he said this. I endeavored to speak without inflection, my pulse racing away. "Mr. Devereux tells me that you believe Jonas's murder has a connection to the gambling clubs and the villains who run them," I said.

"I did think that for a time. But those inquiries have thus far proved fruitless. I have found no firm evidence to support such a link."

"No evidence?" I cried, dismayed. "Mr. Devereux said Jonas was stealing from those men. And that blue carriage was outside my house. My apprentice saw it."

Fielding nodded. "Regrettably the owner of that carriage, a man named Musgrave, has an unimpeachable alibi."

I searched frantically for further arguments that might convince him. "There must be others. Jonas surely had accomplices. He'd never have conceived all of this alone." William's promise notwithstanding, I owed nothing to that wretched man, Mitford Banks. Let him talk his way out of this mess of his own making.

"I'm looking into a number of possibilities." Fielding drummed his fingers on the hat in his hands, his jaw working the tobacco in his cheek. "Upon that point, madam, did Mr. Devereux talk to you about certain other aspects of my investigation? I don't speak of Jonas's money here, but of his more personal dealings."

I looked away. "He told me that Jonas was planning on running away with another woman. That she was with child." My shudder was entirely genuine. "I find it all so hard to believe. That was not the Jonas I knew."

"I assure you it's true," Fielding said, with rather less sympathy than I had hoped. "Then you had no idea what your husband was planning?"

"Of course not," I said. "He was hardly likely to confide in me."

"You seem a resourceful woman," Fielding said. "The sort who makes it her business to find out what is going on."

"If I had known, I would have told you," I said.

Fielding took a turn about the cellar, circling me and the ice-store. "Jonas's mistress believes that you found out," he said. "She believes you killed your husband."

I stared at him, a high-pitched sound ringing in my ears. "How could she say such a thing? I am a victim of this piece. This woman is making up stories, sir. She is hardly a disinterested party."

"I was inclined to believe that too, especially after Mr. Devereux made such an ardent declaration of your good character. But now a second witness has come forward, a gentleman, one who supports the mistress's claim that you suspected your husband of infidelity. I am making no presumptions about guilt or innocence, not at this time, but I'm afraid I do need to ask you some rather indelicate questions."

The cellar seemed to spin around me. William knew that Fielding suspected me—and he had leapt to my defense. Of course he had. He wouldn't have believed for a moment that I could have committed such a dreadful crime. If only he had told me. Then I might have been better prepared for Fielding's visit.

The mallet was still gripped in my hand, a pointer to my guilt. I set it down. "What witness?" I asked, though I feared that I already knew.

"Mr. Daniel Cole," Fielding said. "He says that Jonas told him that you believed that he had other women. *Her damn jealousy is driving me mad*, were the words he used. That's a rather different portrait of your marriage than the one you painted for me."

After I had rejected him, had Daniel conceived a different path to my money? If I was convicted of murder, then he would get everything. I thought about saying this to Fielding, denying my argument with

Jonas had ever happened, but I knew what sort of man the magistrate was. He'd never believe a shopkeeper's widow over a gentleman, not without evidence. Fielding was watching for my reaction, and I hoped he wouldn't see me tremble as I met his gaze. "It was one rare argument. I didn't dwell on it."

Fielding considered. "Yet you professed just now that this was not the Jonas you knew."

"I believed my husband's assertions of innocence," I said. "It seems I was a fool to do so."

"You do not strike me as a fool, Mrs. Cole. Did you know that Daniel Cole has been intercepting Jonas's mail ever since his death? He was worried that you might open a letter from one of his Jezebels—that it would cause you further pain."

I gazed at him, not liking the sound of this. Had Daniel really been trying to spare me pain? More likely he was thinking about the money, afraid that I might take any evidence of its dubious origins to Mr. Fielding. But whatever his motivation then, he certainly wasn't trying to spare me pain now. Quite the contrary.

"The other day," Fielding went on, "Daniel opened a letter that made him consider his cousin's murder in a new light. That's why he came to see me."

Again, that sick feeling, treacle moving stickily through my veins. "What letter, sir?"

"It was from a fellow confectioner, a Beaconsfield man who is looking to move to the city. It seems he'd heard a rumor that Mr. Cole was selling his shop and he expressed an interest in purchasing it."

"Jonas was planning to sell my shop?" I exclaimed, as if this was the first time I had heard of it.

Fielding nodded. "To help fund his new life in Scotland with his mistress."

Not knowing what else to do, I covered my face with my hands. "Forgive me."

"It would make one very angry, I would think," Fielding said. "Losing your home, everything you and your father had worked for."

"Angry? I am bereft. To think that the man I loved . . ."

"Could be so cruel? I tend to agree. You must be thanking Providence that everything has worked out so well for you."

"How can you say that?" I glared at him indignantly. "My husband is dead. If you only knew how I've suffered, sir."

"And yet your shop is safe and thriving. And once probate is granted, you'll be a wealthy woman."

"I didn't know about that money," I cried. "Nor about the sale of the shop. I had nothing to do with any of this. You must believe me."

Fielding didn't reply at first, only observed me with those shrewd eyes. "Your grandfather's watch still hasn't come to light—in case you are wondering. It clearly meant a lot to you. That family heirloom."

His hands were resting upon the side of the ice-store, mere inches from the watch. "I am grieved to hear it, sir."

"Nor have I been able to track down Jonas's friend," Fielding went on. "The one he was due to see on the night he was killed, after the tavern. Did you know all the men he was drinking with that night thought he was heading directly home? The taverner too. Jonas doesn't seem to have mentioned this friend to anyone other than you. Are you quite certain that's what he said?"

"I've said so from the start." I'd told that lie because if the body was ever pulled out of the Thames, I would need the authorities to think that Jonas had good reason for being down by the river. He'd known so many people who lived near Parliament after all.

"So you did." In the silence that followed these words, Fielding peered down into the ice-store. My heart was racing at the speed of a whisk, treacle coating my mouth. "One of those underground rivers, is it? The land around here is riddled with them, I'm told."

"My father said it was an old sewer," I said, faintly.

"People use the term 'sewer' quite liberally, you know. May I?" Fielding spat his tobacco into the shaft, and then tilted his head to listen. "It sounds like a river to me. Most of the ones around here flow into the Thames."

CHAPTER TWENTY-SEVEN

FIELDING CAN PROVE nothing, I told myself in the days after his visit. Whatever he suspected, he had no real evidence. Hadn't he said he was looking into a number of possibilities? Perhaps he spoke to all of his suspects like that? As if they were the guilty party? I'd held up well under his questioning, all things considered. And yet the way Fielding had looked at me, as if he could see the guilt written on my soul . . . I flinched from my memories of that searing gaze. How I wished I could confide all this to William. Listen to his wise counsel, place my life again in his capable hands. But how could I? If William knew about Jonas selling the shop and the things Daniel had told Fielding, he might come to suspect me too.

Under the circumstances, it was madness to keep seeing him. The speed with which I'd taken a lover would be considered further proof of my guilt. And yet those moments when I could be alone with William were the only times that I felt at peace. The shadow of the gallows tree, looming ever more starkly, only made this exquisite new taste of life all the sweeter. Every night, William would unlock his door, and we would fall upon one another. When he spoke of our future together, at the house in Kensington Gore with Teddy, it was all I could do not to weep.

I was a ghost in the shop during the day, exhausted from late nights with William and worrying about Mr. Fielding. But our hordes of customers allowed me little respite.

"You are the toast of the town, Mrs. C," Theo had cried, after a famous actor from Drury Lane had visited the shop with a party of his friends. But I could not bask in my success. The higher I climbed, the dizzier I became.

My new grocer, Mr. Pickering, was working out very well, and unlike Roger Brunsden, never skimped on his measures. Nor did he give me old vanilla pods oiled up to look fresh. I had been in to see him recently, wanting only the very best ingredients for the iced cream I'd conceived for Lord Richard's supper. I'd also bought a new gown to wear that night, far grander than anything else I owned, determined not to look shabby and embarrass William in front of his friends. I probably should have used that money to reduce my debts, but I told myself that probate would be granted any day now, and then I'd never need to worry about money ever again.

The day of the supper finally dawned, and I saw to the last of the preparations in the kitchen. We closed the shop early, and my creation, still in its mold, was placed carefully within a metal pail filled with ice. Oscar and Felix carried it out to the hackney carriage, and I prayed that the jolting of the journey would not damage it. Oscar and Theo rode with this precious cargo to the Marquis of Morrow's kitchens, whilst William came to collect me in his carriage. Seeing my tense face, he smiled. "They will adore your iced cream and they will adore you."

I had anticipated that the house would be grand, but when we pulled up outside one of the largest mansions in Grosvenor Square, with a vast frontage of pillars and windows blazing with light, my nerve almost failed me. A pair of liveried footmen descended upon our carriage, ushering William and me inside with great ceremony. An entrance hall laid with marble led to a pair of black-and-gold gates and a vast staircase hall. The stairs were also made of marble and sported a modern balustrade of ornate bronze. On the galleried landing, a second pair of footmen threw open a pair of double doors, and our presence was announced to the guests inside. "Mr. William Devereux, Esquire, and Mrs. Hannah Cole."

It was the most sumptuous room I had ever seen. The ceiling a deep dark blue, emblazoned with plasterwork stars, the walls hung with gilt mirrors reflecting all the heads that turned to welcome us. I recognized only two of the guests: Lord Richard and Mrs. Parmenter, who ran her gimlet eye over my new lilac-gray silk and sniffed. Yet two other ladies smiled at me and I could detect no trace of scorn in their eyes. Both elegantly attired and bejeweled, I didn't know which one was the Countess of Yarmouth. Of the five remaining gentlemen, only one stood out. His dark skin reminded me of the Lascar sailors who lived in lodging houses down at the docks, except that he was dressed in flowing gold robes, and wore a silk turban embellished with a red stone. He held a chain in his hand, and as my gaze followed it to the floor, I was startled to see a tiger cub nestled at his feet.

"His Excellency takes him everywhere," William whispered, perhaps sensing my unease. "Sometimes he makes a bit of a mess, but he's perfectly safe."

A short, rotund gentleman with a brandy nose barreled up to us. "Devereux," he cried. "And the famous Mrs. Cole. Charmed, I'm sure."

William made a more formal introduction. "Allow me to name Mr. Bennett, the agent of Arcadia, our syndicate. Everyone else here is an investor, aside from Lord Richard, who represents his father, and His Excellency." He looked around. "The Countess of Yarmouth isn't here?"

"Bout of the dropsy," Mr. Bennett said. "A great pity, but it can't be helped."

I was trying to contain my disappointment, when Mr. Bennett drew William aside. "I need to talk to you rather urgently," I heard him say in a low voice.

"This is hardly the time, Bennett. Can't it wait?"

"I'm not sure it can."

They were still speaking in hushed tones, when a gentleman with long white hair and a military posture introduced himself to me with a bow.

"Colonel Watkin-Williams. I must say, it is a pleasure. My wife can talk of nothing but your iced cream. She's been into your shop three times this week."

How odd it was to be lauded by strangers like this. "If you tell her to make herself known to me next time, I will give her a good price." I smiled.

"Oh, I will. I'll tell her to bring the Countess of Yarmouth too, once she's back on her feet."

Were the countess to walk into my shop, I thought, Theo might expire upon the spot.

"As for all the profit you must be making," the colonel went on, "you're in the right company. Devereux has performed marvels for most of us here."

I smiled politely. "My father always taught me that it was safer to save than to invest. Though I imagine that way of thinking is heresy here."

"Not heresy," he said. "Only a crying shame. Why, I wince at all the money you'll be losing."

Gazing around at the happy throng in their jewels and finery, I wondered if he was right. Perhaps my father's way of thinking was outmoded. Even once I'd paid off my loans, I'd still have over four hundred pounds to my name. Perhaps I could risk a portion of it—maybe as much as a hundred pounds? William could advise me on where to place it. Maybe he could even convince the right people—Mr. Bennett? His Excellency?—to let me invest in Arcadia as he had with Mrs. Parmenter?

"Forgive me," William murmured, as he rejoined us. "Do you mind if I steal Mrs. Cole, sir? I haven't yet introduced her to the ambassador and you know how prickly he can be."

"Wouldn't want to start a war, now, would we?" the colonel said, with a grin.

As we approached the young man in the turban, he studied me with a haughty gaze. "Allow me to name His Excellency Nawab Farook," William said. "He is the ambassador to the Court of St. James's from the island of Bentoo. Your Excellency, allow me to present Mrs. Hannah Cole, a very dear friend of mine."

The nawab raised his hand, which was adorned by a ring with a blue stone. Realizing that I was supposed to kiss it, as if he were the pope himself, I lowered my lips, trying to keep as great a distance from the tiger cub as I could.

"Forgive my ignorance," I said, "but I am not familiar with the island of Bentoo."

"It lies in the middle of the ocean, two weeks' voyage south of India," the nawab said, in heavily accented English.

I remembered seeing a prospectus for the company, Arcadia, in William's rooms. An engraving upon the front had depicted a tropical island with palm trees and exotic birds. "Does your island have a connection to Arcadia?"

The nawab frowned, and I sensed that I'd said the wrong thing. I glanced rather anxiously at William, fearing a reaction like that of Jonas on the day of the dinner at the Vestry Hall. But he only smiled. "I promise you, Farook. Mrs. Cole can be trusted." He glanced at me. "You're not going to sell our secrets in Whitehall, or to our competitors, I hope?"

"I should hardly know where to start," I said, bemused.

The nawab studied me for what felt like an eternity, before he seemed to relent. "Arcadia is a colony upon the eastern tip of Bentoo," he said, bending to ruffle the fur on the back of the tiger cub's neck. "My uncle, the maharajah of Paan, opened our doors to the Englishmen ten years ago."

"Our syndicate has leased the land for a period of one hundred years," William said. "It was I who first conceived it, when I visited the island during my travels. Between myself, the nawab, the maharajah, and Mr. Bennett we brought it to fruition."

"It sounds a most impressive achievement," I said. "What do you cultivate there, sir?"

The nawab seemed confused by the question, and I wondered if his English wasn't as good as it had first appeared.

"Spices and sugar for the most part," William said. "The climate is perfect for both. Which is why we endeavor to keep our business quiet. The maharajah's greatest fear is that once the European powers learn about our profits, one of them will send a flotilla to take the island and our colony too."

I learned rather more about Arcadia over supper. We dined in an adjoining room with yellow-silk wallpaper painted with butterflies and a magnificent table laid with elaborate arrangements of fruit and flowers. I found myself seated between the colonel and Lord Richard, and though

William was down the other end of the table, next to the nawab, I could at least catch his eye. Various soups and stews were served, and platters of dressed fish. I'd had to remove my gloves to eat, and I was very conscious of my hands, which were covered with old burns and scars. While we ate, Lord Richard pointed out some of the paintings in the room. I'd only heard of a few of the artists, but the others nodded knowledgeably, and I felt a little embarrassed by my ignorance.

"That jade dragon on the mantelshelf used to be owned by a Chinese emperor. My great-grandfather bought it for a song."

"Don't let the nawab hear you saying that," the colonel cautioned. "He already suspects that we're out to rob his uncle blind."

I studied his face. "You're not, are you?"

"Heavens, no," the colonel exclaimed. "Farook has little enough to complain about, not that it will stop him. Our colony is making his uncle a fortune. We gave him very generous terms, some might say too generous. But William insisted upon a fair deal for all parties concerned, including the colonists."

"Who are they?" I asked. "Where did they come from?"

"Scotland, for the most part," the colonel said. "They indenture themselves for five years, and at the end of it they receive a small plantation. Because they are working upon their own behalf and we can evict anyone whose labor we deem insufficient, our harvests are abundant."

"Then there are no slaves on your plantations?"

"Not one," the colonel said. "William was insistent about that too."

"What a worthy enterprise," I said. "The Atlantic trade has never sat well with me. I would be interested in purchasing Arcadian sugar for my shop."

"We have a shipment due next week," the colonel said. "You should have William speak to Mr. Bennett. I am certain that he could get you a good price."

I resolved to talk to William about it, though I would raise the subject delicately, in case he felt that I was taking advantage of his connections.

There was a lull in conversation while the plates were cleared, and then a peacock pie was served, along with many other platters of meat and beautifully dressed vegetables. The pie tasted just like chicken to me, but everybody made appreciative noises and I joined in. Nervous about how my iced cream would compare alongside such delights, I prayed that Oscar had everything under control in the kitchens. As if reading my thoughts, William caught my eye, and gave me a smile of encouragement.

All around me, the guests were discoursing freely about their wealth—in a manner that would have impressed Jonas, but shocked my father. Lord Richard was buying a painting by Watteau, another gentleman was buying a racehorse, and Mrs. Parmenter couldn't stop talking about a yellow diamond necklace she'd seen in a shop on Bond Street.

"Everybody has a dream," the colonel said, perhaps observing my detachment from the conversation. "Wealth merely opens the door to opportunity. Take Lord Carter down there. He wishes to build a country house that will rival Blenheim in splendor. One that will stand as his legacy for centuries to come. While Mr. Llewellyn there dreams only of winning the Newmarket Town Plate. For my own part, I wish to build an experimental hospital. I have seen too many men die over the years for want of effective treatments. I hope in the future we shall see rather less."

"Another worthy enterprise," I said.

"Don't think me entirely worthy," the colonel said, with a grin. "My wife has her eye on a rather fine house near to the palace. She is a great confidante of the countess, which necessitates court dress and all the rest. I'd be in the Fleet, were it not for Arcadia. Now how about you? What's your dream? Don't tell me you don't have one. Everybody does."

To be free from Mr. Fielding. To be free to marry William. But that was the one thing money could not buy me. I recalled the old dreams we'd had, back in the days when my husband had loved me: Jonas the Great. "In the early days of our marriage, my late husband and I dreamed about buying the shop next door and knocking them into one," I said. "That house fell vacant a few months ago, and nobody has bought it yet. Sometimes I imagine how I would fit it out, all the improvements I would make if money were no object." The thought of it occasioned me a little frisson of excitement. Once probate was granted, I'd have enough money to buy that house, though not enough to fit it out as well. But perhaps if business kept up like this, one day I'd be able to afford to make that old dream a reality.

"Hold on to that ambition," the colonel told me, rather fiercely. "You must be ready to seize opportunity whenever it arrives."

The footmen cleared the plates again, and once they had withdrawn, Lord Richard rose to his feet.

"As you know, my father couldn't be here tonight, but he did ask me to say a few words on his behalf. When our good friend, William Devereux, glimpsed the soft white sands of a distant island amidst an ocean of deepest blue, who might have guessed that it would lead us here. Through Devereux's vision—and Mr. Bennett's diligence—and the trust bestowed upon us by the maharajah and His Excellency, we have created a paradise on earth." He grinned. "A very profitable paradise."

Everybody laughed, raising their glasses.

"In the second year of our syndicate's business, every person here saw a twenty-three percent return. By the fifth year that figure stood at fifty percent. Now we double our money year upon year."

I knew how extraordinary such profits were from my conversation with William on our first trip to the ice house. Little wonder men like Jonas and Sir James had been so eager to be a part of it.

"To celebrate our success," Lord Richard went on, "I asked Mrs. Cole to create us a dessert worthy of Arcadia."

My hands were moist, my breathing shallow. What if the iced cream had melted? Or the mold had not come away easily?

Lord Richard rang a silver bell, a signal for the doors to be thrown open once again. A footman marched in, bearing a plate covered in a silver cloche. He placed it ceremoniously in the center of the table and then whisked away the cloche. There was a gasp from the guests and then a ripple of applause.

My pineapple stood proudly upon the silver plate, fashioned from iced cream, yet nearly indistinguishable from the genuine article. Theo, who had an artistic bent, had painted the eyes with colored dyes, and real pineapple leaves were affixed to the top. I'd had to use a third of the flesh of my pineapple in order to make the iced cream, and the guinea Lord Richard had paid me wouldn't come close to meeting the cost. But sometimes you had to spend money to make money, and I hoped William's rich friends would now patronize my shop. It was only a pity that the Countess of Yarmouth wasn't there.

William beamed at me with pride, as the guests exclaimed their astonishment, and lauded the flavor. Lord Richard proposed another toast, this time in my honor, and I basked as everybody applauded once again. Even Mrs. Parmenter's curt remark that her tongue felt horribly numb couldn't dent my exhilaration at how the night had gone.

Two hours later, at nearly midnight, I was still bubbling with the thrill of my success. We were making our farewells in the entrance hall, when William drew me aside. "I'm afraid that Mr. Bennett has some urgent business he needs to discuss with me. I don't know why it can't wait until tomorrow, but he was most insistent. I said I'd drop him home in the carriage, so we can talk on the way."

"Of course," I said, trying to conceal my disappointment. "I can take the hackney home with Theo and Oscar."

"You will not," William exclaimed. "Once I've got rid of Bennett, I want you all to myself."

I want you. Those words still sent a delicious shiver through me.

The carriage was brought round, and once the three of us were seated inside, William turned to Mr. Bennett. "Now George," he said, "what's all this about?"

Mr. Bennett gave me a sidelong glance, but William waved an impatient hand. "You can speak in front of Mrs. Cole, or not at all."

Seeing that he had little choice, Bennett launched into an explanation: "I received word this morning from Captain Rigby of the *Silver Star*. She's been impounded in Lisbon. The harbor master says we owe him fees, which is a pack of lies."

I could see from Bennett's face that this news was occasioning him great distress. I guessed he had been holding it in all evening, trying to appear unruffled. William greeted the news rather more calmly. "How much does he say we owe?"

"Seven hundred pounds. According to him, the debt dates back eight years and the interest has been mounting all that time."

"Pirate," William exclaimed. "Can't we get the law involved?"

"Of course, and we'd probably win. But the delay, man, the delay. Roseberry is in for three hundredweight and contractually he is bound only until the first of September. We'll lose thousands—and my suspicion is that the harbormaster knows it. Rigby thinks we'll be able to beat him down, but it will cost us five hundred at least."

William thought for a moment. "So pay him. The cargo's worth twenty times that."

"I don't have it, not at the moment. Not with my losses upon the Exchange."

"You should have listened to me upon that score," William rebuked him mildly.

"No need to kick a fellow when he's down," Bennett said. "I'm reluctant to appeal to the syndicate. They'll all start haggling for better terms and it could end up costing us more. I was hoping you and I might handle it between ourselves. If you could lend me the money, I'll pay you back once the cargo is sold, and you can have another three hundred out of my share by way of interest."

William pulled a face. "As it happens, I'm not sure I can. I've just put in an offer on a house."

Bennett muttered an oath. "You can't borrow it?"

"Of course I could," William said. "But the moneymen will want to know what it is for. They've all heard rumors about Arcadia, and I fear they'll want better terms than the ones you're offering."

Bennett sighed. "Nine hundred?"

"More like a thousand."

He nodded gloomily. "I suppose we have little choice."

Perhaps it was all that talk over supper, but as I listened to this conversation, it occurred to me that I might volunteer the money. Probate was due to be granted in a few days, and with my iced cream profits, I could afford to let my debt run a few weeks longer. Then when the ship returned, I would have eight hundred pounds to my name. Even after I'd settled my debts, I'd have enough to buy and fit out the shop next door. Opportunity! For a moment I was tantalized by this dazzling possibility.

But in the next moment, reason prevailed, all my father's words about the risks of speculation sounding in my ears. This harbormaster sounded like a most dishonest man. What if he demanded more money? What if the ship sank? Or the cargo had spoiled because of the delay? And what was I even doing thinking about speculation, ambition, and greed, when Henry Fielding might arrest me at any moment? I almost laughed at the hubris of it all.

Both men had fallen silent, an air of expectancy between them—as if each was waiting for the other to speak. The silence stretched on, to the point where I began to feel quite awkward, turning away to look out of the window at a party of revelers in Golden Square.

Mr. Bennett let out a little sigh.

"Don't lose heart, sir," William said softly. "One way or another, I'll get that money."

CHAPTER TWENTY-EIGHT

Later that same night, at William's rooms, I returned from the dressing room in my stays. William was sitting up in bed, staring out the window with that expression of dark intensity on his face again.

"That bad, was it?" I said.

He smiled. "Forgive me."

"Well, I'm not sure I shall." I raised my hands to pin my hair, watching him in the mirror. "Or at least, I'll make you work very hard to earn it."

"You'll be the death of me, woman," he said. "I shall beg for protection from Henry Fielding. Though knowing your wiles, you'd only talk him round."

What to say to that? I smiled uncertainly, as if this subject didn't concern me in the slightest. "Who said anything about talking? Perhaps Mr. Fielding will be more appreciative of my talents than you are, sir."

He liked it when I said bold things like that. As I listened to his laughter, I realized that I liked her too: this new, rather daring Hannah Cole.

When I knelt on the bed to kiss him, he took my hands. "Do you ever feel tired of London?" he said, gazing at me rather earnestly. "We could live anywhere in the world. Just you and I."

"In Bentoo?" I said, still in that same playful tone. "We could see your plantations? Meet the maharajah?"

He was silent a moment. "I thought rather Paris. Or Florence. Have I told you about the light on the statues? It's really quite something."

For a moment, I entertained the thought. No gossiping neighbors. No Daniel. No debts. No responsibilities. No Henry Fielding. "What about my shop?"

"That's just bricks and mortar," he said. "You could open a new shop in Florence. Show the Italians how it's done."

Was he serious? I studied his face, alarmed by the rather haunted look in his eyes.

"It was my grandfather's shop," I said. "I could never leave it. And what about Teddy? Your house? All your plans."

Another pause, before his smile returned. "Our plans," he said. "But let me dream for a moment about showing you the world."

I wanted to understand him. All the ingredients that made him up: his hopes, his fears, those dark shadows that touched his soul. *But what if he should come to understand you?* That was the demand of my conscience—and yet I was getting good at ignoring that persistent voice.

*

The following evening, Tom brought a note to the shop. William wrote to say that he had been called away unexpectedly, and that I should not come that night. The news concerned me. Had he received bad tidings? Or was he having second thoughts about our future together? Sometimes I prayed that this would happen, that I would be delivered from my desires and my conscience. Yet I also knew that to lose him now would be a torment I could scarcely imagine, a living Tartarus of punishment I surely deserved.

Deserve it I might, but that didn't prevent a rush of relief the following day when William called at the shop not long after we had closed. I fetched him a bowl of iced cream—this one flavored with mint, the color enhanced with a little spinach greening—and when I put it in front of him, I could see from the strain on his face that something was wrong.

"What is it?" I asked, after he'd paid me his usual compliments, but without his customary wit and spark.

"Is it that obvious? I'm sorry. I do not wish to trouble you with my problems."

"How many times have I troubled you with mine?" I cried. "Please, tell me. I might be able to help."

He sighed. "It's Teddy. Or rather it is his mother. I had a letter from her yesterday, asking to see me. She tells me that she and her husband are intending to move to Ireland. I might have said it's the best place for her, except that now she says she's changed her mind, and intends to take Teddy with her."

I stared at him, dismayed. "Oh, William."

He shook his head angrily. "The boy had a bruise upon his face last night. He lives in fear of that brute. You should have seen how relieved he was to see me."

"That darling boy," I said. "Is there nothing you can do to change her mind?"

"As it happens there is," William said, with a hard smile. "Five hundred pounds will do the trick, or so she tells me."

"But that's blackmail!" I cried.

"She didn't even flinch when I called it that. The trouble is, I don't have it at the moment. Not if I buy that house. Ordinarily, I would simply borrow it, but I'm already overextended because of Mr. Bennett and that damn ship. I asked Mrs. Parmenter for a loan, but she says she can't help me."

Too many diamond necklaces to buy, I thought savagely. And after everything William had done for her.

"There's nothing for it," William went on. "I'll have to pull out of the sale. I'll lose my deposit, but I don't see any other solution. Until that ship returns from Lisbon and the cargo is sold, there's nothing to be done. And Teddy's mother refuses to wait that long."

"How much is the deposit?" I asked.

"Three hundred pounds. I don't care about the money. Not really. But the house . . ." He smiled sadly. "I have spent too many hours imagining us living there."

As had I, despite all my misgivings. Nor was I so nonchalant as William about the thought of him losing three hundred pounds.

When he would have the money in a matter of weeks. The very idea offended me.

"You must not do it," I said, with sudden conviction. "Why don't I lend you the money? I'll have it once probate is granted. You can pay me back when the cargo is sold."

He frowned. "I could never ask that of you. A gentleman doesn't borrow money from a lady."

"I'm not just any lady."

He held my gaze. "How true that is."

In that moment, everything felt right. To use this money, Jonas's ill-gotten loot, to save that little boy. To save the house. To bring a smile back to William's face. "You have to take it," I said. "I'm afraid I insist."

"What about your debts?" he said.

"I'll just let the interest mount a little longer. It will cost me another ten pounds or so, but that doesn't compare to the three hundred you stand to lose."

He thought for a moment. "I suppose there's a certain logic to what you are saying . . ."

"It makes perfect sense," I said firmly. "Please, I want to help."

"I shall meet all of your costs—and pay you interest upon the loan at a generous rate."

"You certainly shall." I lowered my voice, though Theo and Oscar were busy in the kitchen, and Felix was cleaning the windows outside. "Only not in coin."

William grinned. "And not even Henry Fielding will be able to protect me."

How at peace I felt in that moment. To be able to do something for him, after everything he'd done for me. A small compensation for all my lies and deceptions.

I saw William to the door, promising that I'd come later that night. Mrs. Brunsden, Mrs. Fortnum, and Mrs. Howard were gossiping outside the Howards' shop, and I tried to act normally, giving them a little wave. Mrs. Brunsden looked away—she wasn't speaking to me because I'd ended my dealings with her husband. Their eyes followed William down the street.

Turning, I spotted one of William's kid gloves on the shop floor. I stooped to pick it up, and hastened after him. Luckily, he had been waylaid by a gentleman down the street, and I was easily able to catch up with him.

"You must remember me," the gentleman was saying. "David Thewson from the Wandsworth Academy."

William gave him a bland smile. "I think you must have me confused with somebody else."

"Really, sir?" the man exclaimed. "You are the very spit of William Everhart."

At that moment, William noticed me. His smile never slipped, but I saw a flicker of something alien in his expression. I knew it at once, both disturbing and familiar: the look Jonas had used to wear when I'd caught him out in a lie. It was there just for a second, and then it was gone.

"Oh, Mrs. Cole, you are a godsend." William took the glove from my outstretched hand.

The man looked from William to me, and back again. He had a pointed nose like a chiseled pencil, salt-and-pepper eyebrows, and rather swollen eyes. In his hand was a parcel wrapped with the distinctive purple ribbon used by Mr. Floris. "Then my apologies, sir," he said. "I shall not keep you." He walked away, but I saw him look back and shake his head. William gave me a bemused shrug. "They say everyone has a double," he said.

CHAPTER TWENTY-NINE

*T*HEY SAY EVERYONE *has a double.* All night I thought about that encounter, even while I coupled with William at his rooms. He hadn't mentioned the incident again, as if it was entirely inconsequential. And yet I kept remembering the man's expression when he'd looked back and shaken his head. He hadn't believed William. I was not sure I believed William. That flicker in his eye, so fleeting I might have imagined it. Had he changed his name at some point in the past? And if so, why? I recalled Felix's coarse laughter. *It's not me she needs to be worrying about.* He'd called me a flat. Was it true? Could I be a flat?

I'd known William just over a month and I was offering to give him all of my money. If he failed to pay me back, then I wouldn't be able to pay off my loans—and even with the profits I was making now, the extortionate interest would cripple me. I'd lose the shop and my home, have to move away from St. James's and everyone I knew. Even thinking about it sent my world into a dizzying spiral. And yet this was William, the man I loved. He'd never even asked me for that money. I'd had to beg him to take it. He was the most honorable man I'd ever met. Wasn't he?

The following day, during a lull in the morning rush, I hurried down to Jermyn Street and Mr. Floris's perfumery. A dark and lively Spaniard, he greeted me warmly.

"You had a customer in here yesterday, a man named David Thewson?"

He nodded. "He has bought his scent here for many years."

"Do you happen to know where he lives? He came into my shop too, and I fear my girl overcharged him by mistake. I'd like to rectify the matter at once." How easily the lies rolled off my tongue these days.

"You are a good woman, Mrs. Cole. I don't know where he lives, but I do know that he works as a secretary for Mr. Pelham."

The king's first minister. I thanked him and returned to the shop, but two hours before closing, when business was a little quieter, I put on my hat again and walked across the park towards Westminster.

Outside the Lactarian, children were playing, while their mothers and nursemaids queued to buy milk fresh from the cow. One little boy with golden curls reminded me of Teddy. I thought of that house in Kensington Gore. It couldn't all have been a ruse. A man as wealthy as William wouldn't go to all that trouble to steal five hundred pounds from a widow. The very idea was ridiculous. Unless he was lying about his wealth, as Daniel had claimed. I remembered how well William had lied in the Rotunda that night at Ranelagh. But the syndicate—their wealth was surely real? Hadn't I dined at Lord Richard's table? He had been in no doubt about William's worth. Unless William had somehow duped him too?

I was still going back and forth on the matter, when I emerged from beneath the Horse Guards' arch onto Whitehall. Everything gleamed in the sun. The Banqueting House, the Cockpit, the Tudor brick of the Holbein Gate, Dover House with its funny little dome like a goose pie. Men strode self-importantly between the government offices. Their ambition made me think of Daniel and Henry Fielding. They were my enemies, I told myself, not William, who had only ever tried to help me.

Nevertheless, I kept walking, taking the turning onto Downing Street and the anonymous brick house at number ten that was the most famous address in the land, apart from the palace. Mr. Pelham—like his predecessors—had never taken up residence, opting to live instead at his much grander mansion in Arlington Street. Daniel had told me that most of the house was given over to government offices. A pair of stout constables guarded the door, and I informed one of them that I wished to see Mr. David Thewson. He permitted me to go inside, where a bored-looking clerk presided over a desk in the lobby. As I approached him, I almost stumbled over a great crack in the marble floor. Indeed, the entire building seemed to be sinking into the earth, the door frames at an angle, the fireplace sloping. The newspapers said it was an appropriate metaphor for Mr. Pelham's ministry, but to me it seemed all of a piece with my buckling world.

I'd anticipated having to make an appointment and return, but as luck would have had it, whilst I was discussing the matter with the clerk, Mr. Thewson himself walked into the lobby in the company of another man.

"Mr. Thewson," I cried out.

"Madam?" He bowed, peering at my face. "Are we acquainted?"

"We met yesterday. Or at least, we were not introduced. My name is Mrs. Cole. I own a confectionary shop on Piccadilly. I was with a customer of mine, a man you believed to be named William Everhart."

"Ah yes, of course." He studied me curiously.

"I wondered if I might speak to you about Mr. Everhart in confidence. It would not take long."

He paused for a moment, considering. "I don't see why not," he said. "Mr. O'Donovan, we will have to have that bottle another time."

Mr. O'Donovan lifted his hat and bowed, giving Mr. Thewson a little smile that suggested he knew only too well why his friend was being so obliging.

"Shall we take a turn about the park?" Mr. Thewson said. "It's too bright a day to be cooped up inside."

Once out on the street, he offered me his arm, pulling me a little too close for comfort. "Now explain how I can assist you, Mrs. Cole."

We walked the reverse of the route I'd taken there, while more lies flowed from my lips. "The man you mistook for your friend is named William Devereux," I said. "He is a customer of mine. And yet you seemed very certain that he was named William Everhart. It made me wonder if Devereux was a name that he might have assumed. I have extended him credit, you see, and if Mr. Devereux has been less than honest with me, then I'd like to know why."

"I see," Thewson said. "When I saw him in the street, I was indeed convinced that it was the man I'd known as Everhart, though it has been many years since I saw the fellow last. But that face." He shook his head. "Everhart had half the girls in Wandsworth in love with him. I don't like to call a man a liar, and I cannot swear for certain that it was him, but if it isn't, then they are as alike as twins."

"Did William Everhart have a reputation for dishonesty?"

"Not as I recall," he said, glancing down at me with a reassuring smile. Yet my proximity seemed to be the limit of his ambition, and he discoursed quite freely as we took a turn about the park, pausing every now and then to sneeze into a large handkerchief.

"Everhart and I were both students at a private military academy in Wandsworth. Over twenty years ago now, though it shocks me to say it. The place was run by a Frenchman, and we spent an awful lot of time studying battles. As I recall, Everhart's father had cut him off with only a small sum, and he hoped to use that money to purchase an officer's commission. He was a very charming fellow, always in the thick of things. I remember one time, in the mess hall—we were all rather the worse for wear—he jumped up on a table and had us all in stitches mimicking the Frenchman. Of course, being Everhart it all went a little too far. There was some sort of dance involved and he fell off the table. Smashed a lot of bottles, cut open his knee, blood everywhere."

I stared into the sun. William had a scar upon his knee. He'd told me he'd got it in India, when he'd pushed a child out of the path of a runaway cart. Surely that couldn't be another coincidence, on top of his likeness and the same first name and that flicker of panic? William had changed his name. I was sure of it now.

But perhaps he'd had a good reason for doing it? Hadn't Mrs. Parmenter said that his father had been a brute? And alongside that scandal involving his mother, maybe he'd wanted to distance himself from his childhood? And yet William had never mentioned a military education and we had talked at length about his past.

"Do you know anything at all about Everhart's life after Wandsworth?" I asked.

Thewson grinned. "She asked me that too."

"She?"

"A lady called on me last month. She was looking for Everhart. Had a list of names of men who'd been enrolled with him at Wandsworth, and I was on it. I told her I hadn't seen him in an age, but that the last I'd heard he was headed for the fort at Tilbury."

"Do you remember her name?" I asked. "This lady?"

Thewson fished a little book from his pocket and turned a few pages. "Mrs. Penelope Felton."

"Do you have an address for her?"

"I'm afraid not. She seemed disappointed by the little I knew, and didn't leave a card."

"Can I ask what she looked like?"

Thewson gave me a bemused smile, but he answered me readily enough. "Black hair. About my age. She wore half-mourning dress."

Another widow. Again, I stared into the sun. "Did she happen to say why she was looking for William Everhart?"

"Not in so many words, but she was very eager to find him. My impression was that a sum of money might be involved."

CHAPTER THIRTY

I TOLD MYSELF that this lady, Penelope Felton, might be looking for William for any number of benign purposes. An outstanding debt she wanted to repay, perhaps, or soliciting a charitable donation. I knew how generous William could be. Again, I took myself through all the valid reasons he might have had for changing his name, reminding myself that he had never done anything apart from this to give me cause to mistrust him. That story about the child and the cart might still have been true, and he'd simply muddled up the incidents in his mind. And yet if it was all so innocent, then why hadn't he told me about his soldiering days? Why had he pretended not to know David Thewson?

I considered raising the matter with him that night, when I went to his rooms. But it would be impossible to do so without revealing my conversation with Mr. Thewson. Then William would know that I had called his trust into question. The thought of having one of those accusatory confrontations with him, like the ones I'd used to have with Jonas, was more than I could bear.

And that evening, while I was in his company, the whole idea of him deceiving me seemed so implausible. After our passion was spent, and I rose to dress, I caught him watching me in the mirror with an expression of such intense feeling, I knew there could be nothing bad in that man's heart.

"I wrote to Teddy's mother," he said, when I met his eye and smiled. "Told her she'd have her money, though it boils my blood to do it. Did you go to the bank as we discussed?"

I had gone there after my turn about the park with Mr. Thewson. The clerk had informed me that probate had now been granted and that I could withdraw the money at any time. "I will be sending my man of business to collect it," I'd told him, not wanting to carry such a large sum upon my own person.

"I'll make a note," the clerk had replied. "You'll need to give him a letter of authorization. And I'll need your signature for my records."

I was on the verge of telling William this, when I hesitated.

"The clerk said there had been another delay," I said. "The wrong signature on the wrong document."

"There's always something," William said. "Did he say how long it would take? I won't sit comfortably until Teddy is removed from that woman's clutches."

"Just a few days, I think."

Perhaps the woman I was before would have wished away her doubts. But I was a different creature now. One who knew how easy it was to deceive others in the commission of a crime. I still believed in William. He almost certainly had had a good reason for changing his name. But I had been a fool for love once, and I wouldn't be made one again. I had to be certain.

*

Felix's voice was sullen, his face unreadable in the early-morning glare of the shop window. "I don't know what you're talking about," he said.

"The other day I heard you talking with Theo," I said. "You called me a flat. I want to know why." Had he witnessed something untoward? Something involving William?

He shrugged, occasioning me a flash of anger at his insolence.

"You need to start being honest with me, Felix. Your position in this household is at stake. A flat is a term for a fool. Someone who is taken advantage of. Who is it you think is taking advantage of me? Mr. Devereux?"

I waited for his answer, my stomach churning. But Felix shook his head. "Just your suppliers."

There, I told myself. All this worry is your own creation. Yet two images of William hovered before my eyes. That longing gaze in the mirror at his rooms. That flicker of panic in his eyes on the street. Despite my desperation to believe, I needed more convincing.

"Yes, well, there will be some changes to come on that score," I said. "Now I have something else to discuss with you, and I want you to think carefully before you answer. Did you ever hear Mr. Devereux or his man, Tom, mention a lady named Penelope Felton? Or say anything about a woman who might be trying to find him in connection with a sum of money?"

Over the past two weeks, Felix had often taken my notes to William's rooms—and Tom had often brought his master's replies to the shop. I'd observed them chatting together on more than one occasion.

Felix considered my question for a few moments, and then shook his head. I restrained a sigh. It was no use asking Oscar or Theo, who had hardly spent any time in William's company.

"Very well, then, we shall say no more about that conversation I overheard. But if I ever hear you speaking disrespectfully about me again, there will be other changes too. Do you understand?"

Felix nodded, his expression dark as December.

"Good. Now find me a hackney carriage to take me to Chelsea."

I'd be gone several hours, and given the crowds of customers, it was unfair of me to leave the counter to Oscar and Theo for so long. And yet faced with my doubts about William, nothing else seemed to matter. Outside on the street, Felix whistled for the hackney and when the vehicle drew to a halt, he whisked the door open for me with unusual diligence. I hoped that meant some small part of my lesson had been learned.

"The Royal Hospital in Chelsea," I said to the driver.

We rattled along to Hyde Park Corner, where we took the road south, skirting the Green Park, towards Pimlico. I resented the cost of the journey, but I supposed I could afford it now, and the threat of highwaymen was ever present on the Chelsea Road. Beyond the turnpike—where I parted with yet more coins—we journeyed further south, past the waterworks. The fields were full of men picking fruit and harvesting crops, their bare torsos browned by the sun. I watched them absently, thinking about the last time I'd traveled along this road, in William's carriage, on the night he'd taken me to Ranelagh. That conversation with Lady Mountford, William's words about me. If William was intending to defraud me, then it meant that whole story was a pack of lies. But why would Lady Mountford tell me something that wasn't true? Could William have lied to her too? Or could she be a co-conspirator in his scheme against me? The thought was so fantastical, I almost laughed. And yet I didn't tell the driver to turn around.

The Royal Hospital occupied a rather grand spot on the bank of the Thames, between Ranelagh and the pretty and prosperous village of Chelsea. An imposing palace surrounded by elegant quadrangles and gardens, it was home to old and maimed soldiers, as well as the office where army pensions and other records were administered. We halted by the main gate, and I paid the driver to wait. Crossing the central quadrangle, I passed strolling groups of pensioners in their distinctive uniforms: scarlet coats, blue breeches, and hats commensurate to their army rank. An impressive white portico with steps led to an octagonal vestibule, where a clerk sat scribbling at a desk. I told him the nature of my inquiry, and he summoned a lurking porter, telling him to take me to the pensions office. We proceeded through a large dining hall hung with the captured flags of enemy countries, down a corridor, and into an office where three more clerks were laboring away.

I approached the nearest fellow, a full-faced man with a dimpled chin, who examined me with an air of beleaguered detachment. "Yes?"

"I'm trying to find out some information about a former army officer who was once stationed at the fort at Tilbury."

"All records are confidential," the clerk said, turning back to his ledger.

I placed a half-crown on his desk, which he studied rather sorrowfully. Sighing inwardly, I added another coin of the same value. The man opened a drawer, swept the coins into it, and regarded me much more pleasantly. "The name, madam?"

"William Everhart," I said.

The clerk disappeared through a door to the rear of the room and returned about ten minutes later with a file in his hand. "Captain Everhart was stationed at Tilbury between 'twenty-eight and 'twenty-nine," he told me. "He was put in charge of guarding the gunpowder magazines there. Following an explosion in which his lieutenant was killed, and his gentleman of the ordinance seriously injured, he was court-martialed for negligence. I don't have an address for him on file, I'm afraid, as he doesn't receive a pension."

"Negligence?" That didn't sound like William, who was diligent to a fault.

The clerk nodded, frowning down at the file. "It says here that he was also charged with theft. The governor at Tilbury seems to have believed that the gunpowder exploded whilst it was being stolen. But Everhart convinced the court that he was innocent of the more serious charge. It sounds as if he was lucky to escape a hanging."

A common thief. A man able to talk his way out of a difficult situation. And yet, I assured myself, maybe William had been found not guilty because he was innocent.

"Do you have an address for the governor of the fort? I presume he draws a pension."

"He died some years ago, I'm afraid. I recognize the name."

"How about the gentleman of the ordinance who was injured? And the dependents of the lieutenant who died in the explosion?" They would surely know the full story behind these allegations.

The clerk looked at me with a vague half-smile, until I reluctantly reached for my purse again. Positively jaunty in demeanor now, he closed his drawer on my coins with a flourish and once more disappeared through the door to the rear.

When he returned, more files in hand, he sat and studied them for a few minutes. "The injured man's name is Richard Britten. He still draws a disability pension, though there is some correspondence here that suggests the matter was in dispute for a time."

"Do you know why?"

"It looks like the governor wanted him charged with theft too. But due to the severity of his injuries and Everhart's acquittal, a decision was taken against it. The governor tried to block his pension, but he failed in that too."

"And the dead lieutenant?"

"His name was Stanley George. Left a widow. She never remarried and still receives his pension. You want both addresses?"

"Yes, please."

As he copied them down, my thoughts were a distressing whirl. But I was certain that I could not give William my money now—not until I knew if there was any truth in these allegations.

*

To my horror, when I returned, I found the shop closed. I unlocked the door and walked inside, trying to restrain my anger. Heading for the kitchen, I gazed around myself in dismay. The floor was unmopped, a blackened pan upon the stove, a dairy order left out on the side to spoil. No sign of any of my apprentices.

My fury drove out everything else—even my fears about William—but it was anger at myself more than anything. All of this was down to my neglect. I found Oscar upstairs, sitting morosely in the servants' hall, a gloomy little room that I'd tried to brighten with some cheap prints of London and a few books.

"He's gone," Oscar said. "Felix. Theo won't come out of her room. I couldn't open up all by myself."

Slowly, I got the full story out of him. "Felix went out not long after you left. I tried to stop him, but he said he'd beat my head in if I tried." Oscar winced. "Theo said he was probably headed for a tavern or the park, and he'd be back before too long. She was right, but when he returned, he said that he'd just come to collect his things, and then he was going for good. He tried to make Theo go with him, but she didn't want to. They had a right set-to, and then he just took his things and left."

I found Theo curled up on her counterpane, her face buried in her arms. "He might come back," I told her, gently rubbing her shoulder. "It's a hard world out there. He'll find that out."

She turned her reddened face to glare at me. "Why couldn't you have left him alone? Always on at him, you were. And now he's gone."

CHAPTER THIRTY-ONE

I SENT OSCAR to William's rooms with a note saying that I could not come that night, using Felix's departure as an excuse. I knew that he'd ask me about the money, and I couldn't bear to lie to him again.

Everything felt as if it was falling apart. I needed to set my mind to the things that really mattered. But the truth was, nothing mattered more to me than William.

Theo returned to work in the shop the following morning, but she answered me in monosyllables and was not much more loquacious with our customers. Even when I made an effort to cheer her up by telling her she could commission some pewter molds she'd begged me to buy so that she could try out a new idea, she hadn't smiled. All my customers were asking for new flavors of iced cream, which I hadn't had time to make. Thank heavens for Oscar, who had poured our strawberry iced cream into lobster molds, the conceit affording everyone much amusement.

"Thank you for everything," I told him, when we had a moment to catch our breath. "I'll make it up to you in your wages, I promise."

I expected another of his long-suffering sighs, but he only looked at me askance. "Mrs. Brunsden and Mrs. Fortnum came in earlier, while you were out back. I heard Mrs. Brunsden say that Mr. Fielding had been in to see them again. He was asking more questions about you and Mr. Cole. And about some underground river that flows under Piccadilly."

Against the prospect of William's betrayal, even the questions of my life and liberty had receded into the background. Another important matter that I was neglecting—and yet what could I do? I told myself that as long as I said or did nothing to incriminate myself, Fielding could prove nothing. "I imagine he's just being thorough."

Oscar's skeptical gaze fell on the hat in my hands. "You're going out again. People have been talking about that too. Theo heard them."

I didn't know which people, and it wouldn't serve me to ask. "Things will be back to normal again soon. I promise."

Of the two names and addresses the clerk at Chelsea had given me, the man injured in the explosion, Richard Britten, lived just down the road in Petty France. Yet the clerk had said that he'd been lucky to escape a court-martial himself, which raised considerable questions about his honesty. If William was innocent of that theft, then Britten might well be the guilty party. And if William was guilty—which I could hardly bear to think possible—then Britten might be his co-conspirator. Of course, the same might be true of Lieutenant George, the man who had been killed in the explosion, but surely a woman wouldn't lie to protect the man responsible for her husband's death?

Islington, where Lieutenant George's widow owned a tavern named the Pillars of Hercules, was about an hour's walk from Piccadilly. I headed through Mayfair, up to Tottenham Court, where I cut east across the fields to Battle Bridge. There I joined the Islington Road, which was thronged with farmers driving their herds into London for slaughter. Though the sun was fierce, there was a scent of rain on the air, and I wondered if the weather would break at last. I hoped it wouldn't dampen my customers' appetite for iced cream. Perhaps I could simply serve them warmer flavors? Coffee, cinnamon, chestnut, marmalade? Iced creams that people might enjoy even in winter?

On the edge of Islington, just past the galleried coaching inn named the Angel, the road forked. I took the upper of the two bustling streets that cut through the village, which was lined with houses and shops and a great many taverns and tea gardens. The Pillars of Hercules looked as if it had been standing there since its namesake walked the earth: the upper stories protruding over the street, casting a shadow over the door which was studded with iron. When I walked into the oak-paneled taproom, the patrons stared, perhaps taking me for a prostitute. Paintings of duck hunts and horse brasses covered the walls, the air thick with tobacco and a smell of fried food.

"This isn't your sort of establishment, miss," the woman behind the bar told me rather sternly.

"It's Mrs. Cole," I told her, crisply. "I'm looking for Mrs. Mary George."

Her features relaxed into a curious, assessing gaze. "That would be me."

Mrs. George's heart-shaped face was lightly lined, her fair hair turning silver, her knuckles already a little swollen with arthritis. Yet otherwise she wore the years well, her skin still taut, her eyes bright. If the tragedy of Tilbury had left scars, then they weren't visible upon her countenance.

"I was hoping to speak with you about a personal matter," I said.

She frowned. "What manner of personal matter?"

"It concerns a gentleman who once served with your late husband: William Everhart."

"I knew William," she said, after a moment. "Though I haven't seen him in a long time. Has something happened to him?"

I paused delicately. "Is it possible for us to talk somewhere more private?"

She studied me a moment longer, taking in my widow's purple. Perhaps the loss of my husband spoke to her, because she called out to a man of about thirty who had just come into the taproom with a tray of glasses. "Mind the bar, will you, Hal? I'll just be outside."

I followed her through a back room, where men were playing skittles. A door led out into a garden, which was much larger than one might have anticipated from the size of the tavern. Gravel walks intersected little squares of lawn, with a hexagonal pond at the center. More patrons sat out here, enjoying their beer in the sun, and Mrs. George led us to a table a discreet distance from the rest. I had already decided that the truth would serve me best here.

"I have recently made the acquaintance of a gentleman named William Devereux," I said. "I had only the highest regard for him and I believed him to be a man of honor. Yet recently I have come to suspect that the gentleman I know as Devereux is that same gentleman who once called himself William Everhart. It is important to me to understand why he might have lied about his background—especially given everything I have learned about his dishonorable discharge from the army."

Mrs. George gave a faint smile. "It must be nearly twenty years since I saw William last. He was my Stanley's commanding officer, though I only met him after my husband died." She sighed. "William was a great source of comfort to me and to Hal, in those sad days after the accident. If he has changed his name, then it does not altogether surprise me. He was in despair about the calumnies that had been heaped upon him."

"You mean the charges? Negligence? Theft?" I tried to still the flutter of hope in my heart.

"Such slanders," she said, with great feeling. "The cruelty poor William endured. It would have made a lesser man bitter, but he was determined to look to the future."

"Please, tell me everything," I said, with a catch in my voice.

Mrs. George massaged her knuckles while she talked. "During their time at Tilbury, William and my Stanley had come to believe that someone was robbing the gunpowder magazines and selling it to the local quarries. They suspected the governor was turning a blind eye and profiting personally from the crime, but they had no proof. That's what they were endeavoring to find on the night of the explosion. William risked his life trying to save my Stanley, but the roof collapsed before he could. He would have died himself, had a man named Britten, who'd been keeping watch, not dragged him out of there." She gazed into the distance. "William swallowed a lot of smoke. He was still in hospital when he was arrested. The governor must have known that they were on to him and decided to use the accident to take care of two problems at once. That's if it was an accident at all, rather than an attempt to silence William for good. There was no real proof of theft against him, of course, which was why he was acquitted. But because of the governor's lies and the stories he spread, few believed him innocent. Due to the strength of feeling amongst the ranks, the court felt they had to find him guilty of something, hence the charge of negligence. In the course of just a few months, William lost his commission, his friends, and his reputation."

Didn't this tale fit with the William I knew? An upright, diligent man? If William had been unfairly traduced, his character blackened, then of course he'd have wanted to change his name. He probably hadn't wanted to think about his soldiering days ever again.

But my head sounded a note of caution. "How do you know all of this?"

"William told me."

My heart sank. "Then you never had any proof that it was true?"

She studied me gravely. "I'm not sure what you're asking me. William Everhart wouldn't have lied to anyone, least of all to me. As I said, he was a godsend. I'm not sure I would have come through those days without him." She gazed at the ducks on the pond. "We still speak of him sometimes. Perhaps you could tell him that?"

I wanted to believe in William as faithfully as she did, but all sorts of suspicions crowded into my mind. Had she simply swallowed William's lies? Perhaps she was even another of his conquests? There was something about her darting gaze that made me wonder if there might be more to her story.

"Mrs. George, forgive me if this is a personal question, but did you ever lend or give William any money?"

She frowned. "You are right, that is a personal question. Look, I have said it before and I will say it again: William Everhart is as good a man as any I have ever met, one who deserved none of the misfortunes that came his way." Her color had risen.

"Who did you say it to before?" I asked. "Did someone else come here recently asking you about William?"

"Yes," she said. "A lady. She was looking for William, but I couldn't help her."

"Was her name Penelope Felton?"

Mrs. George looked surprised. "That's right. Do you know her too?"

"Somebody told me she was trying to find William in connection with a sum of money."

Mrs. George nodded. "I was sorry to disappoint her, as I had the impression that it might be to William's advantage. As it happens, she left me her card. Perhaps you could pass it on to him? And tell him that should he ever choose to visit us here, we will make him a warm welcome."

A sum of money to his advantage. That didn't sound in the least like the scenario I had most dreaded. Yet it was also possible that Mrs. Felton was lying herself, playing a cautious game. Only by speaking to her face-to-face would I know for certain. "Of course I will."

Mrs. George's expression brightened. "William deserves only luck after everything he's been through."

*

The address on the card Mrs. George had given me was for a lodging house in one of the anonymous, yet respectable streets north of High Holborn. It wouldn't take me long to walk there, and with every stride across the fields, I convinced myself that my fears had been unfounded. Mrs. George had said nothing to indicate that William was anything other than a slandered man. Those nerves I had detected in her could have had any number of causes. It couldn't have been easy for her, recalling the events of her husband's death. I would speak to Penelope Felton, just to reassure myself one final time, and then I would set aside my suspicions of William forever.

Gray's Inn Lane was busy with eminent-looking lawyers heading for the chophouses and taverns. I turned into another street, and then another, and soon I was standing before Mrs. Felton's lodging house. Despite all my earlier conviction, as I lifted the knocker, I felt only trepidation. An elderly woman came to the door, and she smiled when I said that I was there to see Mrs. Felton. "She has my best room. Let me take you up."

We climbed a flight of stairs to a landing, where the landlady knocked at a door. A refined voice called out that we might enter, and I walked into a comfortably furnished parlor. A lady in half-mourning dress, her black hair piled and pinned, rose to greet me.

"Mrs. Felton?" I said. "My name is Hannah Cole. I hear that you are looking for a man named William Everhart."

PART FOUR

The Drop

Thus is the prudence of the best of heads often defeated by the tenderness of the best of hearts.

Henry Fielding, *The History of Tom Jones, a Foundling*, 1749

CHAPTER THIRTY-TWO

I'VE ALWAYS HATED waiting. The narrow sense of it, like now, sitting in the Black Lion, waiting for Amy—when your mind can't help but turn to all the things that a job distracts you from. Like Hackney. My father and the millrace. My mother making iced cream, cold fingers stroking my hot cheek. I'd burned those letters from the madhouse, but certain phrases kept coming back to me. They hadn't said exactly how she'd died, but that didn't stop me from imagining. That's the trouble with an inventive mind: too many stories.

I hated the wider sense of waiting too. Especially the wait between the Rope and the Drop. When the money is almost yours, but not quite yet. People kept coming by my table to congratulate me: Sylvia; Crab Jack, who'd played the part of Mr. Bennett with such aplomb; the colonel (we all called him that, even though the only time he'd come close to military service was picking the pockets of the crowd during Trooping the Colour); and young Nazim, who'd only lost his lines once, which wasn't half-bad for a debut. I was curt in response to their compliments. Don't oil the skewer while your rabbit is still in the woods. Though looking at things purely objectively, I had to admit that the Rope had gone pretty well.

The irony of that moment of madness in Hannah's rooms, when she'd kissed me and I'd walked away, was that it had served me well. By the time I saw her again, at the ice house, she was so pliant with loss and longing, it had been the work of a moment to get her into bed. I'd told Tom all about it: how she hooded her eyes and stifled her sighs, how she cried out to God when I took her to the brink and held her there.

He'd grinned. "Your cockstand earns its due, I'll give you that."

I didn't tell Tom how she'd looked afterwards in the candlelight, so exposed, so vulnerable, back to being afraid it was all a seduction and now I'd discard her. How even as I'd built her confidence back up, there was a part of her that remained unknowable, a missing piece that I couldn't quite put my finger on. Sometimes, when she'd talk about herself so frankly, or gaze at me with unabashed lust, or come out with one of those bold comments that made me laugh, I'd wonder if I'd imagined it. But it was always there, a lurking shadow, just out of reach.

Occasionally she said things that caught me off-guard. "Life leaves scars on the soul as well as the body," she'd told me once, as she'd traced the line of knitted tissue on my knee. "Do you ever wish that you could dream them away? I know I do."

"It's the knocks that make up a man," I'd told her blithely.

"Perhaps," she'd said. "But sometimes I wish I could remember the woman I was before the knocks. I think that I'd like to have been that person more."

I'd thought about that afterwards. Maybe I shouldn't have. But I did.

Hannah's unplumbed depths might have occasioned me more concern, but I was in no doubt about her feelings. I'd never told her that I loved her, never said those words out loud to any woman—not since Hackney. I don't know why—after all, it's just one lie like any other—but there you are. She hadn't said it either, but like I said, she didn't need to. A man knows when a woman looks at him like that.

I didn't tell Tom how it gnawed at me. Seeing her in the shop, all flushed with her success. Imagining her sitting in some dark little house, having lost the shop because of me. I'd mulled on it for days, trying to think of a different way.

"Maybe I could run a second job," I'd said to Tom eventually. "Give the proceeds to Musgrave, and leave Hannah a hundred like we planned?"

He'd looked at me like I was mad. "We don't have time for that, Bill.

Nor the money to set it up. And how could you possibly run two jobs at once?"

He was right, of course. Time really was pressing. A week or so after his first visit, Patrick Musgrave had paid me another.

"Where's my money, Billy-boy?" he'd asked me softly, while his golems had clomped about in the background.

"I'm nearly there," I'd said. "I just need a little longer."

"Not too much longer," he said. "I'd hate for us to part company on bad terms."

I didn't have to guess what he meant.

After his first visit, when Musgrave had told me that he hadn't killed Cole, I'd wondered if he was telling me the truth. That alibi might have been cogged, and if I could prove it, then it might be a route out of all this mess. After all, if Musgrave swung for murder, he could hardly come after me for his four hundred pounds. Take it as a mark of my discomfort about Hannah, that I was even considering this.

In any event, I'd decided to have another chat with Cole's co-conspirator, Mitford Banks. I'd gone back down to the courthouse, where I'd discovered Banks hadn't come into work for a couple of days. A bad feeling had crept over me, and I'd spun them a yarn about a lottery win to obtain his address. I'd knocked at the door of his rooms in Fetter Lane, but there was no reply. Eventually, I'd jigged the lock and as I'd walked into his parlor, the smell hit me. I found Banks laid out on his bed covered in flies. Musgrave hadn't crucified him, like the stories said. He'd skinned that poor fuckster alive.

I presumed that meant Banks was in on Cole's double-dealing. It made me think that Fielding might be right to believe that Musgrave hadn't killed Cole. After all, if Musgrave had known about the thefts back then, then why hadn't he gone after Banks before? Why hadn't Cole been tortured to death to send a message, rather than bludgeoned about the head? Thinking of Musgrave's spies in Fielding's office, I hoped to God he hadn't found his way to Banks through anything I'd said or done. I could still taste that smell, still hear the feasting of the flies.

If anything had concentrated my mind on the job, then it was that.

What other choice did I have? Musgrave didn't make threats lightly. If I let him down, then nowhere in England would be safe for me. I'd have to leave the country for good—leave Tom and Amy and all my friends. Wander the continent forever like a damn Gypsy.

All our tricks had played out like a charm: Arcadia, implausible profits, the world dying to get in on the act. A greedy woman would have been begging William Devereux to pull some strings and get her a piece of it. But Hannah was more cautious, and so at Lord Richard's supper, we'd played a longer game, the Rope unfurling loop by loop to draw her in. Money as a means to an end. The house next door, a bigger shop. Then opportunity: an impounded ship, a vast reward there for the taking. Yet deep down, I think I already knew that she wouldn't bite. Which was why I'd decided to put the boy in play.

Darling Teddy. Tom had found that little angel at Covent Garden, begging with a woman who claimed to be his mother. I suspected she'd bought or hired him, and she was eager enough to sublet him to us for the right price. Older than he looked, already a skilled little prig, he'd done everything we'd asked and more. When Hannah had held him in her arms in the gardens of that mansion at Kensington Gore, I'd known this would be our Rope if Arcadia failed. Dreams again. Motherhood and me. I'm not sure I'd even needed that big house. I could have taken her to a little cottage on Well Walk and she'd have reacted just the same. That night I'd dreamed of my mother hunched in a cell, chained to the wall—and when she'd looked at me, she had the eyes of Hannah Cole.

Despite everything—Hackney, Mitford Banks, Patrick Musgrave, the taste of that fucking iced cream—I'd only come close to losing it once. That night when Hannah had watched me in the mirror and caught sight of my mood.

"We could live anywhere in the world," I'd said, and in that moment, I think I'd meant it. Just her and me, far away from Musgrave and the Black Lion and Tom and Amy and Henry Fielding. It was impossible, of course, even if I'd really wanted it, which was a joke. Hannah was my gull, my mark, flat as the fens—see how she danced! Yet my indiscipline that night had shocked me and I'd resolved no more.

Two days later, when I'd fashioned my noose—poor Teddy and his wicked mother, set to whisk him off to Ireland into the hands of his brutal stepfather—Hannah had slipped her neck quite readily into it. But I'd barely had time to relish the moment, before my encounter in the street with that royal fuckster, David Thewson. I'd seen the doubt on Hannah's face and my heart had sunk. The very next night she lied to me, told me that probate had been delayed. My clerk at the court duly informed me that this was horseshit, and it had made for an anxious couple of days. Which was why I was waiting now, in the Black Lion, in such a foul temper. Everything hinged upon this play. The Drop, the money, my life. I didn't want to wind up covered in flies, stinking up the place.

At last, across the taproom, I glimpsed Amy coming through the crowd, Tom behind her. His girl, Beth, had done a good job dressing Amy's hair. She wore half-mourning dress and gloves, not too many stones. Amy had always passed well for a lady, albeit one who didn't bear the slightest resemblance to Penelope Felton. She lowered her face for a kiss. "Not even a bow? Where's your manners?"

"Did she come?" I said, rather roughly.

Amy smiled slyly. "She came."

"And?" I said, still too loud in my agitation.

"Would I ever let you down? She swallowed the lot."

CHAPTER THIRTY-THREE

Hannah's determination was one of the things I liked best about her. There was an iron will there, beneath the softness and the smiles, that I was only just now starting to appreciate. Following our encounter with David Thewson, after she'd lied to me about probate, I'd planned to spin her some yarn about changing my name to assuage her doubts. Give her another day with Teddy, perhaps, to help make up her mind.

Except that the very next day, I'd discovered that things were far worse than I'd thought. I'd left my rooms about ten, and strolled down to the Black Lion to meet Tom. I filled him in on David Thewson and the story I planned to tell Hannah, assuring him that everything was in hand. He'd got that murderous look on his face again, which was getting as dull as David Thewson. "I'm starting to think this job is cursed," he'd muttered.

Across the taproom, Amy was flirting with a rather handsome African, a former footman who worked the blue pigeon lay, stealing lead from off church roofs. I had no doubt that the flirting was for my benefit. What with everything that had been going on with Hannah, I hadn't felt up to much with Amy lately. Turning back to Tom, I was in the middle of talking him round, when I noticed Felix watching us from the bar, a slight smile on his face. He raised his pot of ale in greeting, strolled up to us, cool as Edinburgh, and sat himself down.

Jesus. I almost spilled my porter. Tom's arm slipped inside his coat, where he kept his blade.

"Felix," I cried, betraying no hint of my alarm. "I was just buying Tom here a drink. He tells me this is his favorite tavern. Rather a colorful place, but it has a certain charm."

He gave me a scornful smile. "She's on to you."

Tom and I exchanged a glance. "How do you mean?" I said.

"You put on quite an act. But don't think you have me fooled. I'll warrant you're no more a gentleman than I am. And he's not your coachman, he's your accomplice. You're out to rob her blind."

It was like that scene in Norwich with Tom all over again. But like Tom, Felix wouldn't be here if he wasn't prepared to agree to terms.

"You seem to think you know an awful lot."

"I listen at doors, don't I? That's how I found out about her money. Seems a big coincidence, you showing up just then. Especially what with all the questions he's been asking." He nodded at Tom. "So the other day, I followed you here. Asked around, found out what sort of place it was. This where you come to do all your charity work, is it, sir?" He grinned.

Refusing to panic, I kept my mind on the prize that mattered. "What did you mean when you said she was on to us?"

"Exactly that. She questioned me this morning, asked me what I made of you. Whether I thought you was taking her for a fool, that sort of thing. Then she went off in a hackney carriage."

"Do you know where she was going?"

He gave me a long look. "The question you should be asking, is what did I say to Mrs. C about you and your intentions?"

"I'm guessing nothing yet."

He nodded. "Yet."

I glanced at Tom. His instinct in these situations is usually that a beating serves as better dissuasion than a bribe. Have I mentioned yet that he has a ruthless streak? But I rather liked Felix. He had potential, and I'm not one to crush a young man's dreams. I produced a half-crown from between my fingers. "Might this prove an adequate inducement?"

Felix laughed. "I won't take less than three guineas. There's a man I know has a monkey for sale. Does tricks and dances too. For three yellowboys, he'll throw in his hurdy-gurdy. Reckons I'll triple my money by Christmas."

The monkey was probably diseased and the hurdy-gurdy played flat, but Felix's silence was cheap at the price. It didn't stop me resenting it, watching my profit get smaller and smaller.

"Does your sister know?" I asked, while the lad was pocketing his coins.

He shook his head. "She's a bigger gull than Mrs. C. Thinks you're good for her. Says it's romantic."

"Keep it that way," I said. "So do you know where Mrs. Cole went this morning?"

"Chelsea," he said. "The Royal Hospital. That's what she said to the hackney driver anyway."

I thought for a moment. "She must have talked to Thewson," I said to Tom. "How else would she know I was once a soldier?"

"Then by now she's probably learned how that episode ended," Tom said grimly. "She'll be heading for the same places as that Felton bitch. Dick Britten. Mary George."

"Mary's a good girl," I said. "She won't let us down."

Nor would she. Tilbury had been a sorry business, all told, but Mary had never blamed me. We'd made good money on the black spice lay, her Stanley, Dick, and me. Until the governor had got wind of it and started asking too many questions. We'd been trying to move the gunpowder out in a hurry, when the explosion happened. The evidence against me had been rather damning, but Dick had held his tongue, and I'd talked the court-martial round. A dishonorable discharge for negligence was a good outcome under the circumstances. I'd been to see Mary afterwards, to give her some money to keep her sweet. She asked me to stay for supper, and I ended up staying six months. I know what you're thinking: that I robbed her blind as well. Well, you're wrong. I could have, but I didn't. She was Stanley's missus, and I'm sentimental like that. It did give me professional inspiration, though, and I'll always be grateful to her for that. She'd do anything for me, would Mary. And she made a far more convincing advocate for my trustworthiness than that old drunk, Dick Britten, who could never keep a story straight in his head for long.

"Mrs C asked me something else too," Felix said. "Wanted to know if you'd ever mentioned some lady who was trying to find you. Something to do with some blunt."

Tom and I exchanged another glance. "Penelope Felton," I said.

"That's her." Felix grinned. "Can't think why she might be after you."

Gesturing to Tom that we shouldn't panic, I took a moment to judge the angles. Felix sat watching us, a look of interest upon his face. The initiative he had shown was rather impressive. He also had that hard-headed edge—that a soft-hearted man like me needed from time to time. Or at least, he looked as if he could fake it, which is often enough.

"Tom here is leaving me in a couple of weeks," I said. "Do you think you could do what he does? Dress up? Drive me around? There's better money in the widow lay than in dancing monkeys." I grinned. "Though there're similarities between the two, I won't deny it."

Did I mean it? I'm not sure. Perhaps I just wanted to show Tom how easily I might replace him.

Felix thought for a moment. "Nah, you're all right."

"Can I ask why not?" I said, a little surprised.

He shrugged. "I'm doing this because I don't want to mop her floors no more. But there's better ways to make a living than what you do."

After he'd departed, pockets jingling, I raised my eyebrows at Tom. "It seems even vagabonds find us morally wanting."

"Never mind him," Tom said. "What do we do about Mrs. Cole? Her and Felton are cut from the same cloth. Stubborn fuckstresses, the pair of them. What if she goes looking for Felton in London? Tracks her down?"

Tom was right, of course. Hannah was a force. If she did find Penny, then it would put paid to everything. I thought of Musgrave's yellow smile, the buzz of those flies.

Amy's laughter was distracting me. Still flirting with her African. He had one hand on her knee, unfamiliar with her games. If it was my attention that she was after, she suddenly had it.

"Tom," I said, "I've got an idea."

*

It proved relatively easy to set it all up. That morning we rented the room, and then I went off to Islington to remind Mary George how much she liked me. She agreed to give Hannah a card with the address of "Penny's" lodgings in London and we were good to get on. Tom and I had come up with a story that would weave together all the lies I'd told Hannah into a new tale that would provide a pretty explanation for the uglier truths she'd ferreted out. We installed Amy at the lodging house, all dressed up in gray and lavender silk—and settled down to wait.

"You should have seen her face when she came in," Amy told me now in the Black Lion. "Her eyes all big and round, looking sick with nerves. You didn't tell me she was pretty, Bill."

"I hadn't noticed."

"Liar. She told me why she had come and I acted all serious, like we said. Invited her to sit and take tea and cake and away I went." She put on her best Mayfair voice. "'I have been searching for William Everhart for several months,' I said. 'I wish to return to him a bundle of letters that he wrote to my late sister. I also need to tell him that she went to her grave knowing that she was wrong. That at the end, William occupied a place in her heart.'"

"What did she say to that?" I said.

"Asked how my sister had been wrong, of course. 'Eliza fell in love with William Everhart many years ago,' I said. 'He was then a broker upon the Exchange, making his way in the world. Our parents did not approve of the match, but my sister begged them to reconsider, and between us we convinced them to assent to an engagement. A few weeks prior to their marriage, William told my sister that he had once been dishonorably discharged as an army officer. Though he told her that the charges against him had been unjust, my sister was disturbed by this information and confided in our father. He looked into the matter, and became convinced that not only was William a bounder, he was also a thief. He ordered Eliza to break off the engagement, and though it broke her heart to do so, this she did.'"

"And?" I said sharply, when Amy paused for breath.

"Mrs. Cole breathed very deeply and said: 'I too have heard these rumors. Do you mean to say that William's detractors were wrong?'"

I could picture Hannah saying it, her eagerness to believe.

"'As wrong as anyone ever was,' I said. 'We only learned it years later, when my sister encountered another officer who had served with William. This gentleman told her that it was the governor of the fort who had manufactured the charges against him. That men he knew had been bribed to tell lies about William at the court-martial. That he regretted deeply his own part in the matter, in believing those lies, and how he wished he could find William to make amends.' When I said it, Mrs. Cole clasped her hands together, looking like she might piss herself with happiness. 'I confess I doubted him too. How wrong I was.'"

"Did you give her the letters?" I asked.

"She read them right in front of me, even brushed away a tear."

I'd taken my time over those letters. If I couldn't convince Hannah to her face, the written word was the next best thing. Of course, those words were designed to appeal to Hannah and her doubts and her conscience, as much as to their fictional recipient.

Every night as I try to sleep, I hear your cold speech all over again, remembering the suspicion in your eyes. To know that you went behind my back, spoke words of deception to my face—that you did not trust me—I cannot reconcile any of this with the woman I love. Upon my word as a gentleman, I am an innocent man, unfairly maligned. Those acts of betrayal committed against me by men I called my friends were the worst of crimes. To be shunned, humiliated, my name traduced in public—I thought little could be worse. Yet that pain is as nothing compared to the torment I suffer now. That you believe those lies, despite the love we shared, is the cruelest wound of all.

There was very much more in the same vein. My anger at the governor who'd destroyed my life, more heartfelt pleas that Eliza believe me, despair and regret:

You ask why I did not call those men out, as a man of honor must. The truth is, I blamed myself for everything that had happened to poor Stanley and Richard, good men under my command. I had no desire to see yet more blood and suffering, more children orphaned by my own hand. How I regret that mercy now. I would kill a hundred men in defense of my honor, if it would bring you back to me.

"Women like a man who would kill for the lady he loves," Amy had said.

Are the rumors true? That you are to marry HIM? I fear that they are. I shall not be there to witness it, worry not. I leave for India tomorrow, a distance yet smaller than that which now exists between us. And if I shall never give another man the opportunity to besmirch my honor again, nor will I ever permit another woman to capture my heart. I struggle to accept that I have lost you, dearest Eliza. But I know that I must.

Amy moistened her lower lip with her tongue. "I told her: 'My sister died knowing that her suspicions had destroyed her one chance of happiness. She regretted it until the end of her days. Her guilt at the hurt she'd caused William is hard to comprehend.' And then, get this, Mrs. Cole said: 'I understand now why he did not tell me the full story about his past. Because he once trusted a woman he loved and he lost her forever. I don't wonder that he changed his name. Who wouldn't want a new life after all that pain?' Just like you said, Bill. She danced and danced. I gave her the letters to give to you. Do you think she will? No lady likes her man to be reminded of his lost love. I'd just burn them."

"I doubt it," I said. "She'd have to explain how she found Felton, which means admitting she didn't trust me. Did she ask you about the money?"

"Of course." Amy smiled rather contemptuously. "I said my sister had left William fifty pounds in her will, but that I doubted he would ever take it, for despite his financial talents, he had never been overly motivated by money."

"You sweet beauty."

Amy preened, leaning in for another kiss. "With any luck, she'll be running to her bank as we speak."

"Luck? What's that?" I grinned. "I owe you one, Amy."

"You certainly do," she said, moving my hand onto her breast. "There's a room free upstairs. I already checked."

"I can't," I said, pulling away. "*Carpe diem*, and all that. Mrs. Cole will be waiting to show me how sorry she is."

Amy's smile faded. "It's been over two weeks. What's up with you?"

She was looking at me like I had another girl on the bounce. I decided to tell her the truth—it was better than her imaginings. "It's just this job. Taking the lot. I don't relish doing it, that's all. I like to leave my widows better off, not worse."

She stared at me incredulously. "You don't really believe that, do you? I thought it was just one of your jokes. Jesus, Billy, you break their fucking hearts."

CHAPTER THIRTY-FOUR

RATHER TO MY surprise, Hannah did not come to my rooms that night. Presuming that she was feeling too guilty to face me, the next morning I decided to call in at the shop. A few minutes of my smiles, and she'd soon forget her shame. After all my success yesterday, I ought to have felt as buoyant as a bubble in a glass of champagne—but I felt only a bleak sense of inevitability. I blamed Patrick Musgrave for that. And Henry Fielding and Penelope Felton and Tom for his imminent desertion and Amy for her unkind comment and even that little fuckster, Felix. *There's better ways to make a living than what you do.* Well, good luck with that, I thought savagely. He'd be begging on the street within six months, and unlike darling Teddy, a face like his wouldn't keep you fed and warm.

As soon as I got my hands on the blunt, I'd pay Musgrave and my people, and get out of London for the rest of the year. Bohemia was supposed to be nice. Not too hot, not too cold, plenty of widows come to take the waters. I could earn my way as a puff at the gaming tables, until I found the right woman. Then I'd return to London in the spring, when it would be ripe with fresh fruit. Surely Penelope Felton would have given up by then? As for Hannah, I'd tell her by letter. I knew her face would stick with me if I told her in person that she'd lost all of her money. Hannah would soon find somebody else. Not some cunt like Jonas Cole, someone who'd make her laugh like I had done. A widower, one with children. She'd enjoy motherhood, without the distraction of her shop.

When I arrived at the Punchbowl and Pineapple, I was surprised to see no queues outside and when I tried the door, it wouldn't open. Through the window, I could see someone moving around inside, and I knocked on it, gesticulating that I wanted to be let in.

A large man with a bald head opened the door. "The place is closed. Order of Bow Street."

Behind him, I could see Hannah, sitting at a table at the rear of the shop, another man, presumably a second constable, standing over her. My heart sank.

"Is Henry Fielding here?"

The man nodded. "Upstairs."

I adopted my most peremptory tone: "I wish to speak with him. Permit me entrance, my good man, or you'll be sorry for it."

Before he could reply, I pushed past him. When Hannah caught sight of me, her mouth twisted in distress. "Don't worry," I told her. "I'll deal with everything."

Ignoring the constables' objections, I mounted the stairs two at a time. Theo and Oscar were in Hannah's parlor, seated upon the sofa. Fielding was standing over them, drawn up to his full, impressive height. He broke off when I walked in. "Mr. Devereux, can I help you, sir?"

"I'm intrigued to know what is going on here, Mr. Fielding."

"I'm questioning these children in connection with the murder of Jonas Cole. I think they know rather more than they are telling. Perhaps much more."

Oscar was sniffling softly. Theo appeared to be holding herself together, but only just.

I was ambivalent about the fate of Hannah's apprentices, but it was a distraction I didn't need. If I was to get my hands on Hannah's money, then I needed to get Fielding out of the house.

"Can't this wait?" I said. "Mrs. Cole is losing money every minute her shop is closed."

"I'm afraid it cannot," Fielding said. "This girl's brother has run off. Probably got nervous because I questioned him before. I have to ask myself what made him so skittish. Either he knows something, or he killed Jonas Cole himself."

His interest in Felix alarmed me. If Fielding caught up with the lad, there was a risk that he'd tell the magistrate all about me.

"Then may I watch?" That way at least I'd know what Fielding knew. Perhaps I could find the boy first and warn him. "I have heard of your great talents at eliciting a confession."

Fielding allowed himself a small smile. Self-regarding fuckster. "Very well, but I do ask that you keep quiet. There is an art to unraveling a lie. Please observe." He dropped his gaze to Theo, who flinched under his scrutiny. "As I was saying, you cannot expect me to believe that you have no idea where your brother might be?"

She glared, eyes like little gray pebbles. "I don't. That's the truth."

"But you know something. I can see it. Did your brother kill Jonas Cole?"

"No!" Theo cried.

Fielding raised his voice. "Then why did he run, girl?"

"He didn't like it here no more. There was too much work to do."

Fielding studied her face. "I don't believe you. Was that why you lied about your conversation with Mr. Cole? When you said you'd seen that blue carriage? Were you trying to pull the wool over my eyes?"

"I didn't lie," she said. "Mr. Cole asked if I'd seen that carriage, and that's what I told him."

"I've been to the workhouse," Fielding said. "And to your old neighborhood, where you lived when your parents were still alive. Everyone remembers your brother. Terror of the parish, I'm told. Fighting, pilfering, perhaps much worse. Felix didn't think much of Mr. Cole, I've heard. There were hard words, beatings—he wouldn't be the first apprentice to do away with his master." He drew a breath. "If you don't help me, Theodora, I will scour London until I find him. He won't be such a terror on his hanging day. The toughest ones often weep, did you know that?"

Theo stared at him mutely, her face white. I could see she was about to break.

"I put it to you that there never was any blue carriage. It was a fabrication to protect the guilty party. Confess, girl. Or it will be the worse for you and your brother."

Theo wrapped her arms tightly around herself. "I didn't mean to lie. Not to you. Only to Mr. Cole."

Fielding gave me a swift smile of satisfaction. "Explain yourself."

Between sobs and gulps, he got the story out of her. "One night back in February, Mrs. C took Felix, Oscar, and me to an evening service at St. James's. Only I felt sick, and she said that I could go home. I came in the back way, and I heard talking in the shop. Mr. Cole was in there with another man. I could tell from their voices that they was discussing something serious. Mr. Cole thought they'd been found out in something bad, though the other man said he was imagining things. I listened in case it might affect things for Felix and me. Mr. Cole said he thought he was being watched. He told the other man to look out for a dark blue carriage with brass trim. He seemed to think the owner of that carriage had it in for him. So when he asked me, I told him that I'd seen it outside the shop. But I hadn't. I made it all up."

"It's as I thought," Fielding declared, with another glance at me. "I have been unable to find a scrap of evidence to suggest that the owners of these gaming houses ever even realized they'd been robbed. In view of that, I now believe that the motive for his murder lies closer to home." He glowered at the weeping girl. "Why did you lie to Cole when he asked you about that carriage?"

"Because I didn't like him," she said, with another gulp. "He was mean to me and Felix and he was mean to Mrs. C. He never had a kind word to say about anyone, even Oscar. And he gave Felix a thrashing just for breaking a mixing bowl. I wanted to scare him. That's all."

Jesus, I thought. It was all in Cole's head. Some men get like that, no nerve, can't front it out. They turn into their own worst enemies—though to Cole's mind, no enemy was as bad as Patrick Musgrave. I wondered if the man he had been talking to was poor Mitford Banks.

"Perhaps your initial presumption was correct?" I suggested. "Cole's death was the product of a simple street robbery."

But Fielding wasn't so easily diverted. He turned to Oscar, whose face was slick with tears and sweat and snot. "You didn't like your master either, that much is clear. Was it you who killed him?"

Oscar let out a wrenching sob. "No, sir."

"But I think you know who did. You are protecting the guilty party."

"No, I would tell you if Felix had done it."

"Mr. Fielding," I said, "I can assure you that there was little love lost between those two boys. And Oscar is a very honest lad. If Felix was the guilty party, he'd certainly tell you."

"I'm not talking about Felix," Fielding said.

Oh, Christ. Realization hit me like a hay wagon. Fielding wasn't after the children at all—he was after Hannah. What a damned fool I'd been, thinking I'd closed that suspicion down. "Mr. Fielding—"

"Quiet, sir. I want to hear what this boy has to say. I remind you, young man, that you can hang for perverting the course of justice. That includes concealing what you know, what you saw, what you suspect. Anything you're hiding, I will find it out. And if you've been less than honest, it will go the worse for you. What will your parents think, eh? When they learn you protected a murderer? That you mired them in scandal? Cost them their business? They'll curse the day your mother brought you into this world."

Oscar's words came out in a shuddering gasp: "The cellar floor."

"What about it?" Fielding said.

The boy spoke very fast, as if to expel the words all at once. "The morning after that night—when Mr. Cole went out and never came home—I rose at five o'clock as usual, and went downstairs to the kitchen. I lit the ovens, which Felix was supposed to do before I got up, but he never did. I had to go down to the cellar to fetch some coal. Felix was supposed to clean the cellar floor too, so I expected to find it covered in flour and footprints. But that morning it was clean."

"What did you make of that?" Fielding asked.

"I thought it odd, that's all. I asked Felix when he came down, but he said he hadn't done it. Neither had Theo. So I asked Mrs. C, and she said she'd done it before she came to bed."

"Now hang on a minute, Mr. Fielding," I said. "A clean floor is hardly evidence of murder."

"What else?" Fielding barked, his eyes still on Oscar.

The boy drew another fraught breath. "Two days later, down in the cellar, I moved a sack of flour. There was something lying behind it, on the floor."

Fielding leaned forward. "What was it, boy?"

Oscar wiped his face with his sleeve. "A tooth. It was bloodied. I threw it away."

I stared at him. Could it be true? Had Hannah killed Jonas?

Fielding nodded, his face grim, eyes bright with satisfaction. Then he strode to the door. I hurried after him down the stairs, the sobs of the apprentices diminishing behind us. Fielding strode into the shop and Hannah quailed before his expression.

"Mrs. Cole," he declared, "I am arresting you on suspicion of your husband's murder."

CHAPTER THIRTY-FIVE

Hannah's face was ashen as Fielding's constables dragged her into their carriage. Nobody listened to my protests, one of the constables shoving me back. People came out of the shops and houses to watch. The carriage moved off and I stared after it, despair crushing my viscera. How could I have missed that Fielding still suspected her? Too much distraction. Because of Musgrave. Because of Hackney. Because of Hannah.

I ran all the way to Bow Street, my breathing labored, my chest tight. The air had an edge to it, metallic and sharp, a pewter sky. Before I reached Fielding's house, the first drops began to fall. I sat in his waiting room for almost six hours, listening to the rattle of rain against the windows. Every time I enquired, Fielding's clerk informed me ever more curtly that his master was busy and would see me as soon as he could. I paced the room, my stomach a knot.

When eventually I was shown into Fielding's study, I thought he looked tired. Presumably he'd spent the last hours interrogating Hannah. I'd already seen that he was good at it. The way he tripped people up with their lies, or sensed what would break them.

"You've made a terrible mistake," I told him, still uncertain whether he had or not.

He gave me a sympathetic smile. "I am sure I would feel that way too in your shoes. It must be hard to accept that the woman you love could have committed so terrible a crime."

At my insistence, he took me through his theory: how he believed

Hannah had discovered her husband's affair and his plan to run off to Scotland. How Jonas had intended to sell her shop, which had sent Hannah over the edge. How she'd beat him to death in the cellar with her ice mallet, and then dropped him down an old well into the river. I had to admit, it was a compelling tale, though the evidence was entirely circumstantial.

Guilty or innocent, I had no moral qualms about talking Fielding into letting her go. As far as I was concerned, Jonas had deserved everything he'd got. My heart was racing, and not just at the thought of losing her money. Hannah's lovely neck in a noose. No metaphors, an actual fucking noose. I'd been to many hanging days—the Black Lion always turned out for one of our own. The hood, the drop into darkness, that sickening crack. I refused to let it happen. Not to her.

"Had you been the one to tell her about the mistress, you would not believe this for a moment," I told Fielding. "I saw her face. She was astonished, distraught."

"I don't doubt that she's a good actress," Fielding said.

If she was guilty, then she certainly was. I was still struggling with the very idea.

"We all know how badly you need an arrest in this case," I said. "Don't make poor Mrs. Cole pay the price of it."

He frowned. "You think I would hang an innocent woman to suit my own convenience?"

Careful, Billy, I cautioned myself, endeavoring to speak more calmly. "I simply think you are laboring under a delusion."

Fielding sighed. "I understand your passion, sir, but I fear it is you who has been manipulated and deceived. A good man is always vulnerable to the persuasions of a Delilah. Unwittingly, you've been recruited to Mrs. Cole's cause. I should warn you that her neighbors have paid attention to her movements of late. Going off in your carriage. Late-night visits, coming home at all hours. I'm afraid that it may come out in court."

His judgmental gaze told me that he still saw Hannah and me as a mirror of all that had happened between him and his wife. Yet that mirror no longer reflected the golden light of star-cross'd lovers, but rather the darker reflection of all his second thoughts: a tale of unbridled passion, poor judgment, and duty shirked.

"To love again after loss is not a crime," I said, rather pointedly. "I know Hannah. She's not capable of murder."

"Do you know what I believe?" Fielding said. "That any one of us is capable of acts of great wickedness under the right circumstances. I speak from experience here. When I was a youth, I became infatuated with my young cousin. Her guardian would not consider my suit, and so one day, I attempted to abduct her on her way to church. It was as if I was consumed by madness. Another man entirely. Had I not learned to master my passions, I might have ended up in a hangman's noose myself. Confronted by her husband's cruel design, I believe Mrs. Cole was gripped by a terrible rage. Perhaps she told herself afterwards that the person who committed this deed was akin to a stranger. A possession of body and spirit. I know I did."

For Christ's sake. He was going to hang Hannah because, a hundred years ago, he'd had a cockstand for his cousin?

"You have no evidence, only a theory," I told him. "One boy's story about a tooth, that may not even have belonged to Jonas Cole."

"She will confess, I know she will," Fielding said. "If not today, then tomorrow. My constables are searching her house as we speak. I believe Mrs. Cole kept her grandfather's watch, you see. I think it's hidden somewhere in that house. And when we find it, she will admit to everything. Perhaps then you will accept the truth."

Then Hannah had admitted to nothing yet. That gave me hope. She was tough, I told myself, perhaps more than I'd ever imagined. Yet even the hardest of men could be induced to confess. When they were tired, or manipulated, or they just wanted the questions to stop.

"Go home, sir," Fielding went on. "Try to get some rest. Do your utmost to forget Hannah Cole. This is a blessing, even if you cannot see it yet."

*

I knew they'd be holding Hannah in the cellar of the Brown Bear tavern, opposite Fielding's house. It had been used for years by the Bow Street magistrates as a temporary prison, to hold villains before their transfer to Bridewell or Newgate. The tavern was also where Fielding's constables liked to drink, and I normally gave the place a very wide berth. Not today. I strode through the taproom, rain dripping from my hat, and descended the stairs. In the first room of the cellar, I found the jailer, reading a lewd pamphlet by the light of a lantern. A number of doors reinforced by iron led into the cells, and there was a warren of other rooms and cells further back. From behind one of the doors, somebody groaned.

"I'd like to see Hannah Cole," I told the jailer.

"She's not allowed visitors," he said. "Mr. Fielding's orders."

I produced a guinea, more than he'd earn in a week. "I say differently. Order of King George."

The man hesitated a moment, before his greed got the better of him. He bit my coin, and then slipped it into his pocket. Rising, he took out his keys and unlocked one of the cell doors. "Five minutes," he said, showing me the truncheon on his belt. "There's no way out except past me, so don't go getting gallant."

When I entered the cell and saw Hannah sitting there in the dark, something seemed to tear inside me. A manacle around one wrist chained her to the wall. A grating near to the ceiling afforded a glimpse of black sky. Lightning flashed, illuminating her drawn face. It was like that scene from my dream. My mother, Hannah's eyes.

"Fielding means to hang me," was all she said.

Kneeling, I took her in my arms. "I won't let him do it," I told her fiercely. "I'm going to get you out. But in the meantime, you must admit to nothing, do you understand me? Fielding's constables are searching your house for Jonas's watch. When they don't find it, he'll have to let you go." I hesitated. "But if there is any truth to his suspicions at all, then you have to trust me. I need you to tell me where that watch is."

She gazed at me for a long time and when she spoke, her words were a whisper: "In my ice tub. In the well. Down in the cellar."

I stared at her lovely face, imagining her wielding that mallet. Accepting it took some doing, even then. I recalled that shadowy part of her that I'd never quite been able to understand. Her reticence when

I'd tried to discuss marriage. Her reckless abandonment in the face of this gathering storm.

She'd lied to me over and over. Me, who prided myself on the art of a lie. Used me to point Fielding in the wrong direction. I had to hand it to her, it was nicely done. But she'd lost her heart, despite herself. That must have been a struggle. However good she thought she was, I was better.

"I'll get it," I said. "The watch. Just tell me how."

CHAPTER THIRTY-SIX

I STOOD IN the doorway of the lace emporium opposite Hannah's shop, sheltering from the rain. My hat was pulled down low, and I'd dressed as a laboring man to explain the large sack at my feet. I was pretending to smoke a pipe, but in reality, I was watching the place. It was after two in the morning, but the lamps were lit, and I could see constables moving about upstairs and down. I saw no sign of Theo or Oscar, and I imagined Fielding had thrown them out, so they wouldn't interfere with the constables' search. From the look of it, they were going to keep at it until they found the watch. Which left me only one choice.

Walking swiftly, I headed down St. James's Street to the entrance to the alley at the back of Hannah's house. I walked along it until I reached the door to the yard of the house next door. Slipping my hand over the top of the gate, I released the latch and let myself into the yard. Hannah had told me that the man who owned the place, a taxidermist, had died six months ago. His nephew had immediately offered the house and shop for sale, but he evidently hadn't received a satisfactory offer, because the place was still empty. Crouched in the darkness by the back door, I worked away, getting soaked to the skin, jigging the lock. Eventually it gave with a satisfying snap.

Only when I was inside did I light the bull's-eye lantern in my sack. Directing the aperture away from the window, I almost collapsed from heart failure on the spot. About fifty pairs of eyes were picked out in the beam of light, staring at me from the shadows of the room. Stuffed foxes, squirrels, and the like, all gathering dust on the shelves. Hannah had said that she and Jonas had viewed the house years ago, the last time it was up for sale. The place had the same layout as her own house, and there was another old well down in the cellar. I made my way through the storeroom into the cloakroom, where I descended the cellar stairs.

Holding up my lantern, I made out broken boxes, old sticks of furniture, sacks of God knows what, moldering bits of fur, rusting tools, everything covered with a thick film of dust. Moths swirled around my lantern like a biblical plague. The well had a heavy iron cover, and it took me a few minutes to work the rusting bolts free and open it up. About ten feet down, I glimpsed a rush of roiling water. Hannah had told me that during a storm, the waters surged, but I hadn't anticipated anything quite like this. I'd have to swim underwater, and I doubted I'd be able to see a thing down there. It was only a matter of yards to Hannah's cellar, but ever since that day on the millrace, the mere thought of putting my head under the water was enough to raise my pulse. Yet our lives depended upon it, hers and mine.

I stripped down to my undershirt and buckled my belt around my midriff. From the sack, I took out a coil of rope, a grappling hook, and a billhook. Thrusting the latter into my belt, I secured the grappling hook to the rope, and then looked around the cellar for a suitable anchor. The newel post at the bottom of the stairs was made of oak and when I gave it a few hard kicks, it appeared sound. I tied the rope around my waist, braced the grappling hook against the newel post, and climbed over the edge of the well. Took one last look down into the shaft. Christ.

Slowly, paying out the rope, I walked my way down the wall of the shaft. The stench was foul, and I thanked heaven that I'd been too overwrought to eat that day. The water roared through the culvert below, filling my ears. I was shocked by the chill of the spray, needle points against my skin. *I'm not afraid of anything in this world. Do you believe me?*

Alas, there was no one around to convince except for myself, and I wasn't doing a very good job of it. Steeling myself, I payed out more rope and dropped down into the water. The current heaved against my legs, and would have carried me away had it not been for the rope. Water up to my chest, I waded to the edge of the culvert, where I paused with my hands on the edge. Things floated past me: offal, turds, a dead cat. I took the biggest breath I could, and plunged on in.

The current snatched me up, hurling me into the culvert. I was turned around, everything black, like the millrace. I hit my head on the brickwork, hands scrabbling to slow myself down. If I was carried past the entrance to Hannah's cellar, if the rope broke, I might be swept all the way out to the Thames. Washed up dead on some lonely beach, like Jonas Cole. I was trying to stay close to the roof, my hands seeking an opening. When I reached it, I thrust up my arms, grabbing hold of the edge. For a moment I hung like that, wrestling against the force of the water, using every ounce of my strength to haul myself up. My head broke the surface, and I sucked air back into my lungs.

In the darkness above, I could make out the blacker shape of the ice tub that Hannah had described. A little too high to jump, but that was what the billhook was for. My fingers were so numb with cold that I struggled to hold it. My first blow bounced off the tub, but with my second, the blade sank into the wood. Hannah had said that the winch-and-pulley mechanism had a wooden peg to prevent the tub dropping down into the water. I had to break that peg, and so I jerked the billhook hard. Again and again, until I heard a crack above me and then the tub was traveling towards me at such a speed, I didn't have time to get out of the way. It struck me on the shoulder, knocking me down into the water.

Using the rope to steady myself, I grabbed hold of the tub before it was swept away. Then I heard voices up above, and the shaft filled with light.

"I swear I heard something down here," one man said.

"Probably a rat," another said.

A pause, then a sigh. "Christ, look at this place. It's going to take us hours to search down here."

"You heard what he said. Ten guineas for the man who finds it. I'd search all night for that."

"Hot little piece, isn't she? Do you think she did it?"

Most of the ice had spilled out of the tub when it had dropped down. I slipped my hand through the hole in the funnel, praying that the men wouldn't happen to glance into the well. My fingers made contact with a little package tied up in oilskin with string. I wanted to toss it away, to be carried off on the tides, but Hannah had made me promise not to.

"You can't," she'd said. "Please, it was my father's."

Quickly, I secured the package to my belt with the string. Then I maneuvered myself over to the entrance of the culvert, knowing that the hardest part of this endeavor was still ahead of me. The rope would guide me home, but it would be slow going compared to my journey here, fighting all the way against the current. Taking another huge breath, every fiber of mind and body protesting at having to endure the cold and the dark again, I plunged back in. My muscles ached as I heaved myself along the rope. I couldn't see a thing. Hand over hand, pulling myself on.

Then an impending rush of something large and heavy. It struck me full on. A packing crate, or a broken bit of furniture. I let go of the rope, swept backwards by the current, made a grab for it in the dark, found it again. My chest was fit to burst, lights flashing before my eyes. My strength ebbing, my spirits diminishing, I thought about letting go. Floating away from it all: Hackney and Musgrave and all the lies. Then I thought of Hannah. Who would talk her out of there, if not me? I heaved on the rope again. Pull, fucking pull. Then the rope drew me upwards and my head broke the surface inside the shaft and I breathed that fetid stench like alpine air.

Somehow I found the strength to climb back up. I collapsed onto the cellar floor, my energy utterly spent, and all I could think about was a field of poppies that I'd once seen in the Yorkshire Wolds and how it would feel to make love to Hannah Cole in their midst.

CHAPTER THIRTY-SEVEN

I WENT HOME and stashed the watch, changed my clothes, and headed out to find Tom. As dawn was breaking, we arrived at the Goldfish, where I committed the kind of sin from which some men never recover, and insisted that they get Patrick Musgrave out of bed.

"I need your best lawyer," I told him. "Fielding's arrested my widow."

Musgrave took some convincing not to have me taken to some deserted warehouse down by the river right then and there. The sort of place where nobody can hear you scream and a quick push at the end is all you need by way of tidying up. But I explained the dearth of evidence against Hannah, said he could take the lawyer's fees out of my share. It would leave me with next to nothing, but I was past caring.

"The man's expensive," Musgrave observed. "I won't stand the cost of a trial. And you can be damned sure that I won't wait that long for my money."

"It won't come to that," I said. "I just need Fielding to think I can afford the best. You'll have your money in a matter of days. If I get her out, she'll be begging me to take it."

"By tomorrow," he said. "Or I'm going to come looking for you, Billy-boy."

*

The lawyer's name was Antony Kent, a bear of a man who had a quietness of manner that I quickly learned belied a ferocious line in argument. Fielding wouldn't receive us until gone five o'clock that evening, and from the look on his face when he did, Hannah had stuck to her denials. Fielding's expression darkened as Kent made his case: the lack of any firm evidence linking Hannah to her husband's murder, the lack of any evidence to suggest that Hannah even knew of her husband's mistress. Nor Jonas Cole's plan to sell her shop and run off to Scotland.

"And I will attest to Hannah's complete astonishment when I told her about the mistress," I said.

"I think you'll concur that Mr. Devereux will make for a very credible witness," Kent concluded.

It was very hot in that room and I was feeling dizzy and sick from the night's exertions. Fielding poured himself a glass of claret and drank it down. "I have the testimony of her trade apprentice," he said. "The mopped floor, the tooth."

"A tooth you cannot produce," Kent said, "because the apprentice claims to have thrown it away. For all you know, the lad might have invented the tale to cast blame upon Mrs. Cole to conceal his own involvement in the murder. You have said yourself that Jonas Cole treated his apprentices harshly. And from what Mr. Devereux has told me of your witness, I don't believe I will struggle to discredit his story when he gives testimony."

Poor Oscar. But I could see from Fielding's face that he had his own concerns upon that score.

"You wanted an arrest in this matter to curry favor with the cabinet," I said. "I regret to say that your desire to secure their support for your judicial reforms has blinded you to the truth. Should you persist in this miscarriage of justice, I believe a jury would laugh at your evidence. And the newspapers will raise a clamor. For isn't this exactly what your enemies predicted? Innocent men and women, dragged from their homes on the whim of you and your *police*."

Fielding glowered. I'd hit a nerve there. Somebody knocked at the door and entered. We all gazed at the constable who stood there, his hat in his hands. The man looked at Fielding and shook his head. I suspected he'd been one of the constables searching Hannah's house.

Fielding was silent a long moment. Sweat crawled down my back, and I fought the urge to sneeze. Then the magistrate addressed his constable: "Release her."

I almost felt sorry for him. He'd been so certain that he had his woman. As for me, when I was standing outside a few minutes later, gazing at Hannah in the doorway of the Brown Bear, my breathing was as shallow as a pauper's grave. She crossed the road towards me like a woman in a dream, forcing a passing carter to swerve. I could see the hesitation in her eyes—how would I feel about her now? I wanted to tell her that she could have murdered half of London and I wouldn't have cared.

I didn't think beyond that moment. Not then. I just wanted to hold her.

The warmth of her filled me up. I pressed my face against her hair. "Let me take you home."

Before getting into the carriage, she paused. "Mr. Fielding said they tore the place apart. That Oscar's father has taken him away. That Theo has gone—I don't know where. My customers—" She broke off.

I knew what she was thinking. Word of her arrest would be all around St. James's by now. Would her business even survive the scandal? It was hard to see how.

Tom gave me a look. I knew what it meant. *There you go. She would have lost it all anyway. So wipe that miserable look off your face and get this done.*

"I don't want to see it," Hannah said, and I knew she was talking about the destruction of her shop. "Can we go to your rooms?"

I watched the sharpers in Covent Garden as we passed by. Men selling phials of colored water, wooden nutmegs, forged lottery tickets. "You'll regret it, if you don't," I heard one say. "It might change your life."

Was money all it took? I'd never stopped to think about it before. Always talking. Too many words. Always running—away from what? A black shadow over a millrace, blocking out the light. The lingering scent of my mother's perfume in an empty room. A mirror that reflected too much and not nearly enough.

Once we were upstairs in my rooms, I gave her the watch. She stared at it a moment, and then slipped the oilskin package into her pocket. I'd thought that she'd want to talk. About her husband and the murder. To try to make me understand—which was ironic, because understanding was the one thing I could truly give her. But she only led me into the bedroom, where she kissed me with a desperate passion. When she broke away, I started to say something, but she placed a hand over my mouth. Her eyes bright with tears, she was already unbuttoning her bodice. "Help me forget."

With the ghost of Jonas exorcised, I knew her in every sense of that word. The want, the fear, the grit, the pain suffered and the pain exacted, a price paid in blood. As I thrust into her, she cried out. I was fluent in the language of feeling, but if my heart spoke to me, it was in words that I didn't understand. If there was a point to it all, then it was this—but even as I reached for that thought, it slithered away through my fingers. There was a ferocity to our coupling, two creatures tossed around on a current. I tried to fill myself again with her fire and came up cold.

When I was lying there, catching my breath, she touched my face. "I love you," she said, and her voice was a sigh of surrender.

There were many things I might have said. That truth wasn't enough in a world full of lies. That Jonas wasn't the only ghost. That they were staring back at us right now, trailing the rags of their shredded lives.

"I wish you'd known him," I said. "The man I might have been without the knocks. I think that I'd like to have been that person more."

CHAPTER THIRTY-EIGHT

When I awoke, at a little before six, I thought Hannah had gone. A moment of panic gripped me, before I glimpsed her through the open door. She was sitting at my desk in a pool of morning sunlight. I watched her, just drinking her in, as she finished writing, then sanded and sealed her letter. She came into the bedroom. "You're awake."

I knew all the things I should say—Teddy and all the rest of it—but the words wouldn't come. Then she held out the letter. "Give this to the clerk at the bank at Messrs. Campbell & Bruce. It authorizes you to withdraw my money. They know to expect you."

I gazed at it mutely, picturing Musgrave's yellow smile. A bird was singing outside, and I remembered Hannah at the window of the house at Kensington Gore, her telling Teddy all the names.

I took the letter. "Thank you," I said.

"Just make sure that Teddy is safe," she said. "Nothing is more important than that."

"The arrangements with his mother will take some time," I said. "I may have to stay overnight." I forced a smile. "But I'll call in at the shop as soon as I'm back."

Hannah nodded rather soberly. "Whatever is left of it. I had better go and see how bad it is." She turned, and I was gripped again by that feeling of panic.

"Hannah," I cried, and she turned back.

I wanted to remember her face in that moment, but the sunlight was so bright it dazzled me. "You're worth more than that shop," I said. "You're worth more than anyone I've ever met."

I don't know if it made her smile, but in my mind's eye, it did. Wide and lovely, the sort I used to have to earn. Then there was only sunlight on the bare boards and I heard the door close and all that I had left was the absence of her.

*

Three hours later, I was striding along Haymarket to the bank, determined to be there the moment the doors opened. After that, I'd head home and finish my packing. When Tom got back from Beth's, I'd make a last-ditch effort to change his mind about coming with me. If he refused, then I'd head down to the docks alone and buy passage on the first ship bound for France or Italy that I could find. My mood lightened as I walked. I refused to think of it as a choice. When all was said and done, it was the only course I could take.

At the post office at Charing Cross, I paid for my letter to Hannah to be delivered. "But it's not to go out until tomorrow, do you understand?"

I had taken my time over the writing, determined to give her a story she'd truly believe. I didn't like to imagine her reading it, but I told myself she would survive. She was a fighter, was Hannah. It would take more than me to knock her down.

I wasn't quite the first customer at the bank, and I was forced to wait for a few interminable minutes, tapping my foot on the floor, eyeing the mahogany counter with impatience. When it was my turn, I approached the desk clerk with a smile. "I'd like to withdraw some money from your vault."

Once he'd handed over the blunt, and I'd secreted the notes upon my person, I left the bank swiftly, still battling those second thoughts. I had barely taken two strides along the street, when two large men fell into step on either side of me. Eyeing them cautiously, heartbeat rising, wondering if Musgrave had got impatient for his money or whether this was something else, I gave them my most disarming smile. "Can I help you, gentlemen?"

One of the men nodded to a black carriage that had drawn up outside the bank. The door opened and Henry Fielding gave me a wintry smile. "Mr. Devereux," he said, in a tone pregnant with dark intent. "Let me give you a ride."

CHAPTER THIRTY-NINE

LOVE IS THE midwife of betrayal. A Judas kiss. A knife in the back on the Senate floor. A girl named Annette. Without love, an act of theft or lust or murder is simply that. But betrayal sears the soul and tears apart the human heart. It unravels your world.

Perhaps I would have believed in Penelope Felton were it not for her gloves. She'd been wearing them when I'd arrived at that lodging house off High Holborn, which was odd for a lady at home alone. She might have been preparing to go out, but it hadn't appeared that way when I'd walked in. Rather, she'd been seated, a sampler on the cushion next to her. Odder still, when the landlady had brought us tea and cake, she hadn't removed them. There might have been a good reason for this breech in etiquette. A skin complaint, for instance, or a deformed hand. But I also remembered my own discomfort when I'd dined at Morrow House. My red, calloused hands that I'd tried to conceal. Was it possible that Penelope Felton wasn't the lady she claimed to be?

Then there was her appearance. The woman I met that day was very pretty, her glossy black hair piled, big dark eyes, a shapely nose. David Thewson had not mentioned that she was attractive, and the adjectives he'd used to describe her had been perfunctory at best. Nor had he done any of the things that Jonas had used to do when he'd described a pretty woman: speaking warmly with a little smile, a goatish glint to his eye. I remembered how Thewson had looked at me—he'd seemed that sort of man. He'd also said that Penelope Felton was about his own age, whereas this lady looked younger. It occurred to me then that she might be an impostor. Could William have somehow got wind of my suspicions, and installed her here?

It seemed ludicrous to imagine. I told myself that Thewson might simply have misremembered her. Still writing those stories. Still wanting desperately to believe. Mrs. Felton told me all about her dead sister and her rejection of William over his past, about his heartache and his letters, and her sister's belated discovery that he was the honest man he'd always claimed. As I listened, I said and did everything that the old, credulous Hannah might have done. Nodding gravely, weeping a little as I read William's letters, telling this stranger of my shame. Yet despite all the efforts of my heart to keep that reality alive, my head had conceived a cold clarity of purpose.

When I left the lodging house, I crossed the street, glancing up at Mrs. Felton's window. Seeing that I was unobserved, I concealed myself behind a waiting carriage and kept watch on the place. Sure enough, barely ten minutes after I had left, the door opened and Mrs. Felton emerged, carrying a portmanteau. She walked off down the street and I followed her.

First she turned onto Bedford Street, and then cut down through an alley and a courtyard onto High Holborn. There, on the junction with Lyon Street, she climbed into a waiting chaise. The liveried driver turned to survey the road, before lifting his whip to chivvy the horses. Everything seemed to shudder around me as I recognized the sleek, reptilian profile of William's manservant, Tom.

*

Forced at last to confront the bleak horror of the truth, I walked home in a daze. My stomach spasmed with pain. Had everything been a lie? Arcadia? William's friends? I couldn't work it out. How had he done it? Got inside my head like this? It was a thousand times worse than anything Jonas had done.

I thought of the way William had looked at me with such devotion, all the things he'd said, and my humiliation slowly sharpened to anger. And Teddy! I saw it all now. How William must have examined my life for vulnerabilities, old wounds he could reopen. How he had used a child to obtain my money by false pretenses.

I wanted to make him pay—but how to make it happen? My story sounded so fanciful, not least to myself. Even if I could convince a magistrate to arrest him, it would mean telling the story of my humiliation in court. I'd become a laughingstock: a desperate widow, wanton in her desires, held up as a cautionary tale in the newspapers. By the time I reached Piccadilly, I was no nearer to an answer. Half of me wanted to march directly to Bruton Street, to confront William with all that he'd done. He'd probably laugh at my rage, at my credulity in believing that he could have loved me.

That night, sitting in my parlor, my eyes stinging with unshed tears, I tried to come up with a plan. Play him along? Keep making excuses about the money, have him spend more of his own deceiving me, and then laugh in his face? It seemed so inconsequential compared to his sins. I was still awake when the sky lightened, and the clatter of traffic resumed on the street outside. Not long after that, somebody knocked at my door. When I opened it, to be confronted by Henry Fielding and his constables, I realized that he intended to arrest me.

He made me wait downstairs while he questioned Oscar and Theo, and I confess I thought as much about William as I did the hangman's rope. I blamed him for this too. Had my head and heart not been so full of him, I might have taken further steps to protect myself. When he burst through my door, agitation written large on his beautiful face at the prospect of losing my money, I wanted to run to my kitchen to fetch a knife and skewer his heart. Had it not been for the constable standing over me, I might have done it. Of course, he'd hastened upstairs to try to work his charms upon Mr. Fielding, but the magistrate only thought him a fool for love. The irony of that did not escape me, even as Fielding's constables dragged me out of the shop and into their carriage.

Fielding tried every trick to get me to talk. Reason: the case against me. Lies: a confession might save my life. Threats: that prison would go hard for me, unless he intervened. Persuasion: some old story about a cousin he'd tried to abduct.

Men always assume that you think like them. I wanted to say that Jonas's murder was not a moment of madness. It was the only course left open to me—because of men like him who wrote laws for the benefit of other men. Instead, I kept to my story, weeping as he called me an unfeeling whore. Another irony that William's seduction should be used against me. At last, Fielding gave up, and ordered me taken to a cell in the Brown Bear's cellar.

"But when my men find that watch," he said, "I shall use it to hang you."

And they would find it. I knew that. I sat there in my cell awaiting the inevitable.

Until William came. I hadn't thought he would. I'd judged that he would cut his losses and run. How desperate he'd looked. So much like a man in love, that for a moment, despite everything, I almost believed it true. And yet it was my money that he coveted—and that might be my salvation. He couldn't get it unless I was free—and I needed his help if I was going to escape with my life. So I submitted to his embrace, as if nothing had changed. Locked in our mutual deceptions, we had gazed at one another with new recognition.

"I'll get it," he said. "The watch. Just tell me how."

After he had gone, I'd closed my eyes, remembering that first day in the shop, my gaze meeting William's in the mirror. And that was when it came to me—my plan. Throughout that long night, I'd sat there conceiving how I might do it.

When the jailer unlocked my cell and escorted me upstairs, I didn't know whether it would be William or Fielding waiting for me outside. But as the man had nudged me, blinking, into the light, it was him, my dark Lancelot, standing there.

I told myself that I only went to his rooms because my plan demanded it. But the truth is, I wanted him, despite everything he'd done. One final night when I could lose myself in myth and lies and pretend. "I love you," I'd said, and my words came from a place beyond reason and motive. An abyss into which I willingly plunged, where there were no angels to watch me fall, only the exquisite pain of his touch and the sound of my name on his lips just one last time.

"I wish you'd known him," he'd said. "The man I might have been without the knocks. I think that I'd like to have been that person more."

I believe it was the only true thing that he ever said to me. In that moment, I pitied him. We are all prisoners of our pasts. But we make our choices too, and I had made mine.

In the morning, when I'd approached the bed, holding out my letter of authorization for the bank, there was a moment when I'd thought that he might not take it. The sun pooling all around us, I'd held my breath. But then he'd reached out a hand. "Thank you," he said.

And then there was only one story left to write. I was taking quite a risk with my money, but I'd needed to be certain. It was over two hours until the bank opened. I had time. I felt a curious sense of unburdening, as I walked back to my house to collect the things I needed, and then hailed a hackney carriage on Piccadilly.

"To Mr. Fielding's house on Bow Street," I told the driver.

"Had something stolen?" he said, and I might have laughed.

Only my trust, only my heart, only a child to love and nurture. William had taken my dreams and woven them into a skein of lies. Now I would take that skein and embroider him a shroud.

CHAPTER FORTY

As I'd anticipated, Henry Fielding saw me almost immediately. I imagine he hoped that I'd come to confess. A servant showed me into his study, where I found him in his banyan robe and Turkish slippers, sipping from a bowl of chocolate.

"Something has happened, Mr. Fielding," I told him. "And I don't know what to think about it all. In the end, I decided that you would be the best judge."

He eyed me rather skeptically. "What are you talking about, madam?"

My hands fluttered with agitation, my nerves entirely genuine. "Jonas's friend," I said. "The one he was due to meet after he left the tavern on the night he died."

"What about him?" Fielding's voice was thick with suspicion, which reassured me that I was doing the right thing. He still believed me guilty and his pride meant that he would never let it go. I might spend my entire life waiting for his knock at my door.

"It was Mr. Twisleton who gave me the coat," I said. "He is the clerk at St. James's. I went there to talk to him last month about Jonas's money. I put it away in my cloakroom, because I haven't been able to bring myself yet to get rid of Jonas's things." Here I allowed my voice to waver slightly. "But this morning, I went through the pockets. Jonas used to carry all sorts of nonsense around with him. Comfits and sealing wax and all manner of little notes." I smiled sadly. "Like this one here."

I produced a trade card that I had indeed found in the pocket of that coat. It was covered in Jonas's writing: names, appointments, sums, and reminders. One of which I had carefully added that morning, after practicing my husband's hand. I pointed to it now. "See here."

26 March, ¼ after ten at night, W. D.

Fielding studied it, and then looked at me with raised eyebrows. "You're telling me that Jonas met William Devereux that night?"

"No," I exclaimed, looking distressed. "That is to say, I don't know. Perhaps the appointment refers to somebody else?"

"Do you know any other person with those initials?"

"No," I said. "But I cannot believe that William would have had anything to do with Jonas's death. They were good friends. I know they argued before his murder, but it all seemed very inconsequential."

Fielding considered. "Mr. Devereux did tell me about their falling out, and I'm not sure I'd describe it as inconsequential. He'd discovered your husband's corruption and it made him very angry. They almost came to blows, was what he said. Do you happen to know precisely when this quarrel occurred?"

"Not long before the murder, was all he said." I frowned. "But surely he'd never have told us about their argument if he was guilty of anything untoward?"

See how I'd learned from William? If I'd walked in and insisted that he was the murderer, then Fielding would have suspected my motives. Argue the contrary and—as clever men are wont to do when a woman states her case—he'd start to look for all the ways that I might be wrong.

"Sometimes men volunteer such information if they are concerned they might be found out. It offers the appearance of innocence, as your reaction confirms." Fielding hesitated, and I knew he was thinking of all the evidence pointing to me. The tooth, the cellar floor, the sale of the shop, Annette.

"But Mr. Devereux is kind and calm and courteous," I protested. "He argued for my release. If he was guilty, he'd have wanted me to hang!"

"Not necessarily," Fielding said slowly, as if he was thinking aloud. "Mr. Devereux is a gentleman who prides himself on his honor. If he was indeed responsible—and I posit it only as a hypothesis—then the last thing he would have wanted was for an innocent woman to hang in his place. It would certainly explain how passionately he argued your cause."

See how he already spoke of me in those terms? "But why would he have come to my shop in the first place? Or drawn himself to your attention by persuading you to return my money?"

"Guilt," Fielding said, reflecting. "Seeing how you were left, he may have been seeking to make amends however he could. A gentleman would have considered it his duty to do so."

He studied my face, and I could read the train of his thoughts. Murderess? Consummate actress? Or an innocent woman desperately trying to believe in the man she loved?

I dabbed at my eyes with a handkerchief. "I don't doubt that William was angry, but it doesn't seem plausible to me that he would kill over a friend's misdeeds."

"That's because you don't understand the mind of a gentleman," Fielding said, rather pompously. "It's certainly plausible, though I'd need more than that piece of paper to believe it true. Mr. Devereux considered Jonas a friend. One who'd betrayed his trust in a manner that could have damaged his work and his reputation. To a gentleman, a betrayal of honor demands redress."

"Oh," I exclaimed, then immediately bit back the word.

"Mrs. Cole?"

"It is . . . nothing."

"This is a question of murder," Fielding said. "Whatever it is, you must tell me. Regardless of your own feelings upon the matter."

I looked down at my hands. "When you questioned me the other day, you made certain allegations regarding my conduct with Mr. Devereux. Though I admitted to nothing in my shame, the truth is that he has become rather dear to me. On occasion, I am sorry to say, temptation proved too much and I went to his rooms."

His gaze was censorious. Fat old hypocrite, I thought.

"Go on."

"One night when we there, I opened a drawer of his desk, looking for something—I don't recall what—and he came up behind me and closed it very suddenly. It was most uncharacteristic, and I got the impression that there was something in that drawer that he hadn't wanted me to see. I'm sure you can imagine the direction in which my thoughts trended—especially after everything I'd learned about Jonas."

"You thought Devereux was seeing another woman?"

I nodded meekly. "Then a stranger came up to William in the street and called him by a different name. William denied he was that man, but I didn't believe him. It made me wonder if he might be secretly married and so I looked into it."

"You looked into it, madam?"

"That's right. I learned that William had once been an army officer, and so I went to Chelsea to make inquiries there. Then I spoke to the widow of a fellow officer who'd served with him, and she led me to a lady who was also looking for William. I had thought that she might be his wife, but I was quite wrong. William had once been engaged to her sister, and he had a perfectly innocent reason for changing his name. She gave me these letters to give to him, but I never had the chance."

I took the bundle of letters from my pocket and passed them to Fielding.

"How very industrious of you, Mrs. Cole." He hooked a pair of spectacles over his ears and peered at the letters closely. When he had finished reading them, he studied me gravely. "You did the right thing in showing me these, madam. These letters are not evidence of murder, but they do pertain to motive. As I'm sure, by your reaction, you realize yourself. Devereux was falsely accused in his youth of a criminal act. He lost everything because of it. His commission, his reputation, the woman he loved. His friends betrayed him, providing false testimony against him. He even states here that he would have been prepared to kill in defense of his honor. Now we can pity such a man, even as we can imagine his reaction upon discovering that your husband had been deceiving him—and had led him unwittingly into investing his ill-gotten money. Another betrayal by a friend he trusted, combined with the risk of losing the reputation that he had so carefully rebuilt . . ."

I simply sat there as Fielding talked himself into it. Wants and needs.

William had taught me much about them. The shop too. And just as I wafted a spiced mulberry pie under the nose of a hungry customer, so I dangled temptation in front of Fielding now. Denied a confession, he'd been forced to let me go. And yet he needed a guilty party to shore up his reputation with the cabinet, and obtain his *police*. My story offered him everything he wanted. He only needed to believe.

"Mr. Devereux owns a carriage, does he not?" Fielding said.

"Yes, he keeps it in the stables behind the house where he lodges on Bruton Street." I gave him the address.

"Can the yard be seen from the street?"

"No." I cast my eyes down again. "It is all very discreet."

Fielding would see it for himself when he went there. The perfect location for a secret tryst is also the perfect location in which to load a dead body into a carriage to take to the river.

"But William is a good man," I all but wailed.

"Didn't I tell you that every person is capable of murder, under the right circumstances? A terrible passion can afflict even the best of men, as I know myself."

And so we came to Fielding's own story, his universal thesis of mankind, written to excuse the fact that he'd once tried to abduct and rape his pretty cousin. Well, let him apply that thesis. Let William try to talk his way out of this one.

"That thing you thought he was trying to hide in his desk drawer," Fielding said. "You didn't get a good look at it?"

"No, as I said, he closed the drawer very swiftly."

This information seemed to decide him, for Fielding rose unsteadily from his chair. "Do you know where Devereux is now?"

"He was intending to go to Jonas's bank first thing this morning. Messrs. Campbell & Bruce on the Strand. I'd agreed to let him invest my money, you see." I glanced at the clock on his mantelpiece and bit my lip. "The doors open at nine. If you hurry, you'll be in time to catch him there."

Fielding picked up his hat, and I sensed his determination. "Don't you worry about your money, Mrs. Cole. Leave this with me."

CHAPTER FORTY-ONE

As we drove through London in Fielding's carriage, a string of thoughts ran through my head. Had Penelope Felton been to see him? Had Fielding put two and two together? Surely not. Or had Hannah laid a complaint against me? Had she seen through our ruse with Amy and Penny? But then why would she have given me the letter for her bank? Why would she have told me that she loved me?

"I was going to come and see you, as it happens," I said, ever mindful of the possible angles. "It's Mrs. Cole. I have been concerned for her health quite frankly. I fear her arrest and incarceration might have affected her state of mind. I wanted to ask for your advice, as you'd have experience of such matters."

Fielding didn't reply, and nothing I could say would draw him out for the rest of the journey. Rather to my surprise, instead of Bow Street, they took me to my rooms. "I am very grateful for the ride," I said, mustering all the insouciance I could manage. "Are you coming in to take tea? I see that you are."

Upstairs, Fielding's constables proceeded to tear the place apart. Fielding sat watching them, drinking a glass of my best Geneva.

"Perhaps it would help if you told me what you were looking for?" I said, eventually, confident that I kept nothing incriminating in my rooms. Widows often got curious, started poking around.

The man rooting through my desk drawer caught Fielding's eye. "I have something, sir."

In his hand was the oilskin packet. I stared at it, my heart sinking. The last time I'd seen it, Hannah had slipped it into her pocket. Why on earth had she put it there? When it could incriminate us both? The magistrate held out his hand for it.

"Mr. Fielding, I can explain—"

Christ knows what I would have said. But Fielding only glowered. "There will be time for explanations later," he said.

Taking my quill knife from the desk, he cut the knots securing the package one by one, and then held up Jonas Cole's watch by the chain.

"Mr. Devereux, I am arresting you on suspicion of murder."

*

Fielding gazed at me across the table in his interrogation room. My hands were manacled, the metal cutting into my wrists. A constable was sitting next to me, another guarding the door.

"So why did you hold on to the watch?" Fielding said. "What was it you suggested when you first came to see me? That the killer might have kept it as some sort of macabre trophy? You must have enjoyed that conversation, Mr. Devereux."

Don't panic, I cautioned myself. You've talked yourself out of worse spots than this one. "I've not seen that watch since the last time I saw Jonas Cole."

"The night you murdered him, you mean. We know you had an appointment with him after he left the tavern. Mrs. Cole found evidence of it this morning."

I stared at him. "She did what?"

"She brought it to me, because she didn't know what to make of it. Still convinced you are a good man. It's clear how much she cares for you. Even good men can kill, I told her."

As he took me through his theory about my motives, showed me those fucking letters I had written, I realized how Hannah had made him dance. Jesus, woman. I marveled at her work.

"Look," I said, "I wasn't even in London that night. I'd taken a trip to Bath. My manservant, Tom, can vouch for that."

"A man in your employ," Fielding said. "If I had a guinea for every servant who'd lied for his master, I'd be as rich as you are, sir. I don't suppose anyone else can corroborate this tale?"

Placing my manacled hands on the table, I fixed him with my most appealing gaze. "I give you my word as a gentleman that I did not do this. I don't know how that watch came to be in my rooms, but I didn't put it there."

"Then who did?"

I hesitated. If I implicated Hannah in the murder, she could implicate me right back in the retrieval of the watch from the ice-store. A man could hang for perverting the course of justice. That was even supposing that Fielding would believe me—and from the look on his face, I wasn't sure that he would. Nor did I want to implicate Hannah, despite everything she'd done. There had to be another way out of this. I just needed to find the right angle.

"Mrs. Cole's apprentice, Felix, has been to my rooms. He delivered his mistress's letters. Come to think of it, I left him alone there the other day, when I had to go down to the stables. And I know he didn't much like his master, that Mr. Cole often gave him a thrashing. The lad was from low stock and breeding will out."

I didn't like doing it, but it was either Felix or Hannah. With a bit of luck, Felix had already been sucked into London's murky underworld, where men had evaded capture for years. True, if Fielding caught him, he could implicate me in the widow lay. But I'd have to take my chances, talk my way out.

Yet Fielding wasn't biting. "As far as I can see, Mr. Devereux, you had motive, means, and opportunity. A confession would help you now, not trying to cast the blame onto others. I do have some sympathy for your actions. Cole was a villain, and undoubtedly provoked you. But you have to start telling me the truth."

CHAPTER FORTY-TWO

OF COURSE, I wasn't going to admit to anything that could see me hang for a murder I hadn't committed. Eventually, Fielding tired of my repeated denials and ordered me taken over to the Brown Bear. They put me in the same cell where Hannah had been held the day before. Once the constables had departed, I summoned the jailer. "I need to get an urgent message to my manservant. You'll find him at the Black Lion near Drury Lane, or at his girl's house in the Borough."

The jailer ran his eye over my coat and wig. "It'll cost you, sir. Mr. Fielding said no visitors."

Though they'd confiscated my money when they'd arrested me, I had a few guineas and some silver hidden in the heel of my boot. I paid the man, but despondency swiftly set in. It was clear that Fielding wouldn't listen to Tom alone. I called the jailer back, handing him the card that Tom had given me at my rooms on the night Musgrave had first called. "I need you to send for this lady too," I said.

Two hours later, when the jailer unlocked my door again, I thought it would be Tom. But Penelope Felton had always been eager where I was concerned. She examined me down the length of her hawk-like nose.

"You are a sight for the sorest eyes in Christendom," I told her, risking a smile.

"Sir William Truscott," she said. "Or is it William Everhart? William Devereux seems to be the name they're using here."

"I only changed my name because I was so ashamed after losing your money," I said earnestly. "I've been working night and day to recover it."

"Do you have it?" She didn't hesitate. Penny was one of that glorious breed: a greedy widow.

"Not yet," I said. "But I will. All I want is to put things right between us. I've been so miserable without you, Pen."

"Not as miserable as you'll be when you swing for murder."

The jailer must have explained why I was there. "Please, Pen. I need you to tell Henry Fielding that I was in Bath with you that night. The twenty-sixth of March. Do you remember? We drank champagne. That shooting star."

"I remember. And two weeks after that, you stole my money."

"I told you—"

"I refuse to hear any more of your lies," she said. "And I will drink champagne on your hanging day."

I gazed at her helplessly. "Then do it for the money," I said. "Everything I took from you, plus the interest that I promised. I'll write you a promissory note. You can have me locked up if I don't."

I didn't know how I'd get it, but at that moment, I was prepared to promise her anything.

Penny studied my face and I watched in vain for a softening of her gaze. "Do you remember what you said to me the first time I tried to convince you to let me invest in your foundry? You said: 'There're sweeter things in this world than money.' How you must have laughed at me. Well, it's my turn now. Because it seems that you were right. There are indeed far sweeter things."

*

After Penny had gone, I sat there in the dark and the cold, waiting for Tom. At least I was safe from Patrick Musgrave in here. Even he wouldn't risk murdering me right under Fielding's nose. I'd worry about him another day—once I was out.

But how to get out? As I mulled the matter, considering all the angles, I found myself thinking of Hannah—of all the ways I'd failed to see her coming. I remembered a night we'd spent together, when she'd opened up to me about her marriage. How she'd cried when she'd told me that she couldn't bear a child, and how Jonas had punished her with his cold cruelty over so many years. I'd traced the line of her jaw, brushing away her tears.

"If this should all go wrong," she'd said, "I want you to remember how happy I was right at this moment."

Perhaps I should have seen it then. That she was talking about the murder and the prospect of her arrest. Then I might have realized what she was capable of when a man pushed her beyond her limits.

I thought then of our final night, our frantic coupling. "Help me forget," she'd said. I'd thought she was talking about her time in this cell, but now I wondered if she meant her knowledge of me and what I really was.

"I love you," she'd said and I hadn't seen the truth of that moment either. Not a sigh of surrender, but a declaration of war.

Voices outside my cell dragged me back to the present. "Here," I heard Tom say, "buy yourself a pot of ale."

A key in the lock, the door opened and I grinned up at his familiar face. "Tom," I cried, "come in, sit yourself down. It's not Blenheim Palace, but I think you'll agree it has charm."

The door clanged shut and Tom squatted down on his haunches, his thin face taut with concern. "What the hell happened?"

He listened impassively as I explained, occasionally muttering an oath beneath his breath.

"As far as I can see," I concluded, "there's only one angle left. I have to tell Fielding the truth. Not all of it, but close enough. Who I really am and what I was planning to do. How I never met Jonas Cole. How I fed Hannah a pack of lies from the start. I'll give him the names of some of my widows and when he talks to them, he'll know that I'm telling the truth. Stick to my story about Felix and the watch, and say Jonas's appointment must have been with somebody else."

Judges and juries tend not to treat adventurers like me too harshly. Often they blame the women for being too credulous. A year or two in prison—I'd survive. There was just one problem: Tom. His expression was already mutinous.

"Tell Fielding all of that, and you'll be implicating me," he said.

"I'll swear to him that you knew nothing. That I played you for a fool too."

"He won't believe you. Not once he talks to those widows. He'll know that I've been with you every step of the way." Tom shook his head. "I can't do time. Not now."

"You won't need to. I'll hold off confessing until the morning. That'll give you plenty of time to get out of town. Head for Nice, give those mesdames dowagers my love. I'll come and find you there once I'm free."

"You're forgetting Beth," he said. "The baby. I need to be here for all of that."

Of course I hadn't forgotten. Tom just wasn't seeing the angles, that was all. I searched for the right arguments to convince him, trying to make him understand that it was for the best, that he'd soon have tired of that life anyway. As I talked, he rose and leaned a hand against the wall, resting his head upon his arm, so that I couldn't read his expression.

"I have no choice," I said, at last. "You must see that. It's either this or the Tyburn jig. I can't talk a jury round. Not with that watch."

He turned, emotion working across his pockmarked face. A strange light had come into his narrowed eyes. As his shadow fell across me, his hand slid inside his coat.

"Tom?"

"I'm sorry, Billy," he said. "It's not going to work."

CHAPTER FORTY-THREE

When I arrived back at the Punch and Pineapple, Mrs. Brunsden, Mrs. Fortnum, and Mrs. Howard were at their usual station opposite. I raised a hand in greeting, but they turned away. Walking through the door, I surveyed the smashed jars and overturned tables. I picked up a chair to right it and then sat on it and put my head in my hands. William kept forcing his way into my thoughts—but I refused to dwell on him. There was work to be done.

After I'd set the chairs and tables straight, I went through to the kitchen to find a broom to sweep up the glass. A pail near the back door was filled with broken crockery, and I supposed that at least one of the constables had had the decency to clean up. A jug of cream had been left out on the side, and I was about to take it down to the cellar, when I heard footsteps.

Theo had a broom in her hand. She smiled tentatively when she saw me. "They let you go. I knew they would. Those new molds arrived. I bought a little ice from the dairy and made iced cream."

When I said nothing, her smile faded. "I didn't know where else to go. I can stay, can't I? I like it here."

Crossing the room, I took her in my arms, fighting back tears. "Of course you can stay."

We worked until dark putting everything right. That night a messenger came to my door with a note from Henry Fielding, informing me that William Devereux had been arrested and that my money was perfectly safe. I threw the note on the fire, watched as it burned to ashes, and then went up to bed.

The following day, we reopened the shop, but all that morning, despite the bustle on the street outside, we had only three customers.

"Your arrest was in the newspapers yesterday," Theo said. "But they'll come back. Once they learn that you are innocent. The milkman told me that Mr. Devereux's arrest is already the talk of the parish—" She broke off, looking at me anxiously.

I had winced at his name. I was also quite certain that she was wrong. The neighborhood believed that I'd been the lover of my husband's murderer. I'd have to close up the shop after all and go into the country. As I mulled this dismal prospect, I realized that a little crowd had gathered on the street outside. A rather grand carriage had drawn up there, and as I watched through the window, a lady emerged and came into the shop.

She was about forty-five years of age, with piled brown hair, arresting dark eyes, and an upturned nose. Her open-fronted mantua was richly embroidered with flowers in gold and silver thread. An emerald necklace drew attention to her magnificent bosom. Theo clutched my arm. "It's the Countess of Yarmouth," she whispered.

The king's mistress approached my counter, followed by two maids and three footmen. People clustered into the shop behind her, eager to get a good look at her.

"Mrs. Cole?" she said, in a rather heavy German accent. I bobbed a curtsey. "We have heard about your iced cream and we wish to try it."

I could only presume that the neighborhood gossip hadn't yet reached the palace. Theo ran down to the cellar, while I showed the countess to our best table. Then I went through to the kitchen to plate up the iced cream. The new molds were hinged in two parts, in the shape of a candlestick, and Theo had filled them with a simple vanilla cream to resemble wax. By means of a hole in the top, she'd inserted a real candlewick inside them. I carefully unmolded one onto a gilded plate, surrounding it with cut strawberries and a sprinkling of gold leaf. Then I lit the candle with a taper, and carried it ceremoniously to the countess's table.

"You might wish to blow it out, My Lady," I said. "Before it melts the iced cream."

"A clever conceit," she said. "But it is the flavor that we have heard so much about."

Returning to the counter to serve the long queue of customers wanting to breathe the same air as the countess, I watched her rather anxiously as she ate. Eventually, one of her maids approached me. "My mistress wishes to speak with you," she said.

The countess's plate was empty. "Can I get you anything else, My Lady?"

"No, thank you, but we shall come again tomorrow."

Not once she heard about my scandalous misadventures, she wouldn't. But as if reading my thoughts, the countess gave me a slanted smile. "Reputations come and go, my dear. They say all manner of things about me. But you'll find virtue matters rather less once you are rich." She gazed around the shop at all the curious faces, and then raised her voice. "We like Mrs. Cole's iced cream. We shall tell all of our friends to visit her shop."

The countess rose, but on her way to the door, she turned back, shook her head and smiled. "Iced cream," she said. "What a thing."

*

Just as we were closing, Daniel's boy called at the shop with a letter. Daniel never brought my post himself anymore, and I was glad of it. My breath caught as I recognized the handwriting. What could William Devereux have to say to me now?

Presuming it to be some heartfelt plea from his prison cell, I broke open the seal with trembling fingers. But as I read the date and the first few lines, I realized that William must have written and posted it before his arrest, when he'd thought that I still believed in our love and his lies. He'd spun me some fanciful tale about Mr. Bennett running off with Arcadia's money. *All of which is a long way of telling you that I have been utterly ruined.*

As I gazed at those words, the knowledge of my final victory didn't prevent a tearing of those fragile stitches that held my heart together. Unable to read any more of his lies, I crushed the paper in my fist, and tossed it into the rubbish pail behind my counter.

For the next hour, I busied myself about the shop with mundane labors, as if my cleaning rags could wipe away all memory of him. I was mopping the floor when Henry Fielding arrived. Supposing that he'd come to return my money, I invited him in.

We sat at one of my tables, and I told Theo to bring him a Piccadilly Puff and a glass of angelica spirit. Mr. Fielding produced a little package from his coat pocket and placed it upon the table. "Your grandfather's watch. We found it in Devereux's desk drawer."

I reached out a finger to touch the wrapping. "You don't need it for the trial?"

Fielding hesitated. "I'm afraid I have some bad news upon that score. You'll hear about it soon enough, but I wanted to tell you in person. I regret to say that William Devereux is dead."

I clutched my wrist, my skin suddenly icy to the touch. "That can't be true." Had he pulled some final devious trick to escape justice?

"I am afraid that it is. His body is down in my cellar." Fielding sighed. "It happened last night. My jailer had gone upstairs to buy a beer, and on his return, he checked on the prisoners, which was when he found him. Devereux had stabbed himself in the heart. He must have somehow smuggled in a knife. It was still in his hand."

"No." I shook my head violently, fighting the urge to vomit. "William would never have killed himself. He wasn't that sort of man."

"I imagine it must have seemed like the honorable course," Fielding said. "Better than the shame of a hanging day."

How could I tell him the truth? That the real William Devereux wouldn't have given two figs for honor. That he was fearless, shameless, always ready to talk himself out of a hard situation. I told myself that it wasn't my concern. That however he had died, his death was what I'd wanted. And yet all I could think about was that day at the ice house. The leap of my heart when I'd emerged into the light to see him standing there.

"It should at least reassure you as to his guilt," Fielding went on. "I would have preferred him to pay for his crimes on the gallows, but it is still justice of a sort." He took a piece of paper from his coat pocket. "I also wanted to give you this. We found it at Devereux's rooms. I had to open it. I'm sure you understand. Given the sum of money involved, I didn't want it falling into the hands of any bad characters."

It was the letter I'd written to the bank, authorizing William to withdraw my money. "You found it at his rooms? I thought you apprehended Mr. Devereux as he was leaving the bank?"

"That's right." Fielding took a bite of his pastry. "I think Devereux was planning on leaving the country, probably for good. He must have known it would only be a matter of time before I caught up with him. His trunk was already packed. They told me at the bank that he had withdrawn all his own money—just ten pounds. Perhaps the rest of his fortune was deposited elsewhere, or perhaps he wasn't as rich as he liked to pretend. Either way, the last thing on his mind would have been your financial affairs."

I stared at him. "He didn't take this letter to the bank? Nobody had opened it? Are you quite sure?"

Fielding nodded. "Your money is sitting in the bank's vault, quite untouched. At least Devereux's death means you'll be spared all this unpleasantness coming out in court. Jonas's corruption, I mean. The source of your money. Your closeness to the deceased."

I was hardly aware of his censure, nor of any of the words he said after that. When he left, I walked him to the door in a daze. Theo came in from the kitchen. "What did *he* want?"

"Mr. Devereux is dead." I closed my eyes, remembering his anguished face in my cell, so much like a man in love that I could almost believe it true.

Theo gazed at me concerned. "You should sit down."

His letter. I ran to the pail behind my counter to retrieve it. Smoothing the paper out on the marble, ignoring Theo's entreaties, I read it again—all of it this time. And as my world buckled once more, amidst the realization of all that I'd done, I emitted a cry. William's words blurred before my eyes: lies spun together with truth, like all of his deceptions. But if this one held the echo of a tale he'd told many times before, here it was woven into something new. The last story that William Devereux ever contrived, written to save me from himself.

CHAPTER FORTY-FOUR

My darling girl,
How my heart aches to write you with this news. After you left this morning, I had a visit from Colonel Watkin-Williams. He had just come from the docks, where the offices of Arcadia are located, and he told me that he'd found them boarded up. Having spent the morning making inquiries, I am dismayed to discover that Mr. Bennett has absconded with the syndicate's money. That story about the ship in Lisbon was a concoction, I believe, Mr. Bennett and the ship's captain having conspired to sell the cargo and pocket the profit, along with the money I loaned him in order to secure the ship's release.

All of which is a long way of telling you that I have been utterly ruined. I only thank heaven that I learned this news before withdrawing your money and giving it to Teddy's mother—as I should have been left without any means of paying you back. I counsel you to do what I should have done, and avoid any fast investment schemes, however plausible they might seem. Leave your money in the bank, or put it into government bonds. With your eye for innovation, your talent and hard work, I know that in time you will achieve all of your dreams. I only regret that I will not be there to see it.

You must understand that I cannot marry you now in all good conscience. I have no means to support a wife, and my honor would never permit me to depend upon your undoubted generosity. Our parting will render me the most miserable of beings, alleviated only by the knowledge that neither time nor place can ever deprive me of the memory of our days together. I intend to return to the East, where I shall endeavor to rebuild my fortune—and I think it unlikely that I shall ever return. You must not concern yourself with me, and neither must you concern yourself with Teddy. I have prevailed upon Mrs. Parmenter (who wisely saved more of Arcadia's profits than she spent) to change her mind and pay his mother her five hundred pounds—and she has also agreed to take the boy into her household. I know you do not care for her, but she is a kindly woman beneath it all, and I know that Teddy will be very happy in her charge.

Hannah, since our first meeting, the universe has changed its aspect. The man I was then, and the man I am now are two different people. I anticipate the pain you must be feeling as you read these words and it occasions me more grief than you can imagine. But I also know that a woman of your beauty, wit, and intelligence will not be alone a moment longer than she desires. Choose wisely, dearest. A good man who values honor. One who will give you everything that you deserve and never narrow your world.

In that spirit, I hope you get to travel one day soon. To go to Paris to try their confectionary, or to Italy as I recommend. I hope you will go to the Piazza della Signoria and try the iced cream. Go in the morning, at dawn, as the first rays strike the marble. It is how I shall choose to imagine you, shielding your lovely eyes against the glare. I shall meet you there in every dream, and when I awake I will think of my Hannah and all that you are.

> I love you
> > Eternally
> > > *William Devereux*

HISTORICAL NOTE

Be warned, the following pages contain spoilers . . .

This novel came together in four parts. I have always been drawn to stories about con men and liars. Films like *The Sting*, *The Grifters*, and *Dangerous Liaisons*, novels like *Fingersmith* and *The Talented Mr. Ripley*, and the more recent spate of docudramas about real-life confidence tricksters. Having read much over the years about the colorful world of eighteenth-century "sharpers," I wanted to write a novel about a romantic con man of that era who becomes locked in a gladiatorial battle of wits with his widowed mark. Two dangerous and desperate characters, mirroring one another with their love, lies, and damaged pasts. The central idea of the book came to me as a question: *What would happen if a romantic con man targeted a woman who had murdered her husband?* The answer arrived on a walk two weeks later: she would use his lies to frame him for that murder, an act of revenge and self-preservation that would end in Shakespearean tragedy. Everything else in this book flowed from there.

My plot required that my con man's mark be a woman of means, but one who had everything to lose. The shopkeepers, traders, and entrepreneurs of Georgian London have always interested me—the industrious "middling sort" who grew substantially in number over the course of the eighteenth century, but who are so often left out of portrayals of that period. The many women who owned or ran their own businesses are especially marked by their absence from the costume dramas, not to mention the history books. I decided that my widow would be struggling to run her family's luxury confectionary shop in the aftermath of her husband's death—and when I read about the Georgian craze for ice cream and the curious method for making it, I thought it the perfect recipe to bring Hannah and Billy together.

My plot also required a third character, who would investigate Jonas's murder: a law enforcement figure who is deceived by both Billy and Hannah. Years ago I had read *Tom Jones*, Henry Fielding's most famous novel, and I knew a little about the author's fascinating life. When I realized that Fielding had been the chief magistrate of Westminster at around the time ice cream came to Georgian London, I decided he belonged in my book. Given the plot was already rich with the theme of stories, it felt serendipitous, especially when I came across the novel's first epigraph in one of Fielding's plays: a man shadowing his mistress's mind, described through the metaphor of a looking-glass.

Finally, Fielding's contempt for corruption inspired a backstory about political and judicial abuse of power to explain how Jonas acquired his money. That unexpected fortune is a godsend for Hannah, but it is also the catalyst for both Billy's appearance in her life, and the decision of Henry Fielding to take personal charge of the murder investigation.

With those four elements in place, it only remained to set the scene. St. James's, home to London's finest shops, seemed the obvious location. The parish was centered on Christopher Wren's beautiful church, and encompassed the area between St. James's Park to the south and Oxford Street to the north; from Bond Street to the west to Wardour Street to the east. It has always been one of my favorite areas of London because the city's eighteenth-century history can still be glimpsed there so vividly. Many of the locations in this book can be visited and imagined in their Georgian heyday with only a little effort: the church, St. James's Palace, Shepherd Market, St. James's Square (where a few majestic eighteenth-century townhouses still survive), and most of all, St. James's Street, where several gentlemen's clubs and shops dating from that period flourish today. *Georgian London: Into the Streets* by Lucy Inglis (Penguin Books, 2014) has a fascinating chapter on the history of St. James's and some of the more colorful residents who lived there.

I could not resist incorporating a few venerable St. James's businesses into this novel. The world-famous department store Fortnum & Mason was founded on Piccadilly in 1707 by William Fortnum, a footman at the palace, and his landlord, Hugh Mason. They claim to have invented the Scotch egg in 1738. The perfumier, Floris, on Jermyn Street has been in business since 1730, when Juan Famenias Floris and his wife, Elizabeth, arrived in London from Menorca to seek their fortune. The shop is still run by their descendants today.

R. Brunsden, "tea dealer, grocer and oil man," traded at the sign of the three golden sugar loaves in St. James's Street. His beautiful trade card can be seen in the British Museum's collection. I know little more about Brunsden, and his views on women in trade may have been perfectly liberal, but his hostile opinions in this novel were not uncommon at that time. His rival, John Pickering, ran a grocer's shop in Pickering Place, at the bottom of St. James's Street, across from the palace. I like to think Pickering's attitude to women in trade would have been more enlightened, as his grandmother had founded his business in 1698, and after his father's death, his mother also ran it alone. In 1810, the shop took on the name of a new partner, George Berry, and began to concentrate on wine and spirits. Berry Bros. & Rudd still trades from its original premises in Pickering Place, its cellars extending for two acres under St. James's.

All three of the surviving businesses above hold royal warrants, which have been granted to traders serving the royal family since the fifteenth century. Not long after they were introduced, St. James's Palace was built by Henry VIII, originally as a hunting lodge next to his deer park. King George II (1683–1760) lived in the palace when he was in London, although he traveled frequently to his German dukedom of Hanover (Buckingham Palace, then Buckingham House, was purchased by his grandson George III in 1761). Foreign ambassadors today are still appointed to the Court of St. James's. In 1738, the year after the queen's death, George II installed his mistress, Amalie von Wallmoden, in the palace—to the disapproval of many at court. Born into a prominent Hanoverian family, von Wallmoden became a British subject in 1740 and was granted the title "Countess of Yarmouth," the last royal mistress to be elevated to the peerage.

The River Tyburn, which was gradually culverted over as London expanded, flows under Mayfair, Piccadilly, Green Park, and the forecourt of Buckingham Palace, on its way to the Thames. Old maps from the seventeenth century, when most of the earliest houses in St. James's were built, show a watercourse, the Air Street sewer, flowing under the buildings on the south side of Piccadilly, connecting to the Tyburn, and thence to the Thames. I recommend walking the course of the Tyburn, from its source in Hampstead to its outfall in Pimlico. It takes the best part of a day, but it is a wonderful way to see how the geography of the river shaped London. Alternatively, *The Lost Rivers of London* by Nicholas Barton (Phoenix House and Leicester University Press, 1962) provides an overview of the city's underground waterways.

Another enterprising businessman, Sir Thomas Robinson MP, founded the Ranelagh Gardens, next to the Royal Hospital in Chelsea. Its centerpiece, the Rotunda, was painted by Canaletto, and an eight-year-old Mozart performed there on his visit to London. The gardens were demolished in 1805 and became part of the hospital grounds—the Chelsea Flower Show is held each year on the site that they once occupied. For over three hundred years, the Royal Hospital has provided a home for old soldiers who have served their country. Guided tours of the site and museum are now conducted by Chelsea Pensioners, still wearing their distinctive red uniforms.

The banking house at 59 Strand was known in 1749 as Messrs Campbell & Bruce. It comprised a banking hall with offices and a strong room behind it, with the family living on the floors above. In 1755, James Coutts, a Scottish banker, joined the business, which later took his name. Coutts & Co., bankers to the royal family, still trade on the Strand today, a little way down the street from their old home.

A surprisingly high number of businesses in Georgian London were owned by women—about 10 percent of those listed in commercial directories. Most tradeswomen were widows or married women (the custom of *feme sole* enabled a married woman to trade as if she was single). And of course, a great many more women played an active role in business alongside their husbands, fathers, brothers, and sons. Women who ran their shops and workshops alone faced significant obstacles: financial barriers, legal constraints, and censorious attitudes. *Women in Business, 1700–1850* by Nicola Phillips (Boydell Press, 2006) does an excellent job of dismantling the preconceptions and exploring women's role in trade throughout the eighteenth century.

One common misconception is that women could not own property in Georgian England. Whilst that was largely true for married women (whose property became their husband's, unless legally protected by trusts), single women and widows could and often did own property in their own right. Women were disadvantaged by the inheritance laws, and by the decisions of their husbands and fathers, as many Jane Austen novels attest. Yet husbands and fathers did leave their wives and daughters money and property, and marriage contracts and common law offered women a degree of financial protection. Of course, male heirs routinely challenged these rights in the notoriously corrupt courts—and many husbands similarly attempted to subvert their marriage contracts. Even where a woman was fully within her rights, she needed money to prove her claims, and many wronged widows were forced to abandon such efforts in order to avoid impoverishing themselves.

Mourning in the Georgian period was more relaxed than it became in the Victorian era. Black (or occasionally white) was worn for a varying length of time, before the widow switched to half-mourning, wearing clothes in muted shades such as purple and gray. Whilst some aristocratic women mourned for a year or longer, that simply wasn't practical for most poorer women. Remarrying was the most common route out of poverty, with 35 percent of widows in London remarrying within a nine-month period. Yet many widows did not wish to surrender their property or their autonomy a second time, and it was not uncommon for such women to take a lover. Popular portrayals of widows depicted them as lustful, insatiable, weak, or foolish creatures, the target of rakes and adventurers, who were eager to get their hands on their victim's body or property. *Behind Closed Doors: At Home in*

Georgian England by Amanda Vickery (Yale University Press, 2009) has a chapter that explores the status of widows.

Goods flowed into eighteenth-century London from all corners of the globe, many of them essential to the confectionary trade. Tea, spices, and porcelain from the East Indies; chocolate, sugar, ginger, rum, and coffee from the West Indies; fruits and wine from Africa and the Levant. The popularity of sugar led to a horrifying expansion of the Atlantic slave trade—and to the organized campaigns against the trade at the end of the eighteenth century, in which the use of East Indian sugar was championed, as it did not depend on slave labor. *Emporium of the World: The Merchants of London, 1660–1800* by Perry Gauci (Continuum Books, 2007) is a good exploration of the boom in London's trade, as is *Luxury & Pleasure in Eighteenth-Century Britain* by Maxine Berg (Oxford University Press, 2005), which is also interesting on the growth in the market for personal and domestic possessions aimed at the new, aspiring middling classes.

The Punchbowl and Pineapple was inspired by a real-life confectionery shop opened in 1757 in Berkeley Square by an Italian pastry cook named Domenico Negri. Confectionary was a highly skilled profession, requiring specialist equipment and a beautiful premises fitted out at great expense. Domenico Negri sold all manner of cakes, candies, fruits, and creams, and became the leading confectioner in London. Later, his business was known as Gunter's Tea Shop, which traded until the 1950s. Negri's trade card, even more beautiful than R. Brunsden's, can also be seen in the British Museum's collection.

Ice was crucial to the confectionary trade, both as a means to chill ingredients and as a tool in the manufacture of ice creams. Ice houses became common on large estates during the seventeenth and eighteenth centuries for the storage of ice harvested from lakes in winter. In London, ice was sold by merchants to businesses and private houses, often kept in makeshift ice-stores like the one in Hannah's cellar. "Iced creams," made using the "frigorific" method described in this novel, had been popular in Italy since the sixteenth century. The salt mixed with the ice causes an endothermic reaction that lowers the freezing temperature of liquids, making them much colder. Ice cream was served at one of Charles II's banquets and mentioned in a few early-eighteenth-century English recipes. But it was not until the middle of the eighteenth century that it became commonplace in London shops. Negri was serving a wide variety of iced creams by 1757 and the craze for it quickly spread.

Many popular eighteenth-century iced cream flavors are familiar to modern palates—pistachio, chocolate, strawberry, etc. Yet Georgian confectioners were great innovators and experimented with iced creams flavored with everything from Parmesan to artichoke, molding their confections into the shape of candles, lobsters, pineapples, and all manner of other conceits. Often iced creams were eaten in carriages drawn up outside confectionary shops, enabling men and women to mingle freely in public, in a way that was otherwise prohibited. Ice cream, it seems, was a feminist enterprise! Books that give a good overview of Georgian ice cream and confectionary include *Of Sugar and Snow: A History of Ice Cream Making* by Jeri Quinzio (University of California Press, 2009); *Sugar-plums and Sherbet: The Prehistory of Sweets* by Laura Mason (Prospect Books, 1998); and *Sweets: A History of Temptation* by Tim Richardson (Bantam Books, 2002).

The novelist and playwright Henry Fielding (1707–1754) decided upon a career change later in life, becoming the chief magistrate of Westminster. Responsible for the detection and prevention of crime, as well as adjudicating upon it, he despaired of London's ramshackle and corrupt system of law enforcement. In 1749, the year this novel is set, Henry was lobbying his political masters for change. Many in Parliament were hostile to anything that smacked of the dreaded French *police*, and though Fielding's proposals were much more modest, the bill he drafted that summer "for the better preventing street robberies" was never enacted into law. Towards the end of Fielding's life, he obtained £600 from the Privy Council, and recruited a small band of experienced and trustworthy constables who later became known as the Bow Street Runners, the forerunners of Britain's modern police force.

A complicated and conflicted man, Fielding's brilliance, integrity, and reforming zeal sat at odds with his snobbery, alcoholism, and his stubborn and prickly demeanor. Fielding claimed that the character of Squire Allworthy in *Tom Jones* was modeled on his patrons, George Lyttelton and Ralph Allen. Yet more than one biographer has observed that in his portrayals of Allworthy and Tom, Fielding also captured the conflicting aspects of his own personality. Denied access to high office because of his second marriage to his dead wife's maid, Fielding threw himself into both his work and drink, leading to his early death in 1754 at the age of forty-seven.

In my portrayal of Fielding, I have tried to stay true to his character. All the events of his life referred to in the book really happened: his disreputable father, the riot on the Strand in that notoriously hot summer of 1749, his efforts to take on the gaming houses and combat judicial corruption, the attempted kidnap of his cousin. Although my other characters are not always kind in their thoughts about Fielding, as a fellow author, I like to think he would have been amused by the liberties I have taken. Two of the best books about Fielding's life, both of which analyze the man through his literary works, are *Henry Fielding: A Life* by Martin C. Battestin with Ruthe R. Battestin (Routledge, 1989) and *The Life of Henry Fielding* by Ronald Paulson (Blackwell, 2000). For Henry Fielding's work as magistrate, *A House in Bow Street: Crime and the Magistracy, London, 1740–1881* by Anthony Babington (Macdonald, 1969) is a very readable study of Bow Street under Fielding and his blind half-brother, John, who took over from Henry as chief magistrate after his death.

Corruption was rife in Georgian society. The powerful parish committees, known as vestries, were renowned for the dishonest practices of their members. The character of Patrick Musgrave is loosely inspired by Joseph Merceron (who will be familiar to viewers of *Poldark*), who controlled the Bethnal Green vestry during the late eighteenth century. Having amassed a fortune by stealing from the vestry, he invested the money in taverns, turning many of them into brothels and gambling dens. Bethnal Green became his personal fiefdom and Merceron was said to be worth over £300,000 at his death, making him the equivalent of a billionaire today.

Gaming-house owners bought protection for their businesses from corrupt magistrates and it is certainly conceivable that Jonas Cole could have enriched himself this way. Gambling "hells" enticed men and women of all ranks, from dingy cellars to the splendor of White's chocolate house on St. James's Street, which remains one of London's most exclusive gentlemen's clubs today. The members of White's gambled away tens of thousands of pounds, and it is depicted as "Hell" in Hogarth's *Rake's Progress*. The dice game hazard was popular, as were card games like faro, and E & O (evens and odds), the precursor to our modern game of roulette. An excellent account of the gambling clubs, the efforts of men like Fielding to close them down, and the complicity of corrupt magistrates in undermining those efforts can be found in *The Gambling Century: Commercial Gaming in Britain from Restoration to Regency* by John Eglin (Oxford University Press, 2023).

Confidence tricksters of all persuasions were at work in Georgian England. At a time when a man's credentials were hard to verify, a great deal rested upon how he dressed, spoke, acted, and behaved. If Billy's Arcadian scheme seems overelaborate, consider the case of Gregor MacGregor, who in 1821 created a fictitious country. MacGregor, a Scottish military officer, had served in various armies in South and Central America. Whilst on Nicaragua's inhospitable Mosquito Coast, he persuaded the local Miskito people to give him land to create a colony, which he named Poyais. Returning to England, calling himself the Prince of Poyais, MacGregor set about recruiting settlers and investors. His first step was to publish a 355-page guidebook describing the wonderful life and abundant harvests that settlers could expect to find in Poyais, going so far as to devise a constitution for his fake country, a banking system, and uniforms for the different regiments of the Poyaisian army. He gave interviews to newspapers and hired a publicist, and through these efforts raised over £200,000 in shares. Nearly three hundred settlers embarked for Poyais, and to add insult to injury, MacGregor persuaded them to change their life savings into Poyais dollars before they left. Dismayed on their arrival to discover the bleak reality of their new home, they tried in vain to establish a colony and more than half of them died. Many still refused to believe that MacGregor could have duped them. When the story emerged, he fled to France, where he repeated his scam, raising another £300,000.

The French arrested him for fraud, but he was acquitted of all charges, beguiling the court into believing him the innocent dupe of one of his associates. The full, fascinating story of Poyais can be read in *The Land That Never Was: Sir Gregor MacGregor and the Most Audacious Fraud in History* by David Sinclair (Da Capo Press, 2004).

I found further inspiration for Billy's character in John Hatfield, who attained notoriety as a romantic con man in 1802 when he arrived in the Lake District calling himself Colonel Alexander Hope, brother of the Earl of Hopetoun and an MP. Whilst there, he worked two romantic cons at the same time, a few miles apart. His targets were an heiress of good family, and the beautiful daughter of a wealthy innkeeper. Hatfield was described as "fluent and elegant in his language, great command of words, frequently puts his hand to his heart, very fond of compliments and generally addressing himself to persons most distinguished by rank or situation, attentive in the extreme to females, and likely to insinuate himself where there are young ladies." Eventually, he was arrested and hanged for an earlier crime, having swindled his business partner out of a small fortune. Hatfield's story and those of many other Georgian fraudsters can be found in *Con Men & Cutpurses: Scenes from the Hogarthian Underworld* by Lucy Moore (Allen Lane, 2000).

I found writing from Billy's perspective to be simultaneously great fun and emotionally disturbing. I could all too easily imagine myself in Hannah's shoes, having all my hopes and dreams used against me. To paraphrase Billy, the people who pull off these scams are very, very good at what they do. Many of their tricks now are little different from those they used in the eighteenth century. The prisoner these days is more likely to be Nigerian than Spanish—but the scheme is otherwise unchanged. Wherever there are people who are lost, lonely, desperate, greedy, or simply not paying attention, there will be sharpers hovering to take advantage. *The Confidence Game* by Maria Konnikova (Canongate, 2016) is a disconcerting insight into the psychology and emotional tricks of these devils in disguise who walk among us.

ACKNOWLEDGMENTS

First on the list, as ever, is my agent, Antony Topping, #TeamBilly, who knew how to fix this book when it was broken. I depend hugely on his sage advice, calm words, and delightful gossip. Thanks also to everyone at Greene and Heaton and especially to Kate Rizzo.

My editor, Maria Rejt, loved the idea of this book from the beginning, and I am grateful for her passion for good stories, her ambition for her authors, and her strategic mind. I am equally thankful to Madeleine O'Shea for all her hard work in publishing this novel, and to Michael Davies, the most organized person I know!

I hugely appreciate Lucy Hale's championing of my books—her seal of approval is among those I value most, along with that of Lara Borlenghi, who has been one of my most enthusiastic readers from the beginning. Thanks also to everyone at Mantle and Pan-Macmillan who has worked on this novel: Stuart Dwyer, Becky Lushey, Kimberley Nyamhondera, Poppy North, Rosie Friis, Kate Tolley (the woman who never misses a trick!), Sian Chilvers, Lindsay Nash, Jonathan Atkins, Leanne Williams, Becky Lloyd, Nick Griffiths, Richard Green, Izzy Radakovic, and Emma Pidsley, who designed the cover and created such a standout look for this book.

Just as much heartfelt thanks is due to Kaitlin Olson, my US editor, whose delight in this book and determination to get it into the hands of American readers has been inspiring. Thanks also to Ife Anyoku, Paige Lytle, Lacee Burr, Maudee Genao, Sierra Swanson, Esther Paradelo, Annette Pagliaro Sweeney, Jimmy Iacobelli, Laywan Kwan, and everyone else at Atria and Simon & Schuster. And to Jennifer Weltz and her colleagues at the Jean V Naggar Literary Agency. A special mention too to the editors and translators who have worked on my foreign language editions—it is always a thrill to walk into a bookshop abroad and see myself there.

Several people helped me with my research for this book. Barbara Rich very kindly put me in contact with Rebecca Probert, who was extremely helpful in helping me navigate women's property rights and widowhood in Georgian England. On Henry Fielding, Dan Waterfield generously shared his fascinating research, and Hallie Rubenhold pointed me in the direction of some excellent sources. Sophia Money-Coutts put me in touch with Tracey Earl, archivist at Coutts bank, who told me everything I wanted to know about the bank's history at that time. Frank McGrath helped me devise a plausible background for Daniel Cole. David Schofield (along with my husband) helped me imagine a chemistry show of that era. And a very fond mention to Andy Bagnall, Lee Findell, Sarah Ward, and David Black, who joined me in walking the course of the River Tyburn on a hot summer's day.

Thanks, as ever, to Abir Mukherjee and Anna Mazzola: my first readers, dazzling writers, and partners in crime. To Nicci Cloke and Jo Callaghan, who read this book very swiftly when I needed them to. To David Headley and Goldsboro Books, who have supported my novels since the beginning—I appreciate it more than I can say. And to all my author friends who kept me laughing along the way—you know who you are!

The support of my family for my writing career never wavers and I love them for that and for so much else. This book is dedicated to my niece, Lyla, known to us as Billy, stealer of buttons and hearts. Charming, incorrigible, beautiful, clever, and bold, I know her plots and schemes will carry her far.

My biggest thanks, as always, go to my husband, Adrian. A good man who values honor, and who has never narrowed my world. If life has flies, then he is my swatter-in-chief. My love and appreciation know no bounds.

ABOUT THE AUTHOR

Laura Shepherd-Robinson worked in politics for nearly twenty years before re-entering normal life to complete an MA in Creative Writing. Her debut novel, *Blood & Sugar*, was a Waterstones Thriller of the Month and won the Historical Writers' Association Debut Crown and the CrimeFest/Specsavers Crime Fiction Debut Award. Her second novel, *Daughters of Night*, was shortlisted for the Theakston's Old Peculiar Crime Novel of the Year Award, the Goldsboro Glass Bell Award, and the HWA Gold Crown. Her third novel, *The Square of Sevens*, was an instant *Sunday Times* bestseller, as well as a *USA Today* bestseller, and was featured on BBC2's *Between the Covers*. *The Art of a Lie* is her fourth novel. She lives in London with her husband, Adrian.